S0-CBG-538

EX LIBRIS
UNIVERSITY OF UNIVERSITATIS
ALBERTA ALBERTENSIS

Lost in the American City

Lost in the American City

DICKENS, JAMES AND KAFKA

JEREMY TAMBLING

palgrave

LOST IN THE AMERICAN CITY: DICKENS, JAMES AND KAFKA
© Jeremy Tambling, 2001
All rights reserved. No part of this book may be used or reproduced in any manner whatsoever without written permission except in the case of brief quotations embodied in critical articles or reviews.

First published 2001 by
PALGRAVE
175 Fifth Avenue, New York, N.Y.10010 and
Houndmills, Basingstoke, Hampshire RG21 6XS.
Companies and representatives throughout the world

PALGRAVE is the new global publishing imprint of St. Martin 's Press LLC Scholarly and Reference Division and Palgrave Publishers Ltd (formerly Macmillan Press Ltd).

ISBN 0-312-23840-1 hardback

Library of Congress Cataloging-in-Publication Data
Tambling, Jeremy.
Lost in the American city : Dickens, James, and Kafka / by Jeremy Tambling.
    p. cm.
Includes bibliographical references and index.
ISBN 0-312-23840-1
    1. Dickens, Charles, 1812–1870—Knowledge—America.   2. Dickens, Charles, 1812–1870—Journeys—United States.   3. Dickens, Charles, 1812–1870. Martin Chuzzlewit.   4. Dickens, Charles, 1812–1870. American notes.   5. James, Henry, 1843–1916—Knowledge—America.   6. Kafka, Franz, 1883–1924—Knowledge—America.   7. National characteristics, American, in literature.   8. City and town life in literature.   9. Cities and towns in literature.   10. United States—In literature.   11. America—In literature.   I. Title.

PR4592.A54 T36   2001
823'.809321732—dc21

                                                                    2001034818

A catalogue record for this book is available from the British Library.

Design by Letra Libre, Inc.

First edition: August 2001
10 9 8 7 6 5 4 3 2 1

Printed in the United States of America.

CONTENTS

AUGUSTANA LIBRARY
UNIVERSITY OF ALBERTA

Notes to Editions Used

DICKENS

American Notes   *American Notes*, ed. F. S. Schwarzbach (London: Dent, 1997).

Bleak House   *Bleak House*, ed. Stephen Gill (Oxford: World's Classics, 1996)

David Copperfield   *David Copperfield*, ed. Jeremy Tambling (Harmondsworth: Penguin, 1996).

Dombey and Son   *Dombey and Son*, ed. Alan Horsman (Oxford: Clarendon Press, 1974).

Great Expectations   *Great Expectations*, ed. Margaret Cardwell (Oxford: Clarendon Press, 1993).

Hard Times   *Hard Times* (Oxford: Oxford University Press, 1955)

Letters   *The Letters of Charles Dickens*, vol. 2, 1840–41, ed. Madeline House and Graham Storey (Oxford: Clarendon Press, 1969)

The Letters of Charles Dickens, vol. 3, 1842–43, ed. Madeline House, Graham Storey, and Kathleen Tillotson (Oxford: Clarendon Press, 1974).

The Letters of Charles Dickens, vol. 6, 1850–52, ed. Madeline House, Graham Storey, and Kathleen Tillotson (Oxford: Clarendon Press, 1988).

The Letters of Charles Dickens, vol. 10, 1862–64, ed. Margaret Brown, Graham Storey, and Kathleen Tillotson (Oxford: Clarendon Press, 1998)

Martin Chuzzlewit   *Martin Chuzzlewit*, ed. Margaret Cardwell (Oxford: Clarendon Press, 1982)

JAMES

International Episode, An	An International Episode, in The New York Edition, vol. 14 (New York: Charles Scribner's, 1917)
Ivory Tower, The	The Ivory Tower, vol. 25 of The New York Edition (New York: Charles Scribner's, 1917)
LC I	Henry James: Literary Criticism: French Writers, Other European Writers, The Prefaces to the New York Edition, vol. 1 (New York: Library of America, 1984)
LC II	Henry James: Literary Criticism: Essays in Literature, American Writers, English Writers, vol. 2 (New York: Library of America, 1984)
Letters	Letters of Henry James, ed. Leon Edel, 4 vols. (Cambridge, Mass: Belknap Press, 1984) (referred to by volume and page number)
	vol.1: 1843–1875
	vol.2: 1875–1883
	vol.3: 1883–1895
	vol.4: 1895–1916
Notebooks	The Complete Notebooks of Henry James, ed. Leon Edel and Lyall H. Powers (New York: Oxford University Press, 1987)
Portrait of a Lady, The	The Portrait of a Lady, ed. R. D. Bamberg (New York: Norton, 1995)
Princess Casamassima, The	The Princess Casamassima (Harmondsworth: Penguin, 1977)
Round of Visits, A in Henry James: Complete Stories 1898–1910	A Round of Visits in Henry James: Complete Stories 1898–1910, 7 (New York: The Library of America, 1996)
Washington Square	in Novels 1881–1886 (New York: Library of America, 1985)

OTHER WORKS

Edel	(followed by volume number and page) vol. 1: Henry James: The Untried Years: 1843–1870 (London: Rupert Hart-Davis, 1953)

vol. 2: *Henry James: The Conquest of London: 1870–1883* (London: Rupert Hart-Davis, 1962)

vol. 3: *Henry James: The Middle Years: 1884–1894* (London: Rupert Hart-Davis, 1963)

vol. 4: *Henry James: The Treacherous Years: 1895–1901* (London: Rupert Hart-Davis, 1969)

vol. 5: *Henry James: The Master* (London: Rupert Hart-Davis, 1972)

Kaplan   Fred Kaplan, *Henry James: The Imagination of Genius: A Biography* (London: Hodder & Stoughon, 1992)

KAFKA

America   *America*, trans. Willa and Edwin Muir (1938; Harmondsworth: Penguin, 1967)

Complete SS, The   *The Complete Short Stories*, ed. Nahum N. Glatzer (London: Minerva, 1992)

Dearest Father   in *Stories and Other Writings*, trans. Ernst Kaiser and Eithne Wilkins (New York: Schocken Books, 1954).

Diaries   *Diaries of Franz Kafka* (Edinburgh: Oliver and Boyd, 1967)

J   *Conversations with Kafka*, Gustav Janouch, trans. Goronwy Rees (London: Andre Deutsch, 1968)

LF   *Letters to Felice*, ed. Erich Heller and Jurgen Born, trans. James Stern and Elizabeth Duckworth, including Elias Canetti, *Kafka's Other Trial*, trans. Christopher Middleton (Harmondsworth: Penguin Books, 1978)

The Trial   *The Trial* trans. Willa and Edwin Muir (Harmondsworth: Penguin, 1953)

Preface

Lost in the American City: Dickens, James, and Kafka brings together several interests I have had over the past several years, and as it started as a project from several different compass points at once, I want to name them here.

One of these several starting points was Dickens and how his analysis of the prison in America, so like Bentham's classic Panopticon, might be compared with that of Foucault in *Discipline and Punish*, which necessitated looking at what Dickens said about the American penitentiary, and outstandingly, the panoptical prison in Philadelphia. This led me into further work on *American Notes*, for though the Philadelphia jail gets the most attention out of all the prisons and "institutions" he visited on his American tour of 1842, it is easy to see that the prison becomes a trope that draws toward itself so much of the American experience. I have written about Dickens and the prison before, in my monograph, *Dickens, Violence and the Modern State* (London: Macmillan, 1995), but why the prison—as a triumph of a new form of architecture—should have so inflected Dickens's mode of perceiving the American city, and how far as a trope it worked into that perception and into the writing of *American Notes* I did not then consider.

Further, *American Notes* and the novel that succeeded it, *Martin Chuzzlewit*, another novel that thematizes both architecture and America, have often usually been taken in end-stopped fashion, as though America went no further in Dickens's writings or novels than that (though there was, of course, a return visit to the United States in 1867). I wanted to look further, and to question whether American notes could be found elsewhere in Dickens.

This meshed with a second point of departure, which was Kafka's novel about America. It appeared posthumously with that name, but it should perhaps better be called *The Man Who Was Never Heard of Again* (*Der Verschollene*). That title, whose resonances sound throughout this book, implies that to go to America from Europe is to disappear: hence my title, *Lost in the American City*. But the only part of the novel that was published in Kafka's lifetime, the first chapter called "The Stoker," Kafka saw as being in dialogue with Dickens—specifically with *David Copperfield*. I discuss the implications of this in the first chapter, but I want to draw attention to the hint that there may be something of America in that novel, which seems so distant from *American Notes* or *Martin Chuzzlewit*. Do the traces of America—as a place of trauma for Dickens—inflect more than the prisonous images in Dickens's later writings? Do Dickens's readings of American cities structure his sense of London? Dickens and Kafka appear in *Lost in the American City* as interlocutors, their subject America, capitalism, modernity as these things inflect America and Europe differently.

But Henry James is also here, placed between Dickens and Kafka, and it is significant that he quotes *American Notes,* as a tutor text, in the context of discussing the prison in Philadelphia, during his travels in America that are recorded in *The American Scene* (1907). Writing *Lost in the American City* immediately succeeded my book on James, *Henry James: Critical Issues* (London: Macmillan, 2000), in which I was also fascinated by the Dickens/James relationship. I have continued here with that earlier work, which looked at James, America and *The American Scene,* and James and cities—principally Paris, London, New York, Boston—as indicative of his relationship to "modernity." The same preoccupations are here, save that the only James text I examine in detail is *The American Scene.*

As with Dickens, the architectural image runs throughout James, the city and architecture having their own symbiotic and reactive relationship with each other. *The Princess Casamassima* (1886), which is set in London, came, according to the preface to the New York edition (so James memorializes his achievement by naming it for the major twentieth-century world city), from the "habit and exercise of walking the streets" of London during James's first year of living there (1876). And its hero, Hyacinth Robinson, "sprang up . . . out of the London pavement." In *The Princess Casamassima,* London slums, centered in Islington, then as now one of the most deprived parts of London, are succeeded by a Naturalist-inspired account of Millbank Prison, which had been built in 1821 to a modified Benthamite plan. Its panoptical architecture—it is of the city, so it is called a "draughty labyrinth"—constructs the "Battersea shore,"

> making the river seem foul and poisonous and the opposite bank, with a protrusion of long-necked chimneys, unsightly gasometers and deposits of rubbish, wear the aspect of a region at whose expense the jail had been populated. (*The Princess Casamassima,* 7, 8, 53, 50).

A later description of the river, downstream from Battersea, shows how much London, riverine as New York is not, can be characterized by its

river, and how much the river has taken character from its prison, as
though this was its source:

> The river had always for Hyacinth a deep beguilement. The ambiguous ap-
> peal he had felt as a child in all the aspects of London came back to him from
> the dark detail of its banks and the sordid agitation of its bosom: the great
> arches and pillars of the bridges, where the water rushed and the funnels
> tipped and sounds made an echo . . . ; the miles of ugly wharves and ware-
> houses; the lean protrusions of chimney, mast and crane; the painted signs of
> grimy industries staring from shore to shore; the strange flat obstructive
> barges, straining and bumping on some business as to which everything was
> vague but that it was remarkably dirty: the clumsy coasters and colliers which
> thickened as one went down; the small loafing boats . . . ; in short, all the
> grinding, puffing, smoking, splashing activity of the turbid flood. (*The Princess
> Casamassima*, 392–93)

The impoverishment seems to be set up by the prison, as does the industrial ugliness. I shall comment more in the book on how James draws
from Dickens here, but the descriptions succeed, in inspiration, the characterization of Boston in James's previous novel, *The Bostonians*, as seen
from Olive Chancellor's window (see below, p. 176). James visited Millbank in 1884 and the Philadelphia penitentiary in 1905, two years after
Millbank prison had been pulled down (it closed in 1890, four years after
The Princess Casamassima, to make way for the Tate Gallery). And James
makes clear (see below, p. 156), that the prison in Philadelphia has also
changed from Dickens's day. One form of modernity has replaced another, though the prison remains a trope by which to think of the city, for
any one of three reasons. Perhaps it is because of a sense of being under
control, however benign-looking, or because the city produces a subject
marked by paranoia, from a sense of possible surveillance. Or it is because the city and the conditions of subjectivity it produces cannot be escaped from? James's *The American Scene* is city-dominated from start to
finish. In approaching it, and considering that the experience of being in
America and writing *The American Scene* coincided with James's novel revi-
sions for the New York edition—with *The Bostonians*, that most negative of
his texts about America, not included in this publishing homage to his
birthplace—I have thought of it as working through a central confrontation in James, which could only take place in the American city. America
had made him, and had structured even the alternative life he tried to
make in England; and he also knew that America was leaving him—and
Europe—behind in its relentless modernity.

I have also looked at accounts of America by Basil Hall, Captain
Maryatt, Mrs. Trollope, and Harriet Martineau—mainly hostile, with

the exception of the last—who made their visits in the 1830s, before Dickens; and those of Thackeray and Trollope, in the 1850s and during the Civil War. These were also, predominantly, hostile. In relation to James, I have discussed H. G. Wells, whose *The Future in America* (1906) shows a debt to Dickens and a response to *The American Scene,* much of which Wells read in journalistic form before his book appeared. All of these accounts show the intertextual nature of the European experience of America in the nineteenth century; but Kafka, who provides the fullest comparison between Europe and America, and a revaluation of the notion of travel since he never visited the United States, made the experience of America wholly textual. At first glance, that idea parallels Des Esseintes in chapter 11 of Huysmans's *A Rebours* (1884), who contemplates visiting London, partly on the strength of the Dickens he has read—*Martin Chuzzlewit, David Copperfield, Bleak House,* and *Little Dorrit* for instance. Eventually, however, Des Esseintes concludes, after a day of deferral spent in Paris, that a mere change of locality could add nothing else to the textual experience of London and London types that he had already had. Yet Des Esseintes knew what he was missing in not crossing from one European city to another. America was much more of an "other" to Kafka; yet his account of "America" suggests knowledge of it cannot be empirical; for the empirical is also constructed by the *on dit;* by the turning of "America" into popular representation in the form of guide books, letters, and pictures, the form that Kafka's text plays with. Kafka's book throws back the question that all the writers so far mentioned have been differently engaged with: how to describe the American city.

Lost in the American City begins with the nineteenth-century city, European and English, and with Dickens's place in it. It discusses something of the difference between the European and the American city, and how the latter as the new form of city posed questions for the European writer. Chapter 2 gives a reading of *American Notes* and segues from that into *Martin Chuzzlewit* (chapter 3) and into the contrasted modernities of America and Britain that are opened up by these texts. The inability of the British novelist to read aspects of American life—for example, its feminism, its city culture and the relation of both of these to what W. E. B. Du Bois calls "the color line"—appears throughout, and most markedly in chapter 4, where I add for comparison Thackeray and Trollope. There is a historical as well as ideological overlap between Dickens's response to America and James's, which leads out of chapter 4 through chapter 5 and into my reading of *The American Scene.*

This discussion, buttressed with reference to Wells and to James's Newport-based and unfinished novel *The Ivory Tower,* product of his visit to the United States, is I hope sustained enough to enlarge on those issues that the earlier part of the book suggests. In reading America in the early years of the twentieth century, feminist matters, for which the British writers had shown a certain incapacity, enlarge into gender-questions. The question of race, becomes a meditation on the Civil War and on the invention of history and tradition after that. As for reading city culture, that requires giving a chapter to James's sense of New York, and it becomes a question of looking at alternative possibilities of representing the city, through painting and photography, and so catching and holding it— hence, too, one source of James's interest in American architecture. Thus the question of what new structures of feeling are created in city spaces becomes more intense. Unlike Dickens, James turns to the question of what the tourist can see. This is implied in his sense of the spirit of America being identifiable with the hotel spirit; a statement that while commenting on the outsider as tourist, questions whether the insider can be other than that, within American modernity.

In the last chapter, I discuss *Der Verschollene,* in which the hero is lost in America and lost to Europe, which was, at the time of Kafka's writing (just before and during the First World War), so near to exterminate so many of those who did not belong to a particular construction of a racially pure Europe. Karl Rossmann figures the mass emigration out of Europe to the United States in those years that saw Fascism annihilate the very Europe that Kafka's own people and contemporaries had thought they had a slight hold upon. Europe can claim little over and against America.

This history of writing this book included my own first reading of *The American Scene* before beginning work on my *Henry James,* and then receiving generous travel and research grants in order to work further on it, which I here acknowledge: a big one from Hong Kong's Universities Grants Committee and a second from the University of Hong Kong itself. These grants enabled me to travel over as much of the United States as I could, not for the first—or last—time, of course, but criss-crossing over different journeys, so adding my own itinerary to those of *American Notes* and *The American Scene,* and to those other travelers' accounts of America I have drawn on. I feel I must be relatively rare in having walked round many American cities with *The American Scene* as guide book; but it was a good way to meet many Americans, and I am grateful for conversations with them. Each American city I have written about contains its own memories, which have filled this writing, of people, and of friends made there, of airports and hotels, of museums and old districts and skyscrapers historical and new, of monuments and exhibitions, of downtown areas and suburban places, and of the pleasure of walking the streets, my only way of seeing cities.

It is no longer possible to polarize American and European urbanism as Dickens and James could do; thinking about cities can no longer work within that binary opposition—one of the values of originating each of my visits from Hong Kong was to remind me of that. Trollope could refer to and ignore Chinese cities when thinking about American examples (see below, p. 90). He had to ignore the Chinese city. Its fabled impenetrability to western eyes was even more devastating than the scale and anonymity of the American city, whose modernity even then threatened Trollope's world, as it was constructing the modernity and the city culture whose character is that (to quote Poe) on the "man of the crowd" it refuses to be read. To go to Dickens and to James and to inflect their texts in light of Kafka means tracing an ambiguity of response to that culture—its architecture, its forms of control, its dissolution of forms and creation of delirious spaces—which rendered the European subject "lost."

With Dickens, the loss threatened the stability of the English bourgeois novelist and of his certainties by questioning the boundaries of his thought and of his cultural formation at the moment when his triumph in the old world seemed assured. For James, loss appears in the awareness of having had two existences, American and English/European at once, and of the pain involved in adjudicating between them, especially when the one not chosen is in the ascendant, and the other, the chosen, seems less able to oppose it. James continues to muse over this in *The Ivory Tower,* and also in *The Sense of the Past,* where it is seen that American modernity can learn nothing from England. With Kafka, the loss is also historical. After him, the European can only be lost in the American city, for the European city has already gone. The loss that is common to all is because American cities, unlike European cities, are comparatively new. America may today cultivate its "heritage"—even in 1905 that did not escape James's attention—and besides preservation areas, each city I visited had a comprehensive and often very good, if selective, museum of its history, which was triumphalist in tone, with the memorable exception of St. Louis. Yet to be lost in the American city means being lost in the new, whereas we normally think of being lost in relation to the old. It implies the loss of a particular kind of history and its replacement with another, which cannot be European centered. It implies, as modernity must, a new attitude to the past, as that which no longer has power to construct the subject. The implications of this severance affect Dickens, and make his classic hero, David Copperfield, accordingly posthumous, separated from a certain history to which he need feel no attachment; they make James revalue his own antipathy to America, as bereft of history, as expressed in his book on Hawthorne (1880); and they affect Kafka who knows both the Jewish history and the official history of Europe, and who also knows there may be no European history to hold onto—since what there is in America poses the question: Is there a place there, or is it all a space for disappearance?

I conclude this preface with more acknowledgments, which are also thanks. My Department of Comparative Literature at the University of Hong Kong has pushed me to think more about the culture of cities and megacities, and made me give papers on them, which have fed my interest; the Department of Architecture has also, on several occasions, invited me to talk about architectural theory. My thanks to Ackbar Abbas and N. Matsuda, and to Mario Gandelsonas for conversations on his frequent visits to Hong Kong. The grants I received also paid for two successive research assistants, Adrian Smith and then Ho Cheuk Wing to whom I am grateful. I do not forget any of the Americans I met on my travels, many of them most stimulating company; while those colleagues who helped me with my previous James book have continued being helpful. The English and Italian Departments at Cork University listened to an earlier version of chapter 1, and my friend Jonathan Hall also gave me some help on chapter 1, which was additionally given most useful and astringent comments by my editor at Palgrave, Kristi Long. Chapter 3, in an earlier version, was first published in *English* 48 (1999), and I am grateful to Ken Newton, the editor, for permission to reprint. Chapter 7 received the benefit of a very thorough reading from Iskar Alter in the University of Hong Kong's English Department. For comments on American art I have gained a lot from my colleagues David Clarke, and from Greg Thomas who gave comments on chapter 4. The list of supportive people needs another category all by itself, but it starts and finishes, as always, with Pauline, whose book this is.

Dickens

TALES OF SEVERAL CITIES

Now to astonish you. After balancing, considering, and weighing the matter in every point of view, I HAVE MADE UP MY MIND (WITH GOD'S LEAVE) TO GO TO AMERICA.

—Dickens to John Forster, September 1841, Letters 2:386.

CONFRONTING THE CITY

Why should any English or Anglo-American or European writer be "lost in the American city"? Why should Dickens have been?

The city—be it the newly industrialized, the capital city of nineteenth-century modernity, or the world city of globalization—offers itself first as a problem of how it can be represented, assuming that it should or could be spoken for, which would imply taking up a position outside it or above it. What is there to be seen, and how is that to be read? Is there a way to read the plural and contradictory culture of cities, and the cultures they produce? For English writers coming from Europe, nineteenth-century American cities—lacking monuments to a past, blank and so not quite legible—presented themselves as having nothing to see. For American cities are not only new, they are future cities. What Dickens, writing in *American Notes,* saw in pre–Civil War American cities, in his journey as far as his personal nadir, Cairo, Illinois—of which more later—was akin to Dreiser's sense of Chicago in *Sister Carrie* (1900). He describes a new city, 18 years after its devastating fire.

It was a city of over 500,000, with the ambition, the daring, the activity of a metropolis of a million. Its streets and houses were already scattered over an area of seventy-five square miles. its population was not so much thriving upon established commerce as upon the industries which prepared for the arrival of others. The sound of the hammer engaged upon the erection of new structures was everywhere heard. Great industries were moving in. The huge railroad corporations which had long before recognised the prospects of the place had seized upon vast tracts of land for transfer and shipping purposes. Street-car lines had been extended far out into the open country in anticipation of rapid growth. The city had laid miles and miles of streets and sewers through regions where, perhaps, one solitary house stood out alone—a pioneer of the populous ways to be. There were regions open to the sweeping winds and rain, which were yet lighted throughout the night with long, blinking lines of gas-lamps, fluttering in the wind. Narrow board walks extended out, passing here a house, and there a store, at far intervals, eventually ending on the open prairie.[1]

Cities that are about to be posit the question of the future. The unreadability of that future, and the city's indifference to the European looking for signs of history in its present form—such as monuments or old buildings—make being "lost in the American city" a new experience. Chicago, as Dreiser discusses it, is the modern city for spectacle and for consumption, as the next paragraph of the novel indicates when it refers to Chicago's "large plates of window-glass" that put everything onto display, including the people at work. And to get to that point is to recall how much the city has become the focus of contemporary criticism and of the attempt to read modernity.

The city as spectacle belongs to the criticism of Georg Simmel, in his essay on "The Metropolis and Mental Life" (1903), written just three years after *Sister Carrie,* and to those who have followed Simmel, such as Walter Benjamin, concentrating on Baudelaire, and T. J. Clark, writing on Courbet and Manet. As a current critical trope, it also stems from Guy Debord on "the society of the spectacle" (1967). Benjamin and Clark center on nineteenth-century Paris, and though an exception must be made for Chicago, it should be noted that "the metropolis" as a phrase implies the capital city (the potential world city), rather than the city as the industrial center. David Frisby contends that

the social ecology of industrial cities is not of specific interest to Simmel . . . the fact that capital cities, as institutional and administrative centres are often the location for the cultural hegemony of the bourgeoisie and furnish a large middle class population with a livelihood, is reflected in Simmel's examples of urban social interaction.[2]

Simmel's sociology of the city makes him stress its different social spaces, and urban geography, post-Simmel, characteristically takes the form of mapping space and seeing architecture as constructing different and non-concordant urban spaces that intersect with study of everyday life, one of the topics of Henri Lefebvre.[3]

Urban history criticism has two ancestries. The older, often inflected by a realist Marxism, is reflected in such texts as Engels writing on Manchester in *The Condition of the Working Class in England in 1844,* and it assumes the primacy of production and industry in capitalism and is most conscious of class.[4] Above all, it concentrates on how much of the city could be known—how much of it was hidden from the view of middle-class neighborhoods, how much working-class areas could not be seen.[5] In contrast, criticism following Simmel has tended to be "post-industrial" in emphasis and speaks less about capitalism than about modernity; here, the city commodifies and produces indifference and social isolation (which is not the same as noting separation through the agency of class). Its plural spaces produce another form of unknowability, which extends to its pluralizations of gender and its production of the urban subject as anonymous. The capital city proclaims the nation, but its ethnic plurality gives it a non-relation both to the nation, which as a concept it troubles, and to the notion of definable place, which is, of course, challenged by the idea of the city as global. The furthest development in this sense of the city comes with Baudrillard on the hyperreal, which succeeds the spectacle. The city shows the disappearance of the real—but it was that, in the form of crowds and urban conditions, which first prompted urban history criticism.[6]

Reading the city requires reading signs in a complex and contradictory visual field where signs often indicate an absence or mean that the real has disappeared leaving only the sign behind. The traces of this America, its prehistory, are already to be discerned in James's America, if not in Dickens's. Confrontation with America, which in the twentieth century has often seemed to be the very expression of the hyperreal,[7] exposed Dickens—and James and Kafka, all of them "lost in the American city"— not only to different forms of city life, but to cities requiring both forms of analysis of the city (detailed above), however irreconcilable these critiques are, while refusing any system of thought that would rank-order them in any way (either the cities or the methods). Dickens, writing about America, was able to make half-sarcastic comments about every place in America being a city; he makes the point explicitly in *American Notes* when, referring to any "small town or village," he says "I ought to say city, every place is a city here" (11.165).[8] It is an antagonism to the absence of hierarchy in America, and registers the sense that "a city" has become indefinable because marked, unlike the European city, by expansion, not, like the old European city with walls and fortifications, by containment and enclosure—which also implies containment of the subject.

In England, for Dickens the only city that needed describing was London; indeed, the other capital city to appear eponymously in his work is Paris (though Venice and Rome feature in *Little Dorrit*); while Rochester is anonymous (in *Oliver Twist,* or *Great Expectations*) or is described pseudonymously (as Cloisterham), as is Dickens's virtually single example of an industrial city (Coketown—a composite city in any case, and one which I shall argue derives from an American model). Birmingham, Salisbury, Brighton, Canterbury, and Saint Albans, all appearing in Dickens's novels, do not exist in the same way as does London—but such containment of urban experience to one predominant example, that of London, was not possible in America. Dickens was to discover that during the American trip.

In *Sketches By Boz,* the city might have been unintelligible to any mind but "a regular Londoner's," as Dickens comments when writing about Seven Dials in 1835 in a piece with that name. However, that does not put its "obscure passages" (*SB*, 92)—passages of a labyrinth, passages of the street as text—beyond his interpretation. In *Oliver Twist,* the area of Jacob's Island, one of the "many localities that are hidden in London, wholly unknown, even by name, to the great mass of its inhabitants" (*Oliver Twist,* 50.338) is filthy and a source of disgust,[9] but as a journalist he can still map it, and the filth is localizable. Such ability disappears in America; I follow the suggestion of two of Dickens's present-day editors of *American Notes* that Dickens may have undergone "a form of psychic collapse in America,"[10] which could never be wholly worked through; and I argue that this collapse relates to a feeling of loss of being, or disconfirmation, associated with the American city.

ON BEING LOST IN AMERICAN CITIES

The notion of the European disappearing in American cities finds expression in other writers than Dickens. When Svidrigaylov, murderer and child molester, appears in Dostoyevsky's *Crime and Punishment* at the threshold of Raskolnikov's door, he talks about going to America, as though his future lay there, and he advises Raskolnikov to do the same. Svidrigaylov's last night alive is spent in St. Petersburg at a hotel, "a long wooden building, black with age" on the Bolshoy Prospect on Petersburgsky Island, called "The Adrianople." The tiny room he is shown into with faded yellow wallpaper and a ceiling sloping down obliquely, gives him nightmares, and he leaves and walks out to find himself in a Petersburg covered in a "thick milky mist." He walks back toward the Little Neva, until he stands outside "a large building with a watchtower," which would offer a view of

St. Petersburg. Here, under the surveillance of a Jewish guard wearing a soldier's great coat, and a Grecian helmet that makes the text name him Achilles, while his "eternal expression of resentful affliction" tells a history of displacement—we know how many Russian Jews would later go to the United States—Svidrigaylov says that he is going to America. Pressing the revolver to his temple, he shoots himself.[11]

Associating America with violent loss and internal self-division, which Svidrigaylov embodies, would have been stronger in 1866, when *Crime and Punishment* appeared. America had displayed its own violent self-divisions in the Civil War, which had just ended. The passage in *Crime and Punishment* summons up other texts. While the St. Petersburg mist recalls Dickens's London, most notably in *Bleak House,* the motif of going to America summons up another, earlier, criminal: Vautrin in *Père Goriot,* who tells Rastignac that his idea is to go and live, pasha-like, as "a patriarch on some great estate . . . in the United States, down in the South." To do so he must buy "two hundred Negroes." Practice for living in America comes from Paris, for Vautrin says that "Paris is like some great forest over in America, where there are twenty different tribes of Indians, Illinois and Huron and the rest."[12] Although the destiny of this criminal—degenerate—homosexual is not to go to America, but instead, ultimately, to become a Parisian policeman, it is clear that for Balzac, the analogue for Paris, Walter Benjamin's "capital of the nineteenth century," is America—anywhere in America. Yet to go to America is a radical destiny. Svidrigaylov is succeeded by Mitya Karamazov in *The Brothers Karamazov* (1880), who, given the option to escape exile in Siberia by escaping to America—land of engineers and technicians, as he says—refuses to go, saying how much he hates it and how it would be no better than Siberia.[13] Mitya contrasts with Svidrigaylov in his refusal to be taken in by the power of a newly emerging world power; but he is not alone. Matthew Arnold, in "Civilization in the United States" (1888), quotes the view of an English official who had worked in India, Sir Lepel Griffin, who had said in his book on the United States, *The Great Republic,* that "there was no country calling itself civilized where one would not rather live than in America, except Russia."[14]

For Dickens, whose enthusiasm for America and whose modernity is marked by the point that he visited the United States two years before he ever saw Paris, to go to America was not enough—he had to write about it. A negatively described America, recording, I believe, the failure of the writer to describe it, lives in the pages of *American Notes For General Circulation.* If going to America involves loss, it is worth noting how the writer R. H. Dana, author of *Two Years Before the Mast* (1840) thought that Dickens's American journey "had been a Moscow expedition for his fame" (quoted, *Letters,* 3:348n). That as a possibility and the experience of Svidrigaylov indicate that going to America in the nineteenth century risks a destiny Kafka named, in his title *Der Verschollene.* The destiny is that of becoming "the man who was never heard of again," or even, "the man who died away."[15] Unfinished, and published posthumously with Max Brod's title, *Amerika,* which is not, however, wholly misleading as a title, *Der Verschollene*'s premonitions enable a reading of *American Notes.*

One source for Kafka is Benjamin Franklin's *Autobiography.* Franklin is also referred to, once, in Dickens's *David Copperfield* (14.197). Franklin describes his journey from Boston to Philadelphia, aged 17, in a movement from poverty to successful businessman. It is an urban myth produced as a city narrative. The parallel in *David Copperfield* (1849–50), is the homeless boy's walk from London to Dover, giving something of an American ideology of self-made success, an American unconscious, to the narrative of the rise of the successful English bourgeois, who of course is not the man never heard of again. Benjamin Franklin gets from New York to Philadelphia with the story of being someone "who had got a naughty Girl with Child, whose Friends would compel me to marry her"[16]; and Karl Rossmann, the hero of *Der Verschollene,* is sent to New York from Prague for the same reason. Franklin, aware that his own arrival at Philadelphia may be mythicized, writes to his son, "I have been the more particular in this Description of my Journey, and shall be more so of my first Entry into that City, that you may in your Mind compare such unlikely Beginning with the Figure I have since made there" (*Autobiography,* 20). He makes of his first entry on urban life a literary figure, which affects Dickens, and Horatio Alger's hero, Ragged Dick, the New York boy who blacks shoes, until he gains the favor of wealthy businessman Mr. Rockwell,[17] and then Karl Rossmann.

Kafka possessed Franklin's *Autobiography* and gave it to his father to read, as he reminded him in the undelivered 1918 letter to his father, perhaps because Franklin offered an instance of an American success in relation to patriarchal power, where that power replicates that of the dominant culture:

> You have recently been reading Franklin's memoirs of his youth. I did, in fact, give you this book to read on purpose . . . because of the relationship between the author and his father, as it is there described, and of the relationship between the author and his son, as it is spontaneously revealed in those memoirs written for that son. (*Dearest Father,* 175)

To be in America is to be outside the culture of the European father, as Dickens's David Copperfield, posthumously born, feels he escapes patriarchal influence in England. But whether Europe is escapable is a problem in *Der Verschollene*. Kafka on America relates to Dickens. Gustav Janouch writes of Kafka giving him *David Copperfield,* and Kafka saying, "Dickens is one of my favourite authors. Yes, for a time indeed he was the model for what I vainly aimed for. Your beloved Karl Rossmann is a distant relation of David Copperfield and Oliver Twist."[18] Oliver Twist, David Copperfield, and Karl Rossmann bring into association texts about the orphan with America as the place that automatically orphans the European arrival. Karl Rossmann in America is obsessive about the loss of his parents' photograph—the loss of the substitute memory that would allow him to think that he is not orphaned—but urban America means the orphan condition. It is another aspect of disappearance.

REACTION TO URBAN SPACE

Dickens's urban America was pre–Civil War, prior to the massive modernization that was pushed through as the Northern factories and machines were put in place during the war. Henry James, whose *The American Scene* shows an American reentering the ground of *American Notes,* and partially rewriting it, saw a different country from Dickens, a few years before the United States would be declared to be primarily urban, as happened in 1920.[19] James was followed by H. G. Wells, who in 1906, almost a year after James had returned to England, crossed the Atlantic on the *Carmania.*[20] Wells visited New York, Boston, Niagara Falls, Chicago, Washington, and Philadelphia.[21] His travelogue, *The Future in America,* is excited by American architecture and industrialism, by the profits of Rockefeller's Standard Oil Company, by American wealth, by child labor in New York, by the getting of dollars, by graft, and by American skill and fascination for business.[22]

The Future in America describes crossing the Atlantic, making comparisons for comfort with Dickens's voyage, as detailed in *American Notes,* and realizing how far technological progress has gone since then, just as New York has moved on from the time when Dickens noted that Broadway was scavenged by pigs (1.23). Chapter 2 closes with comments on the assorted immigrants traveling third class: the obsessive fear of *The Future in America.* But among these passengers, constructing urban America, must be imagined Karl Rossmann. What Wells protects himself from, since he is not easy about the rate of immigration or the Eastern European immigrants, is crucial to Kafka, whose question is what lines of flight are open to such a European subject as Karl Rossmann, or himself. For all his enthusiasm for the future in America, Wells draws back from its urban implications, from the question of who would live there.

Thinking of the ship as a "city," with 521 first- and second-class passengers, 463 crew, and 2,260 emigrants "below," Wells measures the ship's size in terms of the city.

> We should only squeeze into [Trafalgar Square] diagonally, dwarfing the National Gallery, St Martin's Church. Hotels and every other building there out of existence, our funnels towering five feet higher than Nelson on his column. (*The Future in America*, 27)

The space of the city has been dwarfed, its fixed identity has been questioned. Chapter 3, "Growth Invincible," begins by contrasting the size of a European city—Liverpool, dwarfed by the liner—with an American city—New York, whose skyscrapers dwarf the liner (27). Thinking that further, greater ships are bound to follow on the trans-Atlantic crossing (the *Titanic* in 1911), Wells thinks of the American belief in "automatic progress."

> It is their theory of the Cosmos, and they no more think of inquiring into the sustaining causes of the progressive movement than they would into the character of the stokers hidden away from us in the great thing somewhere—the officers alone know where. (42)

If the stokers—the proletariat—remain hidden in Wells, Kafka is different. The opening chapter of *Der Verschollene* describes Karl Rossmann entering New York harbor by ship from Europe, and finding the stoker before his rich American uncle. The chapter, "The Stoker," appeared separately in 1913. On 8 October 1917, Kafka noted,

> Dickens' *Copperfield*. "The Stoker" a sheer imitation of Dickens, the projected novel even more so. The story of the trunk, the boy who delights and charms everyone, the menial labour, his sweetheart in the country house, the dirty houses et. al, but above all the method. It was my intention, as I now see, to write a Dickens novel, but enhanced by the sharper lights I have taken from the times and the duller ones I have got from myself. Dickens's opulence and great, careless prodigality, but in consequence passages of awful insipidity, in which he wearily works over effects he has already achieved. Gives one a barbaric impression because the whole does not make sense, a barbarism that I, it is true, thanks to my weakness and wiser for my epigonism, have been able to avoid. There is a heartlessness behind his sentimentally overflowing style. These rude characterizations which are artificially stamped on everyone, and without which Dickens would not be able to get on with his story even for a moment.[23]

This critique makes three aspects of Dickens salient: going to America; being or feeling lost there; and writing *David Copperfield,* the novel that asserts most the characteristics of opulence, prodigality, insipidity, and sentimentality that Kafka feels he must avoid, whose overstatements ensure that Dickens will not be the man who was never heard of again. The qualities in Dickens that Kafka refers to—and which I wish to take as allowing for a symptomatic reading of Dickens—indicate an anxiety about control, which I shall argue his American trip either gave him or symbolized for him. The heartlessness or coerciveness that is behind Dickens's sentimentality would be an effort to make things come right, to assert a control that could not be sustained. America's difference in its cities makes every city problematic, challenging the capacity to speak of it from any standpoint that implies control or that does not make the subject disappear.

The signs are there in *Martin Chuzzlewit* (1843–44), in which, following *American Notes,* Dickens created for the young hero, Martin Chuzzlewit, aspiring architect and lover without a fortune, an American journey. Martin Chuzzlewit, with his servant, Mark Tapley, wants to make his fortune as an architect in America. Occupying about 120 pages in the Oxford Dickens, this expedition to America forms virtually a small book in itself, almost completely separate from the other part of *Martin Chuzzlewit.* Martin arrives at New York, and journeys to Eden, via a city, which in context may be Cincinnati, where he is the subject of a "le-vee" held by the Watertoast Association (chap. 22). The Association obviously expects him to be a man who was never heard of again. After the disastrous expedition to Eden (Cairo, Illinois), Martin Chuzzlewit is on his way back, to the East coast and England. Captain Kedgwick, the landlord, is put out to see him and Mark Tapley back from Eden: the people who hosted the "le-vee" will be displeased to see that they have come back alive. "'A man ain't got no right to be a public man, unless he meets the public views. Our fashionable people wouldn't have attended his lee-Vee, if they had know'd it'" he says. The narrator adds, "Nothing mollified the captain, who persisted in taking it very ill that they had not both died in Eden. The boarders at the National felt strongly on the subject too" (35.537). To have been right in the eyes of America would have required Martin Chuzzlewit's death, an outcome obviously acceptable to these Americans. Svidrigaylov knows that America means disappearance at some level of being; so does Kafka in writing Karl Rossmann, but Dickens defies it with Martin Chuzzlewit.

Martin Chuzzlewit's bourgeois success in England as an architect is repeated in the hero's writing success in *David Copperfield.* There, superfluous people are sent to Australia, and *are* heard of again. But perhaps the price paid in that novel is the overstatement and insipidity that Kafka spoke of. To preserve everyone in Australia (in *David Copperfield*) may be a sentimentalism, whose justification may be the fear of disappearance. It is as though in *David Copperfield* something in Dickens refused to participate in the minority position of being the lost boy, as though Dickens's drive is not toward a Kafkan "minor literature," which would recognize loss and the politics of being dispossessed in the large nineteenth-century city, but toward a coerciveness that sides with the English bourgeoisie.

MELANCHOLIA AND THE CITY

Kafka's title, *Der Verschollene*, receives indirect commentary from the critical attention he has received: from Walter Benjamin; from Deleuze and Guattari, who think Kafka through the concept of a "minor literature"; and from Maurice Blanchot, for whom "the man who was never heard of again" describes Kafka:

> For art is linked, precisely as Kafka is, to what is "outside" the world, and it expresses the profundity of this outside bereft of intimacy and of repose.... Art ... describes the situation of one who has lost himself, who can no longer say "me," who in the same movement has lost the world, the truth of the world, and belongs to exile, to the *time of distress* when, as Hölderlin says, the gods are no longer and are not yet.[24]

To be never heard of again is to be nameless, and aligns with Blanchot's earlier point that writing entails the disappearance of the dominant subject-position:

> Writing is the interminable, the incessant. The writer, it is said, gives up saying "I." Kafka remarks with surprise, with enchantment, that he has entered into literature as soon as he can substitute "He" for "I." ... The writer belongs to a language which no-one speaks, which is addressed by no-one, which has no center, and which reveals nothing. He may believe that he affirms himself in this language, but what he affirms is altogether deprived of self. (*The Space of Literature*, 26)

Perhaps Blanchot's sense of the "space of literature," in view of the temporality implied in Hölderlin's description of "the time of distress," lends itself to historicization. It can be taken as urban. It becomes nowhere because of a prevalent sense of the European and the American nineteenth-century city as the place of crisis, implying the question whether it could be described at all. The modern text traps the subject, because its fate is to be committed to an encounter with the city seen, increasingly, as unreadable.

This is true of the European city as much as the American, and it dislocates the city-dweller, making living there the experience of lacking a place. The St. Petersburg fog in *Crime and Punishment* is to be found everywhere, but it may be compared with the city fog in Baudelaire's "Les Septs Vieillards" ("The Seven Old Men," 1859) in *Les Fleurs du mal*. In this poem, the poet is possessed by the city, rather than possessing it, and his dispossession produces specters who confront him in daytime. Baudelaire's Paris possesses a Poe-like Gothicism—recalling how important the American Poe was to the French poet—and this American context may, unconsciously, infect Baudelaire's Paris with something of the character of an American city.

> Fourmillante cité, cité pleine des rêves,
> Où le spectre en plein jour raccroche le passant!
> Les mystères partout coulent comme des sèves
> Dans les canaux étroits du colosse puissant.
>
> Un matin, cependant que dans la triste rue
> Les maisons, dont la brume allongeait la hauteur,
> Simulaient les deux quais d'une rivière accrue,
> Et que, décor semblable à l'ame de l'acteur,
>
> Un brouillard sale et jaune inondait tout l'espace,
> Je suivais, roidissant mes nerfs comme un héros
> Et discutant avec mon ame déjà lasse,
> Le faubourg secoué par les lourds tombereaux.

(City swarming with ants, city full of dreams, where the specter in full daylight accosts the passerby! Mysteries flow everywhere like sap in the narrow veins of a mighty giant. One morning, while in the sad street the houses, whose height the fog lengthened, looked like the two quays of a swollen river, and when—scenery like that to an actor's soul—a dirty yellow fog flooded the whole of space, I followed, steeling my nerves like a hero and arguing with my already weary soul, through the neighborhood shaken by heavy tumbrils.)[25]

The fog is yellow, and when the first old man is emerges from it, his yellow rags ("guenilles jaunes") imitate the color of the rainy sky. This old man appears as seven old men, as if multiplied seven times, over seven verses. Yellow is the color of bile—the old man's eyes seem to be steeped in bile—and so of melancholy (cp., "green and yellow melancholy" in *Twelfth Night* 3.4.112). Melancholy, as in Baudelaire's "Le Cygne" ("The

Swan"), is a quality of mind associated with city experience and with modernity,[26] and its prevalence, being of the city in depriving the subject of a sense of completeness, associating itself with the subject's disappearance as s/he tries to grasp the city, also makes it impossible to read the city objectively.

Yellow, for instance, becomes a pervasive figure of melancholic infection. It colored the wallpaper in Svidrigaylov's hotel room, as it is the color of typhus, which Raskolnikov's fiancée, the landlady's daughter, died of, and also colors the water Raskolnikov is given to drink after fainting in the police office (2.1.89). All wallpaper in *Crime and Punishment* seems to be yellow, which is (to quote from another Russian novel) "a color associated with insomnia." So says Dudkin, the paranoid and murderous anarchist, in Bely's *Petersburg*.[27] In *Petersburg*, where the city is so much the dominant character that it is also the title, Dudkin suffers hallucinations from the yellow wallpaper. Yellow is also the color of the feared "Asiatic," the non-European in St. Petersburg; hence the paranoia the city induces has to do with the fear of the "alien," always the marker of difference of city space, the secret cause of fear of being lost. However overdetermined, the motif of being haunted by the yellow surroundings is almost identical to that which runs through the American Gothic of Charlotte Perkins Gilman's *The Yellow Wallpaper*. In that short story of 1892, the writer, suffering from a nervous breakdown, which is also a symptom relating to the status of women in late nineteenth-century America, suffers from the hallucination of seeing a woman trapped behind the wall-paper. In *Petersburg*, a face looks out repeatedly at Dudkin from the yellow wallpaper, though by day he can only see a damp spot there.[28] So in the city there is no protection from the look of the other. In Stephen Crane's *Maggie: A Girl of the Streets: A Story of New York* (1893), yellow is the color of the line of convicts distantly seen on Blackwell's Island (used for prisons and for an asylum); yellow is a psychic state when Maggie works in the sweatshop in a state of "yellow discontent," and yellow images her life, as she jumps into the East River, "the river appeared a deathly black hue. Some hidden factory sent up a yellow glare, that lit for a moment the waters lapping oilily against timbers."[29]

Baudelaire's poem "Le Cygne," which immediately precedes "Les Sept Vieillards" in *Les Fleurs du mal*, speaks of "la muraille immense du brouillard" (an immense wall of fog), which though it is only insubstantial fog nonetheless acts as a barrier, defining space and creating the exile. It seems that to be out in Paris streets in the fog is to be surrounded by yellow wallpaper. The same applies to evening: Gervaise, walking out in the old neighborhood ripped apart by new boulevards, in Zola's *L'Assommoir* (1877), notices "the twilight was that dirty-yellow colour typical of

Parisian twilights, a colour which makes you long to die that very instant, so ugly is the life of the streets."[30]

In Baudelaire, the immense wall of fog, substantial and insubstantial at once, demonstrates the double vision of these poems, which means that "tout pour moi devient allégorie," (everything for me becomes allegory) as is said in "Le Cygne." Everything fades in the condition of melancholy (as white paper fades to yellow), into a state where it is real and non-real at once, so the point about the specter confronting the passerby in plain daylight might be rephrased to mean that the city is wholly spectral, yielding to an allegorization, which turns it all into ruins, devastates it. The yellow fog is real and allegorical. Real, it confuses and pluralizes space, increasing the heights of buildings and making the road impossible to see, so that it appears riverine, drowning space. Allegorically, it is like the paper from which hallucinations emerge, as the old man in yellow rags emerges, pluralized seven times in a repetition that denies the possibility of an origin. But if it is yellow, it is old itself, dead, like—to change texts again—the "friend" in Russia in Kafka's short story "The Judgment." The father speaks contemptuously to his son Georg about this friend: "Even three years ago he was yellow enough to be thrown away." (*Complete SS,* 87). No use writing to such a friend: the writing is also dead, finished.

In "Les Sept Vieillards," after he has seen the seven figures, Baudelaire's conjunction of the city as a dead space, apart from the presence of the spectral concludes:

> Aurais-je, sans mourir, contemplé le huitième,
> Sosie inexorable, ironique et fatal,
> Dégoutant Phénix, fils et père de lui-même?
> —Mais je tournai le dos au cortège infernal.
>
> Exaspéré comme un ivrogne qui voit double,
> Je rentrai, je fermai ma porte, épouvanté,
> Malade e morfondu, l'esprit fiévreux et trouble,
> Blessé par le mystère et par l'absurdité!
>
> Vainement ma raison voulait prendre la barre;
> La tempête en jouant déroutait ses efforts,
> Et mon âme dansait, dansait, vieille garbarre,
> Sans mâts, sur une mer monstreuse et sans bords!

(Could I, without dying, have looked at an eighth, an inexorable, ironic and fatal twin, disgusting Phoenix, son and father of himself? But I turned my back on this infernal procession. Exasperated like a drunk man who sees double, I went back, I shut my door, terrified, ill and depressed, the spirit fevered and troubled, wounded by the mystery and by the absurdity. Vainly my reason tried to take over, but the storm destroyed all its efforts, and my mind tossed and tossed, old barge without masts, on a sea monstrous and shoreless.)

He could not look upon an eighth (a renewal of the repeated seven, which forms a unity, just as the eighth day restarts the week). The eighth, new and old together, nonrecognizable and recognizable, would be his twin, the spirit of melancholy, aligning repetition with nondifferentiation, indifference, the state of the fog. At the end, paranoia has been increased and the subject wounded, left like an old mastless barge tossing in a space that lacks boundaries, as the fog has taken away all definition of space. This renders paranoia—locking the door—useless.

Seeing double means that vision has become deterritorialized. It is the condition of the city in plain daylight: the fog is the supplement to bring out what the city does. St. Petersburg where Svidrigaylov dies is the same city that Dostoyevsky's Underground Man described as "the most fantastic and the most intentional on earth," saying that towns could be intentional or unintentional.[31] Intentionality, as in the planning of Peter the Great of St. Petersburg, imposes order, just as, in America's rational cities, it enforces grid formations of streets; and its effects, according to Svidrigaylov, or the Underground Man, are to madden. In corroboration, the translators of *Petersburg* note that "the institutions . . . lining the English Embankment [in St. Petersburg] are painted a pale yellow colour. Because state-owned buildings were often painted that colour, 'yellow house' became a euphemism for an insane asylum; for Russians this is the primary meaning of the expression" (302). There is an alliance here of institutions, and so of bureaucracy and intentionality, of the desire to name, to delineate, to fix identity, even if only by color coding, and to produce madness. Svidrigaylov, referring to St. Petersburg, comments that there are "few places which exercise such strange, harsh, and sombre influences on the human spirit" as this one, having just said that "it's a town of half-crazy people," and adding that it's "the administrative centre of all Russia, and that character must be reflected in everything" (6.3.394).

Urban Fog: Bleak House

Fog makes for the "unreal city," (*The Waste Land*), and the adjective implies that it cannot be "real" while something within it falls outside representation. The unreal is what resists being known, and possessed. Its threat as the unreal is to erase people within its space. In Dostoyevsky's novel *A Raw Youth,* Arkady, thinks that

> On a Petersburg morning like this, decayed, wet and misty, the wild dream of some kind of Pushkinian Hermann from *The Queen of Spades* (a colossal figure, unusual, a completely Petersburg type—a type from the Petersburg period!) it seems to me, should become even stronger, A hundred times, amid this fog, I had the strange but persistent vision: "When this fog is scattered and flies away, perhaps all this decaying slimy town will go away with it, will rise as the fog rises and disappear like smoke, leaving behind only the old Finnish marshes, and in the middle of them, for decoration, there will be the bronze horseman on his driven horse with its burning breath?" In a word, I cannot express my impressions, because all this is fantasy, finally, poetry and therefore nonsense; however a completely senseless question often occurred to me and still occurs: 'Here they all are, rushing about from place to place tossing and turning, but how can we tell, perhaps all this is someone's dream, and there is not a single real, true person here, and not a single real action?[32]

The threat is that there will be no St. Petersburg there, but it is more terrifying to think that this may be the "intention" of the bronze horseman (Peter the Great's statue, the figure of Pushkin's poem *The Bronze Horseman*). The horseman will be left alone in his monumentality, a crazy figure of domination, just as building Peter the Great's St. Petersburg cost thousands of workers' lives. Arkady joins to his perception of the bronze horseman, another Pushkinian figure: Herman from *The Queen of Spades,* who, fascinated by gambling, will not gamble because he wants to maintain control. He wanders round the city, obsessed by the narrative of the countess and her secret of the three winning cards, and "musing thus, he found himself in one of the main streets of St. Petersburg, in front of a house of old-fashioned architecture."[33] It is the house of the countess. And he returns to it "as though some supernatural force"—the conditions of city existence—"drew him there" (164). Herman wants the secret of the cards (which would eliminate chance, and make it possible to construct a logical narrative as the law of life) but ends mad, confirming the narrative direction of his own rationalism. He would impose order—akin to narrative order—on the city, but the city creates him, as Dostoyevsky notes, making him in his madness the man who is never heard of again.

Herman's anxiety to keep control, which means that he wants a life that can be narrativized, not one that has no basis in anything else but chance, is a repudiation of gambling, but perhaps there is nothing else but chance, and city streets illustrate that. In his study of Baudelaire, Walter Benjamin quotes from Alain:

It is inherent in the concept of gambling . . . that no game is dependent on the preceding one. Gambling cares about no assured position. . . . Winnings secured earlier are not taken into account, and in this it differs from work. Gambling gives short shrift to the weighty past on which work bases itself.[34]

Bourgeois work and respectability are mocked by gambling, which nonetheless delivers up to Herman the future that fits his past anxiety. In the image of gambling a number of ideas constellate which link to city space: the chopping up of time into segments and the consequent breakup of memory and of narrative, and therefore of anything that would give stability to the subject.

Arkady's vision is Pushkinian and Dickensian, since these accounts of fog in Paris and St. Petersburg return us to Dickens's London and to *Bleak House* (1852–53), the text that most attempts to see whether the city can be plotted. I argue that traces of a trauma whose earlier place in time was in America work through that account of the London fog and mud; certainly, that experience seems to be repeated in the texture of the first paragraphs of the first chapter, "In Chancery." The pervasiveness of "Chancery," implying the power of canceling, and of what is cancerous, swollen and unrecognizable, monstrous, also implies being under the power of the law, held by a lawsuit, so also committed to a gamble (chance/chancery), where the players are the lawyers. The parties in the case are Jarndyce versus Jarndyce: jaundiced, yellow.[35] The opening word, "London," identifies being "in chancery" with city space. The first two lines give a precise geography for the Lord Chancellor's place for giving judgment, but that presupposes that the Lord Chancellor is above the law, rather than caught up in it. If the whole of London is "in Chancery," all under the law, the space of the law is everywhere and nowhere: writing everywhere present and nowhere accountable.

London. Michaelmas term lately over, and the Lord Chancellor sitting in Lincoln's Inn Hall. Implacable November weather. As much mud in the streets, as if the waters had but newly retired from off the face of the earth, and it would not be wonderful to meet a Megalosaurus, forty feet long or so, waddling like an elephantine lizard up Holborn-hill. Smoke lowering down from chimney-pots, making a soft black drizzle, with flakes of soot in it as big as full-grown snow-flakes—gone into mourning, one might imagine, for the death of the sun. Dogs, undistinguishable in mire. Horses, scarcely better; splashed to their very blinkers. Foot passengers jostling one another's umbrellas, in a general infection of ill-temper; and losing their foot-hold at street-corners, where tens of thousands of other foot passengers have been slipping and sliding since the day broke (if this day ever broke), adding new deposits to the crust upon crust of mud, sticking at those points tenaciously to the pavement, and accumulating at compound interest.

Fog everywhere. Fog up the river, where it flows among green aits and meadows; fog down the river, where it rolls defiled among the tiers of shipping, and the waterside pollutions of a great (and dirty) city. Fog on the Essex marshes, fog on the Kentish heights. Fog creeping into the cabooses of collier-brigs; fog lying out on the yards, and hovering in the rigging of great ships; fog drooping on the gunwales of barges and small boats. Fog in the eyes and throats of ancient Greenwich pensioners, wheezing by the firesides of their wards; fog in the stem and bowl of the afternoon pipe of the wrathful skipper, down in his close cabin; fog cruelly pinching the toes and fingers of his shivering little 'prentice boy on deck. Chance people on the bridges peering over the parapets into a nether sky of fog, with fog all round them, as if they were up in a balloon, and hanging in the misty clouds.

Gas looming through the fog in divers places in the streets, much as the sun may, from spongy fields, be seen to loom by husbandman and plough-boy. Many of the shops lighted two hours before their time—as the gas seems to know, for it has a haggard and unwilling look. (*Bleak House*, I.11–12)

In this passage, which ends with forms of "looming," like the chapter title of the opening of Melville's *Moby-Dick,* "Loomings," the word "London" suggests firstly that this "great" city is the center of empire, which is why shipping appears so much in the second paragraph, as well as the Greenwich pensioners, relics of Napoleonic and Indian wars. "London" implies a date-line and a place for a correspondent to file a present-day report, which is what the anonymous writing sections of *Bleak House* offer; and it signifies the place with which Dickens is most familiar, as though it was Dickens's signature. This is not America, or *Moby-Dick*'s "island of the Manhattoes," but a word and place almost synonymous with Dickens—Dickens's texts create "Dickens's London." The writing is anxious not to let go of its hold over London, but conversely to read it, so that the mud and fog are imposed upon a known topography: Lincoln's Inn Hall, Holborn hill, the waterside, Essex, Kent, Greenwich, the bridges over the river, the fields, and upon things properly named—cabooses, or gunwales. These things must be named, so the writing retains the appearance of ubiquity, as though it took up a place outside the fog; just as the series of anaphorae in the repetition of "fog" rhetorically produce the fog as though in control of it.

The writing produces these things almost *ex nihilo,* just as, in a sentence that is Megalosaurian in length, the flood waters have newly disappeared, leaving only mud behind, out of which a megalosaurus might be produced—as much as then contemporary science generated dinosaurs out of fossil traces. The conditions for thinking about the urban are appropriate for thinking about the dinosaur. Dickens's "London" is a production of writing, as when on the following page the Chancery lawyers in Lincoln's Inn Hall are itemized and then produced by the writing in phrases such as—"as here he is," "as here they are." To begin with "London" is not to start with a place that is known and can be read, but to bring something into textual existence.

While it produces "London," the writing makes the city a place of disappearance: of growing indistinguishability, as the mud comes up and engulfs, and as first smoke, the rain and the black soot come down, and then the amorphous fog. Between the mud and the fog there is nothing; in the city, men are never heard of again, and the crisis point is the corner, where "foot passengers" lose their "foot-hold" in making a right-angled turn, creating a point where everyone, having jostled various umbrellas in order to get by, comes to grief in the mud. It is an indication of what might happen to narrative in this book: the impossibility of turning—or twisting, to pun on an earlier Dickens title set in London. As umbrellas that are up act as a veil, and the crowd who "jostle" each other form a veil, so does the fog: all make description impossible. The fog, which has no origin, has neither inside nor outside, like the notion of "invagination" in Derrida, or the idea of the Moebius strip, and there is nothing to give a center, or sense of time, since the text speaks of "the death of the sun." If "we still believe in God because we still believe in grammar,"[36] then the death of the sun as a force for centering is a possibility in a text that breaks with grammar, refusing determinate events by its absence of verbs, sentences that start but seem unable to make it half way through, as if they too end on the pavement. The fog confounds the distinctions that architecture makes between inside and outside,[37] and creates a vertiginous sense of "hanging," of being between places. To go over the parapet, perhaps in an act of suicide (I shall return to this with *Martin Chuzzlewit*), would be to disappear before you hit the water.

The fog only receives a character as it rolls "defiled," attaining some temporary imprint by that, and then passes that character on, defiling. It figures both the city and writing; the first in being the condition of fragmentary types who also lack inside-outside distinctions, being produced and made to vanish at once. As writing, it is like what Lacan refers to as "the defiles of the signifier,"[38] the writing that contaminates, for there is no subject outside writing, outside the text. The writing makes disappear too, as in the letter from Kenge and Carboy to Esther Summerson, "Our clt Mr Jarndyce being abt to rece into his house, under an Order of the Ct of Chy, a Ward of the Ct in this cause" (*Bleak House,* 3.35). The fate of characters in the letter is the fate of character. Writing, whose act is privative, so that Esther, who in her delirious state (chap. 35) would wish to be the woman who was never heard of again, can say with surprise "As if this narrative were the narrative of *my* life!" (3.35). But its privative nature is also productive, so what is seen is shaped by the fog, like the sun and the gas-lamp appearing through the fog, but not visualizable outside it, so that the fog is like the Derridean text: there is no outside fog.

Bleak House puts spontaneous combustion at its center (in chapter 32, out of the 67 chapters altogether), stopping a realist linear narrative altogether, and ending Mr. Krook's career in mud and vapor, dissolving a distinction between the inside and the outside, for at the end of the chapter his insides are outside, smeared and plastered on the walls, and he is the man who is never heard of—or seen—again. Fog, writing, the city, and the failure of narrative are aligned. That narrative of *Bleak House,* which is not Esther Summerson's, is particularly anonymous in denying a subject position from which to write. *Bleak House* comes ten years after Dickens's visit to the United States, as if not until *Bleak House* can the city which before he thought could be read, be looked at in the decentering terms which align it with the language generated by the sense of America.

DICKENS IN AMERICA

Why should I care for the men of thames,
Or for the cheating waves of charter'd streams,
Or shrink at the little blasts of fear
That the hireling blows into my ear?

Tho' born on the cheating banks of Thames,
Tho' his waters bathed my infant limbs,
The Ohio shall wash his stains from me:
I was born a slave, but I go to be free.[39]

William Blake's proposed itinerary, where the voice in the poem may speak for that of a poor white, identifies London, seat of empire and of the slave trade, with Africa, and the Thames with the Niger. The Ohio, in the newly independent United States, and the frontier of the Western territory, epitomizes freedom from slavery. Dickens's journey, announced beforehand to Forster, with self-confidence as from the man who did not mean not be heard of again, comes fifty years after Blake's poem. As described in *American Notes,* it took him from Boston to New York, Philadelphia, Baltimore, Washington, Richmond, and Harrisburg, then on by canal boat to Pittsburgh and from there by steamboat on the Ohio on to

Cincinnati, then to Louisville and on to Cairo, where the Ohio and the Mississippi meet. He then went 200 miles upstream on the Mississippi to St. Louis and left the river—"never to see it again, I hope, but in a nightmare" (Dickens to Forster, 15 April, *Letters,* 3:195)—by returning from it to the Ohio, and then going back up the Ohio to Cincinnati.

In Dickens's writing about the journey near the meeting point of the two rivers (*American Notes,* chap. 12) the repeated adjectives are "dull," "monotonous," "desolate," "dismal," a breeding place of disease, which read like Marlow's later analogous journey up river in Conrad's *Heart of Darkness.* The listlessness of the company at mealtimes on the boat as a "very recollection" he says "weights me down, and makes him for the moment "wretched." He believes that the "recollection of these funeral feasts will be a waking nightmare" all his life (*American Notes,* 12.176). These points give evidence of the breakdown that has been argued for, so too when he comes to

> a dismal swamp, on which the half-built houses rot away: cleared here and there for the space of a few yards; and teeming then, with rank unwholesome vegetation, in whose baleful shade the wretched wanderers who are tempted hither, droop, and die, and lay their bones; the hateful Mississippi circling and eddying before it, and turning off upon its southern course a slimy monster hideous to behold; a hotbed of disease, an ugly sepulchre, a grave uncheered by any gleam of promise . . . such is this dismal Cairo. (12.177)

There follows the account of the Mississippi, "great father of rivers who . . . has no young children like him!"

> An immense ditch, sometimes two or three miles wide, running liquid mud, six miles an hour: its strong and frothy current choked and obstructed everywhere by huge logs and whole forest trees: now twining themselves together in great rafts, from the interstices of which a sedgy foam works up, to float upon the water's top; now rolling past like monstrous bodies, their tangled roots showing like matted hair: now glancing singly by like giant leeches; and now writhing round and round in the vortex of some small whirlpool, like wounded snakes. The banks low, the trees dwarfish, the marshes swarming with frogs, the wretched cabins few and far apart, their inmates hollow-cheeked and pale, the weather very hot, mosquitoes penetrating into every crack and crevice of the boat, mud and slime on everything.

On the next page, he says that they drank from the muddy river.

The experience was recollected again for *Martin Chuzzlewit,* adding a prevalent melancholy as the travelers approach Eden:

As they proceeded further on their track, and came more and more towards their journey's end, the monotonous desolation of the scene increased to that degree, that for any redeeming feature it presented to their
eyes, they might have entered . . . on the grim domains of Giant Despair.
A flat morass, bestrewn with fallen timber; a marsh on which the good
growth of the earth seemed to have been wrecked and cast away, that from
its decomposing ashes vile and ugly things might rise; where the very trees
took the aspect of huge weeds, begotten of the slime from which they
sprung, by the hot sun that burnt them up; where fatal maladies, seeking
whom they might infect, came forth . . . where even the blessed sun, shining down on festering elements of corruption and disease became a horror; this was the realm of Hope through which they moved.

At last they stopped. At Eden too. The waters of the Deluge might have
left it but a week before: so choked with slime and matted growth was the
hideous swamp . . . (*Martin Chuzzlewit*, 23.375)

The mud and slime, the waters retreating, the foul waters, the affronting
to any sense of individual character or sense of personal centeredness—
these elements of America that so oppress the novelist that they must be
repeated from text to text—reappear in *Bleak House* and suggest that that
text's matrix may be the experience of Cairo, just as Cairo was the point
at which other American experiences of difference and alienation coa-
lesced or found their focus. The wilderness is evoked through allegorizations—Despair, Hope, Eden—and through near allegorizations, such as
"fatal maladies," the "blessed sun," and "corruption and disease," which
attempt to give a face to that aspect of America that resists the English
novelist's attempts to master it in description. In *Bleak House,* there is also
prosopopoeia, but it is applied to those things that resist form and character: mud, smoke, and fog, the last an allegory of allegory, London as an
allegory, London as that which cannot be read.

Returning from St. Louis, Dickens finds the Mississippi repellent
again, a "filthy river" that "seemed to be alive with monsters" (14.191),
and Cairo, already described once, now called a "detestable morass":
terms that anticipate *Bleak House,* especially as the river not only contains
monsters (ready to cannibalize) but also is said to be "dragging its slimy
length." To get from the Mississippi waters to the Ohio waters means
crossing "a yellow line which stretched across the current" (14.192). As so
much in the *Bleak House* passage has also, the yellowness contains a vaguely
excremental sense; but in the contrast with "the clear Ohio," the Mississippi's "sparkling neighbour," the river seems analogous also to the fog. It
is also the monster, the dinosaur itself. It seems to devour parts of Cairo,
which, in terms suggestive of the name Eden in *Martin Chuzzlewit,* Dickens
speaks of in flood as a "floating paradise"; and the hatred appears in the

contrast between it and the Ohio, which makes him hope never to see it again "saving in troubled dreams and nightmares." The repetition of this material from the first journey is the point: the text confesses its own sickness in its need to construct such an image of the disgusting. The Mississippi and Cairo become interchangeable in Dickens's violence of reaction, and the psychic collapse goes with fears of being eaten, or having his identity being sucked under.

Cairo, as the site of a less complete trauma, reappears in the letters of Thackeray written in the 1850s and in Anthony Trollope's *North America,* the record of a journey made at the beginning of the Civil War, and I shall look at their wariness with regard to America in chapter 4. This Cairo, which appears in Melville's *The Confidence Man* (1857), is also the place of crisis in Twain's *Huckleberry Finn.* Jim and Huck were heading for it, so that their raft could turn from the Mississippi and go up the Ohio to freedom, but they overshoot and the raft misses Cairo and continues on south (*The Adventures of Huckleberry Finn* [1884], chap. 15 and 16). Cairo is the missed experience in *Huckleberry Finn,* but Twain's Mississippi is not Dickens's nightmare river, image of the abject. Twain impels upon the reader the reminder that the Mississippi is linked to slavery, and the Ohio not; this does not appear openly in Dickens's prose, but I think it underlies its nausea and sense of unease, including the subject's unease at himself.

The crisis, which in *American Notes* is confronted at one particular spot, at the moment of coming to Cairo, Illinois, seems to work retroactively, casting a light onto American cities and onto American city space, and activating nausea or paranoid fear. Equally, it has been produced out of accumulated sensations of the United States, North and South: Northern urbanism, Southern slavery, from which Dickens has turned away in revulsion. The next novel, *Martin Chuzzlewit,* not only is focused on London, but interrogates city architecture, in both England and America. The city appears as making people crazy, and architects, who think they can control, or stabilize or narrativize city space, or even bring its "unreal" existence into appearance, as craziest of all.

In letting the experiences of Cairo and its riverine memories inform the writing of London in *Bleak House,* no distinction is being made between the "natural" and the city. Dickens feels alienated from the Mississippi and from Cairo, which *was* a city. Cairo, opening onto the Mississippi, questions what city nature is, as European cities cannot, in spite of the alienation—and fascination—with which they are viewed by Dickens, Baudelaire, and Dostoyevsky. By *Bleak House,* there seems no distinction sustainable in Dickens between Cairo and London, or it seems that what informs Cairo may be the same as what forms London, because both are the shape of the modern urban. London, the imperial center, is simultaneously a relapse back to the primeval, to the Deluge or to the glacial melting, and it is also propelled into the future, the time of the death of the sun, which means that, as Benjamin puts it, in the dreams of the bourgeois epoch, the "monuments of the bourgeoisie" are indeed "ruins even before they have crumbled."[40]

It was the American city that made London so illegible. If the European city threatens the subject with being lost, as is clearly the case, it is accentuated as a state when the city is as it is in America—regular, devoid of history, or of an obvious subjectivity, presenting little that was obvious to the eye that seeks for hierarchical markers, and marked by differences in race and class that threaten the European's protected certainties. In the following chapter, I will follow this through by reading Dickens on his American cities.

CHAPTER 2

After Dickens

AMERICAN NOTES FOR GENERAL CIRCULATION

Visiting America and writing about it was common English practice after the Napoleonic wars and after the war with America. Captain Basil Hall, whose *Travels in North America in the Years 1827 and 1828* appeared in 1830, was used by Fanny Trollope, in her *Domestic Manners of the Americans* (1832). Both writers compare America unfavorably with Canada, the obedient colony. Dickens refers to both these, and to Harriet Martineau's *Society in America* (1837), which appeared after her extensive visits to America (September 1834 to August 1836), followed by her *Retrospect of Western Travel* (1838). Captain Marryat's *Diary in America* (1839), deeply unsympathetic, recorded a visit made at the end of the decade, between 1837 and 1838.

In discussing *American Notes,* which in this chapter will take the form of noting its salient features, I confine comparisons with Dickens to the visits made by Mrs. Trollope and by Harriet Martineau—in all, one Tory, one Radical, and one Liberal account.[1] Fanny Trollope left England in November 1827 and returned in August 1831, having spent two years in Cincinnati, Ohio, followed by travel through the East Coast states. Dickens's visit was only a few months. Fanny Trollope's and Dickens's views may be put together in one respect: Both concentrate on America's difference from England. Harriet Martineau, there for two years, sees America as different, but she does not assume England to be the norm. Reading Martineau is a different experience, for she has no separation from what she describes, nor resistance to it. The two others come back repeatedly to the pervasive "spitting" of Americans (spitting up chewed tobacco) as an offense to them: Harriet Martineau dispatches it in virtually two paragraphs, finishing, "I dismiss the nauseous subject."[2]

Each of the three, like H. G. Wells, later, is interested in the utopist possibilities of America. Mrs. Trollope traveled to America with members of her family and with Fanny Wright, who had bought land at Nashoba near Memphis, Tennessee, to educate black slaves for liberty. The party entered America at the mouth of the Mississippi, which Mrs. Trollope speaks of as like the entry to Dante's *Inferno,* and went to New Orleans, where she met William McClure, who had been instrumental, with Robert Owen, in setting up a utopist settlement at New Harmony, Indiana, including a school. They traveled up the river to Memphis, and then to Nashoba, a place of "desolation."[3] That, apart from further references to Fanny Wright's lecturing in Cincinnati and at Philadelphia, and apart from an account of Robert Owen, is all the space that Mrs. Trollope spends on utopian schemes, and the book turns then to a discussion of Cincinnati, where they moved after Nashoba proved impossible, and, after Cincinnati, to East Coast cities. The narrative records the failure of dreams, utopist ones and her own. Harriet Martineau, in contrast, endorses American "institutions" throughout. Dickens's visit to America took the form of visiting each and every institution he could in what reads like a form of repetition, and with a confidence, almost colonial, about his power to judge these.

Writing assumes the power of rendering everything interpretable, and to interpret is also to take away, to destroy, to make the subject of writing disappear. Dickens notes this in retailing a lugubriously funny anecdote about another traveler and his wife on board the same boat as himself, on the journey toward Lake Erie. Dickens overhears the man saying to his wife, "Boz is on board still, my dear," and "Boz keeps himself very close," and then eventually, "I suppose *that* Boz will be writing a book by-and-by, and putting all our names in it!" to which Dickens adds, "at which imaginary consequence of being on board with Boz, he groaned and became silent" (*American Notes,* 14.203).

The evocation of obsessionalism goes with all the other accounts of madness in *American Notes,* but it is all the same an exact metalinguistic account of the book. The fate of being an American meeting Dickens is to be a postcolonial subject meeting someone from the center of English culture, and hence to provide another in the *Sketches by Boz;* and if you have read it, to know exactly how Dickens will do it, how much comic obsessionalism is its metier. It is a cause for fear. Dickens in the anecdote is not Dickens, but the self-styled, fictional Boz, the machinic creator and shaper of machinic identities, and the American's groan and silence at the end shows a pathos as though he has registered his own death—death by being identified in the book ("putting all our names in it"), death by being fixed in a single identity, death by being written about.

Mrs. Trollope focuses on domesticity, as her title implies, but she too, was nearly engulfed by America in a loss of identity, nearly becoming the woman who was never heard of again. One description of her put it, "She was then travelling with her 2 daughters, merely girls, and with a French-man. In what capacity the latter attended her, Hamilton [an English au-thor] could not make out, but from the odd appearance of manners, and her apparent poverty, which hardly admitted her and her daughters being decently dressed, it was conclusive against her being taken notice of by respectable ladies, or treated as one herself."[4] Harriet Martineau, in con-trast to Trollope, is sociological, as the title *Society in America* suggests. Dickens's title, *American Notes for General Circulation,* while it puns on the idea of notes giving a musical tone, like a "keynote," also punned on the expectation that the text would be pirated by American publishers, like forged banknotes, as though American banknotes were likely to be forg-eries.[5] But the title is more ambiguous than that. While his "notes" may be American, the unconscious of the title proposes that they may also be no more than forgeries, not originals of value to be copied, but copies al-ready. The title qualifies the sense of uniqueness in the text.

The doubleness—is this text genuine or not?—recalls Dickens's si-lence in the text of *American Notes* about his motives for visiting the United States. Alexander Welsh, in *From Copyright to Copperfield,* is only one of those who, by discussing what James Spedding in the *Edinburgh Re-view* had to say about the book, have come back to the point that *Ameri-can Notes* says nothing about Dickens's advocacy of international copyright in the United States.[6] Dickens made speeches on this at Boston (1 February 1842) and at Hartford (8 February) and was accused in the American press of being mercenary and tactless in allowing him-self to raise the subject. It had not been long before that English culture had made the judgment, in the words of the Rev. Sydney Smith, "In the four quarters of the globe, who reads an American book? Or goes to an American play? Or looks at an American picture or statue?"[7] And that dominant culture was now demanding to be paid for being read in America! The *New World* newspaper commented that 20,000 copies of Dickens's works were "disseminated every week, throughout the entire land, in the ample pages of the *New World,* calling this "the secret of his widespread fame" (quoted, *Letters,* 3:60n). "Dissemination," in Derrida, is the end of identity, and this loss is associated with the "name" of Dick-ens being known, so the *New World* put it, to "the dwellers in log cabins, in our back settlements," only through the absence of an International Copyright law. Dickens had referred in a speech at Boston to receiving letters about Nell (in *The Old Curiosity Shop*) "from the dwellers in log-houses among the morasses, and swamps, and densest forests, and deepest solitudes of the Far West," written to him "as a friend to whom he might freely impart the joys and sorrows of his own fireside."[8] Now his words, with their protestations of intimacy over a figure whose fate illustrates the coercive nature of sentimentality in forcing intimacy, are turned against him; and the writer has to learn that far from serial publication bringing him nearer to readers, the dissemination of his name in so many forms, pirated and authorized, brings about only the death of the author in a country both urban and so much more amorphous than Britain. Loss of identity—becoming the man who was never heard of again—becomes the fate of writing in urban culture, the place of the production of print.

A third speech on the topic followed, given on 18 February in New York, the place where identity is most dissolved (see letter to Forster, 24 February, *Letters*, 3:81). And Dickens could not have responded well to the point that some of the American advocates of International Copyright were supporting it on the ground that only thus could a new, postcolonial, American literature emerge, for such an argument would, by implication, make his own work nonuniversal, would question its own basis. It becomes a motif later on in the century as part of the establishment of English literature as a consciously colonial construction. Matthew Arnold reacted to an advertisement for a book called *The Primer of American Literature* with, "Are we to have a Primer of Canadian Literature too, and a Primer of Australian? We are all contributors to one great literature—English literature."[9] But before going to America (twice—in 1883 to 1884 and in 1886), Arnold had said that he regarded "the people of the United States as just the same people with ourselves, as simply, 'the English on the other side of the Atlantic.'"[10] Nothing that Arnold saw in America, certainly no contact with America in the aftermath of the Civil War, seems to have made him change his mind.

Dickens's letter of 24 February is not free from self-righteousness, and as he adds that he will not accept any further public entertainments or public recognitions while in America, it seems that there is an unconscious need to protect the self and to guard an identity. If the notion of copyright gives or protects identity, by creating the concept of "intellectual property," the assaults on Dickens from United States newspapers, which accused him of being mercenary after his speeches at Boston and Hartford would have damaged his identity. Loss of identity—becoming the man who was never heard of again—would be a fate shared with his books. America, it seemed, showed for Dickens how unacceptably to the self identity could be constructed, and what was the danger of the obverse: of disappearing into a nondifferentiated city or nondifferentiated wilderness: as surely as disappearing in an urban fog.

AFTER A JOURNEY

In what follows, I follow Dickens's itinerary by breaking it into discussions of the places he visited. He began with New England. When he arrived in the United States of America, Chicago, to take another point of reference for this study, had, like a new plant, only just come into existence about 12 years before with a population of 50. Dickens did not visit it, though Harriet Martineau did, and said she "never saw a busier place than Chicago . . . the streets were crowded with land speculators, hurrying from one sale to another." Predicting an assured future for it, she declared herself "glad to have seen it in its strange early days."[11] By the time James came to America, to visit Chicago but significantly not to write about it, it was the second city, in point of numbers, in America, with well over a million population, and a demonstration of the rapidity with which nineteenth-century America became urban.

NEW ENGLAND

Dickens's America started at Boston (22 January 1842) where he stayed at the Tremont, Boston's leading hotel, which had opened in 1829. "It has more galleries, colonnades, piazzas and passages than I can remember, or the reader would believe" (2.39).[12] So Dickens starts with the hotel, as James will discuss America in terms of the "hotel spirit," and appropriately, for the modern hotel, as distinct from the inn or tavern, may be considered an American invention. The first opened on Broadway in New York in 1794.[13] A little detail at the end of Dickens's chapter on New York notes "the saddest tomb" in a spacious cemetery in a New York suburb (Greenwood, in Brooklyn, which opened in 1838). It was "The Stranger's Grave. Dedicated to the different hotels in this city" (6.104). Not surprisingly, Karl Rossmann works at a hotel, the Occidental.

Boston's 1842 population of 93,000 packed itself into the single square-mile peninsula that the town had occupied for 200 years. Dickens's description misses the overcrowding: "The air was so clear, the houses were so bright and gay; the signboards were painted in such gaudy colours; the gilded letters were so very golden; the bricks were so very red, the stone was so very white, the blinds and railings were so very green, the knobs and plates upon the street doors so marvellously bright and twinkling; and all so slight and unsubstantial in appearance—that every thoroughfare in the city looked exactly like a scene in a pantomime" (3.40). Boston's innocence repeats the traveler's. It is "unsubstantial-looking" (3.41) like its "suburbs"; "beautiful," "handsome," and "charming." But as much as Boston is not regarded as real, the description of it proves equally non-real, as though Boston as a city exists elsewhere—in its institutions, in Harvard, outside the city, and the Perkins Institution for the Blind, founded in 1833, also spoken of as outside the city. Given the prominence it has in *American Notes,* it seems that the Perkins Institution appears as the ideal, focusing on the long account of 13-year-old Laura Bridgman, blind and deaf-mute, and with virtually no sense of smell, and so existing already in a form of solitary confinement:

> There she was, before me, built up, as it were in a marble cell, impervious to any ray of light, or particle of sound; with her poor white hand peeping through a chink in the wall, beckoning to some good man for help, that an Immortal soul might be awakened. (3.46)

The biographical account of this girl, taken from a pamphlet about the Perkins Institute written by its director, Samuel Gridley Howe, and supplemented by further notes on a boy called Oliver Caswell, occupies the next 12 or so pages of *American Notes.* Dickens draws attention to the lack of hypocrisy on the faces of the blind (3.45)—hypocrisy coming about from an awareness of being looked at. "What secrets would come out" Dickens writes, if the sighted could not see they had eyes looking at them. That this is not accidental is shown by its repetition at the end of the visit, when Dickens refers to sighted "hypocrites of sad countenance" (3.58). What is the dream in the visitor to the Institutions, if not of a surveillance that is not looked back at?

The city is not taken seriously; it is dispatched in easy phrases. But that is not the case with the institutions. Dickens passes on to a visit to the State Hospital for the Insane in South Boston, and says that the patients gathered round him were "unrestrained" (3.58). He refers in comparison to the new methods being used at Hanwell Asylum where John Conolly, Dickens's friend, was trying the method of "non-restraint" and appealing to the patient's self-control.[14] Thus "moral influence alone" (3.60) and "decent self-respect" (3.61) activates all the institutions: Dickens passes to the "House of Industry," where the inscription on the walls—an American note—declares WORTHY OF NOTICE. SELF-GOVERNMENT, QUIETUDE, AND PEACE ARE BLESSINGS. I shall return to this very legible writing, which Dickens considered indeed worthy of notice. There is, further, the Boylston School, an asylum for poor and neglected boys, which is intended to get them off the streets, and the House of Reformation for Juvenile Offenders, under the same roof—"but the two classes of boys never come in contact." The social space of the establishment is as carefully managed as the separate parts of a town. Lastly comes the "House of Correction for the State"—the prison that operates on the silent system, of the prisoners not being allowed to speak with each other. These "houses" best represent the city.

The critique of the House of Correction contends that the useful work the prisoners do—as opposed to working the treadmill or picking oakum—means that "in an American state prison or house of correction, I found it difficult at first to persuade myself that I was really in a jail" (3.64). The subject of "Prison Discipline" Dickens declares to be "of the highest importance to any community" (3.65), but here it is missing since the prison is not unambiguously declared to be a prison by the specific discipline practiced there, or even by its architecture, since "it is not walled, like other prisons" (3.65). Up till then, Dickens has surveyed all the architectural arrangements, and approved them in a sense of recognition; but here it is different.

Everything in *American Notes* turns toward regulation of space and people, so that the "oddness" in visiting the Court of Law at Boston is to note that the prisoner in a criminal trial is not to be found in the dock: "that gentleman would most likely be lounging among the most distinguished ornaments of the legal profession" (3.67). It is anxiety-arousing when neither criminal nor prison are clearly distinguishable, as though not properly named. In Britain, this might have become the cause of Dickensian carnivalesque writing; in an American city, it disturbs, as a sign of potential nondescribability. Elements of control are noted, as with the railroad with its gentlemen's, ladies', and "negro" cars on the train, when Dickens traveled to Lowell, Massachusetts (chap. 4), specifically to look at "the American Manchester." This comprised a new factory created in 1822 in a spirit of puritanical paternalism, and by Dickens's time, Lowell was the nation's fourteenth largest city.[15] Dickens looked there at the women—New England farm girls who formed 75 percent of the workforce in the factories, and commented on their boarding houses, mandatory for unmarried female workers. He describes their hospital. The city has no other real existence than that of being managed, disciplined, with different spaces assigned: its other buildings—the church, the hotel—exist as though affirming a public space that is actually not there, since the town is, basically, privately owned, and a contrast to rural life with its "poverty, insanity and alcoholism."[16]

In chapter 5, Dickens spends time in Hartford, visiting the Insane Asylum, where order and control are tested most fully, and from where it seems that most assurance can be found in order to read America. He distinguishes four patients: a "little prim old lady," a male patient with the "faint idea that his talk was incoherent" (5.85), a young man whose love was music who draws attention to the prisonous nature of the institution ("I think I shall go out next Tuesday"), and a woman who asks for his autograph—who presumably, therefore, knows who Dickens is—and who hears voices, which are reason for keeping her in confinement (at this point Dickens makes a joke about Joseph Smith, the Mormon founder). The State prison is also discussed, and a woman pointed out, in confinement for 16 years so far, for the murder of her husband.

These portraits align the novelist's art with that of the prison-visitor and the observation of types with the observation of the mad or the non-free or the criminal. It is evident that all the people thus mentioned have their counterparts in Dickens's novels; in *Bleak House* or *Little Dorrit.* The art of the novel furnishes an example for the description of people, as when one mad woman is compared to Madge Wildfire from Scott's *The Heart of Midlothian* (*American Notes,* 3.59). The novelist by novelizing the people he meets, playing along with their delusions, as he says himself, "humours [the mad] to the top of his bent." The half quotation is from *Hamlet,* "they fool me to the top of my bent"—Hamlet's comment on the spying of Polonius, Rosencrantz, and Guildenstern—and it is strange that Dickens should put himself into the position of any one of those three officers of surveillance. (If he notes it, it is already a sign to him of the awkwardness of his identity in this place.) Why does he play along with the delusions of the Miss Flite-like woman who asks, "Does Pontefract still flourish, Sir, upon the soil of England?" (5.84). In doing so, he confirms the woman in the prison of her delusions, and adopts in relation to her a normalizing stance, which perpetuates a superiority that is national, gendered, and novelizing. It is also strange that the assessments of each of these people should accept that it is right that they should be confined. Dickens's reading of Laura Bridgman is almost wholly taken from the official account of her, and while he registers surprise to learn that the woman who asked for his autograph is confined because she hears voices, there is no questioning of the justice of this, even though reflection tells him that some people who hear voices, or profess to do so, are not locked up. It leads him to the joke that a few "Mormonists" should go that way (5.86), and indeed, the eagerness to visit institutions confirms a sense in *American Notes* that more people, not less, should be confined.

NEW YORK

Traveling through Hartford and New Haven, Dickens reached New York by steamboat on 12 February 1842, to stay at the Carlton House hotel on

Broadway, until 5 March. He was to revisit New York for five days in June, before sailing home.

In 1842, the city's population was approaching 400,000, and though concentrated in the south part of Manhattan, the Battery, Wall Street, Greenwich Village, Broadway, the Bowery, and the poverty around the Five Points area, it was moving uptown, toward Thirty-Fifth Street. New York, every inch of which John Randel Jr. had surveyed by 1810, had been given its postrevolution grid pattern by commissioners who said they "could not but bear in mind that a city is to be composed principally of the habitations of men, and that strait sided and right angled houses are the most cheap to build and the most convenient to live in."[17] They had planned the dozen north-south avenues and the 155 east-west streets that would make New York a city some seven miles in extent, and give it waterfront access.

Dickens's visit came in the interval between the laying out of the grid-iron system and the further laying out of Central Park (Frederick Law Olmsted and Calvert Vaux, 1858). A year after Dickens came, there would be the death of New York's first "millionaire": Pierre Lorillard, a snuff manufacturer.[18] New York had already outstripped Boston and Philadelphia as rivals as a port through the construction of the Erie Canal, enabling goods to be taken right up to the Great Lakes (1825), and one of its material innovations were to be seen the year of Dickens's visit (14 October 1842) when the Croton Aqueduct opened, which after seven years in the planning, was now bringing fresh water to the city.

Just before Dickens arrived, in late July 1841, the body of Mary Rogers had been found in the waters of the Hudson, near Hoboken, New Jersey. Mary Rogers, who with her mother, ran a boarding house at 126 Nassau Street, New York, had probably died as a result of a bungled abortion, but Edgar Allan Poe wrote the case as a murder-mystery, calling it "The Mystery of Marie Roget" in the *Ladies' Companion* in late 1842.[19] In this fictionalization, New York becomes Paris, as if aligning the text to Eugene Sue's *Mysteries of Paris,* which had appeared that year, and all the events are translated into French equivalents. Poe had already written "The Man of the Crowd" in 1840, and set it in London. Poe did not know Paris at all and had only been in London in his childhood. These two narratives of the city are not "about" either London or Paris; they are ways of evoking New York by writing of it as though it was some other city. In fictionalizing and discussing the death of Mary Rogers, and by deepening its mystery, Poe made New York Paris. It is as though the city both requires consideration for its unique deployment of space, but also disallows this since, as Poe seems to see, its character tends toward the international—one of the unsettling aspects of mapping it—and it makes spaces interchangeable, not

only one space an allegory of another space (to be in one city is to be reminded of another), but that space is about to become what Gilles
Deleuze in discussing cinema, calls "any-space-whatever,"[20] space ab-
stracted from the conditions of a distinctive setting. When New York can
be written about in terms of Paris, the city is, implicitly, being defamiliarized, and Poe is deliberately taking it not as a city that was knowable in
terms of size and political importance, but as analogous to a capital—as allegorically, like the "capital of the nineteenth-century." Further, the city,
not quite mappable, is full of crowds whose mobility requires a reading
like that of the detective narrative, following the traces of the city, trying
to establish a coherent narrative at work within it.

Dickens arrived the year William James was born in a house in Washington Square, whose Greek Revival row houses had been laid out in
1828. Fifth Avenue had opened, north of Washington Square, five years
earlier, and its fortunes were already beginning to overshadow the main
street, Broadway. Henry James was born a year after Dickens's visit, but
Washington Square (1879) shows a need to go back—at a time when Washington Square was beginning to lose class and status—with the intention
of writing the city in a way Dickens could not. The main action in the
novel is in the 1840s, but James refers to 1820, the year of Dr. Sloper's
marriage to "a young woman of high fashion," and to "the small but
promising capital which clustered about the Battery and overlooked the
Bay, and of which the uppermost boundary was indicated by the grassy
waysides of Canal Street." In 1835, Dr. Sloper moves up from "an edifice
of red brick, with granite copings and an enormous fanlight over the
door" five minutes from City Hall, to Washington Square, following his
clients, as the downtown houses become converted to offices and warehouses, and where he

> built himself a handsome, modern, wide-fronted house, with a big balcony
> before the drawing-room windows, and a flight of marble steps ascending
> to a portal which was also faced with white marble. This structure, and
> many of its neighbours, which it exactly resembled, were supposed, forty
> years ago, to embody the last results of architectural science. . . . In front of
> them was the square, containing a considerable quantity of inexpensive
> vegetation, enclosed by a wooden paling, which increased its rural and ac-
> cessible appearance. . . . (*Washington Square*, 4, 14, 15)

Architecture is treated in the text with as much skepticism as medical science, and the awareness of dollars underlines the portrait of the square.
Architecture, too becomes an art of irony, like the way Dr. Sloper always
addresses his daughter—in "the ironical form" (22). Nonetheless:

I know not whether it is owing to the tenderness of early associations, but this portion of New York appears to many persons the most delectable. It has a kind of established repose which is not of frequent occurrence in other parts of the city; it has a riper, richer, more honourable look than any of the upper ramifications of the great longitudinal thoroughfare [Fifth Avenue]—the look of having had something of a social history. It was here . . . that you had come into a world which appeared to offer a variety of sources of interest . . .

Dr. Sloper's sister, Mrs. Almond lived further up, in "a region where the extension of the city began to assume a theoretic air, where poplars grew beside the pavement (where there was one) and mingled their shade with the steep roofs of desultory Dutch houses, and where pigs and chickens disported themselves in the gutter." (16)

The difference in 1879 from the then provinciality is the point. James writes that the pigs "were to be found in the memory of middle-aged persons who now would blush to be reminded of them." James gives to the New York society of 1879 a memory, a sense of a past, just as the Dutch roofs imply a past that is further back for the society of the 1830s and 1840s. James's historical writing goes back to New York to assert that there was a past to that America, or that there was a "shadow" to it, even if the effect of historical relativizing, showing how provincial New York's past had been, is also to indicate narrowness in the newer New York of the time of writing.

The house in Washington Square, although different from the housing along the avenues higher up, whose associations with a literal upward mobility Morris Townsend is well aware of (5.26), is geometrical in character, as is Dr. Sloper, who calls himself "a geometrical proposition" (21.109). Dr. Sloper, in other words, as a "modern" figure is not so different from either the bourgeois spirit of New York, which was moving up every three or four years, or from the son-in-law, Morris Townsend, that Catherine, his daughter, would desire for him.

Dickens, however, does not see the geometry of New York, which almost means missing what is American in the city. Though there is a shift in his text when discussing it, as though the certainties allowable in Massachusetts are no longer so possible, it is here that the text most retreats to set forms of writing and types of description picking out idiosyncrasies of the city rather than the development that James read back into it. Dickens later wrote that he had been out at night with the New York police—"and went into every brothel, thieves' house, murdering hovel, sailor dancing place [was this a confrontation with homosexuality?], and abode of villany [*sic*], both black and white, in the town" (to Thomas

Mitton, 22 March, *Letters,* 3:162), but the writing about these things in *American Notes* is more arch. He takes the air along Broadway, noting two Irish immigrants, doing drudge-work,[21] and then, later the number of "foreigners who abound in all the streets: not perhaps, that there are more here than in other commercial cities' but elsewhere, they have particular haunts, and you must find them out; here, they pervade the town" (6.92). There is some discussion of Wall Street, and then, after going along the Bowery ("the stores are poorer here; the passengers less gay") he comes to a "dismal-fronted pile of bastard Egyptian, like an enchanter's palace in a melodrama." It is the Tombs (the New York House of Detention), where Melville's Bartleby dies, and which, designed by John Haviland (1792–1852), had opened in 1838. The choice of the Egyptian style symbolized timelessness, the law as primeval. Describing the Tombs aligns Dickens with architecture, as the text notes the building's functionality:

> A long narrow, lofty building, stove heated as usual, with four galleries, one above the other, going round it, and communicating by stairs. Between the two sides of each gallery, and in its centre, a bridge, for the greater convenience of crossing. On each side of these bridges sits a man . . . On each tier, are two opposite rows of small iron doors. They look like furnace-doors, but are cold and black, as though the fires within had all gone out. Some two or three are open, and women, with drooping heads bent down, are talking to the inmates. The whole is lighted by a skylight, but it is fast closed. . . . (6.93)

From a warder, Dickens elicits information that the ground-floor cells, the most "unwholesome," are used only for colored people. Architectural interest is inseparable from questions of space: for example, where the prisoners can walk to take exercise (they don't). Dickens and the warder walk into the prison yard where hangings take place. Perhaps Melville read *American Notes* and thought of the enclosure of the prison yard for the dying Bartleby;[22] but Dickens, who is told that perhaps the prison's name came about from the suicides there (6.94), and plays on the symbolism in stressing New York's relation to capital punishment, takes the prison more "straight" than *Bartleby the Scrivener* does:

> From the community [the spectacle of capital punishment] is hidden. To the dissolute and bad, the thing remains a frightful mystery. Between the criminal and them, the prison-wall is interposed as a thick gloomy veil. It is the curtain to his bed of death . . . From him it shuts out life, and all the motives to unrepenting hardihood in that last hour, which its mere sight and presence is often all-sufficient to sustain. There are no bold eyes to

make him bold; no ruffians to uphold a ruffian's name before. All beyond
the pitiless stone wall, is unknown space. (6.95)

Architecture confirms the subject-position of the "criminal" whose position is reified in that he is not able to act any part relative to the crowd
in a public hanging. Architecture, by speaking the same language as that
of official justice, confirms the prisoner's abject state. "I thought the
practice infinitely superior to ours: much more solemn, and far less de-
grading and decent" Dickens wrote to Forster, of the method of hanging
(4 March, *Letters*, 104). "Solemn" as a choice of word directs attention to
the desire to confirm a position in opposition to the criminal who is
about to become the man who was never heard of again, and it indicates
ressentiment. Why should it be so important to add the detail that the sentence is carried out solemnly? Is it not enough that it is done? And how
can doing it solemnly be easily distinguished from doing it hypocritically,
in the spirit of, say, Uriah Heep? Are not these two the same?

The chapter turns to Five Points, a slum area since the 1820s, home to
many freed blacks, and to Irish immigrants. Dickens visits this area at
night, as if to confirm or construct a sense of prevalent blackness. He was
accompanied there by New York police, before returning to the Tombs,
which also housed the city watch house, where people arrested during the
night were thrown to await appearance before a magistrate in the morning. The slum, the Five Points, "which in respect of filth and wretched-
ness, may be safely backed against Seven Dials," contrasts with one of the
Sketches by Boz, where the groups of people standing about in Seven Dials
"would fill any mind but a regular Londoner's with astonishment" (*SB*,
92). Dickens feels he can describe Seven Dials as a regular Londoner, not
"the unexperienced wayfarer" (*SB*, 94), but in the Five Points is "all that
is loathsome, drooping and decayed" (12.99). The watch house in the
Tombs in contrast to this laisser-faire America brings out his anger
against a failure in American institutions, since "such indecent and disgusting dungeons as these cells, would bring disgrace upon the most
despotic empire in the world!" Comparisons are made with the sty and
the sewer; this is a failed institution, indicating the failure of city architecture to solemnize, as opposed to degrade.

From there Dickens turns attention to the public institutions on Long
Island and the Lunatic Asylum, the Alms House, the Farm for orphans,
and the Island Jail on Blackwell Island (Roosevelt Island), where he was
rowed by prisoners. Writing to Forster, 6 March 1842, he describes the
prison and includes a diagram of its layout (*Letters*, 3:104), impressed that
by simply walking round, "you see all the cells under one roof and in one
high room," some 400 people. In contrast to this prison, he refers in both

letter and in *American Notes* to the state prisons at Sing Sing, three miles from New York City (founded 1824) and the pioneer prison of the "silent system," Auburn (founded 1819).

PHILADELPHIA

Dickens calls Philadelphia, next visited, and its society, more "provincial" than Boston or New York—which had already overtaken Philadelphia in size, 30 years before. Philadelphia's population was 250,000 and had been built on up to and beyond Tenth Street, away from its port, while many of the people lived outside the old grid system of the city, whose characteristic structure Dickens notes, connecting it to its religious foundation (William Penn's Quaker city). "It is a handsome city, but *distractingly* regular. After walking about it for an hour or two, I felt that I would have given the world for a crooked street. The collar of my coat appeared to stiffen, and the brim of my hat to expand, beneath its *quakery* influence" (7.107). He is caught up in a history of colonial domination, of Quaker rule. Both words I have emphasized connect playfully with the topic of the chapter: the madness of solitary confinement. It is appropriate both that the First Bank of America, which he looked at from his hotel room, marble and Palladian, the work of Benjamin Henry Latrobe, though very different from the brick-built style of late colonial Philadelphia, should also possess symmetry, and that it should have then been shut, thanks to the Panic of 1837: another aspect of this chapter's prisonous theme.

Some of the buildings Dickens singles out are Greek Revival or classical in character, for Nicholas Biddle, Philadelphia's leader, had been in Greece in 1806 and had declared in his diary that "the two great truths in the world are the Bible and Grecian architecture."[23] Architecture seems to have a lot to live up to. Dickens refers to the "handsome" Exchange. This building, with its curving façade, like that which Soane designed for the Bank of England, and its tower in the form of the Choragic Monument of Lysicrates, had been designed by William Strickland. Comments on the abundant water supply refer to the Fairmount Waterworks, designed like Roman temples, and built by Fredrick Graff in the second decade of the nineteenth century. Dickens notes that Philadelphia, like its buildings, is clean, and he mentions Girard College, founded in his will by Stephen Girard for "poor white male orphans" and then built in Greek Revival style by Thomas Walter. But having mentioned other institutions, such as the library and the Post Office, he turns to the nearby Eastern Penitentiary. This, begun in 1821, and like the Tombs designed by John Haviland, had opened in 1830, looking on the outside like a massive fortress with entry through a Gothic archway underneath an iron portcullis. It was the model of the separate system, destined to be copied at a lower level of intensity by Pentonville Prison, which opened in December 1842.

Dickens accuses the prison of a tendency to drive the prisoner mad, with a "slow and daily tampering with the mysteries of the brain" (7.108). He describes being taken to the prison's center chamber, "from which seven long passages [like—but unlike—Seven Dials] radiate. On either side of each, is a long, long row of low cell doors. . . ." The regulated nature of this recalls the grid nature of the streets, and confirms the point that the prison is, for Dickens, as for nineteenth-century government, urban in conception; the city must provide the prison because there is nowhere else that the criminal can go. Putting the prison into discourse does the same for the city. "Standing at the central point, and looking down these dreary passages, the dull repose and quiet that prevails, is awful. . . . Over the head and face of every prisoner who comes into this melancholy house, a black hood is drawn; and in this dark shroud, an emblem of the curtain dropped between him and the living world, he is led to the cell from which he never again comes forth. . . . He is a man buried alive; to be dug out in the slow round of years; and in the meantime dead to everything but torturing anxieties and horrible despair" (7.109).

In using these terms, we anticipate what I have already quoted in chapter 1, the despair in Cairo/Eden, which Martin Chuzzlewit finds. Despair is to be found in the place that is the most humanitarian and rational part of America, Philadelphia, the city of brotherly love, as it is also in the place that is about the furthest west that Dickens visits (for Martin Chuzzlewit in this represents Dickens), and which is the most underdeveloped. "Buried alive" as a phrase appears later in *A Tale of Two Cities,* inscribing that text with something of the trauma that is sensed here, as if in fantasy or in madness, Dickens became the man in solitary confinement, and as though that fate were also imaged in being in Cairo, Illinois. The imprisonment is associated with memory loss: "his name, and crime, and term of suffering, are unknown" and with a loss of spatiality and spatial relations, which is also a loss of identity, for "he has no means of knowing . . . in what part of the building [the cell] is situated" (7.109).

Dickens combines the discussion of the Eastern Penitentiary with a reference to the Western Penitentiary at Pittsburgh, and the rest of the chapter puts the two prisons together as one. The prisoners' faces are "haggard"—the word reappears when the gas lighting in *Bleak House* has a "haggard and unwilling look"—as though the prosopopoeia which turned the lights into faces also made them figures of estrangement, or of physical or psychic maiming: the last point deriving from what it is that specially makes the prisoners' faces haggard—as though they were "blind and deaf, mingled with a kind of horror, as though they had been secretly terrified" (7.118) The idea links back to Laura Bridgman, and to her walled-up state in the prison of her senses, and it connects with what Dickens writes in a letter of 3 April 1842 to Forster about the prison at Pittsburgh:

> A horrible thought occurred to me when I was recalling all I had seen, that night. *What if ghosts be one of the terrors of these jails?* . . . The more I think of it, the more certain I feel that not a few of these men . . . are nightly visited by spectres. I did ask one man in this last jail, if he dreamed much. He gave me a most extraordinary look, and said—under his breath—in a whisper—"No." . . . (*Letters*, 3:181)

This writing puts Dickens into the position of the prisoner. He needs to know that prisoners are haunted, if only by dreams, and like Freud, he takes denial as agreement. He has become the solitary prisoner in his belief that there must be a supplementary absence for the prisoner, the ghost. And like James, later on, Dickens wishes to invent an American ghost in a way that serves to give America a psychic and haunted past. "In every chamber that I entered, and at every grate through which I looked, I seemed to see the same appalling countenance." This resembles Blake's "London":

> In every cry of every Man,
> In every Infant's cry of fear,
> In every voice, in every ban,
> The mind-forg'd manacles I hear.

The "I" that marks faces either with "marks of weakness, marks of woe," or that sees those marks on the faces (but it is undecidable whether interpretation reads in, or whether it merely records), needs the repetition and the totality of the word "every." Dickens does the same. In looking, he gives himself a further vision, which "lives in my memory"—the memory of faces, like those figures of mania Gericault painted. Since horror is ideological, Dickens cannot think that the women are quite as spoiled by what happens, but speaking of men he writes:

> It is my fixed opinion that those who have undergone this punishment, MUST pass into society again morally unhealthy and diseased. . . . [The effect] has . . . become apparent, in some disordered train of thought, or some gloomy hallucination. What monstrous phantoms, bred of despondency and doubt, and born and reared in solitude, have stalked upon the earth, making creation ugly and darkening the face of Heaven! (7.118)

The overwriting in the last sentence leads both into the first page of *Bleak House* and into the criticisms that Kafka made of Dickens. The writing is sentimentally coercive, partly because the critique that is made of the panoptical method—awareness of Utilitarianism appears casually in chapter 6 (97)—is interested in order (hence "disordered") and in morality and is regulatory and so kitsch-like in its generalizing adjectives and allegorical abstractions. Partly, because the issue of madness is being projected onto the prisoners in a way that is coercive in another way, "marking" them as in Blake. If Dickens felt so saddened by the experience of the Eastern Penitentiary, why did he repeat the experience at the Western Penitentiary? That he did suggests a demand for totality, a demand to read America as maddening but also a will toward becoming mad himself. So the generalization follows:

All men who have made diseases of the mind their study, know perfectly well that such extreme depression and despair as will change the whole character, and beat down all its powers of elasticity and self-resistance, may be at work within a man, and yet stop short of self-destruction. (7.118)

To have had to come to America to talk about "diseases of the mind" implies the journey's liminal nature, and its capacity to wound the subject to such an extent that he has to force himself back to an over-centralizing, over-normalizing consciousness in writing the experience at all. This utilitarian discourse will not allow for the possibility that depression itself may even be psychically necessary, and that legislation in relation to it may not work.

WASHINGTON

From 9 to 16 March, Dickens stayed at Fuller's Hotel in Washington. He had come via Baltimore, where, Maryland being a slave state, he noted that he was waited on by slaves. It is a theme for the chapter, for he comments on John Quincy Adams who had attacked slavery in the House of Representatives the week before Dickens arrived; but the anger he expresses originates from a feeling that Adams should have been more listened to as a man who had done the States some service, and the outrage links to Dickens's sense of a failure of solemnity. "It was not a month, since [the House] had sat calmly by, and heard a man, one of themselves [General Dawson of Louisiana—see *Letters*, 3:119], with oaths which beggars in their drink reject, threaten to cut another's throat from ear to ear. There he sat, among them; not crushed by the general feeling of the assembly, but as good as any" (8.128). Dickens narrates this in a far funnier way in a letter to Fonblanque:

the dignity assumed for *American Notes* is another aspect of that sentimentality that is nostalgia for bourgeois order, and is confounded by another older formation in the American South.

Because of that, Washington as a city becomes a place to be criticized. He notes the Capitol, "a fine building of the Corinthian order, placed upon a noble and commanding eminence" (8.123), but it is also relevant that he spends five paragraphs attacking Washington as misplaced in position, the hotel as badly run, the buildings in the street outside the hotel as out of scale and the planning a failure:

> It is sometimes called the City of Magnificent Distances, but it might with greater propriety be called the City of Magnificent Intentions; for it is only on taking a bird's eye view of it from the top of the Capitol that one can at all comprehend the vast designs of its projector, an aspiring Frenchman. Spacious avenues, that begin in nothing, and lead nowhere; streets, mile-long, that only want houses, roads and inhabitants; public buildings that need but a public to be complete and ornaments of great thoroughfares, which only lack great thoroughfares to ornament—are its leading features. One might fancy the season over, and most of the houses gone out of town for ever with their masters. To the *admirer of cities* it is a Barmecide Feast: a pleasant field for the imagination to rove in; a monument to a deceased project, with not even a legible inscription to record its departed greatness. (8.125, my emphasis)

Dickens refers to the capital as planned by Pierre L'Enfant, who had been chosen by Washington in 1791 to draw up a scheme for the city, with diagonals converging on the Capitol intersecting with a grid plan. The financial costs and the war with England that made intentions to build a city like Versailles remain only as dreams, allow Dickens to take the part of an "admirer of cities" who discovers Washington to be an illusory abundance (the sense of "a Barmecide feast"). When Dickens visited, the District's population was 33,000, and the port cities of Alexandria and Georgetown were becoming what Dickens calls Georgetown, a "suburb" (8.131). But Dickens in writing that, puts himself outside the city, in a position of Cartesian separation from it, in the same way that he refers to "the madness of American politics" (8.134) and makes it clear too that he is prejudging its nature. His response to Washington shows aversions, first from the city's incompleteness, its lack of architectural finish, and secondly, in a climactic moment, from spitting—about which he has already had much to say. In a letter to Albany Fonblanque (written between 12 and 21 March 1842) he comes out with the statement, with reference to spitting, which he sees as defiling the "marble stairs and passages of every handsome building" and "the base of every column that supports the roof," that "I can bear anything but filth" (*Letters,* 3:119). Filth defiles the architecture; Washington as a town cannot sustain its dream of architecture. The capital city, to be a "Capital," which is not, however, a word used in this chapter, as the idea of the nation's capital is not an idea motivating the writing of London in *Bleak House,* must be distinguished architecturally. The newness of the White House gardens— "they have that uncomfortable air of having been made yesterday" (8.131) he comments on his first visit when he was presented to John Tyler— pairs with this lack of distinction.

RICHMOND AND BALTIMORE

By night steamer, stagecoach, and railway, Dickens arrived at Richmond on 17 March from Washington, to put up at the Exchange Hotel. Approaching, he noted that "in this district, as in all others where slavery sits brooding, . . . there is an air of ruin and decay abroad, which is inseparable from the system" (9.141, compare the letter to Forster, 21 March, *Letters,* 3:140). It is an identification of the south with slavery and also with the spirit later to be found at its most intense at Cairo. Richmond too, has "decay and gloom," for, "jostling round its handsome residences, like slavery itself going hand in hand with many lofty virtues, are deplorable tenements, fences unrepaired, walls crumbling into ruinous heaps" architecture "hinting gloomily at things below the surface" and "remembered with depressing influence" (9.144–45). The passage hints alike at an unconscious in America, implying that it created an unconscious in Dickens.

Slavery becomes like the state of Laura Bridgman and like the separate system too, so that, recalling both, Dickens speaks of "the darkness—not of skin, but mind—which meets the stranger's eye at every turn; the brutalizing and blotting out of all fairer characters traced by Nature's hand" (9.145). Marks of weakness, marks of woe. The town is the prison, as is the plantation which Dickens also visited. The separate system and slavery were both products of both Christian and utilitarian thought: in a letter to Forster of 21 March, Dickens quotes the "hard, bad-looking fellow" who said to him that it was not in the interests of a slave-owner (a man) to use his slaves ill"; and his reply, "it was not in a man's interest to get drunk, or to steal . . . but he *did* indulge in it for all that" (*Letters,* 3:141). The absence of the power of the rational motive becomes the point. The Utilitarian argument forbids the possibility of an unconscious deciding action, and Dickens comes face to face with it here. In the face of it, he does not go further south, as though doing so begins a trawl through unconscious awarenesses, from which he prefers to shield himself.

After returning for a night to Washington, Dickens moved on to Baltimore (21 March) to stay at Barnum's Hotel, after which he left on 24 March for Harrisburg. In Baltimore he noticed the Washington Monument, "which is a handsome pillar with a statue on its summit" and he investigated both the city prison and the State Penitentiary. In the latter he came across two cases: one of a son who might have murdered his father, unless the murderer was his father's brother, and then a case of a man who repeated the exact crime of theft, which Dickens speculates might be a case of "monomania" (9.147). The writing of *American Notes* swings between the blandness of the word "handsome" and "agreeable streets," and noticing behavior that has no utilitarian basis activating it, which must be recorded as the indication of something symptomatic within America, the marker of some madness by which the novelist could contrast his own stability of being, assuming he had it. When he continues that he bound himself "to a rigid adherence to the plan [of travelling westwards] I had laid down so recently," it is not hard to detect something of the psychopathology of Dickens's own everyday life; monomania exists perhaps in more than one place, if it exists at all. Perhaps Dickens in his patterns was himself becoming obsessive.

Thus in Harrisburg he looked at another prison on the separate system, as well as at the local legislature and "the other curiosities of the town" which gave him the chance to look at the treaties signed with American Indians and to think "how many times the credulous Big Turtle, or trusting Little Hatchet, had put his mark to treaties which were falsely read to him; and had signed away, he knew not what, until it went and cast him loose upon the new possessors of the land, a savage indeed" (9.151).

At Washington (see the letter to Forster, 13 March, *Letters*, 3:126), Dickens had made the decision not to go further south, for example to Charleston, even though urged to do so, as by the Motts, Quaker campaigners against slavery, whom he met in Philadelphia and who "hoped he would not be deceived by the outside appearance—but try to get a peep behind the scenes" (*Letters*, 3:99n). At Washington, he was persuaded that "there is very little to see, after all" (13 March, *Letters*, 3:126). Apart from Virginia, he never saw the states that would form the Confederacy: North or South Carolina, Mississippi or Florida, Alabama or Georgia, Louisiana or Texas, Arkansas or Tennessee. Nor did he see the border states, Missouri or Kentucky.

PITTSBURGH

From Harrisburg, Dickens went by canal boat to Pittsburgh, which had been established as a British settlement in 1758 and laid out as a city in

1784, and by now was well on the way to industrialization. The boat passed "new settlements and detached log-houses" whose "utterly forlorn and miserable appearance" he notes, with not "six cabins out of six hundred, where the windows have been whole" (28 March 1842, *Letters*, 3:171). Pittsburgh, which he virtually spends only one paragraph on, he sees in two ways. Approaching by water, he speaks of "that ugly confusion of backs of buildings and crazy galleries and stairs, which always abuts on water, whether it be river, sea, canal or ditch." The description recalls the meeting place of Monks and the Bumbles in *Oliver Twist*, itself anticipatory of the descriptions of Jacob's Island:

> In the heart of this cluster of huts; and skirting the river, which its upper stories overhung; stood a large building formerly used as a manufactory of some kind. . . . But it had long since gone to ruin. The rat, the worm, and the action of the damp, had weakened and rotted the piles on which it stood; and a considerable portion of the building had already sunk down into the water beneath. . . . (*Oliver Twist*, 38.249)

The undoing of structures from beneath, by water that erodes the scaffolding, is part of a fascination, which this "admirer of cities" has with the vertiginous and the decaying; in the description of Pittsburgh, it is doubled by something else, since he then takes in the town as it appears when viewed, as it were, frontally, using the word "pretty" twice in one paragraph, and speaking of the hotel, which "as usual was full of boarders, was very large, and had a broad colonnade to every storey of the house." The Exchange Hotel had been arranged for Dickens's party by the portrait painter George D'Almaine, who escorted him round Pittsburgh (see *Letters*, 3:148n). The slackness of the writing in *American Notes* implies the absence of desire to speak about the fronts of things, as though they were façadal, as opposed to the backs. Yet, though he shows an interest in writing about the back of the hotel in Washington (8.124), there does not seem to be the desire to deal with the other side of the buildings in this case, where the town abuts on the water. This, in an industrial town, such as Pittsburgh, and unlike Washington, would have resonances, both of the architecture of the blacking warehouse where Dickens worked as a child, which he wrote about in the autobiographical fragment that Forster preserved in his *Life of Dickens* (pt.1, chap. 2) as well as *Oliver Twist*'s manufactory. The urban space, with its symbolic geography, remains comparatively unread.

He pronounces Pittsburgh, on the authority of its inhabitants, as being like Birmingham. The evasiveness means it is not like London; it is not like home. He comments on its smoke,[24] and ironworks, and on the prison that I have already referred to in discussing Philadelphia, and to the man who said it was like London he replied that "the notion of London being so dark a place was a popular mistake" (1 April, *Letters*, 3:178). Perhaps he needed to protect himself against the sense of Pittsburgh being representative of the modern city, for that is not the sentiment of *Bleak House*.

He notes the "villas of the wealthier citizens sprinkled about the high grounds in the neighbourhood" and calls them "pretty enough." But the spatial analysis seems muted. These villas represent the attempts of the capitalists to get away from the smoke and fog that they have created and show, not for the first time, how America was on the way to separating itself into two urban and suburban segments. The same could be observed at Cincinnati, again industrializing fast, and where Dickens, after commenting favorably on the town, refers to "its adjoining suburb of Mount Auburn" (11.169), higher ground looking down on the city and the Ohio, where the capitalists moved in order to evade the consequences of industrialism. These forms of spatial protection, it may be, correspond to something in Dickens's own writing in *American Notes* and its evasiveness about free market capitalism as opposed to the planned forms of it, which he had seen in New England. Certainly no one could have guessed from Dickens the history of labor relations in later nineteenth-century Pittsburgh (including the Homestead riots of 1892); or perhaps, if it could be guessed, Dickens's own comparative silence about Pittsburgh would have to be seen as an aspect of the uneasy conscience of the bourgeoisie.

CAIRO AND THE PRAIRIES, CANADA AND THE SHAKERS

The Messenger, a steamboat, carried Dickens and his party for 500 miles along the Ohio, for three days till they arrived at Cincinnati on 4 April, leaving on 6 April for Louisville, where they slept one night, deciding that the city presented no objects of interest. Then they went onto another steamer down to Cairo, on the confluence of the Ohio and the Mississippi. And then up the Mississippi for 200 miles, to St. Louis, arriving there on 10 April. This is the journey that I have referred to in the previous chapter. It included Cairo, which I shall return to in chapter 3.

Having reached St. Louis, Dickens records going on 12 April to see a prairie, and staying at Lebanon, in the company of the Unitarian minister William Greenleaf Eliot.[25] On the 14th, he turned back, having reached the ultimate point in the journey. Cincinnati, "only fifty years old," he calls "a very beautiful city: I think the prettiest place I have seen here, except Boston. It has risen out of the forest like an Arabian-night city" (the ideal, for Dickens, it seems: see *American Notes,* 8.135 and *Letters,* 3:193). Dickens associated St. Louis with slavery, and he referred to the lynch law in the city—a black burned alive with 2,000 to 3,000 people watching; he also writes of the custom of dueling (*Letters,* 3:202).

Dickens moved on from Cincinnati to Columbus, staying at an unfinished hotel in a town that was said to be "going to be" larger, and on to Sandusky ("a pretty town"), and so on, by Lake Erie, to Buffalo and Niagara. From there, he passed into Canada, which he writes about in chapter 15 with complacency, and then back to the United States, through to Albany ("a large and busy town") and to New York. A last journey up the Hudson follows, to get to Lebanon, near a Shaker village, passing by an "Irish colony" which he saw as filthy. The hotel at Lebanon he compared to a prison (15.217) and the comparison suits the Shakers's settlement also, with the chapel shut, and the woman who ruled the Shakers living, "it is said, in strict seclusion, in certain rooms above the chapel and . . . never shown to profane eyes" (15.219), like the later Miss Havisham. As the community is a "gloomy silent commonwealth" (15.220) both silent and separate systems, and Laura Bridgman's world are all evoked, and Dickens's bile against the Shakers follows, working against "that bad spirit . . . which would strip life of its healthful graces, rob youth of its innocent pleasures, pluck from maturity and age their pleasant ornaments, and make existence but a narrow path towards the grave" (15.220). He had come to see the Shakers, but his writing about them is filled with an anger that nothing in them showed their need of him. Lack of dialogue could be expected in a prison, but this institution had put itself beyond dialogue. Here was another form of existence that was beyond his intelligibility.

Having sketched Dickens's itinerary, the next chapter can go further to draw on Dickens's readings of America in relation to *Martin Chuzzlewit,* and then in the fourth, to bring *American Notes* and *Martin Chuzzlewit* together to form some sense of what it was that might have caused such violence of reaction that could not be separated from, though his contemporaries had apparently no difficulty in making such an adjustment.

CHAPTER 3

City Spaces

MARTIN CHUZZLEWIT

"You will take care, my dear Martin," said Mr. Pecksniff, resuming his former cheerfulness, "that the house does not run away in our absence."

—(*Martin Chuzzlewit, 6. 86*)

"MORAL ARCHITECTURE"

While the nineteenth-century found cities overwhelming, *American Notes* reveals a particular aggression toward American cities, emblems of an existence in movement, its liquidity abject, absorbing, and morasslike. It was particularly sarcastic about the pretensions of Washington, the architectural city, to take hold of the actual form and existence of the city. Architecture has never been able to possess the city, because the latter resists the idea of being seen as a whole, and because architecture can never possess a city in its contingency.[1] However, in contrast to *American Notes,* the successor text *Martin Chuzzlewit,* almost dialectically, reveals an aggression toward architecture, both English and American, in a resistance toward its dream of stabilizing the city. It almost seems to prefer the city as a psychotic space. *Martin Chuzzlewit* I read not as an English novel with some American moments, but as a text whose unconscious is formed by America, and I take these points from it: that if the discourse of nineteenth-century architecture is of control, Dickens wanted this control because of the fear of disappearance he had confronted in America; but that he hated it out of an identification with anti-architecture, and this split showed the abiding challenge of American cities when Dickens returned to a confrontation with writing London, a city changing rapidly under the influence of new architecture.

Pecksniff, architect of bourgeois values, does not want his house to take off while he has gone. Architects are employed to keep buildings and cities stable, to prop up an ideology of property and of familiarity which runs through such Dickens titles as the journal *Household Words* or even *Bleak House*, and in the novel that followed *Martin Chuzzlewit*, whose first page announces that the "House" will "once more be called Dombey and Son." That "House" is at the metropolitan center, relating to British colonies, and it contrasts with the literal fall of the house of Clennam in *Little Dorrit*. *Martin Chuzzlewit*, a novel that "takes off" in many ways, evokes property in its title, which is a "key" to open up the "house" of Martin Chuzzlewit,[2] a house that satirizes the nation and English domesticity. "Your homes the scene. Yourselves the Actors here"—a line similar to "Hypocrite lecteur, mon semblable, mon frère" (hypocrite reader, my twin, my brother)—was at one point intended to be its epigraph. It uses an architect who is also a hypocrite, or a hypocrite who is also an architect, Mr. Pecksniff, for a primary focus, and, for its first five numbers, up to the time when Martin Chuzzlewit goes to America, (to confirm something of what Dickens already knew, and to make the text displaced autobiography), makes him almost its focalizer.[3]

Dickens on architecture draws on buildings autobiographically associated. In *Great Expectations*, Pip recalls a childhood rhyme: "When I went to London town sirs / Too rul loo rul / Wasn't I done very brown sirs / Too rul loo rul" (*Great Expectations*, 15.108). The cockiness of that refrain is rhymed upon later when Joe Gargery finds the Blacking Warehouse in London—his choice of tourist spots—not up to its likeness in the red bills at the shop doors, because "it is there drawd too architectooralooral" (27.222). Done very black (like Dickens in the blacking factory) or done very brown (burned, like Pip), the subject is "done" by being produced through a lying architecture that serves the interests of advertisers. The docile body is produced through the Panopticon—where Bentham is the prototype of architects[4]—which is basic to the prisons and institutions of *American Notes*, and gives the sense of America becoming Panoptical, with even Eden called "an architectural city" (*Martin Chuzzlewit*, 21.353). The name Jefferson Brick, war correspondent of New York's *Rowdy Journal*, and America's answer to Young Bailey (16.261) plays on Jefferson as architect and cartographer of America, and recalls how much building architectural cities was in the national psyche.

Not only in America was the architect busy. In Britain, architectural practice increased after the expenditure on the Napoleonic wars had ended, and credit became easier, so that London soon saw nearly every one of its public edifices rebuilt. Private architecture, too, took on the scale of public buildings. There were new public galleries, schools, hospitals, workhouses, theaters, country houses—complete with brewhouses, lodges, stables, keeper's lodges, and dog kennels—suburban villas such as the cottage *orné,* with rustic overtones, vicarages, churches in cities (produced under a Church Building Act of 1818), banks, warehouses, and covered markets. Daniel Alexander's designs for the London docks changed the river landscape in the years before 1830. Waterloo Bridge (1811–17), Southwark Bridge (1814–19), and John Rennie's new London Bridge (1829–31), as new examples of civic architecture, drove new access into areas south of the river. Swan and Edgar, a drapery shop of 1811, 30 years later was one of the first to have a new shop facade of plate glass giving onto London's Regent Street.[5] Even Mr. Pecksniff, whose interest in architecture is never forensic, can refer to designs for a monument to a lord mayor, a tomb for a sheriff, or a cow house for a nobleman's park, a pump, a lamppost, and an ornamental turnpike, before getting Martin Chuzzlewit to design a grammar school for him (6.87).

These projects, productive of the nineteenth-century invention of history and tradition, are in the service of new money, which is fairly sloshing around in *Martin Chuzzlewit,* shining in the new architectural features of the Anglo-Bengalee Insurance company: "Look at the massive blocks of marble in the chimney-pieces and the gorgeous parapet on the top of the house!" (27.430). Mr. Montague Tigg's apartment in Pall Mall has all the signs of commodity culture: "pictures, copies from the antique in alabaster and marble, china vases, lofty mirror, crimson hangings of the richest silk, gilded carvings, luxurious couches, glistening cabinets inlaid with precious goods: costly toys of every sort in negligent abundance" (28.449). By the 1840s, architecture in England had assumed a national importance, where discussion of what constituted hypocrisy—shams, falsity—in building was part of a debate about the nation's self-presentation. The Institute of British Architects, founded in 1834, received a Royal Charter in 1837, the year of Sir John Soane's death, and became the RIBA. This was a year later than the founding of the New York–based American Institution [later Institute] of Architects. Soane had fought for the idea that the architect should not involve himself in the contracting: John Nash, who had died in 1835, was, in comparison, part architect, part builder, part speculator. The architect in the 1830s, in Britain and America, was becoming defined as a pure specialist, his profession separated from actual building.

These developments, part of the making of bourgeois Britain, had been set in train through the last part of the eighteenth century. The

Royal Academy, two years after its founding in 1768, made Thomas Sandby (1721–1798), self-taught architect and surveyor, its first professor of architecture, his task being to give six annual lectures. William Jones was one of the first to call himself an "architect," when in 1753 he inaugurated the Pecksniffian tradition of taking on an apprentice (craftsmen normally took on apprentices; professional men took articled pupils). Jones received £50 premium for his pupil, and to be articled became the standard route for becoming an architect.

Several events made architecture more pure, more specific. In 1835, 97 designs competed against each other for the new Palace of Westminster, after the old was destroyed by fire. Architecture was linked to historicism and national history, in the arguments over an appropriate style for the Houses of Parliament. The competition for the design made this method of selection fashionable.[6] In 1838, a committee set up by the Institute of British Architects turned away from perspective drawings, which linked architecture with art, in favor of more specific and abstract geometric designs. And A. W. Pugin, who between 1835 and 1837 lived in Salisbury, and would therefore have been a neighbor of Mr. Pecksniff, published in 1836 *Contrasts: or, A Parallel Between the Noble Edifices of the Fourteenth and Fifteenth Centuries, and Similar Buildings of the Present Day; Showing the Present Decay of Taste. Accompanied by Appropriate Text.* Pugin effectively killed Regency architecture with the claim that Gothic architecture was the only style that was morally acceptable. *Contrasts* shows a "Catholic Town in 1440" and "The Same Town in 1840" where, alongside the industrial landscape, in describing the picture, the critic Richard Stein can refer to a "square-enclosed octagonal building squatting low in the foreground. Pugin calls it 'The New Jail,'" but, Stein says, "it is clearly based on Bentham's Panopticon."[7] Nineteenth-century architecture for Pugin shows its alliance with the prisonous and with the official. The "close temporal coincidence" that Robin Evans notes between the reform of prisons and the formation of architecture as a profession is more than that.[8]

Though Pugin might resent Benthamism, architecture was still Benthamite in being elevated to teach, to warn, to memorialize; a dream of architecture led Pugin to convert to the Catholic church. In Pugin, architecture is not "just" buildings: it is a performative statement, trying to pass off as truth an ideological representation. Kenneth Clark quotes from the *Times* obituary for Pugin in 1852: "that very little of the architecture of the last century and the present is beautiful is not the heaviest charge we have to bring against it; the heaviest charge is that it is utterly false. . . . It was [Pugin] who first showed us that our architecture offended not only against the law of beauty, but also against the laws of morality." "Unworthy deception" and "an abominable sham" are Puginesque terms of contempt.

"Perhaps the greatest service has been done by Pugin's unsparing exposure of the system of SHAMS in architectural design" wrote Benjamin Ferrey, Pugin's biographer.[9] Pugin's *The True Principles of Pointed or Christian Architecture* (1841) begins with the "two great rules for design":

> 1st, *that there should be no features about a building which are not necessary for convenience, constitution or propriety;*
>
> 2nd, *that all ornament should consists of enrichment of the essential construction of the building.*[10]

The second of these principles is to ensure that "the smallest detail should *have a meaning or serve a purpose.*" No falsity, no shams, no ornamentation.

Of the "Battle of the Styles," consequent upon the choice of Barry's Gothic for the new Houses of Parliament (the choice was Gothic or Elizabethan), the architect Robert Kerr concluded in 1884, "the chief merit . . . to which the Gothic party laid claim was the resuscitation of the Medieval principle of truthful articulation, or the correct correspondence of the motive of superficial design with the motive of underlying construction. The styles of the Renaissance, they argued, . . . were almost hopelessly entangled in shams, whilst the Medieval, they said, had nothing to conceal or to disguise. . . . False architecture cannot be true art."[11] The standing Pugin gave Gothic may be compared with that given to it by Sir James Pennethorne, Nash's pupil, when discussing the competition for the Houses of Parliament, Gothic, "perfected in this Country, . . . is the most congenial to our climate and feelings, and may be considered essentially NATIONAL; in effect it may be rendered equally grand and imposing with Grecian, and in science is perhaps almost equally correct."[12] Morality, national identity, and correctness make a powerful troika. Thomas Leverton Donaldson, vice president of the RIBA, supplemented Pennethorne by asking in 1847, the year that the Architectural Association was founded: "The great question is, are we to have an architecture of our period, a distinct, palpable style of the nineteenth-century?"[13] Ruskin, two years later, capped both Pennethorne and Donaldson with the Seventh Lamp of Architecture as "Obedience":

> Architecture never could flourish except when it was subjected to a national law as strict and as minutely regulatable as the laws which regulate religion, policy and social relations. . . . The architecture of a nation is great only when it is as universal and as established as its language.[14]

Even *Martin Chuzzlewit* does not escape from idealizing national architecture, when Martin and Mark Tapley return from America (chap. 35). But the deadness of English architecture, unornamented, seriously meaning-ful, expressive of English sturdiness, is Disraeli's theme in *Tancred* (1847):

> Nothing more completely represents a nation than a public building. A member of Parliament only represents at the most the united constituen-cies: but the Palace of the Sovereign, a National Gallery, or a Museum bap-tized with the name of the country, these are monuments to which all should be able to look up with pride, and which should exercise an elevat-ing influence upon the spirit of the humblest. What is their influence in London? Let us not criticize what all condemn. But how remedy the evil? What is wanted in architecture, as in so many things is a man. Shall we find a refuge in a Committee of Taste? . . .
>
> All the streets [of London] resemble one another, you must read the names of the squares before you venture to knock at a door. This amount of building capital ought to have produced a great city. What an opportu-nity for Architecture suddenly summoned to furnish habitations . . . Marylebone ought to have produced a revolution in our domestic archi-tecture. It did nothing. It was built by Act of Parliament. Parliament pre-scribed even a façade. It is Parliament to whom we are indebted for your Gloucester Places and Baker Streets and Harley Streets, and Wimpole Streets, and all those flat, dull, spiritless streets, resembling each other like a large family of plain children, with Portland Place and Portman Square for their respectable parents. . . . [15]

Disraeli's anger, expressed against parliamentary committees, may be part of his repressed awareness that free-market economics had not pro-duced good architecture, and that the nakedness of Britain's venture cap-italism (its imperialist character displayed in *Tancred*) is imaged in empty façades, rows and rows of indifferent houses that give the real dead-end character of English ideology. Dickens's free-marketeer is no better: if a man is known by his house, Mr. Dombey's is "on the shady side of a tall, dark, dreadfully genteel street, in the region between Portland-place and Bryanstone-square. . . . It was as blank a house inside as outside." (*Dombey and Son*, 1.3.23–24.). As Tennyson writes about Wimpole Street—in a line which haunts James in *The American Scene*—"On the bald street breaks the blank day" (*In Memoriam*, 7.12).

In Pugin's "propriety," one of his two principles, architecture sides with property, the proper, and appropriation. It evokes a sonorously moral language, as with Pecksniff or as when Hannibal Chollop says that to like America requires "An Elevation and a Preparation of the Intellect" (33.519). It produces metaphysics, when, in 1834, in the first issue of J. C. Loudon's journal, *Architectural Magazine,* Ruskin referred to the "science of architecture":

The Science of Architecture, followed out to its full extent, is one of the noblest of those which have reference only to the creations of human minds. It is not merely a science of the rule and compass, it does not consist only in the observation of just rule, or of fair proportion: it is, or ought to be, a science of feeling more than of rule, a ministry to the mind, more than to the eye. If we consider how much less the beauty and majesty of a building depend upon its pleasing certain prejudices of the eye, than upon its rousing certain trains of meditation in mind, it will show in a moment how many intricate questions of feeling are involved in the raising of an edifice; it will convince us of the truth of a proposition which might at first have appeared startling, that no man can be an architect, who is not a metaphysician.[16]

The Seven Lamps of Architecture makes Truth the second Lamp—"Do not let us lie at all." It finds three deceits—forms of hypocrisy—in contemporary architecture. It was hypocritical to have "the suggestion of a mode of structure or support other than the true one." So was "the painting of surfaces to represent some other material than that of which they actually consist." A final deceit makes "use of cast or machine-made ornaments of any kind."[17] Changes in the materials for building, such as wrought iron in the 1840s, made the first and second deceptions possible. In the 1820s, buildings used load-bearing brick walls; "it was only after 1830 that the first steps were made towards building fully skeletal outer structures."[18] These structures allowed walls to become false, so that the inside and outside of the building no longer articulated with one another. Such "deception" was not new: it was an extension of tendencies already at work, in the use of facades and blind windows. Stucco, the classic Regency material, designed to give the appearance of stone (Roman cement, used for its manufacture, was invented in 1796), was an example of what was denounced as sham as well as cheap and structurally defective.

Ruskin on the architect as metaphysician compares with Schopenhauer, in *The World As Will and Representation* (1819), who finds the universal Will to objectify itself in one "sole and constant theme" of architecture, that of *"support and load."*[19] The proper philosophic themes of architecture are "gravity, rigidity and cohesion" (2:414); gravity being spatialized in "large masses" (2:414), for Schopenhauer believes that works of architecture cannot be too large. Form, proportion, and symmetry, which are not philosophic ideas, appeal to an a priori faculty of perceptibility; for this reason, Schopenhauer likes the classical for its predictability and dislikes Gothic, where "an arbitrary will has ruled guided by extraneous concepts" (2:417) taking the place of "the purely rational" (2:418). Gravity, rigidity, and cohesion, however, are not arbitrary, but features of the world-commanding Will.

Schopenhauer is anti-ornament in architecture, for ornament belongs more to sculpture (1:215). Nor will he give any place to architecture as an imitative art (2:414). The weight of such words as gravity, rigidity, and cohesion make architecture inherently heavy; Schopenhauer's preferred material for architecture is stone, and in the first volume of *The World as Will and Representation* he adds hardness to gravity, rigidity, and cohesion as those ideas that architecture brings to perception. For Schopenhauer, "the whole mass of the building, if left to its original tendency, would exhibit a mere heap or lump, bound to the earth as firmly as possible, to which gravity, the form in which the will here appears, presses incessantly, whereas rigidity, also objectivity of the will, resists" (1:214). Stone, not wood, brings out this conflict between gravity and rigidity; so does a large rather than a small building. Architecture is to dramatize the imposition of order: it is motivated by a desire for visible control, in the face of loss of control. In starting with the idea of load, the word "gravity" evokes not only moral sententiousness but also the thought of weight that will come crashing down. The support reacts to the power of gravity, as though architecture began not with the idea of building but of *resisting*, as though its structure had nothing spontaneous within it. Gravity and weight in their moral senses are made unattractive qualities each of which will floor the other. In Schopenhauer, the effort that architecture represents denies lightness of being and gracefulness, and asserts by its monumentality its permanence, that it is not likely to be overturned by the chances of time, which erases memory and previous signification. When the Member of Parliament lays the foundation stone for the grammar school that Mr. Pecksniff (read Martin Chuzzlewit) has designed, the inscription is in Latin (35.553): architecture as monumental memorial defies the alterations of time. Architecture sides with *ressentiment*,[20] as if in defying time which takes everything away and so shows that the subject has no ultimate control of events, and cannot establish an autonomy on that basis (for Nietzsche, the source of *ressentiment*). It is suggestive that Pugin suffered a mental breakdown in 1846, dying insane in 1852. His reaction to the 1848 revolutions was reactionary. Calling for muskets to defend himself, he said, "I would shoot any Chartist as I would a rat or a mad dog."[21] The medievalism of Gothic and political reaction may go together, but it is more interesting to posit a relationship between architecture as a form of ordering, prompted by an investment in the monumental, which invites a psychoanalytic reading of its emphasis on the historical, and which seems a reaction from the disorder implied in madness. *Martin Chuzzlewit*—the title means that the text has *something* to do with people's wits—opposes the architecture as rational with an awareness of the city as producing other conditions: split off, hysterical, and melancholic mental states.

In the United States, architecture relates to the American institutions that Dickens so insistently visited. The historian David Rothman shows how Jacksonian America, as opposed to colonial America, invested in institutions in order to preserve the cohesion of the growing urban community: His account shows an awareness of Foucault's *Madness and Civilization,* if also a distancing from his work. Institutionalizing, which means building architecturally, segregates, educates, and provides surveillance. Samuel Gridley Howe (see Dickens's *Letters,* 3:217n) the Bostonian doctor, abolitionist, enthusiast for the separate system and the founder of the Perkins Institution, which Dickens visited in Boston, argued that convicts were produced because of a "faulty organization of society."[22] It followed that the prison as an institution should indeed be organized morally, and Rothman shows the Boston Prison Discipline Society considering architecture to be one of the moral sciences. He quotes: "There are principles in architecture, by the observance of which great moral changes can be more easily produced among the most abandoned of our race . . . There is such a thing as architecture adapted to morals; that other things being equal, the prospect of improvement, in morals, depends, in some degree, upon the construction of buildings."[23]

Accordingly, whereas Walnut Street jail, in Philadelphia (1790), resembled a large frame house, and earlier institutions followed the pattern of the household, new institutions were built to symbolize and to be moral.[24] John Haviland's Eastern Penitentiary in Philadelphia used medieval Gothic because Gothic was Christian (so Pugin) and was castle-like to emphasize seriousness and severity. The moat, the portcullis, and the castellations imaged the necessity for enforcing separation. Within, and quite separate from the Gothic exterior, which was no more than simulacral, the prison was classical in form, emphasizing its own ideology of rational control. Both architectural forms make symbolism inseparable from organization. Samuel Howe condemned the prison system at Auburn for not enforcing isolation. Whereas he makes Laura Bridgman communicate, this "good man" also makes the convict retreat back into his "marble cell." The productions of speech and of silence are both forms of organizational control.

"Moral architecture" summarizes one side of Dickens's America; but could Dickens have wholly admired the morality that supplemented the architecture of the South Boston House of Industry with the legibility of "SELF-GOVERNMENT, QUIETUDE AND PEACE ARE BLESSINGS"? "Moral architecture" describes the creation of Lowell, the industrial town, or Philadelphia, where the prison becomes supplementary to the order of Philadelphia's streets. Fanny Trollope had called Robert Owen's New Harmony projects "hollow square legislations," and she referred to

William McClure's school as "incipient hollow square drilling; teaching the young ideas of all he could catch, to shoot into parallelogramic form and order." She returns to the geometric word in discussing Philadelphia, where "you have nothing to do but walk up one straight street and down another, till all the parallelograms have been threaded."[25] This is not just punning, for the moral architecture of Robert Owen demanded schools built round courtyards in parallelogramic formation, but the prison as supplement to the symmetry of the city shows that symmetry must always be inadequate, and must be repeated by another symmetrical form, in Philadelphia's case the symmetrically built Eastern Penitentiary. Dickens's stated reactions to Philadelphia in *American Notes* repeat Fanny Trollope's sense, just as *Martin Chuzzlewit* parodies "moral architecture" in Mr. Pecksniff.

LYING ARCHITECTURE

In contrast to Schopenhauer, whose interest in gravity and control describes what the nineteenth century thought prison building should be like, Ruskin thought the essence of architecture to be ornamentation and hated the same buildings as Disraeli. The *Seven Lamps of Architecture* begins, "Architecture is the art which so disposes and adorns the edifices raised by man, for whatsoever uses, that the sight of them may contribute to his *mental health,* power and pleasure" (8.27, my emphasis). Of the Lamp of Sacrifice, he says, "that Architecture concerns itself only with those characters of an edifice which are above and beyond its common use" (8.29). Yet while ornamentation in Ruskin's version of architecture seems also *ressentiment,* reacting to what already exists, trying to change it, so what it teaches will be healthful, and a source of rational pleasure, he is also positive. He sees the spirit of play to be vital in architecture, and in contrast to Pugin, in the Gothic. "With the gradual exaggeration with which every pleasant idea is pursued by the human mind, [the Gothic roof] is raised into all manner of peaks, and points, and ridges, and pinnacle after pinnacle is added on its flanks, and the walls increased in height in proportion until we get indeed a very sublime mass, but one which has no more principle of religious aspiration in it than a child's tower of cards."[26] As a footnote to this playfulness, Pecksniff is said "in the garden of his fancy to disport himself (if one may say so) like an architectural kitten" (30.470).

For Ruskin, architects must be metaphysicians who follow nature, so architecture must embody the truth of nature and the nature of truth. But if architecture is also, according to Disraeli, the nation's self-representation, its official ideology, that gives it another role that contradicts the first, since it shows up nature and truth themselves as so much ideology. As though in unconscious deference to this contradiction, Mr. Pecksniff

never builds anything. He is at home with the classical (6.87)—Phiz's illustration, "Mr Pecksniff renounces the deceiver" associates him with Vit-
ruvius and Palladio—and at home with the Gothic (Salisbury Cathedral).
Further, he uses language that caricatures the language of morality in architecture, finding a moral in everything but with the saving proviso that
"there is nothing personal in morality" (2.13).[27] Pecksniff is criticized by
the text for being the kind of architect he is, but in being that he is also the
saving of the text and helps make it anti-architecture. He caricatures the
language of *ressentiment,* which Nietzsche aligns to Christian morality, by
replying, when he has been called a hypocrite, "Charity my dear . . . when
I take my chamber candlestick to-night, remind me to be more than usually particular in praying for Mr. Anthony Chuzzlewit, who has done me
an injustice" (4.56). That is theatrical, and suggests a man who despite his
venality, and partly because of his tendency to pratfalls—which literally
destabilize him—is made not only witty in himself but the source of wit in
others. His position of "architect" opens up the text, shows how its own
proceedings cannot be architectural.

Pecksniff's language is anti-Schopenhauerian in lacking functionality.
His words have nothing to do with load and support. "Mr Pecksniff was
in the frequent habit of using any word that occurred to him as having a
good sound, and rounding a sentence well, without much care for its
meaning" (2.14). The catachreses in his speech (they are also a feature of
Mrs. Gamp's way of talking and they establish links between these two
figures in the text) operate also in the narrative and produce his own lack
of single being, as when he says, "Well well, what am I? I don't know what
I am exactly." Everything about him is performance, put on for others;
there is no single or private self whose existence is guaranteed by his language. "He was a man of great feeling, and acute sensibility; and he
squeezed his pocket-handkerchief against his eyes with both hands—as
such men always do; especially when they are observed" (30.473). This
outside action mocks relationships between inner truth and appearance,
structure and ornament. Everything is ornament, though not in the sense
that anything is being adorned. The elimination of an inside/outside distinction involves questioning the notion of hypocrisy, as though "hypocrite" was a judgment about character (the relation of its surface or its
façade to its interior) that was sanctioned by the concepts and terminol-
ogy of architecture. Mr. Pecksniff's soliloquy, on another reading, suggests also a split subject, a divided state, and this aligns him with the
impossibility of architecture to deliver a single subject or to prevent it
running away, like Augustus Moddle, to Australia—not America—with
his mind "totally unhinged" (54.831). A mind off its hinges has not been
stabilized architecturally.

If Dickens was nearly unhinged by Cairo, at the nadir of *American Notes,* this is repeated in Martin Chuzzlewit (chap. 23 and 33). Cairo had been purchased in 1835 by Darius B. Holbrook, who came to London in 1839 to raise capital for improvements. His claims for the city were supported by a report and plan prepared by the Philadelphia architect William Strickland (1787–1854), who has been already noted in chapter 2 for his Greek Revival Second Bank of the United States (1824) and for his Merchants' Exchange. Strickland also provided a "Prospective View of the City of Cairo" in 1838. The plan shows the familiar grid pattern sandwiched between the two rivers; the picture he produced is done in the customary older nineteenth-century style of rendering the city, showing a distance from it by letting it being viewed panoramically from the countryside. It is that distance from the city Dickens cannot keep, and in European art, it was broken in Impressionism. It shows a busy Ohio, with paddle steamers, sailing boats, and rowing boats, and is imagined from the river's southern side. The settlement in the angle of land between the Ohio and the Mississippi has a church, an obelisk as a memorial, presumably recalling the Egyptian name (and Strickland's own interest in Egyptian style in architecture), and then, set back from the road that runs along the shore, factory buildings in absolute symmetrical form, with here a church spire and there some tall chimneys. There is a Greek revival pediment surmounted by a cupola and a cross, which suggests a city hall, and to the right, castellations that mean a prison, like Haviland's Penitentiary at Philadelphia. Behind all these buildings, the Mississippi can be seen, so that the city looks islandlike: it could be Venice. Or rather, it looks pastoral; no wonder the name Eden chose itself. The design affirmed a relationship between landscape and cityscape. But the design, prospective in every sense of the word, was never realized, the city never became the center for the railroad, as was intended, and James Buckingham,[28] writing in 1840, commented:

> On looking around, however, for "the works already constructed," which are here said to be "considerable," nothing is seen but a few small dwellings of the humblest class of workmen, not exceeding 20 in number, and the whole population of the spot did not appear to exceed 100. So injudiciously conducted were the first operations on the spot, that the infant settlement had already been completely submerged; and but a few weeks since, all its inhabitants were obliged to abandon it, to avoid being drowned![29]

There was the implication that Holbrook had cheated on the investors, and Dickens refers to the "monstrous representations" (*American Notes,*

12.177) that had been made in London to encourage investment. Perhaps the representations included the architectural ones, which is why so much of *Martin Chuzzlewit* is anti-architecture. For architecture seems to be on the side of fraud, architectural façades indicating that no reality is being constructed. Whatever the city is, architecture does not represent it; while city planning is seen as mad connivance at the pretence to order.

ANTI-ARCHITECTURE

Martin Chuzzlewit is anti-architecture in the sense Victor Hugo meant when in *Notre-Dame de Paris* (1832) he says of print media in relation to the hierarchical, monological, and nondemocratic tendencies of architecture, "Ceci tuera cela" ("this will kill that," 5.2).[30] In *Martin Chuzzlewit,* anti-architecturalism appears in a lack of structure. Forster found it improvisatory: "in *construction* and conduct of story, *Martin Chuzzlewit* is defective."[31] This text proclaims its discontinuities throughout,[32] making discontinuity and lack of contact a feature of its plot, such as in the coincidences of perception shared by Tom Pinch and Mr. Nadgett, men otherwise ignorant of each other (38.586). No Dickens novel is more obviously split, less centered than this. Attempts are made to center the text, in terms of "selfishness"—"the *design* being to show, more or less by every person introduced, the number and variety of humours and vices that have their root in selfishness" (Forster, 4.1.291, my emphasis)—or in the plans of old Martin Chuzzlewit to prove his grandson's character. But despite these architectural efforts to give a form to the text, *Martin Chuzzlewit* seems almost plotless. In contrast to *Oliver Twist, Bleak House,* or *Little Dorrit,* no secrets of the past are to be deciphered within it.[33] It works in a perpetual present with a continuing power of exfoliation and proliferation of detail. One narrative is laid within another. As Mark Tapley and Martin Chuzzlewit dream in New York the text changes back to London as though it were "a dream within a dream" (17.297). This *mise en abîme* quality says there is no outside to the narrative. The point appears in Montague Tigg posing the "celebrated conundrum" "Why's a man in jail like a man out of jail?" (4.48). It is a joke about the text: the answer is that there is no answer, there is no way out. Architectural discourse is confounded when Mrs. Gamp is not sure whether the whale is in Jonah or Jonah/Jonas is in the whale, which last signifier slides into other signifiers, wale/vale and veil.[34] Inside the whale? The novel works to reverse such geographical assurances as whether the subject is inside or outside. A man inside a whale is like a man outside.

To be held by the power of architecture is to be held inside ideology, and to be formed by that; and distinctions between inside and outside cannot be taken to mean that what is on the outside escapes control. Mark Wigley, the philosopher of architecture, draws out some of Derrida's implications, when he says that

> to exclude something by placing it "outside" is actually to control it, to put it in its place, to enclose it. To exclude is to include. The very gesture of expelling representation appropriates it. . . . Expulsion is consumption. To lock something up doesn't involve simply imprisoning it within four walls. It is imprisoned simply by being banned. In fact, it is enclosed even before it is officially excluded inasmuch as it can be defined, portrayed as some kind of object that can be placed, whether inside or outside. It is not so much a matter of placing it within limits as declaring that it has limits: "expulsed, excluded, objectified or (curiously amounting to the same thing) assimilated and mastered in one of its moments."[35]

But in a mad, Piranesi-like architecture, the other of the American rationally planned city, the structure includes everything within it and the difference between inside and outside disappears. Exclusion and inclusion become the same. We get a set of Chinese boxes incorporating one thing inside another, but with this difference, that everything may be visible, but its visibility does not matter because it is contained within the system of architecture that incorporates everything. There is no inside. Pecksniff's hypocrisy is visible from the beginning. He is called a hypocrite to his face in chapter 4; his daughters hear him referred to as that in chapter 11 (181). If someone can be so nominated, it is questionable whether the word fits, or the judgment matters. Or take Mrs. Gamp, who is aware of repression, which she calls "fevers of the mind" (29.463). But she also knows that people walk around with their repression highly visible, as the logic of her speech suggests: "we never knows wot's hidden in each other's breasts; and if we had glass winders there, we'd need to keep the shetters up, some of us, I do assure you!' (39.464). Just like Young Bailey, whose extreme youth is obvious while he acts as though he needs a regular shave, Mrs. Gamp seems also unaware of the extent to which she gives herself away. But even open declaration of her secret might do no good, in terms of affecting a change, as when Mrs. Prig announces about the fictitious Mrs. Harris that "there's no sich a person" (49.752). Mrs. Gamp has a huge box going halfway under her bed "in a manner which while it did violence to the reason, likewise endangered the legs, of a stranger" (39.742–43). The obtrusive box symbolizes, though it does not contain, Mrs. Gamp's secrets, and is as obvious as the unconscious that speaks in her speech, as obvious as the box in Hitchcock's *Rope,* just as the effects of the contents of the bottle speak—the bottle that is also on display on the "chimley-piece," as prominent as Edgar Allan Poe's purloined letter. Mr. Pecksniff and Mrs. Gamp reveal what they are on the outside.[36]

Like a Chinese box, Mrs. Gamp's talk incorporates in it the speech of Mrs. Harris, who occupies a special place in Mrs. Gamp's imaginary world, guiding her through her own mental labyrinth, as complex as the one seen in the view from Todgers's. Mrs. Gamp gives a clue to the way she thinks labyrinthinally in her description of how to get to Mrs. Harris: "Mrs Harris through the square and up the steps a turnin round by the tobacker shop" (40.624). Her oddities of speech and behavior are not deceptions, architectural shams, for they form a kind of incorporation of otherness into the self whereby the subject is unaware of what is concealed within it. Needing an other, a support, now that her normal prosthetic—her husband, elevated to the status of a wooden leg (40.625) has gone to his/its reward—she has internalized another. She is a melancholic, or a schizophrenic, unaware that when she talks about Mrs. Harris she talks about herself. In a variation on this, Montague Tigg is Tigg Montague (27.427), and Nadgett has pockets with assorted things in it, including a "musty old pocket book [in which] he carried contradictory cards, in some of which he called himself a coal-merchant, in others a wine-merchant, in others a commission-agent, in other a collector [the secret of all these cards: he collects occupations], in others an accountant: as if he didn't know the secret himself" (27. 446). Perhaps he doesn't know the secret; for he writes letters "but they never seemed to go to anybody, for he would put them into a secret place in his coat, and deliver them to himself weeks afterwards, very much to his own surprise, quite yellow" (27.447). Dead paper, dead letters, yellowness: it is all the city's character. Mrs. Harris and these letters that return to the sender both index schizophrenia. Nadgett is a new type, "a race peculiar to the city" (27.447), like the new "man of the crowd" of Edgar Allan Poe, whose urban nature means that "he does not allow himself to be read," and which makes him the figure "of deep crime."[37] Nadgett as a type of the city is enclosed within the labyrinthine structures of city buildings, which build into their folds and pockets, a whole uncanny.[38] By the end of the novel he is revealed as the detective, but that seems contingent; he could be anything for he has no essential being. The "incorporation" of another, which means that Mr. Pecksniff when drunk (a decentered subject) can claim that the voice of his dead wife speaks in him (9.151) fits with the effects of architecture. Mr. Pecksniff has a Poe-like fantasy of securing old Martin Chuzzlewit's property to himself, his method being: "to wall up the old gentleman, as it were, for his own use" (30.475). Incorporation originates from Freud's notion of the subject being unable to expel a feared object. Unable to repudiate or deny it, the ego copes, as Lukacher suggests, by installing it, in a way that will maintain the smoothness of an architectural front, "in a place inside itself that is henceforth split off from the self and forgotten. Incorporation, then, involves a split within the ego, which forms in effect a secondary unconscious, neither properly inside nor outside the ego, neither properly subjective nor objective."[39]

Incorporation tries to bury some secret within the folds of the ego so completely that it is neither inside nor outside, never to be heard of again. Whatever secrets are encrypted in Pecksniff and in Mrs. Gamp, and imaged in Mrs. Gamp's box, no open exposure will effect change while Mrs. Harris as Mrs. Gamp's creation also points to the heroism of modern life, for she has a schizoid way of coping with a schizoid situation. Hence the banality of the exposure performed by old Martin Chuzzlewit in chapter 52, when he knocks down Pecksniff and threatens Mrs. Gamp with the Old Bailey. Such attempts at clarification and closure try to restore a simple distinction between inside and outside, by excluding Pecksniff and Mrs. Gamp. Martin Chuzzlewit senior here repeats one operation of architecture.

The incorporation of a secret takes place within a larger nonstructure, where everything is labyrinthine, and which was historically already coming into being in the form of the Paris Arcades, "glass-covered, marble-floored passages through entire blocks of houses, whose proprietors have joined forces in the venture. On both sides of these passages, which obtain their light from above, there are arrayed the most elegant shops, so that such an arcade is a city, indeed a world, in miniature."[40] The arcade defeats the ordinary mapping of the city, by the route it takes through houses, while its glass structure puts the outside inside. A labyrinthine structure defeats the organizing attempts of architecture, for it means that there is no inside or outside. Dickensian architecture, as a series of pockets and invaginations, contains its uncanny, and that—the *unheimlich,* the unfamiliar, which is also familiar—returns to destabilize what is ordered and architectural. For "everything is *unheimlich* that ought to have remained secret and hidden but has come to light."[41] This uncanny upsets the homeliness of the home, which is modeled on strict inclusion and exclusion, and the encrypting of family secrets. By suggesting that everything has the strangeness of the dream within the dream, it suggests the impossibility of getting outside the text or the labyrinth. At one point in the plot, the characters comment on "the maze of difficulty" they can see no way out of (48.740). The "view from Todgers's"—Todgers's, with its "maze of bedrooms" (11.171)—is labyrinthine, and the text hints at repressed material folded within it:

> You groped your way for an hour through lanes and bye-ways, and court-
> yards and passages; and never once emerged upon anything that might rea-

sonably be called a street. A kind of resigned distraction came over the stranger as he trod those devious mazes, and, giving himself up for lost, went in and out and round about, and quietly turned back again when he came to a dead wall or was stopped by an iron railing . . . (9.129)

"A dead wall" repeats the description of a "brown wall with a black cistern on the top" (8.128), which at a two-foot perspective is the daughters' view from Todgers's. Since the cistern leaks, providing a damp side to the wall, it suggests the box and the crypt, death and that repression cannot be contained: every box is porous. This London of no thoroughfares exists on several levels, street, cellarage, and roof. Each is strange:

In the throat and maw of dark no-thoroughfares near Todgers's, individual wine-merchants and wholesale dealers in grocery-ware had perfect little towns of their own; and, deep among the very foundations of these buildings, the ground was undermined and burrowed out into stables, where cart-horses, troubled by rats, might be heard on a quiet Sunday rattling their halters, as disturbed spirits in tales of haunted houses are said to clank their chains. (9.130)

London's space evokes towns within towns, enclosures within enclosures, and a sense of infinite recess, *mise en abime*. The top of Todgers's, which looks toward the Monument, evokes a cinematic architecture[42] when things move around the subject, like the "revolving chimney-pots on one great stack of buildings [which] seemed to be turning gravely to each other every now and then." Every detail is uncanny, belonging to urban modernity, unsettling the subject by reversing the assumption of the living subject with dead, mechanical matter all around. The whole is productive of vertigo, so that "the host of objects seemed to thicken and expand a hundredfold; and after gazing round him, quite scared, he [the visitor] turned into Todgers's again, much more rapidly than he came out; and ten to one, he told M. Todgers afterwards that if he hadn't done so, he would certainly have come into the street by the shortest cut; that is to say, head-foremost" (9.132). The only short-cut through the labyrinth where the self is already lost is through suicide: Jonas Chuzzlewit's route.[43] The labyrinth is coterminous with life, and the text is ambivalent about the possibility of mapping it.

The labyrinth has folds within folds. *Martin Chuzzlewit* as constructing the urban and as a novel is porous: a matter of endless holes or mouths or pockets. It hardly seems to matter where you post your letter, as Nadgett knows. The servant Tamaroo at Todgers's is described as "a perfect Tomb for messages and small parcels; and when despatched to the Post-office with letters had been frequently seen endeavouring to insinuate them into casual chinks in private doors, under the delusion that any door with a hole in it would answer the purpose" (32.506). Perhaps the description recalls the Tombs; perhaps Tamaroo's body and clothes encrypting messages is also a prison. Young Bailey, opening the door to Pecksniff and daughters at an unconscionably early hour, greets them with the indescribable sentence: "I thought you wos the Paper and wondered why you didn't shove yourself through the grating as usual" (8.125). Everything works its own way through: in Young Bailey's idiolect there is no room for human agency. This non-architectural body (this labyrinthine city) is full of disconnected openings and pockets.

One image is prominent, the door which both is and is not in place:

> Among the narrow thoroughfares at hand, there lingered, now and there, an ancient doorway of carved oak, from which, of old, the sounds of revelry and feasting often came, but now these mansions, only used for storehouses, were dark, and dull, being filled with wool, and cotton, and the like—such heavy merchandise as stifles sound and stops the throat of echo—had an air of palpable deadness about them which, added to their silence and desertion, made them very grim. (9.130)

This door motif, opening on something unknown, suggests the uncanny in architecture, that which upsets its drive toward establishing the contained and the familiar. It recurs in the house itself:

> But the grand mystery of Todgers's was the cellarage, approachable only by a little back-door and a rusty grating: which cellarage within the memory of man had no connection with the house, but had always been the freehold property of somebody else, and was reported to be full of wealth: though in what shape . . . was matter of profound uncertainty and supreme indifference to Todgers's, and all its inmates. (9.131)

But these doors that lead into other spaces, other areas sealed off from common knowledge, also suggest repression, otherness. The ego contains pockets that are apparently inaccessible. What is on the other side of the door? *Something* is always on the other side, if only the wind, "the ideal inflictor of a runaway knock," which sends Pecksniff flying as he tries to open his front door (2.9). What is hidden returns like the uncanny when Montague Tigg in the inn with Jonas Chuzzlewit (who will later murder him), sleeps in a room with a door locked on the other side, "and with what place it communicated, he knew not."

> His fears or evil conscience reproduced this door in all his dreams. He dreamed that a dreadful secret was connected with it: a secret which he knew

and yet did not know, for although he was heavily responsible for it, and a party to it, he was harassed even in his vision by a distracting uncertainty in reference to its import. Incoherently entwined with this dream was another, which represented it as the hiding-place of an enemy, a shadow, a phantom; and made it the terrible business of his life to keep the terrible creature closed up and prevent it from forcing its way in upon him. (42.651)

The dream continues, with fantasies of trying to keep the connecting door closed, with the aid of Nadgett and "a strange man with a bloody smear upon his head, (who told him that he had been his playfellow, and told him, too, the real name of an old schoolmate, forgotten until then)." In the dream, he gains a knowledge of a name. The dream ends with another name, for the figure on the other side of the door is identified by the man with the bloody smear on his head cryptically as "J"—and then Jonas in waking reality is standing by the bed.

The man with the smear is himself, in touch with his own memories of childhood. That makes the dream proleptic, for when Tigg is murdered, a "dark dark stain" is left behind in the wood, of phantasmagoric proportions (47.722). But the figure is also the person on the other side of the door who must be kept out: the man with the knowledge of names that he has within him, the man who represents a primary violence done to him that must be repressed. The primal scene in this text is an obscure sense of an act of violence, which has been laid down as a memory in a moment of hysteria.

Tigg wakes to find that Jonas has come through the door, as in *Crime and Punishment* (3.6, 4.1) Raskolnikov wakes to find that Svidrigaylov has come through the door. This door "connects" with some secret Tigg both knows and does not know (this is the uncanny). It opens onto a heterotopia, enforcing connection and discontinuity at once. The business of Tigg's life is repression: keeping the door shut. But in moments of madness, different from "ordinary" everyday schizoid states, where the subject has blocked off knowledge, both sides of the door can be made visible. This door typically reappears in chapters 46 and 47, when Jonas, who needs an alibi, says that he will sleep in the back room of his London house, which has a backdoor. He will use that door to go off to murder Tigg, but before going out, hears two men on the street side of it, "a narrow covered passage or blind-alley" (46.716)—another pocket—talking about a skeleton just dug up "in some work of excavation near at hand," supposed to be that of a murdered man, buried—or posted, pocketed, entombed, like a dead letter.

When Jonas has murdered Tigg, he thinks of the dark room left shut up at home, where everyone supposes him to be, in that split-off room within the house, which actually represents himself, equally split off, self-repressed. "His hideous secret was shut up in the room, and all its terrors were there" (47.723). Jonas and Tigg have changed identities: the fear of the room (which Tigg had) and of not being able to get back into the room becomes the same. Jonas becomes his own double:

> not only fearful *for* himself but *of* himself; for being, as it were, a part of the room, a something supposed to be there, yet missing from it. . . . He became in a manner his own ghost and phantom, and was at once the haunting spirit and the haunted man. (47.724)

In such a state, Jonas loses a sense of space, or of his own place, as a ghost has no space, or place, though it tries to have one by its power of haunting—power of possession. Jonas makes it back to the outside door of the room, and as he goes in his fear is of what is on its other side: "What if the murdered man were there before him!" The manuscript reading continues:

> It might be. Such stories were related, sometimes. What if he should see his semblance lying on the floor, or stretched out upon the bed, or seated upright in a chair, or looking down upon him through the patched panes in the skylight, or what if It were hiding now behind the door, to lay its hand upon him as he entered! (4.725n)

The skylight was prepared for by the earlier description of the room (46.716), which recalled a skylight "which looked distrustfully down at everything that passed below" at Todgers's (8.126). Just as it aids the sense of the subject being transparent to surveillance, so it also adds to the room's character as blind: There is no window to see out to the "blind-alley." (A window would be onto blankness, like the "dead wall" at Todgers's, a communication that went nowhere.) But beyond this sense of an anonymous room and anonymous space, the split-off room and a split subject go together. Jonas has lost the stability of place that architecture gives and is caught in the labyrinth, seen here as terrifying, disconnected. Pockets are within pockets and person invades person in the form of the double.

The "semblance" he fears to see may mean his twin, or himself. The double may or may not be other to the self, and being so ambiguous it questions the inside/outside dichotomy: Is the double inside the person, like a Chinese box, or outside? If Jonas can be duplicated, what happens to his original autonomous prior existence? The double's appearance in the skylight, in the position of surveillance, like the nineteenth-century version of the superego, would be truly anxiety creating. As Lacan put it,

"The horrible, the suspicious, the uncanny, everything by which we translate . . . this magisterial word '*unheimlich*' presenting itself through the skylights [lucarnes] by which it is framed, situates for us the field of anxiety."[44] Dickens has already rehearsed the idea of modern life as a paranoid structure in *Oliver Twist* (chap. 34), when the dreaming Oliver wakes to see Fagin and Monks looking in on him. In Cruikshank's illustration, both figures of surveillance are framed since the window has a central dividing bar running down it, which gives the figures their own space. Fagin is known; Monks, "his face averted," is not (34.228); though in another moment Oliver knows he has seen him once before (but does not know his identity as his half-brother). *Oliver Twist* is anxiety making in that these figures who both suggest the father, colonize Oliver's dreams, and mean there is no space between the solid architecture of the familiar house (the room and garden are given a kitschlike pastoral and enclosing setting) and the reappearance of de-territorialized figures of the city, the subversions of bourgeois security. Oliver is in the presence of his relatives in the house (he does not know this yet). Waking up, he is confronted by another relative: someone defined as the same, and different, and capable of making the *heimlich* disappear.

This reversibility intensifies with Jonas, whose fear of what is on the other side of the door replicates Tigg's dream. In this labyrinth, or textual *mise en abime,* one man's dream becomes another man's fantasy. What is repressed becomes "It"—not a single person, or identifiable by a letter, but unnamable, outside representation, that which is always on the point of return.[45] In Jonas's dreams, like Oliver's, the *unheimlich* becomes *heimlich,* for the *unheimlich* is contained in the *heimlich.* What has been repressed has been known all along: as it is known that there is, as with the labyrinth, no point of origin. Subjectivity is taken away in the loss of the origin; the *unheimlich* involves the discovery of lack. The room Jonas hides in is his attempt to give himself borders; in the labyrinth, if there is no inside/outside, there is no separate space that would confer individuality: Jonas is left with nothing but the condition of psychosis, a word that appeared a year later than *Martin Chuzzlewit.*[46]

ARCHITECTURE AND HYSTERIA

In those chapters of *Martin Chuzzlewit* evoking a psychotic state, a way of seeing made possible by architecture is defamiliarized. Architecture tries to mark or map the subject in an attempt to control (Ruskin's approach to architecture was in comparison, undiagrammatic),[47] in a schematicism Robin Evans, discussing eighteenth-century prison architecture, compares to anatomy drawing:

> Plans, sections and elevations—the principal tools of the profession—
> made it possible to see a building from a distance and yet to see its multi-
> farious internal workings at a glance; to survey it from an abstracted,
> privileged vantage point as if it were a dissected body, and to see it so be-
> fore the fact of its construction. (Evans, *The Fabrication of Virtue*, 45)

Architecture, the prison, and anatomy: these are parts of a normalizing
drive, a desire to isolate and to fix, like Mrs. Gamp's practice layout of a
body: "Ah! . . . he'd make a lovely corpse!" (25.410). Control is wanted over
memory and the dream-life. Jonas's dream in the coach as he travels toward Salisbury to kill Tigg takes him into a "strange city, where the names
of the streets were written on the walls in characters quite new to him;
which gave him no surprise or uneasiness, for he remembered in his dream
to have been there before." The uncanny destroys stable architecture:

> Although these streets were very precipitous, insomuch that to get from
> one to another, it was necessary to descend great heights by ladders that
> were too short, and ropes that moved deep bells, and swung and swayed as
> they were clung to, the danger gave him little emotion beyond the first
> thrill of terror; his anxieties being concentrated on his dress, which was
> quite unfitted for some festival that was about to be holden there . . .
> (47.719)

Feelings of shame or personal inadequacy mingle with this sense of the
vertiginous, like the rooftop of Todgers's. What was frightening in the
ordinary situation, becomes almost normal. Jonas in his dream thinks he
has been in the strange city before: he has a memory of what has *not* been.
The modern city threatens the loss of memory. To the examples of
schizoid beings (Jonas, and Mrs. Gamp) who make no distinction between fact and reality, and to all the other characters in *Martin Chuzzlewit*
who show signs of a *deréglement de tous les sens* (their "wits" "chuzzled" by the
labyrinth), may be added Mr. Dick in *David Copperfield*, trying to elucidate
his memories and stabilize his being by writing a "Memorial" (*David Copperfield*, 14.197). Ruskin considered that architecture was to stabilize
memory; and a "duty" respecting "national architecture" he considered to
be "to render the architecture of the day, historical." Memory, the sixth
Lamp of Architecture would help, "for it is in becoming memorial or
monumental that a true perfection is attained by civil and domestic
buildings" (*The Seven Lamps of Architecture*, 8.225). What is monumental
(Latin, *monere*, to remind) creates memory.

Architecture—the monument—memory—these terms elide. Wren's
Monument to the Fire of London (1671), city architecture, hard by
Todgers's, appears in *Martin Chuzzlewit*. It was nationalistic in character

and inscription (blaming Catholics for starting the fire), as indicated in Pope's couplet (*Moral Essays*, 3.339–40) on lying architecture:

> Where London's column, pointing at the skies
> Like a tall bully, lifts his head, and lies.

The couplet is referred to in *Martin Chuzzlewit* (37.577), and is suggestive of the relationship between the monumental and national *ressentiment* and architecture, which asserts in the present both a partial memory that it has created and a national narrative. To *ressentiment,* where memory is engendered by a desire to revenge the past, may be added Freud on hysteria. Saying that "hysterics suffer from reminiscences" he says that hysteria works through mnemic symbols, and asks his American audience to take an imaginary walk through London, first noticing Charing Cross, site of a memorial to a dead queen:

> At another point in the same town, not far from London Bridge, you will find a towering, and more modern, column, which is simply known as "The Monument." It was designed as a memorial of the Great Fire, which broke out in that neighbourhood in 1666 and destroyed a large part of the city. These monuments, then, resemble hysterical symptoms in being mnemic symbols; up to that point the comparison seems justifiable. But what should we think of a Londoner . . . who shed tears before the Monument that commemorates the reduction of his beloved metropolis to ashes, although it has long since risen again in far greater brilliance? . . . Every single hysteric and neurotic . . . remember[s] painful experiences of the remote past, but they still cling to them emotionally; they cannot get free of the past and for its sake they neglect what is real and immediate.[48]

The inscription on the monument was taken off in 1831. Dickens evades the question whether this novel is pre- or post-1831, by referring to Pope but not the inscription, and playing on the question where truth can be found. The Monument is an empty signifier (the past can be changed, the inscription removed) feeding impulses toward hysteria. *Ressentiment* and a kind of madness come together, in a repressed panic/paranoid state marked/instated architecturally. One hysteria is fear of fire, which helps in architecture's production of the obedient and regulated subject. Mrs. Gamp is wakened out of her sleep, expecting to find "the passage filled with people, come to tell her that the house in the city had taken fire" (25.414). Bailey's knock at Chuzzlewit's door is "the like of which had probably not been heard in that quarter since the great fire of London" (28.454) and Mrs. Gamp is aggrieved that she is so much knocked up for her professional duties that landlords have warned her "in consequence of being mistook for Fire" (40.630). The bullfinch, alarmed at the noise of argument in Mrs. Gamp's, is "straining himself all to bits, drawing more water than he could drink in a twelvemonth, he must have thought it was Fire!" (49.754). As part of the psychopathology of everyday life, Mr. Pecksniff, drunk at Mrs. Todgers's, falls into the fireplace, and is nearly singed (9.153). The Anglo-Bengalee Insurance Company has "rows of fire-buckets for dashing out a conflagration in its first spark and saving the immense wealth in notes and bonds belonging to the company" (27.430). These buckets are the defense of architecture against the hysteria of memory, but they are also productive of hysteria. Mrs. Gamp when sick-nursing at night is "glad to see a parapidge in case of fire" (25.410). A parapet was part of the architectural ornamentation of the Anglo-Bengalee Insurance Company's building; it suggests that architecture produces the subject *and* its unconscious by raising tensions and fears in people's minds it then makes a feature of trying to allay. The year 1836 had seen the founding of the Royal Society for the Protection of Life from Fire. The modern subject is constructed as fearful and in need of safeguards. Young Bailey escapes such discipline when on the rooftop of Todgers's. "Contemplating . . . any chance of dashing himself into small fragments [he] lingered behind to walk upon the parapet" (9.132). Even vertigo and opposition to it are produced architecturally.

Perhaps in America, Dickens was bored by his visit to Lowell as an experimental, organized town. It does not show, for in his account in *American Notes,* after comparing it and the conditions of the good girls who go there and then return home after a few well-managed years, he refers to British manufacturing towns, saying that to contrast Lowell with these would move between "Good and Evil, the living light and deepest shadow." Yet he pretends to fall asleep on the rail journey from Lowell back to Boston, and glancing out of the window, says he "found abundance of entertainment . . . in watching the effects of the wood fire which had been invisible in the morning but were now brought out in full relief by the darkness: for we were travelling in a whirlwind of bright sparks, which showered about us like a storm of fiery snow" (4.81).

Lowell as an experiment did not last; and perhaps Dickens "still sensed behind all the rushing purposeful energy of the place some uncontrollable, even destructive potential that time alone would reveal."[49] Something of Lowell appears in *Hard Times,* place of Mr. Gradgrind's "model school," designed on rationalist, experimental lines (and Coketown may be Dickens's transposition of an American planned city into Britain). Mr. Gradgrind, with his "unbending, utilitarian, matter-of-fact face" proposes Mr. Bounderby as husband to his daughter, but Louisa does not respond.

She sat so long looking silently towards the town that he said, at length: "Are you consulting the chimneys of the Coketown works, Louisa?

"There seems to be nothing there but languid and monotonous smoke. Yet when the night comes, Fire bursts out, father!" she answered. . . . (*Hard Times* 1.10.100)

Only when the fire breaks out in the night is anything interesting taking place at all. Lowell's public state could not produce anything of difference. This would make the reactions to social control in *American Notes* ambiguous, stated in language as bland as it is because the commitment to order and intelligibility is not complete.

Indeed, the order is based on repression, as with the penitentiary at Philadelphia, which, though it is placed on the *outside* of the city, away from the parallel arrangement of streets, as an alternative organization, shows that the symmetry depends on a more repressive, violent symmetry elsewhere. The prison creates the well-organized American city, not the city the prison, even if the prison is seen as a model for urban planning—"a grand theatre for the trial of all new plans in hygiene and education." As one prison chaplain, quoted by Rothman, puts it, "Could we all be put on prison fare, for the space of two or three generations, the world would ultimately be the better for it. . . . As it is, taking this world and the next together . . . the prison has the advantage."[50]

Harriet Martineau admires the legible, social order unambiguously. She commented on Jacksonian America that its "fundamental democratic principles" were those of "justice and mercy" by which, she said, "the guilty, the ignorant, the needy and the infirm, are saved and blessed." For Martineau, for whom "guilt was infirmity," the Philadelphia "separate system" of punishment was admirable:

Every one of those prisoners, (none of them being aware of the existence of any other), told me that he was under obligations to those who had the charge of him for treating him "with respect." The expression struck me as being universally used by them. Some explained the contrast between this method of punishment and imprisonment in the old prisons, copied from those of Europe; where criminals are herded together, and treated like anything but men and citizens. Others said that though they had done a wrong thing, and were rightly sequestered on that ground, they ought not to have any further punishment inflicted upon them; and that it was the worst of punishments not to be treated with the respect due to men. In a community where criminals feel and speak thus, human rights cannot but be, at length, as much regarded in the infliction of punishment as in its other arrangements.

Much yet remains to be done, to this end. An enormous amount of wrong must remain in a society where the elaboration of a vast apparatus for the infliction of human misery, like that required by the system of solitary imprisonment, is yet a work of mercy. Milder and juster methods of treating moral infirmity will succeed when men shall have learned to obviate the largest possible amount of it. In the meantime, I am persuaded that this is the best method of punishment which has yet been tried. The grounds of preference were, that they could preserve their self-respect, in the first place; and in the next, their chance in society on their release. They leave the prison with the recompense of their extra labour in their pockets, and without the fear of being waylaid by vicious old companions, or hunted from employment to employment by those whose interest it is to deprive them of a chance of establishing a character.[51]

Harriet Martineau's arguments make criminality, not as something to be allowed an irrational existence, but as infirmity, curable, and therefore intelligible. They preserve the right of a society to condescend to the prisoner, by making cure and correction his destiny. But philanthropy is also a form of violence. Lacan, discussing the negative reaction to be expected from any attempt on the part of a psychoanalyst to show sympathy to an analysand, refers to "aggressive reactions to charity" and shows that such reactions are justified when he continues by writing of "the aggressive motives that lie hidden in all so-called philanthropic activity."[52] The point may be made by considering who philanthropy benefits. "According to a Boston vicar named Cooper, the giving of relief to the poor 'enables our nature by conforming us to the best, the most glorious betters. . . . Charity conforms us to the Son of God himself.'"[53] Philanthropy establishes the ego of the giver, as it constructs the subject of philanthropy—in this case (in the Penitentiary), as an infirm creature needing correction. Dickens only needs to name the architect's daughters Mercy and Charity to illustrate his critique of philanthropy.

The society created in *Martin Chuzzlewit* is being brought under control; the reminiscences that are simulacral memories, created in the present, are not memory but extort control at the price of hysteria. Fear of fire suggests fear of sexuality, or it could imply a primal fear of violence invented in the present. This would account for the text's investment in the desexualized male (Tom Pinch), in the courtship of John Westbrook and Ruth Pinch (near fountains, keeping down the fires) and in the attempts the text makes to make the *heimlich* completely familiar, with no trace of the uncanny within it. These are elements in Dickens of a splitting whereby textual energies are closed off—pinched, to evoke the name of the text's most repressed figure—and where the emotionality and the apostrophes evoking domesticity and simpleness—the virtues of the subject who was so nearly lost in America—become hysterical. At the end of the American sections of *Martin Chuzzlewit,* their craziness and their critique of Britishness, the irrelevance of the British national flag, is all appropriated by a morality preaching decent, bourgeois behavior (as in Martin on the neglect of social observances [34.536]). It makes Kafka's critique of Dickens intelligible; it shows the text siding with the 1840s discourse of architecture, to stabilize itself against those giddy moments when the text realizes that its substance is gaps, discontinuity, folds within folds and space that moves about.

It is not London space versus American space in *Martin Chuzzlewit,* but perhaps America with its polar oppositions of Philadelphia and Cairo posed an irresolvable question for Dickens as subject, so that in *Martin Chuzzlewit,* one textual movement is panic, like fear of fire and a desire for a stable space with the subject inside or outside; in that way it responds to the memory loss (loss of an imagined secure subjectivity) that nineteenth-century urban existence, English and American, implies. Its other move is deconstructive, toward instability, the labyrinth, a structureless structure.

CHAPTER 4

Writing in Reaction
DICKENS, THACKERAY, TROLLOPE

Yesterday I read Dickens' American Notes. It answers its end very well, which plainly was to make a readable book, nothing more. Truth is not his object for a single instant. . . . The book makes but a poor apology for its author, who certainly appears in no dignified or enviable position. He is a gourmand, & a great lover of wines & brandies, & for his entertainment has a cockney taste for certain charities. He sentimentalizes on every prison & orphan asylum, until dinner time. But science, art, Nature and charity itself all fade before us at the great hour of Dinner.

—Emerson, *Journals*[1]

You have given to every intelligent eye the power of looking down to the very bottom of Dickens's mode of existing in this world; and I say have performed a feat which, except in Boswell, the unique, I know not where to parallel. So long as Dickens is interesting to his fellow-men, here will be seen, face to face, what Dickens's mode of existing was; his steady practicality, withal; the singularly solid business talent he continually had; and deeper than all, if one had the eye to see deep enough, dark, fateful silent elements, tragical to look upon, and hiding amid dazzling radiances as of the sun, the elements of death itself. Those two American Journies especially transcend in tragic interest to a thinking reader most things one has seen in writing.

—Carlyle to Forster, on reading his *Life of Dickens*.[2]

DICKENS AND EMERSON

How much excitement was to be had from America appears involuntarily in Dickens's letters. Stimulus flowed from politicians, abolitionists, church ministers, lawyers, penologists, temperance advocates,

theatrical people, local dignitaries, and journalists. Going through the
Letters (vol. 3) for the period: in England, Edward Everett, Unitarian and
former Professor of Greek at Harvard (3n) gave names to Dickens of
people he could call on; and in New England he met William Ellery
Channing, leader of American Unitarianism (16n); Henry Dexter, sculptor (18n); George Bancroft, historian and transcendentalist (19n); W. H.
Prescott (19n); R. H. Dana; Jared Sparks, historian at Harvard (24n); the
poet and journalist N. P. Willis (25n); Francis Alexander, portrait painter
(26n); Cornelius Felton, Professor of Greek at Harvard, who accompanied Dickens round New York; Longfellow, Andrews Norton, Benjamin
Pierce, and George Ticknor (all Harvard, 39n), Washington Allston and
Oliver Wendell Holmes (67n). At some stage, he met Elisha Bartlett,
who lived in Kentucky, and wrote about Lowell and medical education
(198n). In New York, he met William Cullen Bryant, Washington Irving,
and two poets: Fitz-Greene Halleck (73n) and Charles Fenno Hoffmann
(82n). He came across Cornelius Mathews and Evert Duyckinck, advocates for a native American literature. In Philadelphia, he had two conversations with Edgar Allan Poe (106n). In Washington, he was invited
to dine with John Quincy Adams, and the occasion made the Whig Representative Robert C. Winthrop say of Dickens that "he seemed rather
to prefer dining with reporters and newspaper men than with persons in
an official position" (113n). Amongst other members of Congress, he met
Henry Clay and Daniel Webster. He may have met the novelist, librarian,
and journalist of Washington, George Watterston (122n). He saw Washington Irving's secretary of legation, Joseph Cogswell, "a man of very remarkable information, a great traveller, a good talker and a scholar" (17
March, 3:139). In Baltimore, there was Stephen Collins, doctor, essayist,
Presbyterian (202n). On the boat from Pittsburgh to Cincinnati he was
bored by William H. Burleigh, editor, poet, temperance advocate, abolitionist, and supporter of women's suffrage (179n); at Cincinnati he attended a party given by the lawyer and legal writer Thomas Walker and
was bored by the "L.L."s—the Literary Ladies (Dickens to Forster, 15
April, *Letters,* 3:194), who perhaps discussed Poe and feminism—resuming the challenge posed by Boston's "Blue Ladies" (*American Notes,* 3.69).
Two "L.L."s appear in *Martin Chuzzlewit,* both "Transcendental" (34.540).

Many contacts were maintained by letters, and remeetings. Most were
with people with more articulated and passionate intellectual sympathies
than Dickens knew in London, less mediated by class, and requiring an
address to sharper issues than were probably available in England: Transcendentalism; philosophy; the questioning of a national literature and
the questioning of English literature; rights, whether of people of color or
of women; feminism; questions of the function of architecture, above all,

of the new phenomenon of the American city. Confronting America's difference from Britain and its racial difference, he encountered otherness. In Britain he could not have entered, as he did in New York, every "abode of villainy, *both black and white.*" That he did means he could have written a different history of New York from James's *Washington Square,* which gives the official history of New York—the gradual movement uptown, with little sense of what was taking place laterally across the city and presenting a history totally white.

Yet in the encounter with American cities and with America as city space, there appears in Dickens, and much more in Thackeray and Trollope, who I want to draw on for comparison, strategies for avoidance of these implications. Dickens's letters and *American Notes* reveal the limitations imposed by English ideology in encountering or responding to this other. The standard praise of the male or male action is "manly." Reaction to the cities involves qualifiers such as "clean and pretty" (Columbus, Ohio), "handsome," "large and busy" (Albany). Broad streets, improvements, institutions, the survival of the quaint or the picturesque—approval for these things shows that this "admirer of cities" reads the city for what is legible to a consciousness that does not respond to difference. In Boston, Dickens refers to the "sect of philosophers known as Transcendentalists:"

> On inquiring what this appellation might be supposed to signify, I was given to understand that whatever was unintelligible would be certainly transcendental. . . . Mr. Ralph Waldo Emerson . . . has written a volume of Essays, in which, among much that is dreamy and fanciful (if he will pardon me for saying so), there is much more that is true and manly, honest and bold. Transcendentalism has its occasional vagaries . . . but it has good healthful qualities in spite of them, and among the number, a hearty disgust of Cant, and an aptitude to detect her in all the million varieties of her everlasting wardrobe. And therefore if I were a Bostonian, I think I would be a Transcendentalist. (3.69–70)

The informal "Transcendental Club" had met occasionally in Boston from 1836 to 1840, and had given way to the magazine *The Dial* in which Emerson published "The Transcendentalist," which said that "the Idealism of the present day acquired the name Transcendental, from the use of that term by Immanuel Kant," and that "whatever belongs to the class of intuitive thought is popularly called at the present day transcendental."[3] But "The Transcendentalist" had been presented as a lecture in the Masonic Temple in Boston in December 1841; Dickens came in its immediate aftermath. Further, Emerson's *Essays: First Series* had appeared in 1841.[4] Since the term "transcendental" appears in Carlyle's *Sartor Resartus*

(1834), Dickens could not have been previously unaware of it; but by Americanizing it, as though it were foreign, and with no reference to Carlylean thought, he conveys a double position with regard to it. He says he would be a transcendentalist if he lived in Boston (Unitarian and rationalist), yet making fun of it in *Martin Chuzzlewit,* he makes it other, and avoids its radicalism of thought.

In Dickens's summary appears a bourgeois and male suspicion of the imaginative, for the antithesis in the pairing of "dreamy"/"fanciful," with the linked words "true, manly, honest and bold" genders the false as female, like "Cant." The word "unintelligible" needs discussing: for transcendentalism's being is not revealed by its name; which is unintelligible as is the philosophy itself; and *Martin Chuzzlewit* plays on this when one of the L.L.s becomes unintelligibly transcendental: "Mind and matter . . . glide swift into the vortex of immensity. Howls the sublime and softly sleeps the calm Ideal, in the whispering chambers of Imagination . . ." (34.541). The unintelligible is opposed to the "true." The English bourgeois identifies with the latter, but perhaps the modern—signified by transcendentalism—is marked by its unintelligibility, as labyrinthine, as the impossible to map.

"Unintelligible" reappears in Dickens—it is the word he uses on his second visit to America to describe the city of Syracuse (Forster, *Life,* 10.2.789)—noticeably in the opium-den setting that opens *The Mystery of Edwin Drood,* where the waking John Jasper, coming out of his drugged sleep, comments on the mutterings of the woman, and then of the Chinese, and then of the Lascar. All, in their opium-trance, are "unintelligible" (*The Mystery of Edwin Drood,* 1.2–3). What appears unintelligible will perhaps not be so in the context of a "mystery" novel, which will be a detective novel (the nineteenth-century literary form for making the city intelligible). In the last chapter I referred to Poe, in one of the earliest of those detective fictions, "The Man of the Crowd" (1840). This, though set in London probably describes New York, and begins with the comment of "a certain German book" that "*es lässt sich nicht lesen*" (it does not permit itself to be read), which becomes true of both the man of the crowd and the crowd.[5] But in *The Mystery of Edwin Drood,* "unintelligible" shows the limitation of the English Jasper's discourse. The unintelligible exists in urban conditions, in East London, the empire's subjects being found there also, at the very heart of the empire; indeed, the unintelligible is what the colonialist cannot afford to read.

Emerson begins "Nature," founding text of American transcendentalism, by saying that "we have no questions to ask that are unanswerable. We must trust the perfection of the creation so far, as to believe that whatever curiosity the order of things has awakened in our minds, the

order of things can satisfy. Every man's condition is a solution in hieroglyphic to those inquiries he would put."[6] Discussing "Language" in the
same essay, words are declared "emblematic" as are things. "Every natural
fact is a symbol of some spiritual fact."[7] The hieroglyphic nature of reality makes everything intelligible, it allows for confidence in interpretation. Yet since the belief in total intelligibility is also a dream of control,
an aspiration toward panopticism, the point may be turned back against
Emerson. Dickens's word "unintelligible" recalls Carlyle's scepticism in
Sartor Resartus, about the danger of "receiving as literally authentic what
was but hieroglyphically so," and also for the statement "Facts are en-
graved Hierograms, for which the fewest have the key."[8] Emerson's world
is more confident than Carlyle's, but perhaps Dickens's response to transcendentalism, in finding something within *it* unintelligible, resists
something in the project as though it were panoptical; which explains the
duality in his response to it, while he wants to find in transcendentalism
an American other, something outside interpretation.

In *American Notes,* Bostonian ideology brings the unintelligible into
clarity, as with Laura Bridgman, locked within her senses, and the mad,
equally locked in theirs. The text tries to read those whose minds are impossible to guess at because of their isolation in solitary confinement, and
creates an American Gothic by evoking the notion that these minds may
be haunted, and so even more inaccessible to the rational interpreting
mind. *American Notes* becomes contradictory in disallowing attempts at
making legible while attacking the non-readable. Dickens scorns Washington for lacking "a legible inscription." Yet how few statues Dickens
would have seen in Washington—or anywhere—which would give a legible inscription and an identity. American sculpture was, after all, almost
nonexistent before the Revolution, while "before the Civil War one
could walk through most streets or squares without ever encountering a
bronze statue of a departed hero or even a simple stone shaft marking an
historical event."[9] For Dickens, Washington cannot be read: It has failed
to become a capital like the ones Dickens knows, London and Paris. Instead its materiality weighs heavily; this is the city where Dickens says
that he can bear anything but filth. The Mississippi and Cairo are extreme forms of nonintelligibility and the old qualifiers, such as "true" or
"healthful" are inadequate to represent them.

In *Martin Chuzzlewit,* satire against America does not allow New York to
be read as a city, but rather as though it were a frontier town. Broadway is
a "handsome street," but also has pigs (16.266), and all other places mentioned in the novel are fictitious, as though America had no infrastructure.
There are no institutions apparent, though Mrs. Brick is said to go to lectures (the Philosophy of the Soul; of Crime; of Vegetables; Government;

and of Matter) and another lady goes to meetings. With these exceptions, America is profoundly and instantly deterritorializing. Above all, none of the characteristics of the people Dickens met appear, as if Dickens removes whatever forms of reality there were that he or Martin Chuzzlewit could have identified with. The boarders at Pawkins's (punning on pigs) are grotesques, cannibalistic at the dinner table, consuming everything like pigs, and all have fake military titles, or are doctors, professors, or reverends—all fake; all reality gone, so that there is nothing for the subject to cling to. Empty titles correspond to the emptiness of the map of the "architectural city" (21.353). By the end of the first chapter of American experiences, through the commentary of Mr. Bevan, the American whose pro-English sentiments—which make him "manly" (16.277)—we are hearing that "no satirist could breathe this air" (16.276). It is clear that America means not the regeneration of man (21.348) but death.

The presentation of women in *Martin Chuzzlewit* implies that America disturbs Dickens through gender. Martin notices at Pawkins's boarding houses "a wiry-faced old damsel, who held strong sentiments touching the rights of women, and had diffused the same in lectures" (16.273). No woman in the American part of the text gets off better. This feminist represents the American radicalism that made feminism into an offshoot of abolition. W. L. Garrison's (male) Anti-Slavery Society began in 1833, but the Philadelphia Female Anti-Slavery Society followed two years later and the first Women's Rights Convention at Seneca Falls, six years after Dickens's visit. To speak of one means to speak of the other. And Dickens takes up slavery in the last chapter of *American Notes*.[10] He follows examples of oppression in the North—prisoners of the silent system, the mad, people such as Laura Bridgman, the docile bodies at Lowell—with examples of physical mutilation enumerated in descriptions of escaped slaves and examples of slaves bound with chains. Yet was this opposition to slavery not what Emerson described Dickens doing: sentimentalizing over social questions until the great hour of dinner? For *Martin Chuzzlewit* goes no further with the slavery question than to satirize abolitionists for not treating the black seriously (17.288), making them part of the novel's critiques of hypocrisy; but it would be easy to show that the presentation of a black servant in the text is equally patronizing. The text cannot think an alternative; while mocking slavery, its antagonism to women will not allow for a sustained critique that thinks through the implications of both types of oppression and relates them to each other. The English satirist finds his positions shown up as inconsistent by America. Emerson, whose Concord attitudes had a tone "alien, beautifully alien" to those of New York, as James, writing of the 1840s and 1850s noticed (*Autobiography*, 3:358), had the abolitionist's insight and could read something in Dickens's stated social positions. The "hour of dinner" was necessary to center the subject. Dickens in 1842 foreclosed on the project of making further acquaintance with the American South and slavery, as he retreated with revulsion from the American West. Both perhaps threatened his sense of himself, making it possible that identity might be undone altogether, producing the delirious state of being the man never heard of again. The South as the nonurban space of slavery, the North as the urban, with its women less silent than Laura Bridgman—both are spaces to be swallowed up in.

I have argued in chapter 1 that in *Bleak House* city space becomes most a space where everything of previously known identity disappears, and that the writing of this "London" draws much, perhaps unconsciously, from the revulsion felt from America, as if what was furthest from the center and least to be identified with, could actually be identified with the center. The Mississippi waters and the mud violate a subjectivity that is aware of its own threat from a disappearance, or a consumption of which slavery is a prime example, slavery being the most violent form of removal of subjectivity, a form of cannibalism. *Bleak House* situates the house of Mrs. Jellyby in the London fog, and identifies with her and with it a disorganization of space in which everything threatens to fall into chaos. Mrs. Jellyby is Dickens's continuation of the "L.L."s and the feminist figures of *Martin Chuzzlewit,* and significantly, her mission is directed toward black settlements in Africa (Borioboola-Gha). From London as Africa, in Blake's poem "Why should I fear" quoted in chapter 1, there is a subtle and slight shift that effects a complete reversal; London is no different from Africa, but should not relate to it.[11] Mrs. Jellyby's philanthropy does not take American slavery into account, but it may be its displaced subject, which would identify the abolitionist and the feminist as the same and as inseparable from city chaos.

The sections dealing with Mrs. Jellyby were thoroughly controversial, as the character's kinship with Harriet Beecher Stowe became apparent, the symbiotic relationship appearing even within Dickens's language, in his letters. *Uncle Tom's Cabin* had appeared in serial form between 1851 and 1852 and Dickens thanked her for the eventual book when it was sent to him (17 July 1852, *Letters,* 6:715), though in a letter of 22 November 1852, he felt that Stowe had caught "the weaknesses and prejudices of the abolitionists themselves" (*Letters,* 6.808). But the character of Mrs. Jellyby in *Bleak House,* which had begun its serialization that March, was soon associated with her.[12] In a letter on this (20 December 1852, *Letters,* 6:826) Dickens refers to a review that appeared of Mrs. Stowe's work in *Household Words* (18 September 1852), under the title "North American Slavery," which he had in part authored.[13] The article repeats an opposition to slavery, but that hardly seems the point since he accepts neither the abolitionist nor the Stowe position. I find it more significant that Dickens's writing can make no distinction between what he recoils from and from what works against those sources of recoil. The passages about Laura Bridgman are symptomatic of a sympathy so intense that its imbalance disallows an adequate reading of the city space of Boston; making it, indeed, almost kitschlike. Identification with this woman's liberation as he writes these passages is a protection against having to absorb into consciousness any other form of liberation that would bring into question the relationship between identity and liberty, both of which are at the heart of abolitionism and feminism, which both work with the constructed nature of racial and sexual difference. Identity may be a defense against liberty, and Dickens shows his own dissociation from his own nonabolitionist and nonfeminist positions—both protective of identity—by fascination with what is on the other side of identity, with chaos, doubleness, disappearance. That is the contradiction in *Bleak House,* which means that its subject matter is still absorbed by America, even as it takes its heroine's name from the novel whose scarlet letter recalls not only adultery and America, but the crisis of abolition.[14]

THACKERAY AND "THE OLD SOUTH"

"What could Dickens mean by writing that book of *American Notes?* No man should write about the country under 5 years of experience and as many of previous reading. A visit to the Tombs, to Laura Bridgman and the Blind Asylum, a description of Broadway—O Lord is that describing America?"[15]

So Thackeray on *American Notes,* as if seeing the text as a pretext for not "describing America," and as ever, he contrasts with Dickens enough to make comparison worthwhile, while his resentment at Dickens on America needs reading. He knows that the Laura Bridgman sympathy will not do—and he knows that "describing America" is problematic, for it requires the awareness than Dickens—as well as himself—has repressed out of existence. Did he also know that "describing America" is also "de-scribing" America: by adding to America by describing it, taking away in the writing the subject of the writing? That writing, far from adding to the subject of representation, negates it? It is Blanchot's point. Thackeray's agitation about Dickens shows a disturbance about what Dickens has written, which is interesting and shows that "America" is not a given, but is to be created through forms of writing;

yet in Thackeray there is also less of the unconscious; he knows what he is not prepared to admit, and that suggests that for him identity is more protected.

Thackeray made his first of two lecture tours ten years after Dickens, but in an America whose public events presaged Civil War: the publication of the pro-urban, pro-North *Narrative of the Life of Frederick Douglass* (1845) and the 1850 Compromise. By this, California was admitted as a free state and the slave trade was abolished in Washington D.C., but the New Mexico and Utah territories were organized without prohibition of slavery, and the new Fugitive Slave Act required Northerners to aid in the return of escaped slaves, so that everybody became implicated in slavery. *Uncle Tom's Cabin* was part of the resultant protest, and the text spills embarrassingly into Thackeray's work. His first tour took in Boston and New York—where he met Henry James Senior and his family, then living at West Fourteenth Street, near Sixth Avenue, and the young James.[16] In mid-January 1853, he visited Philadelphia, Baltimore, Washington, and Richmond—"the very prettiest friendliest and pleasantest little town I have seen in these here parts" (*Letters of Thackeray*, 3:223)—and Charleston and Savannah, where he visited a plantation (*Letters*, 3:241). He left in April 1853. It seems that he had no recoil from the South, unlike Dickens, and might have thought slaveholding American society no worse than contemporary industrial England.[17]

Yet he also felt when he saw the slaves in Washington that his travels had just begun; the otherness of America affronted him as "queer" and even potentially terrifying; needing every rationalization he could give it:

> there was scarce any sensation of novelty until now when the slaves come on to the scene; and straightway the country assumes an aspect of the queerest interest: I don't know whether it is terror, pity or laughter that is predominant. They are not my men & brethren, these strange people with retreating foreheads, with great obtruding lips & jaws: with capacities for thought, pleasure, endurance quite different to mine. They are not suffering as you are impassioning yourself for their wrongs as you read Mrs Stowe they are grinning & joking in the sun; roaring with laughter as they stand about the streets in squads; very civil, kind & gentle, even winning in their manner when you accost them at gentlemen's houses, where they do all the service. But they don't seem to me to be the same as white men . . . Sambo is not my man & my brother; the very aspect of his face is grotesque and inferior. I can't help seeing & owning this; at the same time of course denying any white man's right to hold this fellow-creature in bondage & make goods and chattels of him and & his issue; but where the two races meet the weaker one must knock under. . . . (Letter of 13 February to Mrs. Carmichael-Smyth, *Letters*, 3:198–99)

The letter continues with reference to the "degradation" the African suffered in his own country; by comparison to the condition of poor whites in Britain; and with the likelihood that Chinese laborers might be "imported" to work at cotton and tobacco better than the slaves, thus making slavery uneconomic (a constantly repeated argument, as much as the happiness of the slaves). For "Freedom pays incomparably better than Slavery; as you cross the frontier & directly you see poor Blacky's face the substantive prosperity of the country diminishes, the manufactures fail . . ." (*Letters,* 3:200).

Thackeray sums up his views on the South from his first visit as

> not so horrified as perhaps I ought to be with slavery, which in the towns is not by any means a horrifying institution. The negroes in the good families are the happiest, laziest, comfortablest race of menials. [The ambiguity of this construction makes the "race" congenitally a servant class.] They are kept luxuriously in working time and cared for most benevolently in old age—one white does the work of four of them and one negro that can work has his parents very likely and children that can't. It is the worst economy, slavery, that can be, the clumsiest and most costly domestic and agricultural machine that ever was devised. "Uncle Tom's Cabin" and the tirades of the Abolitionists may not destroy it, but common sense infallibly will before long . . . in household and in common agricultural estates. (*Letters,* 3:254)

Returned to England, in *The Newcomes* (1853–55), he made fun of Harriet Beecher Stowe, via the "womanifesto" sponsored by the Duchess of Sutherland—a letter signed by half a million women in Britain, and presented to Mrs. Stowe on her arrival there in 1853. Back in America (October 1855 to May 1856) he included in his tour New Orleans and the Mississippi up to St. Louis, then Cincinnati and back to New York via Buffalo. In letters, it becomes evident how much affinity Thackeray feels for Richmond, and how "picturesque" he finds the black population; he writes about Savannah, a "tranquil old city, wide-streeted, tree-planted, with a few cows and carriages toiling through the sandy road, a few happy negroes sauntering here and there . . . (to Kate Perry, 14 February 1856, *Letters,* 3:562), and he describes Augusta with the same enthusiasm. Southern cities receive some description, more than the Northern, even New York.

Thackeray on Southern cities may be compared with Frederick Law Olmsted, who in the 1850s believed that cities were the nation's future environment and the basis for social planning. Olmsted, Northerner and abolitionist, visited the South between 1853–57, with the object of presenting a view of Southern life and manners for the New York *Daily Times.*

He noted how the Southern agrarian was suspicious of Northern urban life; the argument being that cities contained poor immigrants and morally degraded them. In his journeys, Olmsted found only six towns with a "townlike character" in the slave States: New Orleans, Mobile, Louisville, St. Louis, Charleston, and Richmond. Others like Savannah he called "overgrown villages, in appearance and in convenience." The port city of Norfolk, Virginia, had "no lyceum or public libraries, no public gardens, no galleries of art . . . no 'home' for its seamen, no public resorts of healthful and refining amusement, no place better than a filthy, tobacco-impregnated bar-room or a licentious dance-cellar . . . for the stranger of high or low degree to pass the hours unaccompanied by business."[18] No public spaces; no assumption of anything other in the American but business; such was the American city, worse in the South than in the North; but the North with its urbanization was changing and the Civil War was the anger of the nonurban against the successful and pushing urban, against Northern cities whose cultural and democratic capacity Olmsted, with his plans for Central Park, wanted to show. Thackeray has no relation to these arguments. For him, Southerners are "much pleasanter to be with, than the daring go-ahead northern people" (15 February, *Letters,* 3:567). Though he dislikes the journeys in the South, this does not produce Dickens's nausea. Rather, he complains "there is nothing to draw" (*Letters,* 3:575); it is not "picturesque." But this is more of a critique than it seems, for Thackeray's sketches, which Baudelaire implicitly compares to those of Constantin Guys, the "painter of modern life" align him with urban culture, in which context his sketches worked.[19] Thackeray retreats from his own position as urban *flâneur,* not so much when he says that Washington had a "Wiesbaden air,"[20] or when he likes New Orleans because it is like Le Havre (*Letters,* 3:577) but when Charleston is declared "like Europe, with an aristocracy and a very pleasant society, ruling patriarchally over its kind black vassals" (*Letters,* 3:587). It is antimodern and antidemocratic; in accordance with Thackeray's sense of it, South Carolina, which included this European Charleston, seceded first from the Union (20 December 1860).

Going up the Mississippi on an eight-day trip to St. Louis, "in all my life I have seen nothing more dreary & funereal than these streams. The nature & the people oppress me and are repugnant to me . . ." (*Letters,* 3:589). But the difference from Dickens in intensity of feeling will be noted, as also when he comments on "the place they say that was Martin Chuzzlewit's Eden Cairo at the confluence of the Ohio and Miss. such a dreary Heaven abandoned place! But it will be a great city in five years spite of overflows and fever and ague" (*Letters,* 3:591). He calls the Mississippi "the great dreary melancholy stream" (*Letters,* 3:596), and at some level of consciousness, connects this reading of the West with an aversion to democracy—but not slavery—for he says he "couldn't bear to live in a country at this stage in its political existence" (*Letters,* 3:593). From Cincinnati, he traveled for 40 hours nonstop in a return to New York. Though Thackeray left America with enthusiasm, later letters show that he did not rule out a return there. The protests about the dreariness were part of a more general Thackerayan melancholia, which was not specific to the American South and West.

Thackeray's identification with the old South produced his American novel, after his second visit, *The Virginians: A Tale of the Last Century* (1857–59), a novel implicitly reacting to Harriet Beecher Stowe. As his letters did not engage with urban America, *The Virginians* did not connect with the nineteenth century, and certainly not with the city. The Virginians are twin brothers; and for half of the novel (up to chap. 47) the emphasis is on the younger, George, an American innocent amongst corrupt English relations and nearly entrapped into marriage: The theme anticipates what James would do in *The Portrait of a Lady.* The elder, George, is destined to fight for England in the War of Independence, while Harry fights for America. Their home is on a vast estate near Williamsburg, where "the question of slavery was not born . . . to be the proprietor of black servants shocked the feelings of no Virginian gentleman; nor, in truth, was the despotism exercised over the negro race generally a savage one."[21] The tone evokes nostalgia; for example, for old-style hospitality (chap. 9), and the slave, Gumbo, is objectified as much as his choice of name implies.

Is it possible to see Dickens's position with regard to the black and the South, apart from the recoil, as much different from Thackeray's? He could not touch the South, in a visceral reaction Thackeray could never be conscious of, but what did he make of the Civil War? The Southern states proclaimed the Confederacy on 4 February 1861, and bombarded Fort Sumter on 12 April. The Northern blockade of Southern ports came on 15 April, and swung *The Times* behind the South because of the absence of cotton reaching Lancashire; it was the occasion for looking down on America's democratic experiment as a failure. A year into the war, Dickens summarized his views:

> Slavery has in reality nothing on earth to do with it, in any kind of association with any generous or chivalrous sentiment on the part of the North. But the North having gradually got to itself the making of the laws and the settlement of the Tariffs, and having taxed the South most abominably for its own advantage, began to see, as the country grew, that unless it advocated the laying down of a geographical line beyond which slavery should

not extend, the South would necessarily recover its old political power, and be able to help itself a little in the adjustment of commercial affairs. Every reasonable creature may know, if willing, that the North hates the Negro, and that until it was convenient to make a pretence that sympathy with him was the cause of the War, it hated the abolitionists and derided them . . . (to W. W. de Cerjat, 16 March 1862, Dickens, *Letters,* 10:53–54)

The North hates the Negro: not a word is said here about the South hating the black. The argument, following the hostility to the Abolitionists in *Martin Chuzzlewit,* has become implicitly pro-South. Dickens's letters, insisting that the North will not be able to raise the number of soldiers required by conscription, show him boxing himself in to a situation where the North must fail: "I can *not* believe that Conscription will do otherwise than fail and wreck the War" (28 May 1863, *Letters,* 10:254). A footnote adds: "Of course, the more they brag, the more I don't believe them." Dickens willfully misreads and wants the North not to succeed. Edmund Wilson argued that the North's victory over the South was part of an American will to power; he compares Lincoln to Bismarck, and in a separate essay he contrasts the Confederate vice president, Alexander H. Stephens, with Lincoln, drawing attention to the former's total refusal of the concept of conscription, as a refusal of that will to power.[22] Dickens, on this reading of the acceleration of Northern power, draws back from drawing the implications of the North's modernity, even though he had shown his belief, in *Martin Chuzzlewit,* that the American pioneering spirit was quite reconciled to the idea of Martin Chuzzlewit dying in "Eden," and disappointed when he did not. If Dickens thought that the North would not succeed, that may indicate a desire, conscious or not, not to accept the consequences of American modernity. He hesitates in relation to wanting the triumph of the North, and again, in this he shows that doubleness of qualities; a revulsion and a recoil both from what he fears as other to him—the South, slavery—and distaste from that which is hostile to what he fears. It is that doubleness that makes him so hide in the folds of city space, and so create its ambiguity, almost uniquely amongst English novelists, and certainly in contrast to Thackeray or Trollope.

TROLLOPE: NORTH AMERICA

One more comparison with Dickens.

Anthony Trollope visited America during the Civil War (August 1861 to March 1862), beginning with Boston, the "western Athens,"[23] and, circling round the northern states and Canada, finishing at New York. He never visited the secessionist states. His two-volume *North America,* however, is an

index to the state of the war by someone who kept following in the track of
Union soldiers.[24] In *North America* there appears an English ideology uncertain about the value of the city. He is partially aware that America's urban
culture makes a difference from Britain—"Americans live much more in
towns than we do. All with us that are rich ... live in the country" he says in
relation to Cincinnati (2:87). The difference of American towns from English is the American parallel planning, "so distressing to English eyes and
English feelings" (1:41, discussing Portland). He returns to the topic discussing Ottawa, comparing it with the twisting streets of London (1:82–83),
even if he does find Ottowa's new public buildings having "purity of art and
manliness of conception" (1:84)—those typical terms of endorsement,
whose gendering also implies an anxiety about how much femininity might
appear in the city. He gives a sense of how American urbanism works, via
descriptions of Detroit (1:142–43) and Milwaukee (1:146–50), emphasizing the planned nature of each and their unfinished nature; he finds
Chicago the "most remarkable city" in the Union, referring to its growth (by
then 120,000), its prosperity, based on corn, and its expectation of continuing to prosper—"men in these regions do not mind failures, and when they
have failed, instantly begin again. They make their plans on a large scale, and
they who come after them fill up what has been wanting at first. Those taps
of hot and cold water will be made to run by the next owner of the hotel, if
not by the present owner" (1:195). Yet Trollope, though responsive to
American "wondrous contrivances"—including the elevator (1:140)—is unable to say anything about America's urban modernity. So, "Montreal is an
exceedingly brisk commercial town and the business there is brisk. It has
85,000 inhabitants. Having said that of it, I do not know what more there
is left to say" (1:74).

That blankness of response to urban space appears with New York.
He begins, "Speaking of New York as a traveller, I have two faults to find
with it. In the first place there is nothing to see; and in the second place,
there is no mode of getting about to see anything. Nevertheless, New
York is a most interesting city. It is the third biggest city in the known
world;—for those Chinese congregations of unwinged ants are not cities
in the known world" (1:227). "Nothing to see" means that Trollope writes
as the European for whom what is to see is defined by the past, who cannot see that the present is also part of history, and cannot see the challenge New York offers to a European capital:

> How should there be anything to see of general interest? In other large
> cities ... there are works of art, fine buildings, ruins, ancient churches,
> picturesque costumes, and the tombs of celebrated men. But in New
> York, there are none of these things. Art has not yet grown up there. One

or two fine pictures by Crawford are in the town,—especially that of the sorrowing Indian at the rooms of the Historical Society—but art is a luxury in a city which follows but slowly on the heels of wealth and civilization. (1:241)[25]

He estimates New York's size as a million (of which 800,000 lived in the city itself: it may be added that 70 percent of that population lived in the 15,000 tenements that represented the city's poor neighborhoods) and in doing so, he casually puts down China. The limitation is basic to his European perspective, making it predictable that he begins the chapter with negatives, just as writing about Chicago he thinks that the city must undergo inevitable failures. Try comparing the spirit of Trollope—or of Thackeray—with Whitman to get the effect of the reactiveness.[26]

Trollope sees New York as more American than any other city in its "free institutions, general education and the ascendancy of dollars." The negative tone of the opening returns in his distaste for "very large shops," referring to A. T. Stewart's Department Store, which had been newly built to designs by John W. Kellum, between Broadway and Fourth Avenue, at Ninth Street, and occupying a whole block. "For I confess to a liking for the old-fashioned private shops" he writes (1:253). In the same context, he mentions "Harper's establishment for the manufacture and sale of books" with a sense of the place as a vast factory. Harper's, built in 1854 to designs by James Bogardus, was, like Stewart's, an example of new cast-iron building, and with five stories and outside walls that had no load-bearing function, represented a new architecture in New York, which Trollope's sense that there was "nothing to see" disallowed him from seeing. Instead, like his mother discussing Philadelphia, Trollope refers to the "taste for parallelograms" in the design of the streets (1:253); but he finds "good architectural effect" in the houses on Fifth Avenue, which he compares to Belgrave Square, Park Avenue, and Pall Mall, and also in the churches, showing a preference for Gothic over the new. He closes the chapter with reference to Central Park, newly landscaped (New York by then was built up as far as Sixtieth Street), but he refuses the eulogium that would compare it to London parks (1:258).

The prose will not confront something not yet confronted. He finds Baltimore more like "an English town than most of its transatlantic brethren" and refers to fox hunting and to an old inn sign that could have come out of Somersetshire (1:372–73). Baltimore, because of its English look, is where he would choose to live in the States. (2:183). He dislikes Washington for its unbuilt state, and criticizes the idea of a planned city—"commerce, I think, must select the site of all large congregations of mankind" (2:6). He finds the city "melancholy" (2:7), a word repeated several times. Turning to the six principal public buildings of Washington, he finds in most of them their success as buildings "more or less marred by an independent deviation from recognized rules of architectural taste" (2:8). It is a reactive comment. He gives attention to the Capitol; Robert Mills's Corinthian-style Post Office; William P. Elliott and Mills's Patent Office, with Doric façade, just completed when Trollope saw it; the Treasury (George Hadfield); the President's house (James Hoban and Benjamin Latrobe); and the Romanesque Smithsonian Institute.

Recognized rules of taste are what he criticizes the Capitol by, and it means that he has no sense of the building having a history, developing over time, and therefore embodying conflictual interests and ideologies: from William Thornton's design, then that of Benjamin Latrobe and Charles Bulfinch supplementing that, and then the radical change made in 1851. At this time, Thomas U. Walter added extra wings to either side of the building, and a new cast-iron dome replaced the older wooden one (a dome implying national unity, and not as colonial as a cupola, steeple, or spire). The sculptures for the pediment were by Thomas Crawford, who had expatriated himself to Rome to practice neoclassical art; they were to illustrate "The Progress of Civilization." Trollope saw them before they were put in position; equally he did not see the completed dome that took 16 years to complete.

While Trollope likes Crawford's work, he finds the statuary in Washington monotonous, and he does not care for Horace Greenough's statue of Washington, in the grounds in front of the Capitol ("stiff, ungainly, and altogether without life"). Greenough's neo-classical sculpture, based on the imagined reconstruction of a lost Phidias Zeus, was not designed for the open-air. Its partial nudity offended, however, when it was placed in the Capitol in 1841, and its classicism was compromised by the publicly felt requirement to use a naturalistic head, which was based on the portrait made by Houdon for the statue in the Virginia State House at Richmond. The statue, then, needs a cultural reading, in that it shows the marks of a contradictory history, and while Trollope's criticism of it is easily made, the critique does not respond to the crisis in nineteenth-century art, especially American, which makes sculpture use forms reflecting modes of thinking alien to America, but which does not yet license a distinctively American art. Similarly, he faults the new wings of the Capitol for destroying the symmetry; and in this argument appears a preference for abstract fixed structure over historical change, and an assumption that assumes the validity of the European classical for America: he sides with those who want the nation to be already defined, he does not respond to American otherness.

The same argument appears in his reference to the Smithsonian Institute, designed by James Renwick, as "bastard Gothic" (2:16, 17), "subversive of architectural purity." He ostentatiously refuses to consider it as Romanesque, which it was specifically thought of by its planner (Robert Dale Owen in 1849 in *Hints on Public Architecture*) because Romanesque was "less ostentatious [than Gothic] and if political character may be ascribed to architecture, more republican."[27] "Bastard" in itself is suggestive. Further, there was Trollope's critique of Robert Mills's unfinished obelisk to Washington, and if finished, says Trollope, "what would it be even then as compared with one of the great pyramids? Modern attempts cannot bear comparison with those of the old world in simple vastness. But in lieu of simple vastness, the modern world aims to achieve either beauty or utility. By the Washington monument, if completed, neither would be achieved" (2:17). Trollope's judgement is pre-emptive; nor is it clear why the modern cannot compete in terms of simple vastness: American buildings or the Brooklyn Bridge could soon disprove him. But the substantial point is the impoverished sense of the modern, or a hostility toward it, which implies *ressentiment* (as in the word "attempts"), and so the diminishing of Washington continues throughout the description given. Despite Trollope's feeling of futility, the monument *was* dedicated (in 1885); while Washington was to be relandscaped at the beginning of the twentieth century. Trollope considers, in the light of the events of the war, that Washington, designed to be at the center of the nation, may turn out to be at its border (2:1, 2). And in another sense from the one he meant he is right; the architecture of Washington reveals unresolved contradictions that characterized American art. The classicism revealed something of the nostalgia that tolerated the existence of slavery; this architecture is antagonistic to the thought of plurality.

Yet in criticizing the monumentality of Washington, and seeing something not quite fitting in the statuary, Trollope came near to articulating a contradiction at work—which appears in the juxtaposition between white buildings and surrounding mud. And there is something else in Trollope's description, apart from his *ressentiment* to historicize his own perception, which has to do with awareness of a new militarism, which co-opts everything for the war, of which the obelisk is itself the anticipative symbol, both for its self-advertising grandeur and for its warning of nonfulfillment:

A sad and saddening spot was that marsh as I wandered down on it alone one Sunday afternoon. The ground was frozen and I could walk dry-shod, but there was not a blade of grass. Around me on all sides were cattle in great numbers,—steer and big oxen—lowing in their hunger for a meal. They

were beef for the army, and never again I suppose would it be allowed to
them to fill their big maws and chew the patient cud. There, on the brown,
ugly, undrained field, within easy sight of the President's house, stood the
useless, shapeless, graceless pile of stones [the obelisk]. It was as though I
were looking on the genius of the city. It was vast, pretentious, bold, boast-
ful with a loud voice, already taller by many heads than other obelisks, but
nevertheless still in its infancy,—ugly, unpromising and false. (2:18)

To fault Trollope's anti-modernity is possible, but it is also true that in
the atmosphere of a city co-opted by the military, he identifies city planning with militarism—as with Paris, at that time undergoing Hauss-
mann's modernizations. In Baltimore, he had met the Unionist General
Dix, who took him to the summit of Federal Hill, from which his troops
could destroy the city. Dix said that "this hill was made for the purpose"
(1:370)—to which Trollope registers dissent, thinking of the dispossessed
"poor of Baltimore."

Yet we can turn back to his superiority to American cities by looking
at his description of Cairo. Visiting it, he refers to *Martin Chuzzlewit*—he
refers to this text again in satirizing "Mr Jefferson Brick" (2:348)—but he
misses the point by assuming that Mark Tapley—with whom he compares himself several times over the following pages—enjoyed himself in
Cairo/Eden (2:121). The misunderstanding—a lack of irony—makes him
magnify the disaster he felt Cairo to be and to emphasize the ruin into
which it was sinking since Dickens's days; yet he has gone to observe its
"warlike character" (2:125), and so he sees a city become a garrison town,
and he emphasizes mud—"every street was absolutely impassable from
mud. I mean that in walking down the middle of any street in Cairo a
moderately framed man would soon stick fast and not be able to move . . .
along one side of each street a plank boarding was laid, on which the mud
had accumulated only up to one's ankles. . . . at the crossings I found con-
siderable danger and occasionally had my doubts as to the possibility of
progress" (2:123). This makes "progress" allegorical. The passage's texture
recalls the opening of *Bleak House* (mud and people "accumulating at compound interest"), so unconsciously returning that text to its source in this
very city, Cairo. And mud, which unconsciously evokes the battlefield,
becomes also the way in which Trollope views the West. He contrasts
Yankee "hard intelligence" with Southern "more polished manner" but
finds in the Western states men "gloomy and silent—I might almost say
sullen. . . . They care nothing for the graces,—or shall I say the decencies
of life? They are essentially a dirty people. Dirt, untidiness, and noise,
seem in nowise to afflict them. Things are constantly done before your
eyes which should be done and might be done behind your back" (2:117).

This response to dirt, which compares with Dickens's "I can bear any-thing but filth" is not distaste in itself. Pittsburgh, despite its soot and filth, "the dirtiest place I ever saw" (2.84), does not alienate him, perhaps because, unlike Cairo, he can relate it to English industrial towns; he rather finds it "picturesque": "I was never more in love with smoke and dirt than when I stood [on the bridge over the Monongahela] and watched the darkness of night close in upon the floating soot which hov-ered over the housetops of the city" (2.81). Again, there is a difference from Dickens's Pittsburgh. And Trollope reverts to the presence of mud in Washington when he says with regard to his later visit that the city's inhabitants are "in thrall" to "King Mud." The mud surrounds govern-ment buildings and makes passage from one to another, like crossing the streets at Cairo, impossible; and Trollope recalls the presence of the army as a source for it (2:187) before allegorizing the mud in terms of the peo-ple who have profited from the war.

Reading this material in the light of *Bleak House* enforces differences between Dickens and Trollope. Mud which is most central to London (this is confirmed in *Our Mutual Friend*) disconfirms identity in Dickens, but not for Trollope, who gains his own Englishness from combating it. Mud impedes but it does not stick to the European traveler, who has seen dirt elsewhere (Trollope instances Egypt, old Spain, Spanish America, and Connaught in Ireland, and various monasteries elsewhere as places where he has been "educated to dirt"—before saying that it was all as nothing to the Western states of the United States). It seems that mud belongs to the colonial settlement and to the new capital; so it remains other to Trollope, and that by which he asserts his separateness. It implies inadequate urbanization, which means that although he can speak of it in terms of its symbolism, yet that symbolism is what he has the freedom to give to it. The mud does not already signify something to him, whereas for Dickens the abject reactions it produces, threatening to make reality formless come from the point that the mud *already* symbolizes. It takes away identity through the invasive power of its signifying, since it means that the subject is not in control of the power of signification. Like the *Bleak House* fog, the mud is that against which single utterance must strug-gle, because it is of the very entropic character of signification itself.

Trollope is superior to the mud because of that antimodernism that characterizes British attitudes to nineteenth-century America.[28] He is on the side of the North in the war, though opposed to abolitionism (2:68), but he does not hold that the black is the white man's equal: "I see, or think I see, that the negro is the white man's inferior through laws of na-ture. That he is not mentally fit to cope with white men . . . and that he must fill a position simply servile" (2:70). Dickens felt some form of threat, which kept him from the South; Thackeray identified most with the South and reacted away from the urban North; Trollope accepted the North but could not warm to it, either on account of its Americanness, or on account of its new incipient militarism. In each of these cases may be seen a complex reaction to the urban culture that was other to the nonurban South.

DICKENS IN 1867

America meant death in *Martin Chuzzlewit,* and perhaps in *American Notes,* yet 25 years later, Dickens, by now fighting against illness, returned for a second tour (November 1867 to April 1868).[29] Boston, which he compared to Edinburgh, had enlarged, "grown more mercantile . . . like Leeds mixed with Preston, and flavoured with New Brighton" (Forster, *Life,* 10:1.766) — "on ground which he had left a swamp he now found the most princely streets"—the Back Bay area. It is an example of Baudelaire's sense in "Le Cygne" of how "la forme d'une ville / Change plus vite, hélas! que le coeur d'un mortel" (the form of a city changes, alas, more quickly than the heart of a mortal), that in New York, a week passed before he could map the city in relation to his past visit. But with this difference: for Baudelaire it was "le vieux Paris" (the old Paris) that was no more; for Dickens, it was the *new* city of the 1840s that was gone. He writes: "the only portion that has even now come back to me is the part of Broadway in which the Carlton Hotel (long since destroyed) used to stand. There is a very fine new park in the outskirts [Central Park] and the number of grand houses and splendid equipages is quite surprising" (*Life,* 10:1.769).

Brooklyn, where he gave readings, is called "a kind of sleeping-place for New York" (*Life,* 10:2.777). Dickens comments badly on the Irish in New York City (10:2.779) and he reads the black presence in Baltimore, where "the Ghost of Slavery haunts the town" wholly negatively (10:2.782–83). His expectation is that the black "will die out fast . . . [for] it seems, looking at them, so manifestly absurd to suppose it possible that they can ever hold their own against a restless, shifty, striving, stronger race" (10:2.783)—a mistake as gratuitous as his assumption that the North could not win the war, and showing, like his belief that the Irish could be seen in separate terms from other Americans of New York, a desire not to deal with American urban existence as plural, mixed. Yet what he writes about upstate New York and about Massachusetts, including his account of Portland, burnt down three years previously, but through the "astonishing energy" of the people, nearly recreated again (10:2.793) shows his interest in "the rise of vast new cities" (10:2.795). So too his awareness that traveling to Chicago, Boston and New York in one week by train is not exceptional (10:2.778), implies a fascination with the drive toward speed and the elimination of time and space within American modernity.

His response to this modernity at first seems to have nothing of the quality of detachment or objectivity that Simmel discusses in the modern urban dweller's outlook.[30] As a response to America, everything seems frenetic, machine driven, as though Dickens was bound to a machine that he could not be taken off. Yet in another way, perhaps his reaction *was* also objective, and this is something Emerson noticed, after one of his readings, when he concluded that Dickens "has too much talent for his genius; it is a fearful locomotive to which he is bound and can never be free from it nor set at rest. You [James T. Fields] see him quite wrong, evidently, and would persuade me that he is a genial creature, full of sweetness and amenities, and superior to his talents, but I fear he is harnessed to them. He is too consummate an artist to have a thread of nature left. He daunts me! I have not the key."[31] Emerson's earlier comments on Dickens are reversed; Dickens is now the modernist whose lack of nature gives him the same character as America's own modernizers. The interest in the poor and the imprisoned does not come out of a sympathy with nature: Emerson had been suspicious of its origins in Dickens's earlier visit. It comes, rather, from a professionalism that is outside the subject, with which the bourgeois subject is in conflict, as if not quite aware of the difference that has been created. It links urban and machinic America—immediately after the triumph of the Civil War—with the modernist in Dickens.

On this visit, James met him. That November 1867, Dickens had been taken by Fields, editor of the *Atlantic Monthly*, from 28 Charles Street in Boston to dinner with Charles Eliot Norton at Cambridge. James, then living there, was asked to come for an introduction after the dinner. In *Notes of a Son and Brother*, James makes the occasion illustrate "the force of action, unless I may call it passion, that may reside in a single pulse of time." The two met for a moment in a doorway, and James's "dumb homage"— they did not shake hands—was matched by "a straight inscrutability [the word is repeated in the description], a merciless *military* eye . . . an automatic hardness . . . which at once indicated to me, and in the most interesting way in the world, a kind of economy of apprehension."

James describes a transfer of power. His word "economy" attributes to Dickens a Jamesian quality: the older novelist is not the author of loose baggy monsters. In this transference, James continues that "no accession to sensibility" could have compared, for penetration, "to the intimacy of this particular and prodigious glimpse." It seems that James is describing the power of Dickens's look, but the next sentence shows it is rather the power of James's: "It was as if I had carried my strange treasure just exactly from under the merciless military eye—placed there on guard of the secret" (*Notes of a Son and Brother: Autobiography*, 388–90). James looks at Dickens, and feels that he has taken something away from him, despite the military bearing, which James has set up in the description, and which suits—whether James was aware of this or not—the idea of Dickens as the colonial writer. The older, English novelist is by then on "the outer edge of his once magnificent margin" and knows it and the doorway meeting—like the reversal of power on either side of the door in James's dream of the Gallerie d'Apollon—allows for the transfer of power to the younger American writer.[32] If Dickens is Svidrigaylov, James is not Raskolnikov, or if Dickens is Jonas Chuzzlewit, James is not Tigg. In that way James shows his allegiance to America. Dickens on the margin can be taken more fully. America continued to put Dickens on the outer edge of the margin he had always written from; and in so doing, increasing his decenteredness, fulfilled something in him; it contrasted with James, then at the center, being at home. James, growing older himself, and unwell, writes *Notes of a Son and Brother* also on the edge of a margin, and also disturbed more than he could easily summarize by the America he revisited in 1904, and described in *The American Scene*.

Both Emerson and James note how much Dickens was driven physically to the edge; Forster calls the illnesses that waylaid him "the constant shadow that still attended him, the slave in the chariot of his triumph" (*Life*, 10:2.780). The image, like Emerson's of Dickens being bound to a "locomotive," is odd, double; as if the slave was not being led in triumph but was—because it triumphed in the end—triumphant. To the Hegelian implications of this, it could be added that slavery becomes in the image an uncanny driving force, a representation of something divided, double, or misplaced in the subject. The full range of ambiguities also account for Dickens's own ambiguities about race: anti slavery, anti abolition, anti North, anti the perceptions of race hatred that he saw in Baltimore and Brooklyn, and yet fundamentally antipathetic to the black as other, as the other in America he could not recognize, and yet could feel aware of enough to feel that his own English, colonial, identity had been brought into crisis, in a way that might have happened earlier, since there is no beginning of trauma, but that was now unavoidable.

Carlyle's reading of Dickens in America, quoted as an epigraph to this chapter, emphasizes the significance of two journeys in constructing Dickens. Carlyle allows for a reading that makes a comparison with the Freudian desire to repeat, as though going to America for the second time was going "beyond the pleasure principle," as a death wish, as if Dickens not only desired to be consumed by the American appetite, but wanted to push himself as close as he could to death in giving his readings. That was the challenge America posed. His inability to read America, which pushed him into contradictions, pointed up his own constituted subjectivity as split, showing the subject as not in control, and aware of that as a source of danger. At the center in English society, Dickens now put himself at his outer margin, as if something in America, despite the feeling of being above it, produced the desire to be the man who was never heard of again.

CHAPTER 5

James, Trauma, and America

Returned to Boston in 1881, after seven years of being in Europe, Henry James wrote of a dilemma he faced that there was nothing he could do with it:

> With this vast new world, *je n'ai que faire.* One can't do both—one must choose. No European writer is called upon to assume that terrible burden . . . The burden is necessarily greater for an American—for he *must* deal, more or less, if only by implication, with Europe: whereas no European is obliged to deal in the least with America. No one dreams of calling him less complete for not doing so. (I speak of course of people who do the sort of work that I do; not of economists, of social science people). The painter of manners who neglects America is not thereby incomplete as yet; but a hundred years hence—fifty years hence perhaps—he will doubtless be accounted so. (*Notebooks*, 5.214)

In 1881, no European writer had to decide between taking America and Europe as subjects: Europe sufficed. Twenty-five years later, far sooner than the fifty years he had thought might be necessary, James felt the need to describe America as the new society whose modernity rendered Europe needless, and which therefore implied that the years he had spent away from America were also wasted, years of being the man who was never heard from again.[1] *The American Scene* is full of that awareness, which makes it a text implicitly aware of trauma. Trauma, in Freud, is registered retroactively, through a later event that codes a former—imaginary or not—as traumatic. In Lacan, trauma means a missed encounter with the real.[2] If Eliot speaks about the "unreal city" in *The Waste Land,* trauma would be a later recognition that the city, here the American city, had within it something of the real that had not been described. The figure for this in James is always the ghost. In Lacan, the traumatic is the perception of a hole in the network of signifiers that keep the subject in place with regard to the world; the ghost, neither subject nor the world, is the something other that breaks that continuity. James's fascination for ghosts may be read as a desire for trauma, which makes *The American Scene* dual, both opening itself up to otherness as well as conservatively self-protective. But however divided his sympathies, America is written with the awareness that to the extent that it means something, it puts his own past existence into question. As Dickens found America something that went beyond his subjective understanding, James found that America questioned his being as a "European."

In contrast to *American Notes,* written when Dickens was 30, *The American Scene,* which is in its shadow, and which quotes it, comes out of a return visit to America made when James was over 60. *American Notes* looked at a pioneer society, just beginning that modernization, which would take it beyond Europe; Dickens, though overwhelmed by it, was also able to patronize it, as did Thackeray and Trollope. He could not envisage a future in America; that appears in his comments on Washington, the planned and incomplete city. And the empty spaces of America he read negatively, as he was also appalled by the psychic spaces into which the Ohio and the Mississippi Rivers seem to reach. The difference in *The American Scene* is that 60 years after Dickens, America cannot be seen in any inferior way to Europe. But its unlikeness to Europe points to a future that can only take it further away from it. Its difference is most registered in its cities, though these also show differences from each other, which mean that America's future cannot be settled either; its past is equally present, making a single account of the country impossible.

James gave signs from 1900 onwards that he wished to revisit America for an "eventual belated romance" (*The American Scene,* 1.6.42). He had not felt like that earlier—Paul Bourget in his *Outre-Mer: Impressions of America* recorded how James had told him before his departure for the States in 1893 how he would want to return by the next steamer,[3] as though contemplating America required a new psychic energy and ability to reread, and to read beyond appearances. James's readiness to do that appeared when ten years later, he met Edith Wharton. He had already "admonished" her in correspondence to write "the American Subject," and the hints of trauma are already there:

> Profit, be warned by my awful example of exile and ignorance. You will say *j'en parle à mon aise*—but I shall have paid for my ease, and I don't want you to pay (as much) for yours. . . . *Do New York!* The first-hand account is precious.[4]

James had described himself as *"New Yorkais d'origine"*[5] and New York generated three attempts subsequent to *The American Scene* to "do" it, as well
as the New York edition—his own attempted identification with the city.
F. O. Matthiessen gives as the texts that came out of the visit *Julia Bride,*
The Jolly Corner, where Spencer Brydon comes near to throwing himself
out of the window and becoming the man who was never heard of again,[6]
Crapy Cornelia, and *A Round of Visits.* Then there was the American novel
with its Hawthornian title, *The Ivory Tower,* written in 1914, left incomplete, and published posthumously.[7] The settings of these texts are New
York and, for *The Ivory Tower,* Newport, though the notes James wrote for
The Ivory Tower (pp. 278, 354) show him also considering, as well as Newport and New York, the state of California, Boston, and Lenox for the
closing scenes.

The American Scene risks several dangers. Nostalgia, since it looks back
to 1883, from the time when James had left America virtually for good—
even though he was to continue writing about it. Secondly, it comes
from someone who had shown allegiance to Europe. T. S. Eliot wrote
that "it is the final perfection, the consummation of an American to become, not an Englishman, but a European—something which no born
European, no person of any European nationality can become."[8] The
sentiment is perhaps glib, registering failure, not achievement—the
American cannot become English, but might become that synthetic
thing, a European. As Kafka knew, to be a "European" is a fiction, a
nonexistent category; Europe was already showing itself divided over the
category of what was a true European through its anti-Semitism. The
desire for the American to become either English or European is a
marker of postcoloniality, feeling that to be an American is not enough.
James the postcolonial neither quite identified with America, nor with
England, nor with any other category. In *The American Scene,* he tries to be
American and European, comparing the Capitol with Michelangelo's
Rome; the Hudson with the Rhine; Concord with Weimar; Charleston
with Venice. These European comparisons are, however, those of the
tourist of the European scene, whose views are formed by landscape art,
like Lambert Strether in Paris. In relation to England or Europe, he is
the outsider, the American accessing a culture from which he must remain on the outside, like the tourist. Dickens had also been an outsider
from that bourgeois and aristocratic London culture, as with his experiences in the blacking factory, and his distance from Thackeray's class and
club milieu. But Dickens's fame had given him congruence with that
culture. James desired it, though he also wanted something else to criticize it. In relation to America he was the outsider, but burdened also
with a historical remembrance of the place that while it can criticize,

also misreads, in that it finds it difficult to let America assert its difference from Europe, where assertion of difference also threatens identity.
In *The American Scene,* a text struggles with its own conservatism, which
would judge America both by a sense of the past and a relationship to
Europe. Another danger in it is to speak from the position of the privileged white, alienated from mass immigration into America, and unable
to relate to the question of race, despite traveling through the South.

The extent of James's itinerary is not obvious in *The American Scene,*
which is only half of what was planned as a two-volume work. The book
discusses New England and New York (September to December 1904)
and then records an itinerary south to Florida, finishing with him in the
Pullman riding northwards out of Florida again. If he had gone on, it would
have been to give an account of the Midwest. On 4 March 1905, he left for
a tour of the Midwest, going to the Mississippi and St. Louis, where he read
a lecture on Balzac, and on to Chicago. Indianapolis was followed by
Chicago again, till the evening of 19 March, giving him a little under a week
there. He wrote that "this Chicago is huge, *infinite* (of potential size and
form and even of actual); black, smoky, *old*-looking, very like some preter-
naturally *boomed* Manchester or Glasgow lying beside a colossal lake (Michi-
gan) of hard pale green jade, and putting forth railway antennae of
maddening complexity and gigantic length."[9] Edel supplements the record
by saying that James spoke, as he rode by train with Robert Herrick, the
Chicago novelist, "through the smudged purlieus of the untidy city into the
black gloom of the Loop" of "monstrous ugliness"—yet while also noticing
the interest of meeting Americans "who had never thought of themselves
as belonging to any class—a thing impossible in feudal Europe."[10]

From Chicago, he took the Pullman again—a Chicagoan creation—
bound for Los Angeles, past Kansas, Arizona, and New Mexico. In a letter he describes the Pullman having "barber's shops, bathrooms,
stenographers and typists,"[11] like a hotel, part of the pervasive "hotel-
spirit" of America. Yet his reaction is not negative, for the same letter
praises the University Club in Chicago for its "so excellent room, with
perfect bathroom and w.c., of its own, appurtenant (the *universal* joy of
this country, in private houses or wherever; a feature that is really almost
a consolation for many things)." Arrived at California, and staying first at
Coronado Beach, near San Diego,[12] James visited Monterey, San Fran-
cisco, and traveled up the Pacific Coast to Seattle. From Seattle, he returned, via Chicago, through Albany, to New York, for a three-week stay.
In late May and June, he lectured at Harvard, Baltimore, and Bryn Mawr.
On 17 June, he was in Maine, visiting Dean Howells. After further time
with Edith Wharton, he left Boston nine days later on 4 July 1905 for
Liverpool. His impressions of America began to appear while he was in

the States. "New England: An Autumn Impression" came out between April to June 1905 in *North American Review.*

The completed text of *The American Scene* fuses several separate visits to particular cities, without necessarily suggesting that they are separate, and attempts contrasts, as between New England, "An Autumn Impression," and New York, "New York and the Hudson: A Spring Impression." New York is succeeded by a chapter on Newport, the modern city by the personal reminiscence. The projected second book on the Middle West, "California and the Pacific Coast," and on American universities was given up by the Spring of 1907, when *The American Scene* had appeared. Fred Kaplan argues that the omitted sections did not appear because these regions of America could have little autobiographical force for James.[13] While that does not account for the presence in the text we have of the chapters on the South, which James was visiting for the first time, the element of truth in it implies that James desired to stay on the side of familiarity—which differentiates the text from *American Notes,* where everything treated is new. *The American Scene* is an amputated text, not the complete double book, and consideration of it should also look at what James cannot or will not include.[14] Admiration for what James makes of the diversity and plurality of American modernity, one of Ross Posnock's themes, needs to come back to those things omitted from the text. Not to mention Chicago, for instance, means that the America he writes about is shorn of half of its modernity. Giuseppe Giacosa, one of Puccini's librettists, said in 1893 that anyone who ignored Chicago did not understand the nineteenth century, for that city had become its "ultimate expression."[15]

Perhaps one clue to why James stayed with the familiar comes from his travels to the Midwest in March 1905. Edel records his conversation at a reception held for him at the University Club of St. Louis. It included a discussion of Wilde, who had lectured at St. Louis in 1883: Perhaps some members of the audience remembered his visit. James on this occasion called him "one of those Irish adventurers who had something of the Roman character—able but false." He said Wilde had returned to "the abominable life he had been leading" after leaving prison and his death was "miserable."[16]

James had met Wilde in America, in Washington, in January 1883, near the start of Wilde's controversial year-long lecturing tour of America. James's revulsion to Wilde in 1883—"a fatuous fool, tenth-rate cad," "an unclean beast"—is often read in relation to James's repressed reaction to Wilde's homosexuality.[17] Another hint, making the reaction overdetermined, appears in his reference to Wilde as Irish. In touring the United States, James followed on from Wilde, the reminder of British colonialism and the ghost who would warn James of what he, as the member of a postcolonial society, had linked himself with. The states that James wrote about were those where the English alliances were strongest. In St. Louis, he pronounced on English literature, but Wilde as a precursor could challenge the body of power that he and Dickens spoke from, as well as the assumptions on which he valued that literature. Dickens as English, and the author of *The Old Curiosity Shop,* which completed its serialization when Dickens was in the States, and of which Wilde said that no one could read the death of Little Nell without laughing (a reaction Kafka would have understood), was vulnerable to subversion. And James, who was not even English, had had his own marginality shown up by Wilde. In conversation in Washington in early 1883, when James said that he missed London (home of British imperialism, and the capital city in contrast to Washington), Wilde girded him with "You care for places? The world is my home."[18] The expatriate, like the colonized subject, has no place. Perhaps Wilde, after being sentenced to prison and dying later in Paris in virtual exile, could not have maintained throughout his life the buoyancy of saying that the world was his home. The following century showed how no one could or can feel either that the existence of a center, or that distance from that center, means anything, and the point is already there in Kafka's *Der Verschollene.* Peter Szondi, writing about Walter Benjamin's "City Portraits," and the point that they ceased being written after 1933 says that "at that time a story was circulating in the emigrant community about a Jew who planned to emigrate to Uruguay; when his friends in Paris seemed astonished that he wanted to go so far away, he retorted, 'Far from where?'" Szondi adds the point that "with the loss of one's homeland, the notion of distance also disappears."[19]

Wilde was saying what James already knew—that being an expatriate imposed a psychic loss, and that no expatriate can secure an identity by thinking back to a place. *The American Scene,* noting in the America it covers the removal of once familiar places, also shows that attachment to places is impossible in America, which, full as it is of immigrant peoples, people whose place was elsewhere, dispenses with the uniqueness of places. In New York, James's birthplace had disappeared. In Boston, he goes to find a house he had lived in for two years at the end of the Civil War:

> The two years had been those of a young man's . . . and the effort of actual attention was to recover on the spot some echo of ghostly footsteps—the sound as of taps on the window-pane heard in the dim dawn. The place itself was meanwhile, at all events, a conscious memento, with old secrets to keep and old stories to witness for, a saturation of life as closed together and preserved in it as the scent lingering in a folded pocket-handkerchief.

But when, a month later, I returned again (a justly-rebuked mistake) to see
if another whiff of the fragrance were not to be caught, I found but a gaping void, the brutal effacement, at a stroke, of every related object, of the
whole precious past. Both the houses had been levelled and the space to
the corner cleared; hammer and pickaxe had evidently begun to swing on
the very morrow of my previous visit. . . . (7.1.170)

James thinks he could have read the impending destruction in the
"poor scared faces" of the houses—traumatized and feminized. Feeling
that he has realized how fast history could be "unmade . . . it was as if the
bottom had fallen out of one's own biography, and one plunged backward
into space without meeting anything" he now feels that this break, this
hole, is the "figure" of his whole relationship to America; there is no relation, there is a gap between the subject and the world. The house he has
known, with its folds (like the folds of James's own prose, like the
Deleuzean "fold"), had a double interest, a space for a ghost, for a rich
American past; but to return to the site, having missed the destruction of
the house, gives the traumatic sense of feeling that the categories of history no longer apply and that space exists without reference to time, as a
"gaping void," an image of his own unghosted past. The ghostly footsteps
he had imagined had been positive; now his own ghostly, disconfirmed
existence makes the figure of the ghost more disturbing.

James considered two titles for the book. One, *The Return of the Native,* impossible on account of Hardy, another *The Return of the Novelist.*[20]
Native—however ironic—or novelist; both words describe his own
self-stylization, and imply the coincidence of place, time and subject.
The word "return" means that you have a place to come back to, and
your reappearance can be marked in time. The title *The Return of the Native* depends on those things supporting each other. With no time nor
place to return to, the native is not a native, and if the subject cannot
assert a self-identity over time, from the time of birth, in order to be
a native, there can be no return. *The American Scene* wrestles with the
implications of the failure of these things to support each other. One
symptom is not writing about Chicago, which, rebuilt after fire in 1871,
was native to no one, and denied anyone in it a settled history. The
text shows that the illusion of having a center to speak from proves un-
sustainable, as time and place have their existence hollowed out, which
in turn hollows out the native novelist. James approaches his projected
title when calling himself "the restored absentee" (3.1.93; 7.1.175). Absence, like the "gaping void," is a trope throughout *The American Scene:*
America is full of things not there, or not there fully. And James has
been absent, though he is unlike many expatriates who remain

unrestored (7.1.175). But he is no more "present" now that he is in America than he was outside it. An absentee, a ghost, he too is likely to be the man who was never heard of again.

Yet the nostalgia, or the retreat from American modernity meets something else. Gertrude Stein in *The Autobiography of Alice B. Toklas* fused her admiration for James—"whom she considers quite definitely as her forerunner, he being the only nineteenth century writer who being an American felt the method of the twentieth century"—with her sense of the American century. "Gertrude Stein always speaks of America as being now the oldest country in the world because by the methods of the civil war and the commercial conceptions that followed it, America created the twentieth century, and since all the other countries are now either living or commencing to be living a twentieth century life, America having begun the creation of the twentieth century in the sixties of the nineteenth century is now the oldest country in the world."[21]

Stein, like James in his study of Hawthorne, sees the Civil War as the caesura—which would make it the trauma—marking American modernity. Discussing war and education with Bertrand Russell in 1914, "she grew very eloquent on the disembodied abstract quality of the american character and cited examples, mingling automobiles with Emerson, and all proving that they did not need greek . . ." (*Alice B. Toklas*, 165). Charles Caramello links Stein's interest in automobiles, the First World War (taxis were used in the battle of the Marne), and the Civil War, writing that "Stein knows that the American Civil War . . . inaugurated a specific mode of production . . . uniform standards of measurement enabled interchangeable parts enabled line assembly enabled serial production—and that Henry Ford adapted that mode for the mass production of automobiles; she also makes the link between wars and cars. . . ."[22] There are several hints here. The Civil War—highly modernizing and producing a new militaristic drive to factory production, as already noted in relation to Dickens—engenders an atomistic technology of interchangeability and abstract disembodiment both as far as possible from any European history, which is why Americans do not need Greek (a culture associated, too, with the production of the humanist subject). The place given to interchangeable parts is important for cubist art, a subject of *The Autobiography of Alice B. Toklas,* and it explains why individual buildings could disappear as fast as the James family house in Boston. *The American Scene* responds to "the disembodied abstract quality" of America ambiguously, sometimes by recording in America a prevalent emptiness, or by noting the sense of the abyss into which James's biography has been hurled. If he has been denied a history or a biography, as also at his birthplace, which is now not his birthplace, he is indeed new, a twentieth-century character indeed. Something of that awareness is in *The American Scene,* so that a text with a tendency to look back is always asserting the impossibility of doing this. Going back will be "a justly rebuked mistake." He possesses a memory that does not fit present conditions. The house, which he thought kept its secrets within it, like a scent, which he visited as though it were something to be kept as a relic or as a fetish, has gone and been replaced by an abstraction, so that now the memories—the ghosts, the scent, have a new abstract condition, in that they are now internal to him, part of invisible cities that are only to be caught through writing.

James's descriptions in *The American Scene* take three forms and imply a disarticulated text. There are accounts of places that he recollects from over 20 or 30 years back. There is the sense of a new place, as with New York, that has abolished the old. There are the places he sees for the first time. The first form of writing encourages a danger of nostalgia, while the second reinforces the sense of America as disembodied and abstract, where buildings that exist may only be contingent and not an essential part of the cityscape. The third sense makes James speculate on America and the future in America. In the three chapters that follow, I want to give a reading of the text, occasionally using for comparison H. G. Wells's *The Future in America,* already referred to in chapter 1 of this book.

The first, my chapter 6, focuses on New England (*The American Scene,* chap. 1—one of only two sections not named for a city), and specifically on Newport, Boston, Salem, and Concord (*The American Scene,* chap. 6, 7, 8). These are the chapters where going back is most discussed and where the past has been most denied. The text that comes out of the visit, the unfinished novel *The Ivory Tower,* set in Newport, and discussed in relation to it, projects most James's contrasted sense of the American future. In contrast to the pulled-down house in Boston, James's examination turns on the new American home, subject of *The Ivory Tower,* and on what America is building. This rebuilding contains what *The American Scene* calls a "perpetual repudiation of the past" (1.6.43). Such repudiation denies him a place. The house, the product of architecture and so of planning, is the machine whose design looks toward the future, where that is a way of repudiating the notion of the past, so that the past exists as "eternal waste" (2.3.86).

Perpetually repudiating the past includes several significances: first, America would cease to be if it could not modernize, that this is what America does; and that "repudiation," being a term with psychoanalytic implications, allows a way of thinking about America's unconscious motivations. "Repudiation" translates Freud's word *Verwerfung* ("rejection" in the Standard Edition) and it is different from *Verdrängung* (repression).[23] "Repudiation" in Lacan is a psychotic condition, a sign that the ego is not under the power of the superego, and ready to repress the desires of the id, which would produce repression, but a sign that the ego is under the sway of the id, and ready to break with reality. America's repudiation of the past—in the South, this takes the form of remaking the old past of white supremacy, just as tourism, as in Salem, repudiates the past by remaking it in simulacral form—contains its own splitting, its loss of reality. It is a schizophrenic state, and schizophrenia first appears as a word naming a clinical condition a year after *The American Scene*. Lastly, the term is oxymoronic; a perpetual repudiation of the past means that the past keeps reasserting itself, it can never be repudiated. Building, in *The American Scene*—architectural images appear and reappear throughout the text—reflects on the power of a trope in American literature, for "Build, therefore your own world" was Emerson's demand in his essay *Nature*.[24] Equally, building and rebuilding, constant urban renewal, is a form of repudiating the past. From this comes James's interest in two points of America: the *city* and the *house,* and his fascination with architecture.[25]

The city—New York (*The American Scene,* chap. 2, 3, 4, 5)—is the subject of my chapter 7. Like Boston, it has denied James a past—there is no birthplace—but the writing of the city in all its difference from European cities, which makes previous models of writing inadequate, is an encounter with the sublime, which overturns all powers of analysis. The city is impossible to know, which means that it harbors other possibilities, and which James's writing of New York is aware of. The city cannot repudiate the past if that means setting a single direction for its future because it contains so much of difference, focused in the numbers of immigrants from Europe, their backs turned on their past, but forming a new and unknowable city. In contrast to this newness, chapter 8 looks at the cities described in *The American Scene* chapters 9 to 14, covering James's journey through Philadelphia southwards into the American South. With the exception of Washington, the cities here—Philadelphia, Baltimore, Richmond, Charleston—reveal symptoms of the past not being faced, the actual past repudiated and replaced with a substitute past, and the consequence being a failure to become cities, if a definition of the city includes not only plurality and difference, but means that it cannot be a museum to an imagined past. Each of these cities shows signs of a trauma not worked through, and James's writing, though it never makes the point, I believe is informed by the insight that this denial of the past compares with the threat to his own past that the then present-day America posed. The book is well aware of a contrasting power in America to co-opt the past to its own purposes. The chapter on Washington finishes with a Jamesian *coup de théatre* as he reflects on the power of the state capital to absorb into its system the dispossessed past—the American Indian—to repudiate it by including it in its own triumphalism. The last chapter of all, on Florida, returns to what America is building, and finishes with a sense of how much of the past America simply discards, and how much it homogenizes, within its triumphal hotel spirit.

CHAPTER 6

The American Scene—I

BUILDING AMERICAN HOUSES

NEW ENGLAND

ailing on the *Kaiser Wilhelm II,* James left Southampton on 24 August 1904, "emerging from the comparatively assured order of the great berth of the ship" (*The American Scene,* 1.1.5)[1] at Hoboken, New Jersey, 30 August. Met by his nephew, he crossed to New York to look at Washington Square, Union Square, and Gramercy Park (the earliest moments of *The American Scene*), and stayed at New Jersey, with George Harvey, publisher of *North American Review* and *Harper's Weekly,* which would take some of James's essays. He traveled to Cambridge and Boston by train and up to Chocorua, to see William James. During this New England period he spent ten days with Edith Wharton at The Mount, at Lenox, her "exquisite French chateau mirrored in a Massachusetts pond,"[2]—which she had designed, accompanying her co-authorship with Ogden Codman of *The Decoration of Houses* (1897).[3] A movement through various unsatisfactory house interiors has often been noticed to structure Wharton's New York novel *The House of Mirth* (1905); as the title implies, houses and interiors, rather than the exterior space of the street give her representation of the city. There is a feminine investment in the notion of the house. In her short story, "The Fullness of Life" (1892), one character says she has

> sometimes thought that a woman's nature is like a great house full of rooms: there is the hall, through which everyone passes in going in and out; the drawing room, where one receives formal visits; the sitting room, where the members of the family come and go as they list; but beyond that, far beyond, are other rooms, the handles of whose doors perhaps are never turned; no one knows the way to them, no one knows whither they lead; and in the innermost room, the holy of holies, the soul sits alone."[4]

This throws light on James's "house of fiction," which it implicitly genders, but it also implies a reading of American houses, as a response to the construction of gender in the time of the "American Renaissance." Accordingly, a Wharton-like interest in the American house runs through *The American Scene.*

New Jersey possesses the summer houses of rich New Yorkers. It allows a first, displaced sense of the city and of American modernity. All "New England: An Autumn Impression" is a prelude to seeing New York, for the chapter sets up contexts and establishes keywords. Often, James makes the dumb or the silenced speak in an act of prosopopoeia, so that the huge new houses—James seems often to address houses or to be addressed by them—are made to say, "Oh, yes, we were awfully dear for what we are and for what we do" (1.1.10). Architectural façades speak from behind "smart, short lawns," and lawns are images of suburban solidarity and of individualism, framing the house, as they also speak of a nature that has been framed, and define a space between the public and the private. The façades note that they have a certain pointlessness, for only the occupants of the houses see them, since no one else passes by. In contrast, James notes "the big brown barracks of the hotels," and "the bold rotunda of the gaming-room," called, in a Hawthornian note, "monuments . . . of a more artless age, and yet with too little history about them for dignity of ruin." The cottages where Grant lived and James Garfield died had been "left so far behind by the expensive, as the expensive is now practiced; in spite of having been originally a sufficient expression of it." The only history to be read is of successive waves of richness. Money "exert[s] itself in a void." Like "absence" and "vacancy" (1.1.13), "void" resonates through *The American Scene.*

A further subject appears: "the air of unmitigated publicity," which the houses' façades are made to project. Behind them is "no achieved protection, no constituted mystery of retreat, no saving complexity." As James notes the road, he comments on the few pedestrians (1.1.11). Pedestrians suggest private lives and the refusal of publicity. The houses are made to speak further, when they call themselves only "instalments [new installations, but only provisional ones], symbols, stop-gaps . . . expensive as we are, we have nothing to do with continuity, responsibility, transmission, and don't in the least care what becomes of us after we have served our present purpose" (1.1.12). They betray the cynicism of architecture, because they declare its hidden project—not to create a space for privacy, which would require history, but to suggest the need for the buildings' future abolition as they come to symbolize too little.

In the second section he finds New Hampshire "Arcadian," for "in Arcady you ask as few questions as possible" (1.2.14). There is little to be

asked, for the place has not developed a history—it can be seen as "ex-
quisitely . . . Sicilian, Theocritan, poetic, romantic, academic . . . from . . .
not bearing the burden of too much history." The words recall Fenimore
Cooper and W. C. Bryant's idealizations of this landscape, and the Hudson River School, of which Asher B. Durand's 1849 picture "Kindred
Spirits" (Thomas Cole and Bryant above a river valley) may be taken as
representative. The landscape is Arcadian since it has no history—only
that of the "classic abandoned farm," and the local legend of the Indian
who committed suicide off Chocorua mountain—and the lack of history—which implies lack of inwardness—lies behind James's characterization of New England nature as feminine (1.2.18), for throughout *The
American Scene* the feminine codes both that which is ignored by the
American business mentality and that which has been mauled or constructed by that business mentality. It includes the doomed facades of the
houses. Again, in this characterization, James gives a voice through
prosopopoeia to the inanimate, the land marked by "the hard little historic record of agricultural failure and defeat" (1.2.19)—the victim of a
demand for increased profits that has left it used rather by "summer people" for second homes so that "the disinherited, the impracticable land"
threw itself "on the nonrural, the intensely urban class" (1.2.20). The
spirit of New York works in the rural scene.

In contrast to New Jersey, James notes that "a sordid ugliness and
shabbiness hung, inveterately, about the wayside 'farms,' and all their ap-
purtenances and incidents" (1.2.21). Commenting on an absence that
makes even a farmhouse "almost penally clean and bare" (1.3.26), he
finds in Farmington, Connecticut, something missing. The church
steeple as a monument "appeared to *testify* scarce more than some large
white card, embellished with a stencilled border, on which a message . . .
might be still to be inscribed" (1.5.36). In contrast, "the present, the positive, was mainly represented . . . by the level railway-crossing." It is the
second time James notices the power of the railway; earlier he noted that
"the country exists for the 'cars,' . . . and not the cars for the country"
(1.3.24). The railway crossing imposes on the scene "a kind of monotony
of acquiescence."

It is the same impression as that which pronounces, at Farmington,
that "the conditions of the life" are "the same conditions as everywhere
else" (1.5.35). In the same way, James notes the response of the guest to
the American hostess asking him what kind of people he would like to
meet, "Why my dear madam, have you more than *one* kind?" (1.7.52). He
went by car with Edith Wharton (the Ford Motor Company had been
founded in 1903) to the Shaker settlement at Lebanon that Dickens had
visited, noting the blankness of "the rows of gaunt windows polished for

no whitest, stillest, meanest face, even, to look out, so that they resembled . . . parallelograms of black paint criss-crossed with white lines" of
doll's houses (1.5.40). Here was "mortification made to 'pay.'" The regu-
larity of the life recalls the "parallelograms" Mrs. Trollope and Dickens
referred to when discussing Philadelphia. But James has already asked
about the New England villages what secrets they kept (1.5.36); on an occasion where they came across a house full of Impressionist pictures
(1.5.37) James was reminded of what he had had missed so far—"the sov-
ereign power of art"—but was also led to reflect, by Edith Wharton, on
the "whited sepulchre" nature of the villages, so "the village street and the
lonely farm and the hillside cabin became positively richer objects under
the smutch of imputation [of sexuality]; twitched with a grim effect the
richness of their mantle, shook out of its folds such crudity and levity as
they might, and borrowed, for dignity, a shade of the darkness of Cenci-
drama, of monstrous legend, of old Greek tragedy, and thus helped themselves out for the story-teller more patient almost of anything than of
flatness" (1.5.38). Flatness is deadly, though at Hudson, even the straight
street can be evocative (1.5.41)—James invents an American Gothic in
the face of this "flatness," as a reminder that even this rural America contains a past with "folds."

Words pervasive in *The American Scene* appear in relation to Farmington: firstly "universal acquiescence"; the Miltonic oxymoron "visible vacancy," "thinness," "passivity," and "absence of the settled standard"
(1.5.36). Section 6 of the first chapter links the blankness of America to
James's self-discovery, in his retrospective journey, of blanks, things never
noticed in his previous life in America, "which were to live on, to the
inner vision, through the long years, as mere blank faces, round, empty,
metallic, senseless disks" (1.6.42). The writer says, implicitly, that the
things not noticed must have been there, in his absence from them,
working in him though not realized. Those non-inscribed details reappear here, and are gendered as feminine. Here he finds the "perpetual repudiation of the past, so far as there had been a past to repudiate, so far
as the past was a positive rather than a negative quantity. There had been
plenty in it, assuredly, of the negative . . . yet there had been an old conscious commemorated life too, and it was this that had become the victim of supersession." So, the past "was consenting to become a past with
all the fine candour with which it had tried to affirm itself, in its day, as a
present . . . with a due ironic forecast of the fate in store for the hungry,
triumphant actual" (1.6.43).[5] This image, not the sense of the past consuming the present, but the present as cannibalistic, recalls the passage
on New Jersey houses as "instalments," and affirms the stop-gap nature
of American civilization, its endless metonymic displacements. Noting

the endless replacement of things is appropriate in the context of reading the generalizable "'business-man' face" of the American male (1.8.51), but we can go further. James registers blanks of memory in himself, as though he were like America, or as if America had not "taken" in his consciousness, as though his sensorium had remained like the Farmington steeple, still uninscribed. This failure in himself of a memory parallels the American progressiveness that removes the past, and recognizes the present as transient, buildings as signifiers without a signified, substitutional only. It suggests trauma, for not only has the past been taken away, but what was in the past has not been registered, it has not taken hold. The facades of houses that cannot quite speak, but must be supplemented by James, are paralleled by a Jamesian sense that he cannot articulate what has been in America's past.

As James refers later to Cambridge ghosts, they cannot quite be named, so that "it was . . . a question . . . of what one read *into* anything, not of what one read out of it" (1.9.53). The past cannot be read for a punctual history that yields itself to memory; memory rather takes the form of both noting blanks and then retroactively filling them with possible significances. He comments later, offering his impressions of Central Park as history, "history is never, in any rich sense, the immediate crudity of what 'happens,' but the much finer complexity of what we read into it" (4.4.136–37). The change from a nineteenth-century approach, which reads the text of history as though it were intelligible, *lisible,* to one constructing that history in a manner that is *scriptible* is modernist, and witnesses the absence of a deep signified to the scene. American architecture, American building and rebuilding, all reinforce this. Yet a blank in America relates to or threatens an equivalent blank in the subject who writes America. The ultimate blankness is California, which he does not write about.[6]

James alludes to America in Nietzschean terms as the place of the "will to grow" (1.6.43), "at no matter what or whose expense." This is linked to the workings of American democracy, and "democratic institutions"(1.6.44), and he finds attendant on it "something deficient, absent." He calls it "the aching void," on whom, or on which, the pressure exists to be "striking and interesting" (1.6.44). Because of this James attributes a voice and speech to dumb houses, as though his function is not to lift a repression, which would imply a history, but to bring something into existence that was not there. In James, the real is, like Harvard, in confident "possession" (1.7.45); "it massed there in multiplied forms, with new and strange architectures looming through the dark; it appeared to have wandered wide and to be stretching forth, in so many directions, long, acquisitive arms." The description recalls Chicago's railways. Architecture, however, as the reference to "older New England domestic architecture" (1.5.34) shows, while it seems to establish a present, fails to do so, since the present is disappearing, and it fails to cover over absence. Architecture is also unreal for James, as is indicated punningly when he catches sight of an old friend from Newport (John Chipman Gray) working in the Harvard Law Library, but feels that "to go to him I should have had to cross the bridge that spans the gulf of time, and, with a suspicion of weak places, I was nervous about its bearing me" (1.7.47). Here, architecture becomes ghostly, private, an instrument or aspect of memory. It is weak, or "thin," like the walls of Harvard, "extemporized and thin" (1.8.49).

The account of Harvard notes "the intersexual relation" (1.8.51). The men are businesslike, and it will be remembered from *A Small Boy and Others* (*Autobiography*, 1:109, 121), how this ascription excludes James and his family. The women are "of a markedly finer texture," "less narrowly specialized . . . less commercialized, distinctly more generalized"—the word contrasts with the men having "extraordinary actualities," which are trained and focused on one thing alone. The phrase should be compared with the earlier "triumphant actual," which displaces so much of the past. The incompatibility here between the sexes is one of America's chief ironies, and the small place given to the women underpins the chapter. It has been implicit in noting the refusal of privacy, or anything behind the facades of grand architecture, or when the feminine represents the land, to which American settlement has not been able to accommodate itself, save by dominating it and then deserting it. Women suggest a history refused in favor of a commercially-driven favoring of the "stop-gap," so that they remain the unwritten, the blanks of American culture. The church steeple can be raised up but there is not the power to inscribe it. The blanks make women the ghosts in this masculine culture. Harvard is gendered as female, but "the light of literary desire is not perceptibly in her eye" (1.9.54), which implies that the woman's life is unformed, directed instead by the university's adherence to business and the business school.

These considerations of Harvard are prompted in James by consideration of James Russell Lowell (1819–1891), and his belief in a *genius loci* attached to Harvard, a spirit of place, which to cultivate would require an attention to the feminine; and then further by reference to W. D. Howells. James finds his access to the places that might allow thought of the *genius loci* blocked—by the country club, "verandahs and golf-links and tennis-lawns, all tea and ices and self-consciousness," and the country becoming the "Park System," all aspects of "the eternal American note . . . of the gregarious, the concentric" (1.9.56). James refers to F. L. Olmsted creating a ring of parks (the "Emerald Necklace") to encircle the city from Boston Common to Franklin Park.[7] James returns to the idea of the

American lawn, which has now been seen in two contexts, framing the house, where it acts as a form of surveillance, guarding private space, and in a sports context, where it lends itself to rationality and control, speaking of engineered nature, always green, always cut. There is nostalgia in the farewell to Fresh Pond, fitting the note of "autumn," even though James does not commit himself to the view that what his friends—aspects of the feminine—stood for necessarily had survival value, or that they achieved, or could have achieved then, what they intuited. Noting how everything in America is under change, he has a narrative to account for personal loss, but he also tries to suggest that everything, even the signs of present active social life (he has already referred [1.9.54] to "momentary gregarious emphasis") are only momentary, stop-gaps.

NEWPORT AND "THE IVORY IDOL"

A part of New England to which James devotes a chapter of *The American Scene*, Newport changed from being a port, until the Revolution, to a tourist center in the nineteenth century, with hotels and summer "cottages." The James family lived there from 1858 to 1862, and James described it first in 1870 and set part of *An International Episode* in it, as if complimenting the "faintly European expression" of "fine old Leisure" that his writing had located in it.[8]

In 1870, he felt that "Nowhere else in this country . . . does business seem so remote, so vague, and unreal. It is the only place in America where enjoyment is organized" (*Travel Writings*, 761–62). The examples of American life in *An International Episode* (1879) show America in process of change. The ship that takes the English travelers from New York to Newport "struck them as a monstrous floating hotel" (*An International Episode*, 2.292). A description of the inn at Newport shows it perforated with immense bare corridors along which the women can be seen to pass and with a verandah, and this is succeeded by the villa along the avenue, which is similar, with its verandah "of extraordinary width" all round, "and a great many doors and windows standing open to the verandah. These various apertures had, together, such an accessible, hospitable air, such a breezy flutter, within, of light curtains, such expansive thresholds and reassuring interiors, that our friends [the English travelers] hardly knew which was the regular entrance . . . and presented themselves at one of the windows" (2.298). The irony notes the lack of privacy: The house's openness denies the possibility of an interior. In that context, the English travelers are told by the women that in America "there was no leisure-class and that the universal passionate surrender of the men to business-questions and business-questions only, would have to be stemmed" (3.327).

In 1870, James comments on the villas recently built and thinks they give hope for "a revival of the architectural art." Contrasting old "crooked and dwarfish wooden mansions" with newer "matter-of-course modern houses," which while improving the area also "injure it as an unexpected corner," he says that

> enough of early architecture remains . . . to suggest a multitude of thoughts as to the severe simplicity of the generation which produced it. The plain gray nudity of these little warped and shingled boxes seems to make it a hopeless task to present any positive appearance at all. But here . . . the magical Newport atmosphere wins half the battle. . . . It simply makes them scintillate in their bareness. Their homely notches and splinters twinkle till the mere friendliness of the thing makes a surface. Their steep gray roofs, barnacled with lichens, remind you of old barges, overturned on the beach to dry. (*Travel Writings,* 764)

Between James in the 1870s and "The Sense of Newport" in *The American Scene,* the New York architects McKim, Mead, and White moved in, like Richard Morris Hunt (1827–1895), an architect trained at the École des Beaux Arts. They were part of the "American Renaissance," the movement in architecture and urban planning that began around 1880 and continued to the outbreak of the First World War. The American Renaissance—nationalistic, patriotic, imperialist—appropriated European Renaissance styles for itself, and built pseudo-palaces, monuments, and statuary, organizing public spaces and attempting to design whole cities—as in the "City Beautiful" movement[9]—in the effort to assert an American order. Many of the features of art and architecture James comments on in *The American Scene* are American Renaissance in style and ideology. Hunt designed a François I style of chateau on Fifth Avenue for William Kissam Vanderbilt (1849–1920), grandson of Cornelius Vanderbilt, who had created a rail empire, and for his wife Alva Vanderbilt. 11 years later, in 1892, came a further Vanderbilt commission, Marble House, a Newport "cottage" of the 1890s, like "The Breakers," which Hunt built for Cornelius Vanderbilt, the eldest grandson (1843–1899). What James saw on his visit in 1904 made him refer to Newport's "beautiful little sense to be read into it by a few persons, and nothing at all to be made of it, as to its essence, by most others" (6.1.157). The (feminine) essence disregarded, Newport had been added to by cottages becoming villas and palaces, evoking James's comments on American gregariousness: "These monuments of pecuniary power rise thick and close, precisely, in order that their occupants may constantly remark to each other . . . that it *is* beautiful, it *is* solitary and sympathetic" (6.1.158). But he notices in June 1905, traveling the length of the "ocean drive" that he sees not another vehicle, or rider, or pedestrian. (At the end he returns to the point that no one walks in Newport.) He takes this as a sign of a turn in fortune: Perhaps Newport will have its rich inhabitants "blown out."

James writes of the "old town" and of the society that existed up to the 1880s. As he says that the inhabitants "casino'd" (6.2.164) he includes for approval the Casino built in 1881 by McKim, Mead, and White, as "Shingle"-style architecture.[10] The older style of inhabitants, who actually lived in Newport, comprised "the detached, the slightly disenchanted and casually disqualified," united by "having for the most part lived in Europe . . . sacrificing openly to the ivory god whose name is leisure" and having "a critical habit." (6.2.165). The ivory idol contrasts with the "great black ebony god of business." James calls the houses fronted by white marble, with their overlarge classical porticos, "white elephants" (contrasting with the black ebony god, business, and the ivory god, leisure). He says that "they look queer and conscious and lumpish—some of them, as with an air of the brandished proboscis, really grotesque—while their owners, roused from a witless dream, wonder what in the world is to be done with them." James differs from Hunt's sense that he built on the architectural principles of "harmony, dignity, and repose."[11] And "there is absolutely nothing to be done but to let them stand there always, vast and blank . . . for reminder . . . of the particularly awkward vengeances of affronted proportion and discretion." This last word recalls "sense" in the chapter title. Good sense (proportion, a sense of what is fitting) has gone; little sense is left; behind the blankness are the *scents* that James tries to capture. The American owners of the cottages, imitated European models but could not get Newport's "sense," when they used the cottages for European display, as with the celebration of the engagement of Consuelo Vanderbilt at the Marble House to England's Duke of Marlborough (1895). Unlike other rich houses, these cannot be pulled down and replaced by others. Richness can go no further—and indeed, Newport's distinction as a place for a two-month residency for summer cottagers was to begin to fade after America entered World War I.

For George Washington Vanderbilt (1862–1914), art-collecting younger brother of Cornelius and William Kissam, Hunt designed Biltmore in North Carolina in French Renaissance style, like chateaux at Blois or Chambord; F. L. Olmsted landscaped it and it was completed in 1895. James stayed in the "bachelors' wing" in early February 1905 (*The American Scene*, 13.1.292).[12] The house favored advanced technology, including a master-clock on an electrical circuit like those used in railway stations, enabling a factorylike approach to coordination that reflected the railways' adoption in 1883 of standard time and that was supplemented by other industrial devices—such as the estate-manager putting in a telephone system with six stations in each departmental office and a hotel-like bell system,[13] cementing an alliance of industry, railways, and hotels. Biltmore's sculptures were by the Austrian Karl Bitter (1867–1915), who had also worked at the Marble House, at the Breakers, and in New York houses. A simulacral Europeanism appears in the statues of Joan of Arc and Saint Louis, on the exterior of the stair-tower, as if reinforcing "Frenchness," but the simulacral becomes more intense by the carving in relief, in the banquet hall, of scenes from Wagnerian operas.[14] The Europeanness and medievalism disguises American technology, while the technologizing of a European style represents American domination over it.

THE AMERICAN RENAISSANCE AND THE IVORY TOWER

Alva Vanderbilt, after divorcing William Kissam Vanderbilt and becoming Alva Belmont, commissioned Richard Hunt Jr.—who had traveled to China at her request—to build her a Chinese teahouse overlooking the Cliff Walk at Marble House. The opening ceremony took place in July 1914. James could not have seen the teahouse, but the opening of *The Ivory Tower* (1914), which embodies much of James's reaction to America and American architecture, indicates that the novelist's imagination of Newport houses—derived from writing *The American Scene*—anticipated what the teahouse implied. Rosanna Gaw, daughter of the millionaire Abel Gaw, crosses the avenue at Newport "making no other preparation than to open a vast pale-green parasol, a portable pavilion from which there fluttered fringes, frills and ribbons that made it resemble the roof of some Burmese palinquin or even pagoda" (*The Ivory Tower,* 1). Rosanna's umbrella not only evokes the British empire, and delicately implies European and American intervention in China and Japan, lands of pagodas, but also the oversized nature of everything of the millionaires in Newport: It is of a piece with her own largeness and that of "the florid villa, a structure smothered in senseless ornament" (2), which gets new attention at the end, before James broke off writing.

At that stage, the newly enriched Gray Fielder is walking round Frank Betterman's house. Betterman, his millionaire uncle, has died, and has left his money to Fielder because, living in Europe, he has not been tainted with the money madness of Americans. Fielder has now, since his uncle's death, had to get used to the wholly mechanistic lawyer, Mr. Crick. Rosanna Gaw, for her own good reasons, has withdrawn from Betterman's house to her own, where she has been left alone by the death of her father Abel Gaw (Betterman's former partner, and, after some business swindle, then rival). Now that the innocent Fielder has been enriched, he is about to become the victim of Horton Vint, the Merton Densher-like figure (from *The Wings of the Dove*), in whose character Gray Fielder, like Milly Theale, is and will be deceived, and of Cissy Foy, this novel's Kate Croy. And as betrayal becomes the topic of the narrative, so there appears the topic of the American house, which, as an image of the future, claims precedence over the past, as part of the American "perpetual repudiation of the past":

> [Fielder] had taken to pacing the great verandah that had become his own . . . and it might truly have been a rush of nervous apprehension, a sudden determination of terror, that quickened and yet somehow refused to direct his steps. He had turned out there for the company of sea and sky and garden, less conscious than within doors, for some reason, that Horton was a lost luxury; but that impression was presently to pass with a return of a queer force in his view of Rosanna as above all wanting, off and withdrawn verily to the pitch of her having played him some trick, merely let him in where she was to have seen him through, failed in fine of a sociability implied in all her preliminaries. He found his attention caught, in one of his revolutions, by the chair in which Abel Gaw had sat that first afternoon, pulling him up for their so unexpectedly intense mutual scrutiny, and when he turned away a moment after, quitting the spot almost as if the strange little man's death that very night had already made him apparitional, which was unpleasant, it was to drop upon the lawn and renew his motion there. He circled round the house altogether at last, looking at it more critically than had hitherto seemed relevant, taking the measure, disconcertedly, of its unabashed ugliness, and at the end coming to regard it much as he might have eyed some monstrous modern machine, one of those his generation was going to be expected to master, to fly in, to fight in, to take the terrible women of the future out for airings in, and that mocked at *his* incompetence in such matters while he walked round and round it, and gave it, as if for dread of what it might do for him, the widest berth his enclosure allowed. (*The Ivory Tower*, 265–66)

The house is linked to a failure of judgement on Fielder's part, with regard to both Rosanna Gaw and Vint. This adds to its uncanniness, as if it becomes like the pagoda that Maggie Verver in *The Golden Bowl* creates in her thoughts: in which case it even compares with the parasol of pagodalike proportions carried by Rosanna. The sense is that the parasol and the house are machines—a parasol is not just a parasol, but in its overdisplay, a force of aggression, of empire. If the house is aligned with the feminine, the house will generate the "terrible" woman; there is an intense gender politics at work, and the writing possesses its own hysteria, stressing the violence of America's future out of its own traumatized sense of having lost any relation to this America. While the pagoda, like James's "house of fiction" and like Osmond's villa in *The Portrait of a Lady*, are all images of enclosure, implying the uncanny because they do not allow penetration,[15] the house Fielder walks round is different; giving the sense of easy access. It will be noticed how the action in *The Ivory Tower* provides for people crossing from house to house, including Abel Gaw "perching" on the threshold of Betterman's house, waiting to get news of his death. Nonetheless, the openness is also deceptive.

The title *The Ivory Tower* seems to evoke the opposite of these American houses, referring firstly to the ornament that Fielder evokes as having as its meaning "the most distinguished retirement" (147) and that is described as something that might pass

> on its very reduced scale, for a builded white-walled thing, very tall in proportion to the rest of its size and rearing its head from its rounded height as if a miniature flag might have flown there. It was a remarkable product of some eastern, probably some Indian, patience, and of some period as well when patience in such causes was at the greatest . . . It consisted really of a cabinet, of easily movable size, seated in a circular socket of its own material and equipped with a bowed door, which dividing in the middle, after a minute gold key had been turned, showed a superposition of small drawers that went upwards diminishing in depth, so that the topmost was of least capacity. The fine curiosity of the thing was in the fine work required for making and keeping it perfectly circular, an effect arrived at by the fitting together, apparently by tiny gold rivets, of numerous small curved plates of the rare substance, each of these, including those of the two wings of the exquisitely convex door, contributing to the artful, the total rotundity. The series of encased drawers worked to and fro of course with straight sides, but also with small bowed fronts, these made up of the same adjusted plates. The whole, its infinite neatness exhibited, proved a wonder of wasteful ingenuity. . . . (148)

The description might have derived from the description of the architecture of Charles Bovary's hat at the opening of *Madame Bovary*; like the cap, this tower is not to be pictured; its excess of description and its ambiguities gives, as in Flaubert, the triumph of the signifier over the signified, as *lisible*, not visible, and implying that something in James's writing is responding to the imperatives of style, so that the ivory tower evokes Gerard de Nerval—who originated the phrase—and Flaubert's ivory tower, which implies escape into style: "The ivory tower! the ivory tower! and the nose pointing to the stars above!" (Flaubert, to Louise Colet, 20 June 1853).[16] Significantly, the ivory tower is not mentioned in the "Notes for *The Ivory Tower*," which follow the text, as though its significance cannot easily be paraphrased.

But several implications appear in it. As an image of enclosure, analogous to a house, it suggests the feminine as Wharton discussed it; but that possibility is contradicted by its second association: the assertiveness of the American skyscraper. It links that architecture with the building of the white elephants in Newport, which the ivory tower also suggests, so that its evokes the power of American urban culture, while appearing as the "ivory tower" to escape that urban. Secondly, it implies American imperialism, by recalling Rosanna's pagoda and its roundness (which is stressed), linking it to ideas of enclosure, and to secrecy and the uncanny. The ivory tower, to speak about the novel's plot, becomes the place in which to put the unopened letter written by Abel Gaw to Graham Fielder, which probably contains damaging information about Betterman and the money he has left to Fielder, detailing the corruptions that have produced the wealth that actually bought the ivory tower as it also financed building the houses. This letter is further commented on in dialogue with Vint (219–30). The ivory tower, then, becomes a way to repudiate the past, by concealing it, much as new American houses conceal what has been there before.

The ivory tower, however, is in Fielder's mind, rather than anywhere else, for the description of the artifact means that the ivory tower is *not* because of that a symbolic "ivory tower," a symbol of retreat or disengagement: equating the two accords with Fielder's literalism, but missing the point that his reading shows an underestimation of the America he has returned to. The tower's associations are with American architecture and ideology in its dominance and its resistance, and in its enclosure, to questioning. It is unsurprising that the text ends with Fielder circling the house, for it too is the ivory tower, as the ivory tower is "really" an artifice that incarnates America's technological drive; and the comment about the "wasteful ingenuity," which is in both tower and house parallels Veblen's critique of the new "leisure class." Fielder has put the incriminating letter within the ivory tower, and the complex symbolism of this means that this new America with its architecture of modernity—such as the White City exhibition in Chicago (1893)—the work of F. W. Olmsted, Hunt, Daniel Burnham, McKim, Mead, and White, and Adler and Sullivan,[17] which anticipated the "City Beautiful" movement, contains within it the guilt of the past. James could not have been unaware of the Chicago Fair—just as he was in St. Louis in early 1905, right after the end of the rival World Fair in that city (1904).[18] The celebration of the ordered city suppresses the memory of such acts of oppression as the Haymarket riots (1886) in Chicago and the Homestead riots (1892) in Pittsburgh, and so represses its own uncanny. Chicago, with its grand style architectural designs and its display of technology for the future, marks a caesura in America, in that it poses the question what the future in America will be, which is Fielder's obsession at the end of *The Ivory Tower*. The Chicago Fair, the culmination of much of the American Renaissance architecture that James saw,[19] was the exhibition of which Henry Adams wrote, "Chicago asked in 1893 for the first time whether the American people knew where they were driving. Adams answered, for one, that he did not not know, but would try to find out. On reflecting . . . under the shadow of Richard Hunt's architecture, he decided that the American people probably knew no more than he did; but that they might still be driving or drifting unconsciously towards some point in space . . . Chicago was the first expression of American thought as a unity; one must start there."[20]

The absence of an interior in the American house was carried through with the open floor plan of Frank Lloyd Wright houses; it created an outside space inside,[21] associating street space and public space with the house, and contrasting with European houses. Walter Benjamin in relation to these speaks of the "phantasmagorias of the interior" they contained, which "represented the world for the private citizen." He goes on to make a statement about *art nouveau* at the turn of the century:

> And yet *art nouveau* . . . appeared . . . to bring with it the perfecting of the interior. The transfiguration of the lone soul was its apparent aim. Individualism was its theory. With Van de Velde, there appeared the house as expression of the personality. Ornament was to such a house what the signature is to a painting. The real significance of *art nouveau* was not expressed in this ideology. It represented the last attempt at a sortie on the part of Art imprisoned by technical advances within her ivory tower. It mobilized all the reserve forces of interiority. They found their expression in the mediumistic language of line, in the flower as symbol of the naked, vegetable Nature that confronted the technologically armed environment. The new elements of construction in iron—girder forms—obsessed *art nouveau*. Through ornament, it strove to win back these forms for Art. Concrete offered it new possibilities for the creation of plastic forms in architecture. Around this time the real centre of gravity was displaced to the office. The de-realized centre of gravity created its abode in the private home. Ibsen's *Master Builder* summed up *art nouveau*: the attempt of the individual, on the strength of his interiority, to vie with technical progress leads to his downfall.[22]

Before taking this further, we should recall James's enthusiasm for *The Master Builder* (1892).[23] In Ibsen's play, Solness hopes to build towers upon homes—an idea whose contradictoriness reveals a mad motivation which comes about from the point that history ("the younger generation" as

Solness calls it) is about to overtake him with its superior technology. The Master Builder seems to know little of New York and Chicago's skyscrapers, which render his quest for achievement, the perpetuation of the ivory tower, while he is trying to work with powerful forms of technology, already nostalgic. The parochialism of what the master builder seeks to do may be contrasted with Nietzsche, who could be commenting on the Vanderbilt commissions and on their like, and on America's aspirant architecture when he says that

> the architect represents neither a Dionysian nor an Apollonian condition; here it is the mighty act of will, the will which moves mountains, the intoxication of the strong will, which demands artistic expression. The most powerful men have always inspired the architects; the architect has always been influenced by power. Pride, victory over weight and gravity, the will to power, seek to render themselves visible in a building; architecture is a kind of rhetoric of power, now persuasive, even cajoling in form, now bluntly imperious. The highest feeling of power and security finds expression in that which possesses *grand style*. Power which no longer requires proving; which disdains to please; which is slow to answer; which is conscious of no witnesses around it; which lives oblivious of the existence of any opposition; which reposes in *itself*, fatalistic, a law among laws; *that* is what speaks of itself in the form of grand style.[24]

The Schopenhaurian echoes of this [see page 55] are evident; architecture reveals something of *ressentiment* in its effort to make a statement, hence Fielder senses himself to be intimidated by the statement made by the houses at Newport. The conflict that Benjamin notes in art nouveau is between the cultivation of the interior, and the sense that architecture's masculinity has no time for interiority, since the real center of gravity has been displaced to the office. That relates to what James says about the American home; its values have nothing to do with those of the American woman, or with values outside those of business. As such it has become a machine, expressive of American competition and of aggressive control.

BOSTON

From Newport, James turns to write about Boston, following in a pattern that replicated the James family moves: from Newport, where the family lived from 1858 to 1864, to Boston (13 Ashburton Place—the house that was destroyed while James was there) for the years 1864–66. This chapter in *The American Scene* and the next on Concord and Salem are autobiographical, and illustrate shifting positions regarding history, including James's own history, and the present. He looks to Boston to see if the place preserves what he remembered. What he says about that older Boston, which he last saw when he returned between 1881–83, is ironic as he comments on the old "mildly tortuous" roads at the rear of the State House, which served for "an ancient and romantic note." That old Boston was not marked by plenitude or presence; it is ironized in *The Bostonians,* and something of its oppressiveness appears in the opening of the short story *The Patagonia* (1888). However, the romanticism is gone, and he speaks about the "great raw clearance" of older Boston that took place with the enlarging of Charles Bulfinch's 1797 State House—an extension six times the size of the original building. These rebuildings took place between 1889 and 1895, but work was still in progress in 1904, so that James, as we have already noted, saw the old house in Ashburton Place, which two days later had been demolished.

He comes back to the State House and to Park Street Church (*The American Scene,* 7.1.171), which, as a recall of Wren's spires, he says was still "*present,* on the Boston scene" (7.2.177). He speaks with disfavor of the American shop and shop front, which stands both for "'protected' production and of commodities requiring certainly . . . every advantage Protection could give them" (7.1.174); the lack of charm of American shops leads him into discussion of the importance of American money. Why have so many "absentees" from America been "unrestored"—unrepatriated? It is because America's basic postulate is that of "active pecuniary gain . . . to make so much money that you won't, that you don't 'mind,' don't care anything— that is absolutely, I think, the main American formula." If you make no money, you know that "America is no place for you" (7.1.175–76). The knowledge of this, speaking as the "restored absentee," makes him feel that the Athenaeum of Edward Clarke Cabot, though built only comparatively recently (1847–49) has been brought so low by the "tall building" that it no longer counts for anything in Boston (7.1.172–73). Looking for something else, he walks down Mount Vernon Street (where his father died) into Charles Street, passing the door of Fields' house, with its ghosts "from faraway Thackeray down" (7.2.181). The "new splendours" of Boston, which include the Back Bay area, filled in and laid out from 1857 onwards, he finds "a tract pompous and prosaic" and continues with this theme in the third section. Marlborough Street in Boston makes him think of Tennyson on London's Harley Street and Wimpole Street: the "long unlovely street" (7.2.183) where "on the bald street breaks the blank day," a line already quoted in relation to *Martin Chuzzlewit* and resonating through much of *The American Scene.* We can compare the phrase "the blankness of the American street-page" (7.2.181). Yet James prefers London and says that Marlborough Street fell on his sense "with the thinness of tone of a precocious child." The Back Bay area speaks of "a vast commercial and professional bourgeoisie left to itself," homogeneity without any contestation (the bourgeoisie does not have to define itself against an aristocracy).

James cannot quite say for what "imperturbable reasons or its own" he found Marlborough Street break his heart; but it seems to have been as psychically wounding as Dickens's Cairo and helps account for the letter to Edith Wharton that says, "Boston doesn't speak to me, never has, in irresistible accents, or affect me with the sweet touch of an affinity. My want of affinity with it is so almost indecent that I have to resort to concealment and dissimulation" (18 November 1904, *Letters*, 4:333–34). It is a discovery of a nonrelation—this in the novelist who says in the Preface to *The American* that "relations stop nowhere." Blankness can go no further; the novelist fails in finding any ghost and must substitute for this by "concealment." And such indifference has acted throughout his history, and is confirmed here as something increasing. Negativity about the Back Bay area accounts for his mixed feelings toward the public library, "the Florentine palace by Copley Square," in the heart of the Back Bay. McKim, Mead, and White's library was about six years old when James saw it, across from and facing Richardson's Trinity Church (1877), which was put up at the same time as the now demolished Ruskinian Gothic Museum of Fine Arts (John H. Sturgis and Charles Brigham). James's reactions to the library are ambivalent. While he comments on its speaking of the "the power of the purse"—the form under which cultural monuments exist at all—he notes that it gives evidence of "that democratic way of dealing which it has been the American office to translate from an academic phrase into a bristling fact" (*The American Scene*, 7.3.184), which makes him comment on its lack of *penetralia*—and so of forms of privacy. This public deployment of space in architecture belongs to a democracy both social and political, unlike London museums, which show that democracy is only political. The Boston library, in comparison, is a product of thinking that produces, rather, in its form of democracy, panoptical space, which means the denial of privacy, and the perpetuation of this space as blank, indifferent. The bustle the place encourages that James compares to a railway station (7.3.186) makes him reflect on how works of art are made to exist in no special aura or protectedness; he refers here to the murals of Puvis de Chavannes, and John Singer Sargent, and the Pre-Raphaelite-like designs of Edwin Austin Abbey and the Boston artist John Elliott. It is also the moment when James finds himself reduced to silence by the commemorations of the Massachusetts Volunteer regiments on the staircase in the library, as also by Saint-Gaudens's "noble and exquisite" monument to Robert Gould Shaw, which was then only eight years old, the reminder that the first regiments of freed blacks in the Civil War were formed in Boston.[25] Both of these act like Barthes's *punctum* to disturb the surface that the city is; to break up its appearance of smoothness.[26]

The chapter on Boston closes with a visit to the Museum of Fine Arts and a comment on the transplanted Aphrodite there: James says it is worth crossing the Atlantic to see in "the American light" the "genius of Greece." The passage echoes *The Last of the Valerii*, for America is displaced by the Greek statue; but Aphrodite also brings out what the American light is. Commenting on the nature of American institutions to be, essentially, provision of "more lands and houses and halls and rooms, more swimming-baths and football-fields and gymnasia, a greater luxury of bricks and mortar, a greater ingenuity, the most artful conceivable, of accommodation and installation"—places waiting people, "individuals of value" rather than individuals creating places—he concludes with a reference to one particular individual, when he praises the new Isabella Stewart Gardner Collection, in a palace just two years old when James visited.

James's negativity about Boston may be compared with H. G. Wells's, in *The Future in America,* chapter 13, "Culture." Boston is introduced architecturally as having

> rows of well-built, brown and ruddy homes, each with a certain sound architectural distinction, each with its two squares of neatly trimmed grass between itself and the broad, quiet street, and each with its family of cultured people within. I am reminded of deferential but unostentatious servants, and of being ushered into large, dignified entrance-halls. I think of spacious stairways, curtained archways, and rooms of agreeably receptive persons. I recall the finished formality of the High Tea. (168)

Bostonian culture has gone dead, fixed in Victorianism, which makes the electric light illumination of the Massachusetts State House—"the admission of the present, of the twentieth century"—incongruous, and leads to the charge that "the intellectual movement has ceased. Boston is now producing no literature" (170). Boston symbolizes much in the modern world, and is the reverse of America, so that Wells concludes that "the capacity of Boston . . . was just sufficient, but no more than sufficient, to comprehend the whole achievement of the human intellect up, let us say, to the year 1875 AD. Then an equilibrium was established. At or about that year Boston filled up" (172). So, "culture, as it is conceived in Boston, is no contribution to the future in America" (175). If Boston has wasted its leisure and energy in giving too much to the past, this leads to Wells's discrimination: "New York is not simply more interesting than Rome, but more significant, more stimulating and far more beautiful, and the idea that to be concerned about the latter in preference to the former is a mark of a finer mental quality is one of the most mischievous and foolish ideas . . ." (175).[27]

James finds more that is modern in Boston than Wells, who in comparison looks as though he is caricaturing the city, but the sense of the city making a fetish of its history can be compared with the chapter that follows, "Concord and Salem," looking at two Boston suburbs that Wells does not write about. It involves James's sense of American history, the past of the Concord Fight (1775), and of Emerson and Hawthorne and Thoreau. James concentrates on place; though he recalls hearing Emerson lecture, he says little of Emerson. Dickens's America is people; James's is places. When he comes to Salem, he asks directions of an Italian (which succeeds his comments on the Italian immigrants in Boston [7.1.172], who represent that which has "obliterated" his old small "homogeneous" Boston). The separation of this time from an American history becomes obvious, especially since what James had been searching for had been the "New England homogeneous," for a vision he had had, which as a "memory had been, from far back, a kept felicity altogether; a picture of goodly Colonial habitations, quite the high-water mark of that type of state and ancientry, seen in the clear dusk, and of almost nothing else but a pleasant harbour-side vacancy, the sense of dead marine industries, that finally looked out at me, for a climax, over a grass-grown interval, from the blank windows of the old Customs House of the Introduction to *The Scarlet Letter*" (8.2.197). Yet this passage illustrates not just nostalgia, but the point that there *was* nothing in that past. The Salem that he recollects was dead then; as indeed "The Custom House" introduction to *The Scarlet Letter* virtually says. The reappearance of the familiar word "vacancy" is now in a different context. Whereas before it marked an absence of history in America, it stands here, alongside the word "blank" for the loss of history, the point that when James came before to Salem, presumably in the 1860s, it was, virtually, as a tourist. What was dead then—because Salem's days as a port were long gone and Hawthorne's duties at the Custom House a sinecure—is certainly no less dead in 1904.

The intuition of Salem as having been then and now excluded from history, so that nostalgia for it is inappropriate, is scripted in James's Dickensian portrait of a an old lady whom he says he once knew (not from Concord or Salem), whose memory was frozen at the time of the Romantics, and who talked about Lamb, Hazlitt, Byron, and Scott as though they were still alive, but who forbore to speak about people who fell ill (8.1.192–93). In referring to her as "Dickensian," the point emerges that James repeats one aspect of *American Notes* in writing about New England, as he also invites a rereading of its noticing of the mad, people frozen in time and institutionalized. This woman stands for an attitude to history that cannot speak about the present or recognize the pastness of the past. "Only death had beautifully passed out of her world," James writes—but it is the woman who is thereby dead in her very different form of repudiation of the past, denying that it is past. As James comes back to Salem, it is appropriate to think of the woman again, for the town stands for "reconstituted antiquity" (8.2.199), while at the same time it has a new "untidy industrial quarter," which he notices— whose effect is surely to ask what is meant by "Salem," since the tourism of the Hawthornian part of the town, with the putative "house of the seven gables" and the adjacent Hawthorne birthplace, moved from its original site, depends on keeping away the "smoky modernism"—just as the old lady forecloses on the illnesses of people in the present. But the industrial town makes it clear that the tourist's Salem is nothing and viewing a site gives nothing but the tourist's Hawthorne. As James goes to visit the "house of the seven gables," led on by a boy with the manner of a professional guide, he sees that nothing in modern Salem can evoke Hawthorne and *The House of the Seven Gables,* just as nothing in past Salem could have produced Hawthorne. James returns implicitly to the "individuals of value" argument that concluded "Boston," and in emphasizing dislocation between the place and the person and the history, makes it clear that going to the place can say nothing about the past. Going to the house designated as the "house of the seven gables" is another "justly rebuked mistake"—a rebuke to the tourist spirit, an implied rebuke to himself for his interest in his own past houses, and a comment on the blankness that he detects in the American city; even, perhaps, a rebuke to his hysteria about what the modern American house is building.

CHAPTER 7

The American Scene—II
JAMES AND NEW YORK

After New England, James returns to New York, the subject of four chapters, which, at a hundred pages of writing of varying intensity, virtually comprise a small book. They mark James's fascination with the city, and his recognition that it was different from anything he had known it to be in the past and different from anything European he knew in the present. How could it be described, how encompassed? The different sections of the chapters, which I map below, changing subjects and focus and sometimes "restless" in character, like the "restless analyst" and sometimes relaxed, have contrasting densities to match those of the city in its non-homogeneity. By the end of the chapters—and the discussion of New York remains implicit in the rest of the book—it has become the city James writes most about of all the cities he ever discusses.[1]

Nor was the "small book" all. In one of two novellas written after *The American Scene* that can be used for comparison, *Crapy Cornelia* (1909), White-mason, who appears to have been born in New York around 1850 (when New York's population was around half a million) and to have remembered it in what he considers its most ideal form in 1868, contemplates marriage to the society hostess Mrs. Worthingham in 1898 (when New York assimilated the boroughs round it and increased its population to three and a half million). She is the modern and upper-class New York, with shades of the social world of Edith Wharton, which he rejects when he renews contact again with his sisters' friend from the 1860s, Cornelia Rasch. He decides that he is "old," and opts for companionship—not marriage—with her instead. White-mason accepts that Mrs. Worthingham may know "other things" than he does, but, at the last, he does not want to know them (4.247–48). He turns away from her "high modernity" (2.227). The novella dramatizes the problem of reading the new New York, but the reading comes from a repression embodied in the name: White-mason; whose antimodernity makes him a builder of that white America that rests upon ignorance of the other. In *The American Scene,* in contrast, the pervasive topic is "the alien." *A Round of Visits* (1910) recalls a subject that is at the heart of New York in *The American Scene:* as James says, "the immediate expression [of New York] is the expression of violence" (*The American Scene,* 4.5.141). It dramatizes the business "deals" of New York, ending with the suicide of one American fraudulent dealer, Newtown (New town—New York) Winch. Its tensions borrow from detective fiction and the tone anticipates Hollywood cinema: as when the police are ringing at the door: "the pressed electric bell again and for a longer time pierced the warm cigaretted air" (*A Round of Visits,* 7.923). The metonymies in their fragmentariness are indicative of the attempt to find a new form of writing to engage with this New York, which at the beginning of the novella shuts itself round the Europeanized artist, Mark Monteith, with the force of a prison, and imposes upon him the task of communicating with people in this world whose intensities are those of a hot-house.

New York Revisited

The American Scene chapters are structured by alternations between seeing the city in winter (how he begins), and seeing it in early summer (how he ends). At the start, New York is the "terrible town" (2.1.57).[2] J. G. Ballard in *Empire of the Sun* (1984), thinking of the repetitions of trauma in wartime Shanghai, since, as he writes, "wars come early to Shanghai," finishes the novel by calling it "this terrible city."[3] Perhaps alliance of war with the city is not coincidental: Colonial American cities were built for garrison purposes, as the name Wall Street recalls, and New York's or Los Angeles's capacity to fend off alien attack is the theme of America in Wellsian science fiction and cinema. New York is aggressive, unfriendly, which is how James first describes it here. Its tall buildings, part of the sense of New York as a vast "machine room, with its bridges like pistons (2.1.59) are some of America's "terrible things" (2.1.60). James approaches the skyscrapers—"the last word in economic ingenuity" (2.1.61)—from the water, from a "trainbearing barge," carrying him in another form of economic ingenuity. He begins with the diminished visibility of Wall Street's Trinity Church, but he sees New York through a winter mist and fog, which hung round the upper reaches of the skyscrapers, each "a swarming city" (2.1.64). The adjective recurs through the chapters; James is translating, consciously or not, Baudelaire's "four-millante cité" ("Les Sept Vieillards"). Can one city be described through another? The question has already been asked in relation to Poe describing New York: in turn, Poe's New York (a displaced topic) affects Baudelaire's Paris. James thinks of Zola, whose novels respond to a need to say something in the face of the city of Paris, which, torn down, planned, manipulated into another mode of existence, was the driving force in framing nineteenth-century European urban existence. What could Zola—whom James says wrote "the modern novel,"[4] particularly in L'Assommoir—have made of New York, as opposed to Paris? L'Assommoir influenced Crane's novella, Maggie: A Girl of the Streets (1893), as much as Zola's sense of the city had influenced Howells's A Hazard of New Fortunes (1890), which has been called "one of the first major novels about New York City."[5] Howells had settled in New York at the end of the 1880s, like the American Impressionist painter, Childe Hassam, who returned from Paris, having previously lived in Boston.[6] The subject of A Hazard of New Fortunes is relocating to New York from Boston (all the people in the novel have come to the city from other parts of the United States—none are indigenous New Yorkers). Other attempts to "do" New York include Dreiser's Sister Carrie and Edith Wharton's The House of Mirth. Wharton asserts her readiness to confront the up-to-the-minute character of the city by starting it in the very masculine space of Grand Central Station, rebuilding of which had only begun in 1903. James confronts New York—the city—with the sense that in contrast with the diminished scale of Parisian apartments, New York's "monstrous phenomena" seem, with their "immense momentum," to have "got ahead of . . . any possibility of poetic, of dramatic capture" (2.1.65). They defy representation. New York has not yet been adequately described—and how could it be since it is a city on the move?—but the inadequacy of the subject to describe the city is matched by an equal incapacity to grasp the language, which coming into play with the expansion of the city, is needful for any representation. Perhaps some sense of the inadequacy of representation appears with the American Impressionists (the Ten) in their attempts to render New York, for instance, Childe Hassam's Late Afternoon, New York: Winter (1900). There the softening, and the low angle of vision, which draws the viewer into the scene, give no sense of alienation or of energy that cannot be commanded, energy James is fascinated by.[7] Yet in Hassam, the city is only partially seeable, and this draws attention to the city as invisible, as not to be caught by an attempt to render it whole.

Perhaps the newest art-form for the city was photography. Alfred Stieglitz (1864–1946), returned to New York in 1890, had created images of New York in "snow, mist, fog, rain, deserted streets"—those things that remove the city's hard edges, and that show it as resistant to single definition. Stieglitz, like others trying to read the new city, wandered the streets of New York downtown, "around the Tombs, the old Post Office, Five Points. I loathed the dirty streets, yet I was fascinated."[8] It is the response to the city Trollope could never have had, but it is Dickens's, however much the fascination might also be horror, and it is James's. Stieglitz's images of New York contrast with Lewis Hines (1874–1940) who between 1904 and 1909 photographed immigrants arriving at Ellis Island. Hines photographed images of urban society and made his photographs imply a narrative.[9] Along with Riis's photographs of the tenements, these provide different senses that to get at the distinctiveness of the modern city, with its machinic force and nonhuman scale, another technology is required.[10]

Since James invokes Zola, whose mode of seeing the modern city was so influential in Naturalist writing, even if James felt it could not do New York, we should ask what does *L'Assommoir* do to try to make itself equal to Paris, the European city? One answer: Zola de-centers the city, makes it other to the reader by setting his action literally in the suburbs, just outside the newer octroi walls (in what would become the Eighteenth arrondissement). A second point: he shows the city in action, its spaces changing within time. A third is his sense of the changing relationships between people and city spaces. On Gervaise's wedding day, around 1850, the wedding guests go down into Paris through the Faubourg Saint-Denis[11] and later, after suffering the alienating experience of the Louvre—"lost as in the labyrinth of Crete" (James, *LCI*, 897)—climb up the tower at the Place Vendôme and see the landmarks of the tourist's Paris, which mean nothing to them. At the end, around 1869, Gervaise, who "without any principle of cohesion" (James, *LCI*, 892) represents the older form of the city that is replaced by the city planning of Baron Haussmann, becomes a streetwalker. She wanders into the new Boulevard Magenta and the Boulevard Ornano (now Barbès); these roads have taken away the octroi wall it is noted (*L'Assommoir*, 406) and so have abolished the then city/suburb distinction, and the old landmarks, the old buildings known from the earlier parts of the book, including the old abattoir (410) have either been torn down or are left desolate. She wanders onto the bridge that overlooks the Gare du Nord; but she cannot see the train nor be aware of anything save the impression of sound and smoke and the sensation of being shaken (410).[12] Street existence means being enframed by boulevards whose capacity to reduce to indifference is reinforced by the snowfall, which makes things now not yellow, but gray: "Grey walls imprisoned her. And when she stopped and looked round in hesitation, she could sense, beyond that icy veil, the great expanse of the avenues, the endless lines of lamp-posts, the dark, deserted, unmeasurable vastness of the sleeping city" (417). At that point, she is actually within her old neighborhood. As Paris had become its own suburbs, so too New York, in 1898, had done the same—incorporating its four outer boroughs, including Brooklyn, then America's fourth largest city. New York is the consuming, cannibalistic creature, and James picks up on its "appetite."

By 1904 James, with none of his earlier resistance to Zola's urban art, is challenged by New York's appearance of exceeding representation. As the New York of *A Round of Visits* is the New York of a fierce March, James evokes a March morning in New York near Wall Street, where the mist makes for one kind of invisibility, and the skyscrapers, stretching away overhead make for another. That the skyscraper that dwarfs "poor old Trinity" (Richard Upjohn's Gothic revival church of 1846, more recent than *American Notes*) was commissioned by the church's trustees indicates something of New York's "pitiless ferocity" (that Zolean note). In the following passage, James's commitment to Dickens's *Bleak House*, to Zola, and to Impressionism appears as he writes that:

> the vast money-making structure quite horribly, quite romantically justified itself, looming through the weather with an insolent cliff-like sublimity. The weather, for all that experience, mixes intimately with the fulness of my impression; speaking not least, for instance, of the way 'the state of the streets' and the assault of the turbid air seemed all one with the look, the tramp, the whole quality and *allure,* the consummate monotonous commonness, of the pushing male crowd, moving in its dense mass—with the confusion carried to chaos for any intelligence, any perception; a welter of objects and sounds in which relief, detachment, dignity, meaning, perished utterly and lost all rights. It appeared, the muddy medium, all one with every other element and note as well, all the signs of the heaped industrial battlefield, all the sounds and silences, grim pushing, trudging silences too, of the universal will to move—to move, move, move, as an end in itself, an appetite at any price. (*The American Scene,* 2.1.65)

Invisibility as the churches disappear in relation to the skyscrapers invokes a loss of distinction, which echoes in different ways Dickens and Zola. *Bleak House,* first recalled through the word "looming" echoes through that novel's "mud" in the reference to the horse manure implicit in the phrase "the state of the streets," while "the will to move," Nietzschean like the earlier "will to grow," fuses with a Dickensian repetition of the words "move" and "appetite" and recalls the earlier reference to the significantly gendered "hungry, triumphant actual." New York pigs may have gone, but the passage is full of signs of the cannibalistic, the consuming, which annihilates identity. The skyscrapers going upwards are only part of a general "pushing" (the word is repeated). They are the sublime in challenging representation. Old "meanings" disappear and the senses register a plurality of signs. The reference to sounds, first in the word "note," which evokes Baudelaire, "la rue assourdissante autour de moi hurlait" ("the deafening street around me cried"; ["A une passante"]) indicates the impossibility of registering separately different aspects of what is going on here, in this "muddy medium." It is clear that the spectator can be nowhere. The crowd is not under the control of the male gaze; rather as male itself, it pushes, obliterating the spectator, male or not, who would look at it, and the word "push" recalls its sexual implication in the New York edition of *The Portrait of a Lady*, when Isabel Archer reflects on Caspar Goodwood: "there was a disagreeably strong push, a hardness of presence, in his way of rising before her."[13]

In *An International Episode* two Englishmen, Percy Beaumont and Lord Lambeth, arrive in New York in a torrid summer. They are immediately surrounded by the hotel comforts and the high degree of American civilization, which can make such heat bearable.[14] The March morning in which the "terrible town" shows the signs of a "heaped industrial battlefield" contrasts with this presentation, where the English were shown wholly amazed by the accommodating spirit of New York. James catches two aspects of the city and of American life; but he also registers that the city of 1874, which was mappable and walkable at least in part by his Englishmen, now dwarfs representation. But as with Dickens and *Bleak House*, James still tries to encompass the city, and the next paragraph moves to the "terrible little" Ellis Island.[15] In 1904, it received a million immigrants—people on the move—coming to the United States. The weather's harshness is an apt correlate for its official proceedings, and *The American Scene* reaches again to Dickens to describe the activity of sorting out the immigrants—"marshaled, herded, divided, subdivided, sorted, sifted, searched, fumigated" (2.1.66). The observer—never mind the immigrant—has "a thousand more things to think of than he can pretend to retail." At this point both Dickens and Zola become inadequate in their accounts of London or Paris to describe the other city—New York. Its reality may be imaged in Ellis Island, with its arrivals of what James calls the "inconceivable alien." Accounts of Zolean "naturalism" in America have to come to terms with the homogeneity of Zola's Paris in contrast to this, and James returns to it again and again, as in his treatment of Southern cities, he turns to the presence of the Afro-American.

The presence of the "alien" challenges what is meant by "American." The Anglo-Saxon American "had thought he knew before . . . the degree to which it is his American fate to share the sanctity of his American consciousness, the intimacy of his American patriotism, with the inconceivable alien"—but knowledge is dumbfounded through Ellis Island. The American, as much as the English Dickens, has lost his identity, because the "alien" is also American, and this challenges any foundationalism, any sense of the pure subject, pure from his origins. "So is stamped, for detection, the questionably privileged person who has had an apparition, seen a ghost in his supposedly safe old house. Let not the unwary, therefore, visit Ellis Island." The presence of the ghost is not the alien; it is the awareness of otherness characterizing American identity from the beginning; the ghost dispossesses the haunted person of the illusion that he or she was there first. The American, who has missed this at the beginning (the missed encounter with the real) must be the haunted, the traumatized. James (if we read autobiographically) has returned to America to attempt to articulate an American "relation," but as "relations stop nowhere," so the relation (which has the added sense of narrative representation) cannot be made. Reinforced by the uncanny experience of Ellis Island, for which James's own text, *The Turn of the Screw* is the intertextual model, the section returns in an ABA, sonata-like formation to the city, and to the "settled possession" that the "alien," uncanny, ghostlike, makes in New York, itself ghostly in the fog. People move between "possession and dispossession," where both ends of the seesaw imply ghostliness, lack of being (being possessed by the other, like a ghost; lost as far as having any title or status is concerned). James expands the pun when he adds that "this sense of dispossession . . . haunted me so" (2.1.67). The psychic life of New York crowds betrays, under its will to move, its lack of secure being, its provisionality.

The next sections seem to move away from this confrontation with otherness, but concentrate on other aspects where representation—which if it is mimetic, requires a "relation" to a previous model of writing—is challenged. They concentrate on the area between Washington Square[16] and Fourteenth Street, with discussion of City Hall (whose official functions had diminished with the changes to the status of New York in 1898), and develop a case against the skyscraper for its removal of the past—disallowing even the possibility of memorial plaques, thus differentiating New York from European cities. The text makes fun of their pervasive use of windows, since "it takes[s] in fact acres of window-glass to help even an expert New Yorker to get the better of another expert one" (1.2.74). The satire on windows follows a comment on John La Farge, whose stained-glass windows decorated Richardson's Trinity Church in Boston (1876) and whose painting of the Ascension (1886) in the Church of the Ascension on Tenth Street, James admires.

La Farge, with his interest in Japanese art, represented the spirit of *art nouveau,* with its femininity and non-utilitarian value; the absolute contrast to the skyscraper.

For James, New York buildings suffer from "absence of margin," "meagreness of site," "brevity of the block," and "inveteracy of the near thoroughfare." These leave building styles "at the mercy of the impertinent cross-streets, make detachment and independence ... an insoluble problem, preclude without pity any element of court or garden [no chance of New York providing a space for a non-Venetian version of *The Aspern Papers*], and open to the builder in quest of distinction the one alternative, and the great adventure, of seeking his reward in the sky" (1.3.77). Two things oppose each other: the old planning of New York— its "old inconceivably bourgeois scheme of composition and distribution ... with no imagination of the future, and blind before the opportunity given them by their two magnificent water-fronts"—and the new demands of grandeur. Caught between these two exigencies, the skyscraper becomes a compromise formation.

James's reaction to the skyscraper, however, brings out a conservatism that fails to see them as a problem rather than as something whose worth could be settled one way or another. It would be interesting to compare his reaction to that of John Corbin, in a 1902 article in *Scribner's,* "The Twentieth Century City," with photographs by Stieglitz. Corbin finds of Daniel Burnham's Flatiron that "there are times when the building seems no more than what it is called, a flat-iron, or ... a clothes-peg that served to fix Fifth Avenue and Broadway on the line of Twenty-Third Street. But there are times when it seems one of the most striking monuments of modern civic architecture—a column of smoke by day, and by night, when the interior is lighted, a pillar of fire."[17] (These images require Stieglitz's photographic work, with its diffusion of hard edges.) What is implied is the impossibility of reading the skyscraper, which is of the city in that it belongs there, but not of it in that it grows away from it (hence it disdains the city history that would give plaques), and the point that the skyscraper, because it cannot be seen whole, emphasizes that the city is the place of fragmentary vision, itself a source of resentment. Something of that is at work in James. Trachtenberg also quotes the architectural critic Montgomery Schuyler, in 1903, calling the skyscraper a "civic problem," and "like Frankenstein, we stand appalled before the monster of our own creation." These responses indicate that the skyscraper could not be settled as a fixed issue, as James wishes to do so, especially when he tries to relate it to the prehistory of the tall building, by connecting it to the growth of New York streets—where all the dislike of city "blankness" comes out. At this point, we may regret the more his exclusion of

Chicago from *The American Scene,* and the feeling that having not dealt with its skyscrapers—which had no history behind them since all of Chicago had to start again from nothing after 1871—he both compromises his own treatment of the city, for the other cities he chooses to write about are no match for New York, and he becomes too attached to the idea of the development of the skyscraper as something determinate, almost foreseeable, within New York's history.

The longitudinal avenues are the American "original sin," James adding that their creation means the denial of squares, or gardens, or nooks, or a "casual corner." The image of original sin had been implied when referring to the visitor to Ellis Island as "having eaten of the tree of knowledge" (1.1.66), just as the Hawthorne study saw the Civil War acting as "the tree of knowledge" for the American (*Hawthorne,* 135). But James now goes further back to the establishment of the grid system of New York at the beginning of the nineteenth century, and locates a fault in the American city there. We may be skeptical of the idea of the origin; the postcolonial Americans who laid out New York above Houston Street replicated colonial planning. To recall a novel discussed in chapter 2, Dr. Sloper, in *Washington Square,* a "geometrical proposition" as he calls himself and born in 1793, represents the alliance of patriarchy and science that at the beginning of the century had laid out New York on such a regular basis. He moves up into the gridded part of the town. Sloper embodies something of the founding spirit and the founding sin of the nineteenth century. James could have gone further back; that planning system only perpetuated what was practiced in the colonial setting up of American cities. James reads it as an acceptance of meanness and narrowness (he refers to "pettifogging consistency"), which the bourgeois and Utilitarian spirit imposed on the city, confining its vision so that it cannot look outwards toward the sea (as it would, had the avenues run east-west). Where the city provides no escape, the only refuge is the hotel, which, symbolized by the Waldorf-Astoria (1893 and 1896, built on 11 and 16 stories respectively in Beaux-Arts style by Henry J. Hardenbergh). This, on Fifth Avenue between west Thirty-third and Thirty-fourth Streets, appears in the third section and makes James ask if "the hotel spirit may not just *be* the American spirit most seeking and most finding itself" (1.3.79).

The insight is startling, but it is not said for the first time. In 1859, Amory Mayo, Unitarian clergyman from New York, had written that an American city was different from a European capital. Old cities abroad were "the centres of imperial influence, a court, a palace, a royal army. . . ." an American city was always "representative." "Its money is the acumulation of the country's industry; its commerce is the exchange of

the products of the prairie . . . and its institutions of philanthropy and re-
ligion are supported by . . . men and means from the sects that spread
over entire States." So, "an American city is only a convenient hotel,
where a free country people come up to tarry and do business, with old
recollections of nature." And the foreigner would halt at the city and
then push on to the far West.[18] Yet James's use of the image leads to several theories about America. Perhaps the hotel is the most disembodied
and abstract state in which America finds itself. James returns to a word
used in the New England chapter of *The American Scene* when he says that
the hotel expresses the "gregarious state" (2.3.79, 80) that breaks down all
barriers except money and tells the gregarious "member of the flock" to
be "respectable," or "not, discoverably, anything else." Yet what are hotels
if not invitations to anonymous sexuality? What other substantial use has
Hollywood, post-James, found for them?[19] James, hardly aware of film, is
aware of the ironies: The hotel looks like the place of respectability, but
it is the place of sexual "adventure." He plays on the word "promiscuity,"
for the hotel promotes both sexual and social promiscuity, representing
the triumph of surfaces. The American hotel-spirit is Utilitarian, providing in it "the greatest happiness of the greatest number" (2.3.80). The
following paragraph ("The sense of these things . . .) is cinematic in
noticing the metonymic details of a hotel lobby: the "circulation" of people, the décor, the "inimitable New York tune," the simulacral flavor of
European aristocratic taste, the "American genius for organization," and
the soft focus of "a gorgeous golden blur"—James's awareness of how, in
Fitzgerald's terms, voices are "full of money." The hotel spirit lends itself
to abstraction, to separation from the world outside. In *A Round of Visits,*
Montieth begins his "visits" in his hotel, the Pocahontas—i.e., the Waldorf-Astoria—and the hotel "was a complete social scene in itself, on
which types might figure and passions rage and plots thicken and dramas
develop, without reference to any other sphere, or perhaps even to anything at all outside" (*A Round of Visits,* 2.899).

Outside the hotel, James walks up Fifth Avenue, and the chapter concludes by acknowledging his fascination with the city, noting how it treats
itself and its buildings as "provisional," or, using the word applied to
houses in New Jersey, "stop-gap."[20] Buildings, all less than 50 years old,
are torn down, with the warning not to make yourself at home in their
successor buildings: "we defy you even to aspire to venerate shapes so
grossly constructed as the arrangement in fifty floors" (2.3.86). Fifty
floors will soon be outmoded. But if the present—"that perpetual passionate pecuniary purpose which plays with all forms, which derides and
devours them" (2.3.85) is so insistent on the provisional character of its
own forms, that leaves open the thought that it is so because it has no be-

lief in them any more than it has in the past, and the cannibalistic image, which James notes so often, suggests not only violence but willingness to consume itself, nihilistically making itself disappear, and this nihilism not separate from the drive within Europe that Nietzsche identifies.

NEW YORK AND THE HUDSON: A SPRING IMPRESSION

Though James opens by finding continuities and affinities between one part of Manhattan and another, he has to confess that he cannot relate neighborhoods to each other. The failure of homogenization is associated with the presence of the "alien." He recalls the "babel of tongues" heard in Central Park, and nonencounters with Italians in New Jersey and an Armenian in New Hampshire. The future in America is to make all these immigrants "American." Consideration of this makes

> the great "ethnic" question rise before you . . . once it has set your observation, to say nothing of your imagination, working, it becomes for you . . . the wonderment to which everything ministers, and that is quickened well-nigh to madness [this is the complete "othering" of James, as Dickens was made "other,"], in some places and on some occasions, by every face and every accent that meets your eyes and ears. The sense of the elements in the cauldron—the cauldron of the "American" character—becomes thus about as vivid a thing as you can at all quietly manage, and the question settles into a form which makes the intelligible answer further and further recede. What meaning, in the presence of such impressions, can continue to attach to such a term as the "American" character?—what type, as the result of such a prodigious amalgam, such a hotch-potch of racial ingredients, is to be conceived as shaping itself? (3.1.92).[21]

His own character, his history, like his birthplace, has been taken away; shown up to be nothing; there can be *no* representing America since it negates its past. His birthplace had gone unmarked, leaving him "amputated of half" his history (2.2.71). Single identity has been taken away; the "meaning" of "American" character will be that it has no single meaning, no self-identity. The "syllables [are] too numerous to make a legible word" so the "illegible word" hangs in the vast American sky (3.1.93). While America is "too large for any human convenience"—so that it confounds humanism—at the same time, James adds, "goodness be thanked . . . for the bigness" (3.1.94).[22] It is that which dispels any single, monadlike existence. While he feels he can establish "no personal relation" (3.1.94), which returns to the impossibility of representing America, he feels able to wait to see what will happen, in a mood that has renounced analysis.

Perhaps the term "alien" is racist: it is not to be defended, nor the treatment of different groups in the singular. Nonetheless, James, asking "who and what is an alien?" (3.2.95), the mirror question to "what meaning can be attached to the American character?" shows that all Americans, save the native Americans, are immigrants and "aliens," and that if he has been made to "gasp" at their numbers, something unimaginable in Britain, nonetheless the immigrants were "at home" as much as himself, the repatriated American (3.2.96). Perhaps they were more at home. America may talk the language of "assimilation," a word, that, like "ethnic" and "American," he puts within speech marks, testing its ability to expunge otherness, as if seeing the language of "assimilation," which works from a basis of different ethnicities and forms a single Americanness, as homogenizing. But in the electric street cars on Broadway and the Bowery, he feels his own isolation and registers his fascination (3.2.96–97); as he speaks of the "interest, in the American world, of what I have called the 'ethnic' outlook"—the question of difference; "outlook" becomes a pun; including both the present and the future gaze, and the future cannot be guessed at: "the cauldron, for the great stew, has such circumference and such depth, that we can only here deal with ultimate syntheses, ultimate combinations and possibilities" (3.2.99). The future is plural, like the present "foreground."

The "ethnic" question had been implicitly raised by Howells in his use of accents in *A Hazard of New Fortunes,* and by Jacob Riis in *How the Other Half Lives* (1890), which had employed the methods of *American Notes* in investigating the Five Points area of New York to probe the tenements and photograph the inhabitants of the Lower East Side. In a chapter called "The Mixed Crowd," Riis had looked at Italians, Chinese, Russian and Polish Jews, Germans, and Bohemians, and had referred to himself as the "curious wanderer"—James's phrase "the restless analyst" contrasts with this—noting, as if for a tourism readership, what is there to be consumed by a middle-class white readership; so, he says, "Chinatown, as a spectacle, is disappointing."[23] James does not raise the question of "ethnicity" in that he is not interested in the fiction of racial typology, which intersects with Zolean questions of heredity. Those forms of connection, and that homogenization of the other are both relatively absent in *The American Scene.*

We can compare James's sense of the "alien" with H. G. Wells, in *The Future in America,* on "The Immigrant," the title of his chapter 8. Wells has said that he went wanting to know "what is going to happen in the United States of America in the next thirty years or so?"(*FA,* 2). He draws on James discussing the "great mansions" of Fifth Avenue (*The American Scene,* 4.1.121), so that James provides him with his title. Wells quotes:

"It's all very well," [James] writes, "for you to look as if, since you've had no past, you're going in, as the next best thing, for a magnificent compensatory future. What are you going to make your future *of*, for all your airs, we want to know? What elements of a future, as futures have gone in the great world, are at all assured to you?" (*FA*, 4)[24]

Wells associates the skyscrapers with "incompleteness" and with growth in progress, but that progress, signs of which he sees everywhere in terms of technology, is disabled for him by immigration.

He begins "The Immigrant" with "polyglot slums" (101) "a hundred yards south of pretty Boston Common." He gives the immigration figures as in 1906, nearly a million people, focuses on the Jewish quarter in New York "a block or so east of Fifth Avenue," and on the population of Staten Island. He alludes to James (*The American Scene*, 7.1.171–72) on immigration in Boston, disturbed by it and by the immigrant's apparent success in becoming like an "American," even adopting "what naturalists call 'protective mimicry'"—but not being American, for all that, in language. So he cannot answer positively the question what future America could have, because he cannot accept the difference from Europe, where national difference is fixed. He acknowledges himself at odds with American confidence in the ability to accept immigrants (all except the Chinese), arguing that the earlier immigration of "illiterate Irish" degraded political life. But that was preferable to "the immigration of today . . . largely the result of energetic canvassing by the steamship companies; it is, in the main, an importation of labourers, and not of economically independent settlers, and it is increasingly alien to the native tradition. The bulk of it now is Italian, Russian Jewish, Russian, Hungarian, Croatian, Roumanian and Eastern European generally" (105). This is a peasantry, "rather dirty in their habits"—this point is repeated—being converted into an industrial proletariat. While trying to say that this issue of who comes over is different from the question raised by a ten million black population already in America, he also uses that as an example of America's failure to "assimilate" and he relates it to a spreading of "ignorance" in the population generally.

Wells carries with him a sense that America cannot be America because it cannot cease to be Europe. His pessimism is a *ressentiment* about Europe, and it remains, even if qualified by a visit to the central school of the Educational Alliance, "that fine imposing building in East Broadway," run for "the Hebrew immigrant," in a street whose squalor he emphasizes. The chapter ends with the optimism of the woman running it, whom he calls "the spirit of America incarnate," but *The Future in America* distances itself from such a feeling about the future.

In contrast, James shows a fascination with otherness when being taken by the Yiddish playwright Jacob Gordin to the East Side, to Rutgers Street, and to the New York ghetto in a section devoted to "Israel" in America.[25] The passage is full of signs of withdrawal, as with the desire to see his experiences of immigrants and of other communities as "phantasmagoric" (3.3.101) because he cannot read them; but he cannot feel that he can "have done" with such difference—and that he cannot, his last chapter on New York, "The Bowery and Thereabouts" will show. The passage registers anxiety, as when the section finishes by indicating his feeling that it will not be English that will be the language of the future, a thought relativizing the "man of letters," and it is equally implicitly anxious about "Israel" and about New York as the New Jerusalem, as appears in a reference to the "everywhere insistent, defiant, unhumorous, exotic face" (3.3.103) of the people in the streets.[26] James notes the street perspective with its "complexity of fire-escapes with which each house-front bristles, and which gives the whole vista so modernized and appointed a look. Omnipresent in the 'poor' regions, this neat applied machinery has, for the stranger, a common side with the electric light and the telephone, suggests the distance achieved from the old Jerusalem" (3.3.101).[27] In parenthesis he sees this as showing how "in the terrible town, on opportunity, 'architecture' goes by the board," and he compares the fire escapes to cages, with bars and perches and swings. Beverly Haviland suggests that the inhabitants are not living as humans, "they are crowded into structures that degrade them to the status of captive animals."[28] The "terrible" is the surrender to opportunism, to the profit motive. "The very name of architecture perishes, for the fire-escapes look like abashed afterthoughts, staircases and communications forgotten in the construction." Here are buildings whose poverty—not according with New York's skyscraper reputation—means that instead of being pulled down, they are defaced by the addition of iron staircases. This is another form of modernity. These points are valid, even if it is remembered that the fire escapes became balconies, and aided in a communal spirit, and that they did offer a literal form of escape. James's observation occurs while discussing the tenements, where he notes that (as if in contrast to Zola with Parisian tenements) there were "grosser elements of the sordid and the squalid" that he never saw. Aware of how the tenement exploits the tenant, James speaks of how large the "small fry" "massed" on "that evening of endless admonitions" (3.3.104). Yet sitting in cafés with friends, he also acknowledges: "the Yiddish world was a vast world, with its own deeps and complexities, and what struck one above all was that it sat there at its cups (and in no instance vulgarly the worse for them) with a sublimity of good conscience that took away the breath, a protrusion of

elbow never aggressive but absolutely proof against jostling" (3.4.105–6).
It is, again, an atmosphere that cannot be assimilated to a writer like
Zola; James is led on further and further in the sense that nothing can
help in anticipating or recognizing the American future.

This chapter, "New York and the Hudson," describing the "huge
jagged city" (3.4.106) cannot be centered; it moves from the alien and the
Jewish quarter to a winter ride to Riverside Drive on the Upper West
Side, Olmsted's park laid out after 1875, with James lamenting its "sub-
urbanizing" name and the elements of the "meagre, bourgeois" in its settlements. (It includes the area where Cornelia Rasch, in *Crapy Cornelia*,
appears to live.) He speaks of the "grossly defacing railway" that clings to
the river bank, so that after the landscaping of the green slopes and hollows, the "good thing" is completed "ironically"—which James finds a familiar thing in America. Urban spaces cannot be given a single reading.[29]
He notes the provisional aspect of New York's modernity, with everything in process—even Columbia University has moved its position
twice, the last time in 1897. The tomb of Grant (designed by John H.
Duncan, dedicated in 1897), has "a manner so opposed to our common
ideas of the impressive, to any past vision of sepulchral state, that we can
only wonder if a new kind and degree of solemnity may not have been arrived at in this complete rupture with old consecrating forms" (3.4.110).
That is one aspect of modernity, and it produces modern manners. The
tomb works by "lack of reserve," in fact by "publicity, familiarity, immediacy," which the people who walk in and out of it with hands in pockets
and hats on heads allegorize. So the mausoleum resembles a hotel, and
the new question that emerges in America is whether this is a new sensibility, or a reworking of an old one. Much of this chapter turns on manners and practices and existences that seem surprising to James, and yet
which seem so unconscious, spontaneous, as though the person who
found them odd was odd.

In the following section, he comes down the Hudson valley to New
York by train in the spring from his visit out West, through Albany, where
he had lived from the age of three to five. He regrets that he is showing
no respect to the river by not using the boat—but saving time as a practice has "long since made mincemeat of the rights of contemplation;
rights as reduced, in the United States, today, and by quite the same argument, as those of the noble savage whom we have banished to his nar-
rowing reservation" (3.5.112). There is nothing for it but acquiescence in
modernity. The last section refers to Rip Van Winkle as a formative
memory for him, which makes him discuss Sunnyside, Washington Irving's home, place of "the quite indefinable air of the little American literary past" (3.6.117). And he is Rip Van Winkle himself, noticing

constant difference after so long an absence, for he comments on this scene as no longer so accessible, "for 'modernity,' with its pockets full of money and its conscience full of virtue, its heart really full of tenderness, has seated itself there under pretext of guarding the shrine . . . the primitive cell has seen itself encompassed . . . by a temple of many chambers, all dedicated to the history of the hermit" (3.6.117). James returns to the theme of Grant's tomb. Not just that "the American world" is "positively organized to gainsay the truth that production takes time, and . . . the production of interest . . . most time" (3.6.115), which gainsaying appears in the organization of monuments, with their instant tradition. With these monuments, interest centers on the present they promote. Interest has gone out of the past and into the present.

NEW YORK: SOCIAL NOTES

Focusing on Fifth Avenue and Central Park, the third chapter begins with a sense of prevalent waste, "squandered effort" in New York's aristocracy of money; the "particular pathos" in New York's wealth is that "pecuniary power beat[s] its wings in a void" (4.1.120). The houses in uppermost Fifth Avenue, "bristling with friezes and pinnacles" (4.1.122), have an "absent future" and "an absent past," dependent on the fortunes of Wall Street (4.1.121). After instancing a dinner party in New York for a sense of prevalent emptiness, James turns to the "intersexual" question again, for the social life (the opera is the example) is "poor in the male presence" (4.1.124). The equation between women and the interior of houses, which is apparent, entails the familiar American downplaying of interiors. Thinking both of houses and of clubs, James speaks of "the vagueness of separation between apartments, between hall and room between one room and another, between the one you are in and the one you are not, between place of passage and place of privacy" (4.2.125). The last pairing repeats a gender distinction. The interior seems to have its right to exist denied; there seems a guilt that interiors exist. "Young, fresh, frolicsome architecture" abets in playing down sexual differences. There is "the indefinite extension of all spaces and the definite merging of all functions; the enlargement of every opening, the exaggeration of every passage, the substitution of gaping arches and far perspectives and resounding voids for enclosing walls, for practicable doors, for controllable windows," which would aid in conversation. James continues the image of voids and absences, as the visitor sees "doorless apertures, vainly festooned, which decline to tell him where he is, which make him still a homeless wanderer" who is therefore required to say everything not in private but for the benefit of the whole house. The house is like the club, to which James turns, where he reproduces the note of his Hawthorne study: "it takes an endless amount of history to make even a little tradition." He adds to "tradition" "taste" and "tranquillity" (4.2.127). These terms take on a feminine quality.

The city has sexed itself as male, co-opting the female toward male ends. This appears in James's critique of the Saint-Gaudens monument to Sherman (1903), in Grand Army Plaza, where Fifth Avenue meets Central Park. The monument, on a McKim pedestal, images a military advance (Sherman's march through Georgia). But "the Destroyer is a messenger of peace, with the olive branch too waved in the blast and with embodied grace, in the form of a beautiful American girl, attending his business" (4.3.130). The American girl has no other existence than to disguise the brutality of the advance: cynicism is at work, concealing "horrors" and playing on the availability of American women to symbolize—not difference, but what will add to the glory of the militarized male.[30]

Central Park is gendered as a woman in having to "do" everything that is "amiable" in New York (4.4.131). James joins to his sense of the comedy of how many types of landscape Central Park must include within itself a sense that its visitors were equally diverse, "polyglot." On a Sunday afternoon, in May or June, he says, all languages could be heard in Central Park, and for James, the air of "hard prosperity" becomes entirely positive. The city creates ghettos, yet in Central Park, an alternative space is found, which he says makes up "a little globe" (4.4.133), and which is therefore the site for racial difference, for everything that is other. By the early summer, James had been, as he says, throughout the States, and had noted poverty, but here he speaks positively of the upward mobility of Americans—mostly immigrants—as seen in Central Park, significantly noting it more in the women. This section of *The American Scene* reads the city by picking up on American attention to teeth—hence the "'Californian' smile" James refers to—and to footwear. Both are aspects of presentation, and of exteriority; the teeth recall the prevalence of consumption in America, and the footwear speak of a self-conscious pride, of a wish not to be out of place. The hat he thinks has no such unifying function in comparison to footwear (James notes, implicitly, the female *flâneuse,* but it is a question whether his comment on hats applies to fashions in women's hats). In Central Park, heterotopic to the grid structure of New York, urban existence finds its justification, as the "awful aliens" (4.4.137) are integrated there, the subject at ease with regard to the "'social question'" (4.4.133). In *Crapy Cornelia,* which starts in Central Park, as a rooted part of the New York that had come into being in the 1850s and 1860s, White-mason, in the text's indirect free discourse uses the phrase "the daughters of the strange native—that is of the over-whelmingly alien" (1.221). Neither irony nor etymological purity can jus-tify the adjectives put in front of "alien," nor the feeling that he need not worry any more about integration after seeing Central Park, but James requires the irony in the awareness that these new Americans are, unlike him, at home, and moving upwards, in a way that he, at this stage of his career, as the particular kind of expatriate novelist that he was, cannot. Irony becomes a means of self-protection, that which urbanism threat-ens, as it denies also the power of interiors. Central Park tests to the ut-most his ability to welcome difference. It epitomizes the "modern," (4.4.137) in being a place that can "bid for the boon of the future." The city's "modernity" is in its willingness to buy and sell everything, and James compares its overflowing quality with a Veronese painting. While his comparison patronizes the New Yorkers, he has to acknowledge that Veronese's Venetians were no more than "the children of a Republic and of trade" (4.4.138). James begins to retreat from the comparison, but hav-ing made it, it remains in *The American Scene* as a reminder that modernity enforces a rereading of history that de-idealizes it.[31]

The fifth section begins with a walk back along Fifth Avenue, past a Palladian-style Tiffany store on Thirty-seventh Street, just opening at the time of James's visit, and back toward the Croton Reservoir (Fortieth to Forty-second Streets), which in his youth was as far as people went up Fifth Avenue. The reservoir, which opened the year Dickens visited, was demolished at the end of the century. In *Lady Barbarina* (1884), Mrs. Lemon, the "old New Yorker," "amiable daughter of Manhattan," recalls the prewar world where "the normal existence of man, and still more of women, had been 'located,' as she would have said, between Trinity Church and the beautiful Reservoir at the top of the Fifth Avenue" (*Lady Barbarina,* 113). But now the "top" of Fifth Avenue had changed its posi-tion, and when James visited, the site of the Reservoir was being redevel-oped for the new Library, which he sees under construction, glad that it will not be a high-rise, so it will not require elevators ("intolerable symbol of the herded and driven state and of that malady of preference for gre-garious ways . . . by which the people about one seem driven"). He com-pares elevator doors to the guillotine (4.5.140). After commenting on the Presbyterian hospital, which makes him say that "if the *direct* pressure of New York is too often to ends that strike us as vulgar, the indirect is capa-ble . . . of these lurking effects of delicacy. The immediate expression is . . . of violence, but you may find there is something left, something kept back for you, if that has not from the first fairly deafened you" (4.5.141).

He closes with the Metropolitan Museum (Eighty-first Street and Fifth Avenue since 1879), replacing a museum that James had remembered on West Fourteenth Street, when the family had lived there (from 1847 to 1855). Saying nothing of the contents of the Museum, he comments on the money that backs it, and that has allowed for so much fake art—"the penalty of old error" (4.5.144) given by previous donors. Now the museum was dedicated to education, and the money was to go for "the most exquisite things—for *all* the most exquisite except creation, which was to be off the scene altogether; for art, selection, criticism, for knowledge, piety and taste." The education of beauty requires the dumping of old "acres of canvas" and "tons of marble" in order to establish a new identity, the old history is banished. James's irony is fine: "the Museum in short was going to be great, and in the geniality of the life to come, such sacrifices, though resembling those of the funeral-pile of Sardanapulus, dwindled to nothing."

THE BOWERY AND THEREABOUTS

The final chapter of this "short book" on New York is a coda that returns James to the East Side, and to his fascination with that and with the quality of difference opened up by New York's racial mixture. The visitor is in each case a spectator, a figure of superiority to the events witnessed, as his observation of poverty, for instance, has been that of the outsider; yet in each case he is not left entirely with a sense of cultural supremacy. He begins with a midwinter trip made one Saturday afternoon to the Windsor Theater, on Canal Street and the Bowery. The theater, which James speaks of as having known in his youth, had been built in 1826, and had gradually become more "popular," more working class in the years after 1839, when the "elite" theater district moved away from the area. The second section is on a German drinking hall on the East side, encountered in early summer, and the last begins with a Yiddish theater, also encountered in the summer night and then a little "establishment," a café specializing in Slav "local colour." The difference in the Bowery theater from the time he knew it before is that the audience then were homogeneous, though with plenty of Irish, but now are all immigrants, an "Oriental public."

A journey to the Bowery by electric car he characterizes almost cinematically as "like moving the length of an interminable cage, beyond the remoter of whose bars lighted shops . . . offered their Hebrew faces and Hebrew names," and he sees the journey as going "through depths of the Orient" (5.1.146).[32] In the theater, the real spectacle is offered by the audience, whose candy consumption (it recalls James on American teeth) leads to a meditation on the "material ease" with which candy is invested and on the smartness of American marketing—"the solicitation of sugar couldn't be so hugely and artfully organized if the response were not clearly proportionate. But how is the response itself organized . . . ?" (5.1.147). Again, the audience are at home, even though the play— American melodrama—is completely conventional, its "representation" quite removed from "the truth and facts of life." His question is whether the audience will submit to this form of schooling and accept these American tricks in entertainment. He gives a plot detail, which acts as an image for him of American tricks and traps and superior Yankee machinery—noticed in the hotel and the elevator—"a wonderful folding bed in which the villain of the piece, pursuing the virtuous heroine round and round the room and trying to leap over it after her, is at the young lady's touch of a hidden spring, engulfed as in the jaws of a crocodile." The machinery points up the skill in America for entrapping the immigrant into existent American platitudes, and ways of seeing. Or will there be a return of something repressed in this audience, resisting the Yankee machinery?

The second section implicitly recalls Dickens and Zola; James is not going into the "policed underworld"—as Dickens used to do—but nonetheless he is wandering, like a naturalist into poverty, into a subterranean beer cellar, which sets him wondering "of the forms of ability *consistent* with lowness; the question of the quality of intellect, the subtlety of character, the mastery of the art of life, with which the extremity of baseness may yet be associated" (5.2.150). The host of this cellar has no English, as the beer cellar sells no beer, and James comments on the achievement of the place, that its "charm," its "note of the exclusive" had been arrived at with a "beautifully fine economy" and that despite the tendency of "the American air" to reduce "so many aspects to a common denominator," certain "finer shades of delicacy and consistency" had recovered their rights. The section points to the idea of the inhabitants of this beer cellar as preserving an "unquenched individualism"; preserving in New York their difference and their integrity. In the last section, James recalls Yiddish theater, and a Yiddish actor from the East Side who appeared on Broadway, again posing an issue where the audience cannot recognize the language. James concludes, "Marked in New York, by many indications, this vagueness of ear as to differences, as to identities, of idiom" (5.3.153).

The last "establishment" James refers to lays on "local colour" and on the summer night James visited, he notes middle-European bourgeois immigrants there, and then speculates on how they are also "remote and indirect results" of the bourgeois American revolution. In contrast, the "exotic boss" with his modern "plans for the future" stands for an "inward assimilation of our heritage and point of view"—which means an ability to turn it in his own direction. This world of custom James thinks of as different from anything known at Delmonico's, the New York Swiss restaurant of the 1830s, which, on Madison Square, had represented a far different form of European immigration.[33] The passage finishes with an evocation of the establishment at night—the note is new in the writing of the city; the realization that the city has a 24-hour existence is a point James shares with Dreiser. Chicago and New York in *Sister Carrie* are nighttime cities; city lights best embody city energy. The description could recall a Degas or Manet picture of a café-concert, or even *The Bar at the Folies-Bergère*. Certainly, James gives the "impression" he has had, and then supplements it in memory,—but the contrast is nonetheless acute, firstly because the quality of "indifference" (the concept has been noted already) that marks out the urban scene in Paris is not there. T. J. Clark's influential reading of the new attitude of the self toward the public within urban space that he derives from a reading of Manet's *Bar at the Folies-Bergère* is worth recalling. Following in the spirit of Walter Benjamin, who used Simmel to theorize how the modern urban dweller exists in the city,[34] Clark quotes Simmel's essay "The Metropolis and Mental Life," which was written the year before James went to America, discussing the "blasé" outlook:

> an indifference towards the distinctions between things . . . the meaning and value of the distinctions between things, and therewith of the things themselves, are experienced as meaningless. They appear to the blasé person in a homogeneous, flat and grey colour with no one of them worthy of being preferred to another. This psychic mood is the correct subjective reflection of a complete money economy to the extent that money takes the place of all the manifoldness of things and expresses all qualitative distinctions between them in the distinction of "how much." To the extent that money, with its colourlessness and its indifferent quality, can become a common denominator of all values it becomes the frightful leveller—it hollows out the core of things, their peculiarities, their specific values and their uniqueness and incomparability in a way which is beyond repair. . . .

Clark compares this European perception with one of James's own figures: the telegraphist in the novella *In the Cage*.[35]

New York is unlike a European city in not being blasé. James even uses the word "innocent," as if thinking of his "American girl." He thinks, too, that this scene has never yet been reduced to literary notation—which again returns to Zola, and to a consideration of those American writers who had treated the East Side; and to think in the tailpiece at the end of the chapter, of what has so far been missed casts light on his own attempt to "do" New York, to face the challenge of what has never been represented yet. His feeling that the subject is too big for him gives him his form of being lost, but he is happy to be so. Here is the "tailpiece":

Who were all the people, and whence and whither and why in the good New York small hours? Where *was* the place after all, and what might it, or what might it not, truly, represent to slightly fatigued feasters who in a recess like a privileged opera-box at a *bal masque,* and still communicating with polyglot waiters, looked down from their gallery at a multitudinous supper, a booming orchestra, an elegance of disposed plants and flowers, a perfect organization an abyss of mystery? Was it "on" Third Avenue, on Second, on fabulous unattempted First? Nothing would induce me to cut down the romance of it, in remembrance, to a mere address, least of all to an awful New York one ... the ambiguity is the element in which the whole thing swims for me—so nocturnal, so bacchanal, so hugely hatted and feathered and flounced, yet apparently so innocent, almost so patriarchal again, and matching, in its mixture, with nothing one had elsewhere known. It breathed its simple "New York! New York!" at every impulse of inquiry; so that I can only echo contentedly, with analysis for once quite agreeably baffled, "Remarkable, unspeakable New York!" (5.3.155)

CHAPTER 8

The American Scene—III

THE PAST AND FUTURE
OF AMERICAN CITIES

PHILADELPHIA

James visited Philadelphia several times in early 1905, and his writing of the city begins with a prelude, distinguishing it from New York, and St. Louis from Chicago. Neither New York nor Chicago can be represented, but Philadelphia and St. Louis can. Their "sense" or "essence" (James plays with the word "sense") can be picked up (like scents), but of the first two cities, the "cluster of appearances can *have* no sense." James felt that in going south from New York—his direction for the rest of *The American Scene*—he will be able to make more sense of the city—and so he feels when he is staying in Rittenhouse Square. "Philadelphia was the American city of the large type, that didn't *bristle*"; he adds that Chicago, in comparison to St. Louis, "bristles" like a porcupine. It cannot be got at; while bristles also implies skyscrapers.[1] In Philadelphia, James notes that the place is not so much perpendicular but horizontal, so that he is not so often "hoisted or lowered by machinery." He notes that if Boston is not so much a place as a state of mind, Philadelphia is not so much a place as a state of consanguinity, a settled society. He notes in Philadelphia the "homogeneous" (9.2.208); that which he had looked for in Salem (8.2.197). (Homogeneity is not said to be a characteristic of St. Louis, which was then the fourth largest city in the United States.) Philadelphia brings together two states, "sane Society" and parallel to this, the "pestilential City"—a structure that he feels to be representative of American cities. It shows the "good neighbouring of the Happy Family and the Infernal Machine" (9.2.209), the family "indifferent" to the nature of the city.

James's response to Philadelphia is ambivalent. He refers to the old charm of William Penn's layout of streets, which made the city "homogeneous" and gave him the sense of a "vast, firm, chess-board . . . covered *all* over by perfect Philadelphians" (9.2.208–9). The layout meant the exclusion of the "alien," in that it defined "Philadelphia." Immigrants, he says, "may have been gathered in their hordes, in some vast quarter unknown to me, and of which I was to have no glimpse" (9.2.208). What counts as the city is not the city; in a spirit of irony, James thinks of the society at Philadelphia as like the ancien regime. The "coherence" (9.1.202, 9.4.218) is unreal, contrived. The third section speaks with pleasure of Independence Hall (1731–53, designed by Andrew Hamilton) as having given Philadelphia a start, architecture so right that it might be said to have suggested the celebrated *coup* of the Declaration of Independence. The building, with its heritage, has kept Philadelphia from being "vulgar"; it has been like the "nice family" every family should know—and which is not present in New York. Admiration for Robert Smith's Hall of the Guild of Carpenters (1773) follows; its attractiveness is that it is somehow hidden from the parallel structure of streets so that he feels that he could not find it again. The pleasure this gives: of secrecy, of something "behind," allows James to finish the section with a comparison to the city of London. It is an example of what James means in the last section, which begins with Philadelphia's old churches, Benjamin Franklin's grave, and the French artist Duplessis's portraits of Franklin, of "those shy things that speak, at the most . . . but of the personal adventure . . . of one's luck and of one's sensibility" (9.4.219). As with Boston, James criticizes what is epitomized in "a vast vacant Philadelphia street, a street not of Penn's creation and vacant of everything but an immeasurable bourgeois blankness" (9.4.220). Again the Tennysonian note; the street gives the other side that Philadelphia society denies—"gregariousness." As James looks there and at the University of Pennsylvania, he speaks of what he has noticed as typical of Philadelphian society in using the image of "the happy family given up, though quite on 'family' lines, to all the immediate beguilements and activities; the art . . . of cultivating, with such gaiety as might be, a brave civic blindness" (9.4.220).

The one excrescence on this "large smooth surface" that he comments on is the Pennsylvania Penitentiary, and here James refers back to *American Notes*. Like Dickens, James relates the prison to the city, "this huge house of sorrow affected me, as uncannily, of the City itself, the City of all the cynicisms and impunities with which my friends had, from far back, kept plating, as with the old silver of their sideboards, the armour of their social consciousness. It [James alludes to Haviland's castle design for the prison] made the whole place, with some of its oddly antique aspects and its oddly modern freedoms, look doubly cut off from the world of light and ease" (9.4.221). The syntax makes the "place" "uncannily" both Philadelphia and the prison. The "uncanny" seems to have so much of its Freudian senses and links with the idea of the haunted house. The prisoners ghost the people of the city; the prison is of the city, though it has been moved out from its center. The prisoners are the ghosts. The uncanny is that which ought to have remained hidden but which has come to light.[2] James has spoken of the "alien" who is not visible; but what is excluded from Philadelphian bourgeois life returns in imitative form (in a compulsion to repeat, which is also part of the uncanny). James seems overwhelmed by the comparison so that he adds that "the suggestions here were vast, however; too many of them swarm, and my imagination must defend itself as best it can." It defends itself, however, not by a tighter form of writing, but by letting the grammar apply to both things at once. The structure of Philadelphia is prisonous, armored against the other—Lacan speaks of "the armour of an alienating identity," making identity itself a neurotic structure[3]—so that the word "bristled," at first said *not* to be appropriate to Philadelphia, turns out to be the right word to apply to that which maintains an identity—which is, nonetheless, to recall James's discussion at the beginning of the chapter, indescribable, unrepresentable—in a prisonous or militaristic way. Philadelphia appears a city of repression; just as its prison combines medieval castellations and a medieval moat to protect itself against the other—as an image of the city of Philadelphia, with its organized "society"—or, to keep the other out of the city.

The prison contains oddly antique aspects (the separate system) and oddly modern freedoms. James comments on those freedoms when he notes that inside the prison is the atmosphere of a club. The writing is Dickensian, following parts of the treatment of the Marshalsea in *Little Dorrit,* and it adds to the sense of how the prison replicates city society. One "charming reprieved murderer" brings out in his club manner just how much "smooth surface" is at work in both city *and* prison. James compares the prison atmosphere to "the harmony of a convent" (supplying another prisonous image, as in *The American* and *The Portrait of a Lady,* the convent being also dedicated to the cultivation of the surface). He adds that if it were not for the prison atmosphere, there would be no suspicion that the prisoner was a criminal; "the fact of prison" (9.4.222) produces, defines the criminal, a point that resonates with Foucault's *Discipline and Punish.* The space delineated architecturally as a heterotopia constructs the criminal, but it also acts as a critique of the city, which has wished to separate its criminality from its own organized being. It is on the basis of such exclusion and such production of the criminal other that the city maintains its sense of coherence, its representability. James finishes the chapter on Philadelphia with a reminder of hospitality at an old country house, "virtually distant from town," again, allowing for a repression of the city and its doubles. In this company, he is carried back to the atmosphere of an "Irish society of the classic time," existing in "fiction and anecdote"—a last reminder of something non-real in the Philadelphia he sees. Although the chapter has opened with an affirmation of Philadelphia's being as coherent and homogeneous, and James is drawn to this, that is based on a refusal of an "uncanny," which makes the chapter ultimately discard such a wish that the city could be seen as representable. It is a move that will reappear in discussions of later, Southern cities, as in January and February 1905, he traveled south in the States, before returning to New York to go west.

BALTIMORE

Traveling south was to get some sun in winter, but almost failing since snow persisted as far south as Charleston. The American Scene takes this as a hint that "the American land and the American people . . . abhor . . . a discrimination. They are reduced together, under stress, to making discriminations" (10.1.225). So, the way to the South in the Pullman was "monotonous"—a "crude universal white." The journey south, into a region that had resisted American urban modernization before the Civil War, and had been virtually destroyed by the North's will to power during the war, was into a present trying to revive a past that still required a "perpetual repudiation" since the past to be revived, in a spirit of willed melancholia, could only be a repressed one, confirming more and more a sense of absence in America. The final absence is in Florida, whose economic triumph as a tourist venue leads him back, via a discussion of its hotels, to what he had said about New York, which is a reminder of New York's hegemony in relation to the United States. As James spends time in cities whose current and historical repression forbids them to be cities, he becomes consciously more disturbed by America, while his perception of Florida is of a single drive, which brings out forcibly something within New York; a push toward progress that does not allow for alternative lives or possibilities.

Baltimore had to be seen a second time, after the snow, in June, which provides the conditions under which James writes about it. His sense of the city is of an absence of "friction." It has no resistance to offer to him (this is worse than Philadelphia's absence of "bristle"), so much that it appears "a sort of perversely cheerful city of the dead" (10.2.229), a thought that goes with the recollection that this is a Southern city under the shadow of the Civil War; indeed, it was Baltimore prosecessionists who had first shot the Union soldiers (19 April 1861). And what "connection" did that violence have with the present city? The peacefulness of Baltimore James attributes to the peace since the war—which would make it highly repressed. He continues that in June, the town season was over and houses closed up. Baltimore architecture is presented in genteel terms ("little ladylike squares"), which leads him to speak of the city's "virtue"; not just the absence of "vice" but an "absence of the conception of the imagination of it." And at that point James draws in "the European scene" (10.2.230) for comparison, providing a rationale for his text. The European scene (by which he means the European city, as the American scene means the American city) looks "as perverse as it practically is." The American substitutes for that form of sophistication: "the cash-register, the ice-cream freezer, the lightning elevator, the 'boy's paper.'" James's idea of the "south," premised on Naples or Seville, is sexualized, but America's "citronic belt" is "Protestantized," producing "a Methodism of the subtropic night, a Methodism of the orange and the palm" (10.2.231), and implicitly opposing American "vice" to European "perversion."

James returns to the thousand "European" values that are absent in the South, but he allows that America does not admit of the idea of "privation," and he speaks of other values that arise in their place "the marked character of which, for comparative sociology, is that they are not at all as other values" (10.3.236). Here James names his discipline: comparative sociology. Looking for other things different from Europe, he gives as an instance the "Country Club" (sec. 4), which provides him with a metonymy for what "Democracy, pushing and breaking the ice like an Arctic explorer, is making of things." The country club, outside the town, and so again redefining the identity of the city, is based on "the conception of the young Family as a clear social unit," and the Family in America is lateral, not perpendicular, as in Europe—i.e., "expressing itself thus rather by number than by name," making no distinction between old and young, and not beset with the European emphasis on "differences."

WASHINGTON

With "Washington," James opens by saying that he visited the city twice, firstly for a week after Philadelphia, on the way South, which Edel and Kaplan describe, detailing particularly James's meeting with Roosevelt (Edel, 5:264–67, Kaplan, 487–89) and secondly in late April 1905. Before that, James had been in Washington in early 1882 (Edel, 2:458–64), and he had written about the city in the short story *Pandora* (1884), which, he wrote, would give him the "chance to *do* Washington, so far as I know it, and work in my few notes, and my very lovely memories, of last winter. I might even *do* Henry Adams and his wife."[4] In 1905 he stayed with the widowed Adams. Perhaps the first substantial novel based on Washington had been *The Gilded Age: A Tale of Today* (1873) where Twain and Charles Dudley Warner give a guided tour to the city in chapter 24, "The City of Washington." The style owes much, like the rest of the book, to *American Notes* and *Martin Chuzzlewit,* but without the anticolonial note, making fun of the Capitol and its murals ("the delirium tremens of art"), the mud, the Washington Memorial (still uncompleted, so "a factory chimney with the top broken off") and then satirizing members of Congress, such as Senator Dilworthy, who was based on a Kansas senator trying to buy reelection. *Pandora* is also satirical about Washington, and mildly so about the president (probably Chester A. Arthur). Writing about it in 1905, James's tone is different; and he realizes that he cannot attribute all of the charm to that of Nature.

He begins with George Washington's home at Mount Vernon, which had been acquired by the Mount Vernon Ladies' Association at the end of the 1850s and restored during the rest of the century. Commentators on Mount Vernon have noted its relation (as James does) to the picturesque, on account of the landscaping of the building and the idea of a connection in Washington's mind between liberty and the discovery of natural beauty, which might connect with Washington's link, in writings of 1785, between architecture and "the republican style" of living.[5] Something of this seeps through the whole chapter on Washington. James notes the presence of smiles as a "medium of exchange" both at Washington's home and at the capital city; in the city he says that the park atmosphere in May covered up the "unsurmounted bourgeois character" of the place, so that the bronze generals (James borrows from Wilde here)[6] can be nearly imagined as great garden gods. Mount Vernon with its "rich interference of association" (*The American Scene,* II.1.248) gives him so much that he feels able to say that the place is not just Washington's, but Washington, which means that the chapter's title has several referents: the city, Mount Vernon; the character of America as summed up in George Washington; Washington as a signifier of America.

Returning to the city, he notes that it has two faces; one the public, official and monumental, monological, "overweighted by a single Dome and overaccented by a single Shaft" (II.2.250); this part of Washington he still finds provisional, "never emerging from its flatness, after the fashion of other capitals, into the truly, the variously, modelled and rounded state." The other Washington is "a small company of people engaged perpetually in conversation and . . . singularly destitute of conspicuous marks or badges." This is also "the city itself, *the* national capital," and within this plurality of referents for "Washington" James adds that "the charming company of the foreground . . . which referred itself so little to the sketchy back-scene, the monstrous Dome and Shaft, figments of the upper air, the pale colonnades and mere myriad-windowed Buildings, was the second of the two faces" (11.2.251). The "properest name" of Washington—displacing its imperial functions, decentering it, so that it is not a "proper" name—is "the City of Conversation"; so James said he had known it from his previous visit, perhaps because of the presence of Adams and, more, his wife, Marion "Clover" Hooper. It is as though the city's function is to make him forget for an hour "the colossal greed of New York"—America's other capital.[7]

Yet Washington's subject in talking is itself; and here James distinguishes the city from London, which cannot get away from itself because everything is in it; in contrast, Washington is "in positive quest of an identity of some sort" (11.2.253), trying to become something not monological; hence James helps it with drawing out the significance of the plurality of identities in the city and by the plurality of referents in the chapter title. Yet that identity is also non-American in the sense that the conversation here, which would provide elements of the plurality implied in what Bakhtin calls dialogism, is not business related, because the people of Washington are not in business. "From the moment it is adequately borne in mind that the business-man, in the United States, may . . . never hope to be anything *but* a business-man, the size of the field he so abdicates is measured. . . . It lies there waiting, pleading from all its pores, to be occupied—the lonely waste, the boundless gaping 'void' of society; which is but a rough name for all the *other* so numerous relations with the world he lives in that are imputable to the civilized being." The Jamesian theme of an absence at the center returns; and it is a space to be filled by the woman, who must, then, represent the other of the monological spirit that also threatens Washington.

The third section turns, then, to the American woman, continuing the gendering of the American scene, implicit in the discussion of New England and returned to in describing Baltimore. James refers to the power of advertising when he says the woman has been made "a new human convenience" like the "stoves, refrigerators, sewing-machines, type-writers, cash-registers" that have done so much for "the American name." Yet he also refers to her advantage in not having had to deal with "a hundred of the 'European' complications and dangers . . . in which she had . . . to take upon herself a certain training for freedom." Kept in a position from which criticism of this was consistently absent, she arrived on the American scene "the least criticized object," and here, in Washington, James feels that she is the figure who may appear in some new light, since up till now the American male has allowed the woman to represent everything unrelated to business, but in Washington, something has had to be learned by the male. But can the male catch up with the woman? James cannot answer even for the "Washington group."

The fourth section turns to the White House (so renamed by Theodore Roosevelt), and to the 1902 McMillan Commission plans for improving Washington as the federal capital (I will return to this), and to the "wondrous" new Library of Congress, an example, James thinks, where "the violent waving of the pecuniary wand *has* incontinently produced interest" (11.4.261).[8] Admiring the White House, and the Clark Mills statue of Andrew Jackson on a rearing horse (1852), "as archaic as a Ninevite king, prancing and rocking through the ages," he finds it possible to think of ghosts in relation to the White House and, through the statues of Lafayette and Rochambeau lately set up in Lafayette Square (the work of the French sculptors Alexandre Falguière and Antonin Mercié, and of Ferdinand Hamar), of the possibility of "fantasticating" the national past (11.4.262)—giving it a double meaning, giving it, effectively, an uncanny. Concerning the new plans for the "artistic" federal city, which were derived from F. L. Olmsted Jr., Burnham and McKim, all working in the spirit of the Chicago World's Fair, and modeling the "City Beautiful" of parks and boulevards, he wonders what effect this architecture will have on the "civic consciousness." He is not sure whether it will multiply the possibilities of plurality in Washington, but he adds:

> It comes back to what we constantly feel, throughout the country, to what the American scene everywhere depends on for half its appeal or its effect; to the fact that the social conditions, the material, pressing and persuasive, make the particular experiment of demonstration, whatever it may pretend to, practically a new and incalculable thing. This general Americanism is often the one tag of character attaching to the case . . . the thing is happening, or will have to happen, in the American way . . . which is more different from all other native ways . . . than any of these latter are different from each other; and the question is of how, each time, the American way will see it through. (11.4.263)

James defines a kind of modernism different from the European, and this registers the sense that whatever future America has, it is unpredictable, but that America has always worked on such an uncertain future. The new architecture will have to occur, despite the playful statuary memorializing the past, "in the historic void," whereas in Europe, new building takes character from what is already there. "The danger 'in Europe' is of their having too many things to say, and too many others to distinguish these from; the danger in the States is of their not having things enough—with enough tone and resonance furthermore to give them" (11.4.263). James is drawing conclusions, without any of Dickens's or Trollope's negativity about Washington; but one of his "liveliest" impressions of Washington is that "there is not, outside the mere economic, enough native history, recorded or current, to go round" (11.4.264). It is a point that will recur in his consideration of the Confederate cities, especially Richmond.

As he had started with Mount Vernon, he finishes with the Capitol, where "association" reigns; his generosity of feeling toward it shows in the un-ironic comparison he makes with St. Peter's in Rome. He speaks of the Capitol's power of "democratic assimilation" (11.5.265), making everything in and of the States unify; this is in the context of a discussion where it seems like a massive national opera house, like Garnier's Paris Opera: James speaks of "the great terraced Capitol hill, with its stages and slopes, staircases and fountains." He speaks of the impression given of a "large, final benignity in the Capitol, giving the impression of a "huge flourishing Family" running a business, "where, in a myriad open ledgers, which offer no obscurity to the hereditary head for figures, the account of their colossal revenue is kept" (11.5.266). James could almost have had in mind Degas's 1873 picture of his New Orleans relatives in the cotton-buying office, *Portraits in an Office, New Orleans*[9]—a study of white cotton, white newspapers, and black clothes, of cotton being teased out like the sperm oil spreading everywhere in *Moby-Dick* (chap. 94), and dollars being dumped into a wicker basket—except that James's sense of the family (which repeats an emphasis in "Baltimore") does not envisage Degas's division of labor—there are no women in Degas's picture. The domesticity of the image is James's way of recording the power of the ideology that the Capitol embodies. Turning from the "inner aspects of the vast monument for the outer" he thinks of it as "visibly concerned but in immeasurable schemes of which it can consciously remain the centre," those schemes being linked with the future expansion of Washington, with "the great Federal future." The Capitol's capacity is to make the subject feel at the center, to draw him in within a "marble embrace" (the implications are of death), which is the other side of the "vast democratic lap." James's surprise is to see one morning, while walking around, "a trio of Indian braves, braves dispossessed of forest and prairie, but as free of the builded labyrinth as they had ever been of these; also arrayed in neat pot-hats, shoddy suits and light overcoats, with their pockets, I am sure, full of photographs and cigarettes" (11.5.267). The description seems patronizing, but it is not quite that: it follows, rather, the way these Indians have been made "specimens"—museum pieces—"on show, of what the

Government can do with people with whom it was supposed to be able to do nothing." They have been got out of their habitat of "forest and prairie" and been put into cheap suits, exemplifying the power of American government so to reduce people to exhibition status (the Capitol is no longer the theater, but the stage itself, a space for display—like the Paris Opera). It also makes them tourists in Washington, confirming while it seems to assimilate their marginal status.

James concludes: "they seemed . . . for a mind fed betimes on the Leatherstocking Tales, to project as in a flash an image in itself immense, but foreshortened and simplified—reducing to a single smooth stride the bloody footsteps of time. One rubbed one's eyes, but there, at its highest polish, was the brazen face of history, and there, all about one, immaculate, the printless pavements of the State." The ability to polish recalls the section on the prison in Philadelphia, and the sense of that city as a smooth surface; now, the final victory of the white American population over the Indians is told in this reduction of them to tourists, in the subordination of a history of oppression to the state's "printless pavements"—covering over, as if by white marble, effacing a past, and making the other walk on state ground as the dispossessed.[10] It is the power of centralizing monological control, against which James can only put the resistance of Washington as the "city of conversation."

THE SOUTH: RICHMOND

In 1883, when at Washington, James had meant to travel into the southern states, but did not. A hint of his fascination with the South as the other appears, however, in the use of Basil Ransom, from Mississippi, in *The Bostonians.* But it was Virginia that was at the center of glamorizings of "the Lost Cause" and of novel writings, such as those of lawyer John Esten Cooke, biographer of Lee[11] and author of *The Virginia Comedians: Or, Old Days in the Old Dominion* (1854), source material for Thackeray's *The Virginians.*[12] With Cooke, and with Thackeray, the "legend" of the Old Dominion began before the war: James plays upon it when he refers to "the old Virginian dignity" (12.3.279).[13] James came upon the scene of the very center of the mythologizing of the old Confederacy, and he sees Richmond as "thin" in the poverty of the idea and the poverty with which the idea was dressed.

James stayed for the first three days of February at the Hotel Jefferson at Richmond, Virginia,[14] the old Confederate capital, one of the cities of the "supreme holocaust" (12.2.272), registering the War as the national trauma; and looking for the South's "latent poetry" (12.2.271).[15] Finding Richmond a blank, a void, he reflects on this as the irony that spells out the emptiness of the Southern idea, which he describes as "a world re-arranged, a state solidly and comfortably seated and tucked-in, in the in-terest of slave-produced cotton" (12.2.275)—a rural society, a fake pastoral. James's source for his southern history is the Cleveland indus-trialist James Ford Rhodes, *History of the U.S. from the Compromise of 1850,* which in seven volumes (1893–1907) reached 1877, the end of Recon-struction. James recalls how the "Slave-scheme" required a rewriting of "the reality of things"—of American modernity. "History, the history of everything, would have to be rewritten *ad usum Delphini* [for the use of the Dauphin]—the Dauphin being in this case the budding Southern mind" (12.2.275). James does not think of the Southern mind as dying out; rather, it is "budding" with the markers of an alternative modernity, but requiring, as in the North, the "perpetual repudiation of the past." Such repudiation takes the form of "a general and a permanent quarantine . . . the eternal bowdlerization of books and journals . . . all literature and all art on an expurgatory index . . . an active and ardent propaganda; the re-organization of the school, the college, the university, in the interest of the new criticism." This reaction away from modernity James calls "queer and quaint and benighted" and "rococo," and he repeats the word "provincial" three times to comment on this culture's antagonism to any drive toward plurality in Northern urban culture.

James has moved from the consideration of immigration in thinking about Northern cities, to the Indian in considering Washington, and now to the Afro-American in writing about the South. He writes how his own subjectivity has felt threatened by the sight of the black at Washing-ton "'in possession of his rights as a man'"—a reminder of the power of Jim Crow legislation that kept the black invisible in the city, only to be seen by James at the railway station, that most democratizing of places. From his own loss of ease, he intuits how the black was "on the nerves" of the South, and he intuits the South allegorically as "a figure . . . impossi-bly seated in an invalid-chair" (12.2.277)—a figure frozen in time, a Dickensian image; or one anticipative of Rosa Coldfield, in Faulkner's *Absalom! Absalom!,* trapped for 43 years in her home, in the "office," as her father had called it—the word recalls Isabel Archer, when she is first seen in her father's home in Albany in *The Portrait of a Lady.* This invalid figure compares with the woman referred to in the passage on Concord, ignor-ing the presence of death (*The American Scene,* 8.1.192–93), and the image intensifies in the section on Charleston.

At that point James looks down at the James River, and at the water-side industries, and recalls that the Libby prison (for Unionist soldiers) stood there. It is the second prison of *The American Scene:* its ghosts still there, though the structure was gone. He remembers "a wide, steep street,

a place of traffic, of shops and offices and altogether shabby Virginia vehicles, these last in charge of black teamsters" (machines controlling people), which brings back upon him with "violence" the meaning of "the
negro [sic] really at home." He turns to Jefferson's old State House, then
under reconstruction, but has little to say about Jefferson, that "excellent
architect out of books," as Latrobe called him,[16] in contrast to the way he
had situated Washington and Mount Vernon. He passes Thomas Crawford's Washington Monument, which was begun as a commission in 1849
and completed by Randoph Rogers during the Civil War years. The
sculpture places Washington on horseback on a pedestal high above
standing heroic figures—famous Virginians, James notices—and seated
allegorical figures and military trophies round the base. The whole is a
"pyramidal accumulation of pedestals, layer after layer,"[17] breaking with
neoclassical monumentality, and the equestrian statue, new in America,
shows a new preference for sculptural realism over an architectural monument, in an effort to co-opt the national hero (Washington) for Southern values, and as a monumental hero. James picks up on a moment of
crisis (over abolition), which uses the sculptural to monumentalize a previous century in the interest of serving that crisis. This makes the sculpture of its period, "indescribably archaic" and its context, the world of the
mid-century, seem "remote and quaint and queer" so that he adds, thinking of the relationship between ideology and the form of statuary, that "it
is positive that of the 'old' American sculpture, about the Union, a rich
study might be made" (12.3.279).[18] He sees Jefferson Davis's "ample white
house, a pleasant, honest structure in the taste of sixty or eighty years
since," which had been Davis's official residence during the war, and he
looks at an American church, which leads him to a point he had already
noted in Washington; that that city "bristles" with "national affirma-
tions"—which he lists—but one thing is missing: "the existence of a religious faith on the part of the people is not remotely suggested" so that the
city shows as if a figure was painted but the "white oval of the face itself
were innocent of the brush." Again, the whiteness, as though this is symptomatic of the way an American city shows itself publicly. "The field of
American life is as bare of the Church as a billiard-table of a centre-piece"
(12.3.281). It is another reminder of how shallow the history is; how little
that particular interest has told, in comparison to Europe. James then reverts to the particular church Jefferson Davis attended and whence he was
called from his pew on 2 April 1865 with the news that Richmond could
no longer be defended and must be evacuated.[19] James is told this story by
an old Confederate soldier, serving as sexton. He sees it as an example, in
"melancholy Richmond," of how the leaders of a "great movement," as
they supposed, made themselves "not interesting." The city stands for "the

trivialization of history," and no accretion of "legend"—no writing, no future literature, no inscription (another meaning of "legend")—can supplement this absence; this point that the history is gone and cannot be "nursed" (12.3.284, 285) into life, by however much "rancour" (12.3.284)—which is the predominant spirit of the South, and its cause of melancholy. James's word "rancour" is exactly Nietzsche's *ressentiment,* the driving spirit of the bourgeoisie.

He passes back to Jefferson Davis's White House, then a museum of the relics of the Confederacy, the work of the Daughters of the Confederacy.[20] He is shown round by a little old lady and he finds looking at the same sad glass case a farmer, "for all the world like the hero of a famous novel—a gallant and nameless, as well as a very handsome, young Virginian." Perhaps James thinks of The Virginians, and Harry Warrington fighting for the Old Dominion in the American War of Independence—as his like would fight the Civil War. This farmer is still ready to fight the Union soldier, though "platonically," James feels. Yet "it came to me that, though he wouldn't have hurt a Northern fly, there were things (ah, we had touched on some of these!) that, all fair, engaging, smiling, as he stood there, he would have done to a Southern negro" (12.3.286). James leaves the section with this allusion to white supremacy. In the library—containing *penetralia,* unlike the Boston library—James finds an "old mutilated Confederate solider," which leads him to consideration of the monument to General Robert Lee (1807–1870), set up in 1890, 20 years after his death.

This statue was the work of sculptor Antonin Mercié, who worked on the statue of Lafayette in Washington that James admired. The sculpture, implicitly compared with Crawford's monument to Washington, is placed at the end of a long residential street (Monument Avenue), virtually in a suburb of Richmond, at a meeting of roads, "somehow empty in spite of being ugly, and yet expressive in spite of being empty" (12.4.289). The emptiness of the surroundings comments on the futility of Lee's riding high (on a pedestal, designed by the Beaux-Arts architect, Paul Pujol), his attempt to be above it all.[21] "As I looked back, before leaving it, as Lee's stranded, bereft image, which time and fortune have so cheated of half the significance, and so I think, of half the dignity, of great memorials, I recognized something more than the melancholy of a lost cause. The whole infelicity speaks of a cause that could never have been gained" (12.4.290). James walks away, leaving the image indeed stranded. The "lost cause" refers to the rhetoric deployed in the years after the war that sacralized Jackson, Davis, and Lee, and made out that the past did not need to happen the way it did. James's dry "cause that could never have been gained" refers to the sense that the South has repudiated its past; still rewriting it in denial of its trauma.

CHARLESTON

On 10 February 1905 James arrived at Charleston, having begun his "induction as to the nature of the South." He came from Biltmore, the Vanderbilt estate carved out of 200 square miles taken from black sharecroppers, by Pullman (the first time he refers to this train) from which he feels his separation from both the black and white population. It is the moment when he reflects that in America, you become professional in doing most things for yourself, whereas in Europe, you remain an amateur. Waiting for two hours for a train, he reflects on the South giving him the sense of "open gates"—unlike the North's "closed" gates, of a "Margin" open before him. These open gates seem to offer a promise that the South has not taken up; James thinks that with all that America has taken up thus far, there is still much more, and "the fact that, with so many things present, so few of them are not on the way to becoming other, and possibly altogether different, conduces to the peculiar interest and, one often feels tempted to add, to the peculiar irritation of the country" (13.1.296). The lack of otherness, the absence of difference, is the clue to these last sections of *The American Scene*.

In Charleston, looking for "the South before the War" (13.2.297)—Thackeray's Charleston—he compares the houses with Italian provincial—the word again—*palazzi*. He is attracted by the houses' real walls and real gardens, unknown in the North, but which allow for the feeling of being "*within*"; so that, he says, "one sacrificed the North, with its mere hard conceit of virtuously meeting exhibition—much as if a house were just a metallic machine, number so-and-so in a catalogue—one sacrificed it on the spot to this finer feeling for the enclosure" (13.2.297). The house as the machine is *The Ivory Tower* theme; James rejects in the Northern house the necessity for a façade (a "hard conceit") and its denial of privacy. The façade sets up a false appearance in relation to the outside, while also not allowing separation inside. The house at Charleston, built with the side, not the front, to the street, places its "deep gallery" or verandah out of sight, beyond the entry through a door in the garden wall, and the life beyond the garden wall may be imagined to have gone on as before, unchanged since the "great folly" of the war.[22] James admits to having tried to think of his hotel in the same way, as a *palazzo*, where in his room "the ghost of a rococo tradition, the tradition of the transatlantic south, memory of other lands, glimmered generally in the decoration" (13.2.298). And that draws James back to the topos of the American hotel, which "constitutes for vast numbers of people the richest form of existence," and he includes the Pullman in this, as hotel-like, and so carrying in its amenities, "almost *all* the facts of American life."[23] Nothing is hidden, American life can be seen as it is; but the absence of critique James thinks this implies makes everything "provisional," an "instalment, a current number, like that of the morning paper . . . like the hero of a magazine novel . . ." (13.2.300). These comments relate to those on New York skyscrapers (2.1.61), as those on the hotel return to the Waldorf-Astoria and emphasize that *The American Scene* is urban critique throughout. The dominance of the hotel upon the people in it had appeared at Richmond, and is noted here: "the strong vertical light of a fine domed and glazed cortile,[24] the spacious and agreeable dining-hall of the inn, had rested on the human scene as with an effect of a mechanical pressure" (13.2.300). The section continues with a joint emphasis on Charleston's charm and on "thinness," and on the city's "deficiency of life"—a note that continues through to his calling Florida "weak" (13.2.303) as far as gaining from it any sustained impression is concerned.

James describes looking out to Fort Sumter from the battery, fired on by the Confederacy (12 April 1861), and thinking of the words of his companion in Charleston. This was Owen Wister, author of the Wild West novel, *The Virginian: A Horseman of the Plains* (1902) and of *Lady Baltimore* (1906), set in Charleston. Wister said, "Filled as I am . . . with the sadness and sorrow of the South, I never . . . look out to the old betrayed Forts without feeling my heart harden again to steel." The aggression is a reminder of Wister's friendship with Roosevelt, and of the masculinity that made Wister entitle the first chapter of *The Virginian,* "Enter the Man." Something which accords with his use of Basil Ransom, made James relate to *The Virginian,*[25] whose hero is a compound of Washington, Lincoln, and Roosevelt (the novel's dedicatee), but it points to a splitting at the heart of that cult of masculinity, part of its sentimentalizing, and associated with its rejection of Northern cities with their immigrants and mixed population—which made it prefer Wyoming—that it also reveres the old aristocracy of Charleston. It makes a fetish of the matriarchy of the old town, its women insisting on their bereavement and on the lost cause. "Lady Baltimore" is the name of a type of cake consumed at the tea house known as the Woman's Exchange, where James was taken by Wister (13.3.306). Neither masculinity nor the feminine are inspected in Wister's conservative modernity: modern in that it pushes into the West, conservative in that it dislikes urban culture.

James, who certainly does not criticize Wister, in comparison to Wister's modern aggressivity, calls firing on Fort Sumter the "antique folly" and cannot take the place so seriously, cannot imagine it rousing such emotions. The city does not fit with its historical past; it gives no hint how to read that past. He has already compared Charleston to "a handsome pale person . . . prepared for romantic interment" (13.2.301) and

here he continues to characterize Charleston as "a city of gardens and absolutely of no men"—the women being seen behind garden walls makes
him think of "the byways of some odd far East, infected with triumphant
women's rights" (13.3.305). The conceit is witty, but it still means that
"the little melancholy streets" are "clad in a rigour of mourning." He
notes St. Michael's Church, built in the mid-eighteenth century, with its
"high, complicated, inflated spire," which he likes and finds has an "air of
reality" (13.3.310), and he admires its churchyard, as he admires the
Cemetery on the edge of the lagoon (to call it the "possible site of some
Venice that had never mustered," is to draw attention to missed chances,
as the cemeteries confirm the sense of sadness and sorrow: James makes
the place altogether suggestive for another version of *The Aspern Papers*).
He visits a country club, and the "Exchange," principal setting for *Lady
Baltimore,* which leads him to speak of Charleston as "feminized"
(13.3.307). Thinking that the only book of distinction to have appeared
from the South was W. E. B. Du Bois's *The Souls of Black Folk* (1903),[26] as
contrary a text to Wister's texts as possible (though Wister came from
Philadelphia, he had a Southern context as well), he concludes that the
South's only interest had been slavery, collapsing the place into vacancy,
and that anything of value in Charleston had predated the South's
"monomania," which no little "modernism" now could replace.

Charleston was the first American city to designate an historical district (in 1931), but James reads it, like other cities in the South, as in-
validlike, holding on in a present that enables no sense of the past. The
writing implicitly lets it go; just as it recognizes that it could not assume
an existence at all as a city, without letting go of its own repression (of
race), which has made it the tiny unformed being it is. In James appears
the strongest rejection of Thackerayan values.

FLORIDA

The chapter on Florida, detailing his "pilgrimage to Palm Beach," opens
with James's comments on the breakdown of social existence in the
South, with comments on the absence of personal service from the black
population and on the prevalence of "bagmen" and "drummers"—commercial travelers. A "drummer," Bartlett's *Dictionary* noted in 1860, was "a
person employed by city houses to solicit the custom of country merchants." Both types speak of the hegemony of a certain American urban
culture (Drouet, the "travelling canvasser for a manufacturing house" in
Sister Carrie [p. 3] is called a "drummer") and James, in Dickensian mode,
comments on their prevalence at hotel breakfasts—when he is not noticing the "lone breakfasting child" in the restaurant with the "'run' of the

bill of fare" (14.1.313). James thinks of these figures occupying a gap in the "social landscape," pointing to the absence of "other possibilities in man than the mere possibility of getting the better of his fellow-man over a 'trade'" (14.1.315). He calls the drummers "unformed, undeveloped, unrelated," an instance of how far distant James is from Dreiser, who could find novelistic interest in such a type. These considerations that imply his own alienation come to fullness while he is waiting at the station at Savannah in Georgia: all that he saw of that city, which he reads by the young women and men who say "more about American manners than any other single class" (14.2.316). Consideration of the woman, brought forward in "the great glare of her publicity" leads to comparison with the bagmen "for affirmation of presence, for immunity from competition" and James imagines the woman pleading on her behalf in her defense that she has been overparted, because she has to provide all the grace, all the interest "that isn't the mere interest on the money." The "American social order" becomes "a great blank unnatural mother." While the daughters of the system (literal and not) have emerged, the "American mother" (14.2.318)—a support system that would recognize the woman in American society—remains "blank."

Via the "great moving proscenium" of the Pullman, which confirms an alienated gaze on the traveler, as James's view at Savannah was also alienated, James arrives at Jacksonville, and becomes a *flâneur,* smoking in a little public garden outside his hotel in "such a Southern sky as I had dreamed of"—where "it mattered not a scrap that the public garden was new and scant and crude, and that Jacksonville is not a name to conjure with," while the river and "the various structures, now looking through the darkness, that more or less adorned its banks" allow him to think Byronically, i.e., in a nonfocused way, about the place, where any one view has the capacity to "figure . . . any old city of the South" (14.2.319). Such is allowed by "the velvet air, the extravagant plants, the palms, the oranges, the cacti, the architectural fountain, the florid local monument, the cheap and easy exoticism, the sense as of people feeding, off in the background, very much *al fresco,* that is on queer things and with flaring lights." Two points suggest themselves: the importance of looking at the city at night; secondly, that James himself is constructed as a Southerner by the experience of Jacksonville, as the romanticism indicates and the archaeology of Southern romanticism depends upon having a confused sense of Italy (thus we note that James misquotes: it is not Byron who asked where he was in Italy, but Samuel Rogers; not at all the same romantic).

From there, James heads in the Pullman for Palm Beach, the resort that had been developed in the 1890s by the Gilded Age Standard Oil businessman Henry Morrison Flagler in Standard Oil, as a terminus to his East Coast Railway (he was to go on to Miami and Key West).[27] Palm Beach was to be another Newport. James recalls the world of the English adventure novelist Mayne Reid's *The War Trail,* and of the fictitious Florida of "the Seminoles and the Everglades, of the high old Spanish Dons and the passionate Creole beauties" (*The American Scene,* 14.3.322). Mayne Reid had been in the United States and fought in the Mexican War, and glamorized the frontier, the mustang, and settlement in the West; and James recalls Reid's appeal to think in how many ways the South preexisted for him in romantic form. He stayed at The Breakers, a wooden hotel designed for Flagler by McDonald and McGuire (1896), shut in within the "great sphere of the hotel . . . covering one in as with high, shining crystal walls"—an image of enclosure that recalls the machine-world, and the sense of America being "hotel civilization" (14.3.323). The difference between this hotel world and that of New York is that here there is nothing else; the "'national' life"—a life bound by class, as James makes obvious—has become "the sublime hotel spirit." James takes the occasion of the hotel accidentally not having any food for him at the time of his arrival to note how the hotel practices upon "the great national ignorance of many things," which it then converts into "extraordinary appetites, such as can be but expensively sated." Tastes that the hotel spirit has not nurtured, it cannot satisfy. James picks on this to note how America produces "the all-gregarious and generalized life," exactly what the hotel symbolizes. It is another form of imprisonment; James speaks of being "beguiled and caged" (14.3.325), caught in "the common mean . . . [in] the reduction of everything to an average of decent suitability"—and learning this comes over to him as a "betrayal" of what he has come to Florida to find: there is nothing else in Florida but the hotel spirit.

The next section looks at two superior buildings, the Royal Poinciana Hotel (1894, built for Flagler by McDonald and McGuire) and Whitehall, Palm Beach's first mansion, built for Flagler's third wife, both buildings facing Lake Worth, as opposed to the Atlantic, on which James's hotel looked. He feels that only a hotel, given the "general indifference" toward the American scene (a theme returned to in the last section of the chapter), could frame, or bring out what was in the landscape; the hotel was leading the way in discriminating in favor of the beautiful and the "refined" and represented a "desire for taste." He also feels that the "American future" may show no more than this "pathos of desire" (14.4.328), for with all material advantages, able to put to shame Italian objects of beauty, something lacks. Yet, "new with that consistency of newness which one sees only in the States, [the hotel] seems to say, somehow, that to some such heaven, some such public exaltation of the Blest, those who have conformed with due earnestness to the hotel-spirit, and for a sufficiently long probation, may hope eventually to penetrate or perhaps actually retire" (14.4.329). The hotel becomes, then, "the ideal form of the final home" (14.4.330), and he speaks of Palm Beach as Vanity Fair, quite unlike Newport, which has "comparative privacies and ancientries," as comprising everybody—all the "boarders"—under one glass, the world to which the visitor on an organized excursion to the Florida jungle, carried in a machine that seems to be a combination of perambulator and bicycle operated by a black (an "afromobile") is promptly returned. Vanity Fair, in the fifth section of the chapter, is a labyrinth of shops within the hotel; James sketches out what could be bought at the Royal Poinciana, and notes the absence of tea (the marker of the European) and the presence of iced drinks.

Yet James notes that his impression of the boarders has faded; like Prospero's vision, it "leaves not a wreck behind." American impressions exist only in the present; whereas the European vision "has behind it a driving force—derived from sources into which I won't pretend here to enter—that make it, comparatively, 'bite'" (14.5.334). The types at the hotel become one type: gender distinction disappears. The type is the businessman, produced from one generic "business-block," and his "indulged lady." Worse, there is the uniformity; the "neutrality of respectability" (this respectability neuters, of course, so that James can write, "there were the two sexes, I *think*"—my emphasis). This simplified typology "gave it all to the positive bourgeois propriety, serenely, imperturbably, massively seated, and against which any experimental deviation from the bourgeois would have dashed itself in vain" (14.5.335). Color and outline run together in this pictured existence; there is nothing of what Blake calls "the wiry bounding line;"[28] no difference. Here, we can return to the analysis of T. J. Clark on the blasé quality of urban life. New York was not blasé, but to come south to Florida is to enter the real cynicism of the urban world: as though Florida might be the truth of things American in the future. It becomes apparent however, that in thus implicitly distinguishing what he says about New York as the urban space from Florida, there can be no single theme or direction to *The American Scene*.

From Palm Beach, James returned via St. Augustine, staying at the Ponce de Leon, which Flagler had commissioned from Carrère and Hastings. He has been brought up on "romantic" stories of the old town of St. Augustine as the oldest "planted" in America, and as full of interesting details, but he blames the black-and-white photographs for their misrepresentation of the place, and he comments on this "heritage" aspect of America, as it would now be called, that the country's "aesthetic need" is more than "its manners, its aspects and arrangements, its past and its present, and perhaps even future, really supply"—an ominous note at the end of a text. So, as the aesthetic need is intermixed with a patriotic yearning, the heritage has to be "faked" (14.6.336). The nation is engaged, James says, in constructing a romantic past, in producing a "vast home-grown provision for entertainment . . . superseding any that may be borrowed or imported, and that . . . begins . . . to press for exportation" (14.6.337). The Ponce de Leon, "in the Moorish style" substitutes for any memory of the Spanish. James mentions the old Spanish fort, where he wandered for meditation, though "it is not congruous with the genius of Florida . . . to permit you to wander very far," but he sees the fort as the ghost of a ghost, unable to give any sense of association.

The Pullman, "inflated again with the hotel-spirit and exhaling modernity at every pore" (14.7.339), takes James north again, and looking from the window of the train, which affirms "a general conquest of nature and space," he thinks how white progress has dispossessed the Indian of land, and of land despoiled, waste. South of Washington, he has seen virtually nothing that could be called a road, so that this progress leaves nothing behind it, while the agent of progress boasts of its ability to conquer bigness—to make "but a mouthful of the mighty Mississippi" (14.7.342)—which was to be his next impression when he moved out West to St. Louis. A reduced Mississippi, a figure of the production of the indifferent that James intuits in this last chapter, was the reverse of what Dickens feared. James's ending seems to have people excluded from it, as much as place has been negated; a quiet desolation concludes the text.

JAMES AND WELLS ON AMERICA

The American Scene has virtually two endings: one for the chapters on "remarkable, unspeakable New York," and this one, on the destructiveness of American modernity, which is as it were a projection into the future. James needs at least both. Wells has only one conclusion. In *The Future in America* chapter 14, he is in Washington, "this magnificent empty city," which is "architecture and avenues . . . a place of picture post-cards and excursions, with sightseers instead of thoughts going to and fro" (178). He singles out the "stupendous unmeaning obelisk (the work of the women of America) that dominates all Washington." Remembering James calling Washington the "City of Conversation," he sees this as diversion only. Told to visit Mount Vernon (he doesn't), he reflects on America's "historical perspective" as longer than Europe's; America's inspiration is still eighteenth century so that "in many ways America fails to be contemporary" (180). There is a slippage between American technology and American retrospectivism; a failure to be absolutely modern. Wells comments on Congress's inability to make a political impact: this failure of democratic institutions he sees making liable a future "Caesarism" (i.e., fascism). Wells sees America having no future without socialism: "in face of the teeming situations" (the adjective implies immigrants) America does not know what to do; but the trend is away from "anarchistic individualism" (187). The argument asks for more order and feels threatened by its lack.

He describes meeting Roosevelt, "the seeking mind of America displayed" (185), a man on whom "traditions" have no hold—which makes him in this directness, "the mind and will of contemporary America," not characterized by thought, but assimilating it, delocalizing it, and reverberating it. The president seems to personify what is most distinctive about American achievement. Roosevelt had been wholly negative about James as insufficiently masculine, going straight for the gender jugular, but also calling him a "miserable little snob," whose "polished, pointless stories about the upper social classes of England" made "one blush to think he was once an American."[29] In Roosevelt's acceptance of Wells appears a readiness to take seriously the "pessimism" of *The Time Machine* (1895), where, as Wells describes it:

> I drew a picture of a future of decadence, of a time when constructive effort had fought its fight and failed, when the inevitable segregations of an individualistic system had worked themselves out and all the hope and vigour of humanity had gone for ever. The descendants of the workers had become etiolated, sinister, and subterranean monsters, the property owners had degenerated into a hectic and feebly self-indulgent race, living fitfully amidst the ruins of the present time. He became gesticulatory, and his straining voice a note higher in denying this as a credible interpretation of destiny. With one of those sudden movements of his he knelt forward . . . and addressed me very earnestly:
> "Suppose after all," he said slowly, "that should prove to be right, and it all ends in your butterflies and morlocks. *That doesn't matter now.* The effort's real. It's worth going on with. It's worth it. It's worth it—even then." (*FA*, 188–89)

Wells and Roosevelt associated America's future with science fiction, which continues the project of America's utopianism, and continues Wells's question, which was asked in the context of his meeting Roosevelt, whether America, a "giant childhood" or a "gigantic futility," is anything other than an "experiment" (*FA*, 188). In utopist thinking, the issue turns on city planning, as in Edward Bellamy's *Looking Backward* (1888), where Boston, perhaps inspired by Olmsted's designs for the city, is envisioned in 2000 in terms analogous to a "City Beautiful," and in its turn prompting the "city" to be laid out at the Chicago World Columbian Exposition:

> At my feet lay a great city. Miles of broad streets, shaded by trees and lined with fine buildings, for the most part not in continuous blocks but set in larger or smaller enclosures, stretched in every direction. Every quarter contained large open squares filled with trees, along which statues glistened and fountains flashed in the late-afternoon sun. Public buildings of a colossal size and architectural grandeur unparalleled in my day raised their stately piles on every side. Surely I had never seen this city nor one comparable to it before. Raising my eyes at last toward the horizon, I looked westward. That blue ribbon winding away to the sunset—was it not the sinuous Charles? I looked east—Boston harbour stretched before me within its headlands, not one of its green islets missing.[30]

Bellamy's model for Boston, which does not include people in its vistas, contrasts with *The Bostonians,* which appeared two years earlier. The view of Boston from Olive's room shadows Dickens in the accumulation of unrelated urban details:

> [It] took in the red sunsets of winter; the long low bridge that crawled, on its staggering posts, across the Charles; the casual patches of ice and snow; the desolate suburban horizons, peeled and made bald by the rigour of the season; the general hard, cold void of the prospect; the extrusion, at Charlestown, at Cambridge, of a few chimneys and steeples, straight, sordid tubes of factories and engine-shops, or spare, heavenward finger of the New England meeting-house. There was something inexorable in the poverty of the scene, shameful in the meanness of its details, which gave a collective impression of boards and tin and frozen earth, sheds and rotting piles, railway-lines striding flat across a thoroughfare of puddles and tracks of the humbler, the universal horse-car, traversing obliquely this path of danger; loose fences, vacant lots, mounds of refuse, yards bestrewn with iron pipes, telegraph poles, and bare wooden backs of places. Verena thought such a view lovely, and she was by no means without excuse when, as the afternoon closed, the ugly picture was tinted with a clear, cold rosiness. The air, in its windless chill, seemed to tinkle like a crystal, the faintest gradations of tone were perceptible in the sky. the west became deep and delicate, everything grew doubly distinct before taking on the dimness of evening. There were pink flushes on snow, 'tender' reflections in patches of stiffened marsh, sounds of carbells, no longer vulgar, but almost silvery, on the long bridge, lonely outlines of distant dusky undulations against the fading glow. These agreeable effects used to light up that end of the drawing room, and Olive often sat at the window with her companion before it was time for the lamp. (*The Bostonians,* 20.156–57)

But this, as a vision of desolation, is not shared by the feminists, nor quite by the narrator, and if there is irony in "these agreeable effects," it indicates that to read city space adequately, the self needs to be other, as James's lesbians are "other"; since the city makes the subject other. City space is feminine, as those references to color—"red," "rosiness," "pink," and "silvery" may imply; and because Basil Ransom reflects that "he had never seen an interior that was as much an interior" as Olive Chancellor's home (*The Bostonians*, 3.14), a relationship is possible between this feminine interior and the cityscape. Verena and Olive Chancellor—and James, in *The American Scene*—do not look for a utopia in the city, the implications being that attempts, like Bellamy's, to see the city of the future as different from the present, will be kitsch or evasive, or science fiction. Because Bellamy picks up on a utopist, futurist drive inherent in American city design, so his Boston of 2000 has skyscrapers, as the Time Traveller in *The Time Machine* notes something American in the buildings of the year 802,701: "I saw great and splendid architecture rising about me, more massive than any buildings of our time, and yet, as it seemed, built out of glimmer and mist."[31]

The year after *The Future in America*, Wells wrote *The War in the Air*.[32] Its hero is a South London bicycle mender, Bert Smallways, who finds himself implicated in German plans to bomb the United States. Something of Theodore Roosevelt's paranoia about Germany in his foreign policy, which produced the "Roosevelt corollary" to the Monroe doctrine, activates the novel. Smallways is put onto a German plane crossing the Atlantic and bombing American warships (including the *Theodore Roosevelt*). A year before Bleriot flew over the English Channel, Wells imagined the New York skyscrapers being bombed aerially, which gives point to his imagination of them as transitory. The pessimism of *The War in the Air* shows the people of New York grown complacent, like the Elois, blasé, unable to imagine war, so capitulating easily. As the German plane goes overhead, "seen from above [this is cinematic] it was alive with crawling trains and cars, and at a thousand points it was already breaking into quivering light. New York was altogether at its best that evening, its splendid best" (267). Bombing the Brooklyn Bridge, the city hall, the post office, and the rest of downtown New York follows:

> All this [Bert] saw in the perspectives of a bird's-eye view, as things happening in a big, irregular-shaped pit below him, between cliffs of high building. Northward he looked along the steep canyon of Broadway, down whose length at intervals crowds were assembling about excited speakers; and when he lifted his eyes he saw the chimneys and cable-stacks and roof spaces of New York, and everywhere now over these the

watching, debating people clustered, except where the fires raged and the jets of water flew. (271)

The natural landscape suggestion in the word "canyon" reappears in "the architectural cliffs of the city" (274). But New York architecture is ideological, serving a community divided up like the Eloi and the Morlocks:

> In one quarter, palaces of marble, laced and crowned with light and flame and flowers, towered up into [New York's] marvellous twilights beautiful beyond description; in another a black and sinister polyglot population sweltered in indescribable congestion in warrens and excavations beyond the power and knowledge of government. (274)

Wells presents the growth of the skyscraper as like science fiction, the discovery of a fantastic development produced out of dire emergency, with architects as scientists. But the continued upward growth after the need has finished is the marker of decadence, like the Eloi, and the marker of a continued desire for separation between the classes:

> It was the peculiar shape of Manhattan Island . . . that first gave the New York architects their bias for extreme vertical dimensions. Every need was lavishly supplied them—money, material, labour; only space was restricted. To begin with, therefore, they built high perforce. But to do so was to discover a whole new world of architectural beauty, of exquisite ascendant lines, and long after the central congestion had been relieved by tunnels under the sea [sic], four colossal bridges over the East River, and a dozen mono-rail cables east and west, the upward growth went on. (262)

Film, science fiction, and the future of America coalesce in Wells's and perhaps in Roosevelt's imagination. Thinking of skyscrapers as transitory, Wells brings them near to architecture for film; and a vision of New York's harbor was used in the architecture for the film *Metropolis* (1927).[33] Here, buildings are seen as menacing machines, which links with the technologization of workers, in the process of "Taylorization."[34] Like *Looking Backwards, Metropolis* is set in 2000, and envisages a strong leader to unite workers and bosses (coming himself from the boss class: Freder, the son of the Master of Metropolis). Lang based the film on his wife Thea von Harbou's novel, *Metropolis* (1926), which used *The Time Machine* for its distinction between the bosses and the workers who live underground.[35]

Wells's work implies that if architects build upwards, in the machines suggestive of the power James visualized in *The Ivory Tower*, which also associates the American house and the plane, then these "Towers of Babel" will be mapped by film and flattened from the air. Wells reads the skyscraper as embodying a form of nihilism indicated in its provisionality—as in the point that a skyscraper's chief function is the celebration of its own power, and that, since it must be capped, logically produces war in the air. Mapping the city by film in such a way that defeats architecture creates a new space, for "in the air are no streets, no channels, no point where one can say of an antagonist, 'If he wants to reach my capital he must come by here.' In the air all directions lead everywhere." (*The War in the Air*, 300). The logic of this is the ending of the notion of the localizable capital and the creation of new space guessed at in terms of technology and the technologizing of the air. A desire for this makes Wells associate skyscrapers with a mystique of progress just as he regards immigrants as akin to Morlocks: two views inducing panic or hysteria and a belief that the future is definable in terms of catastrophe. That appears in his admiration for Roosevelt's adoption of the language of science fiction for thinking about American politics. Roosevelt thinks himself part of the plot of *The Time Machine*, and Wells endorses that. The unreality allows for an escape from the presence of the other within America.

Unlike James, Wells was not ready to read anything into America as other, so James's duality of response misses him. *The American Scene* is also fascinated by what future America is building and can only answer the question in contradictory ways. America cannot build a future, because it repudiates the past, but it seems also committed to a sense of the past as dispensable, finished with, which insight puts such a writer as James nowhere. *The American Scene* works with these two contradictory insights in a struggle to keep at bay the temptation to hysteria.

CHAPTER 9

The States and the Statue

KAFKA ON AMERICA

NEW YORK HARBOR

Bartholdi's *Liberty Enlightening the World*—the Statue of Liberty—assumed its place in 1886 on Richard Morris Hunt's neoclassical pedestal, as a rival to New York's new tall buildings.[1] From now on there could be no sense that America lacked monuments or did not sign itself. The statue brought out New York, affirmed its premier position as a port and a city in America, and indeed, in the world. James does not refer to the statue, whose appearance at the moment of maximum immigration to the United States gave strongest emphasis to the rhetoric of liberty, and implied the question whether the statue could be identified with America, in its past or present or future. Perhaps his silence responded to its triumphalism, as part of an American Renaissance, which makes the language of "liberty" itself so ambiguously coercive.

Wells, however, thinking of New York harbor, focuses on the disjuncture between the statue and America, comparing the "mechanical, inhuman growth" of the skyscrapers with the Statue of Liberty, her arm "straining upward, straining in hopeless competition with the fierce commercial altitudes ahead" (28). *The Future in America* finds it symbolic that the statue "is meant to dominate and fails absolutely to dominate the scene. It goes up to about three hundred feet, by standing on a pedestal of a hundred and fifty, and the uplifted torch, seen against the sky, suggests an arm straining upward, straining in hopeless competition with the fierce commercial altitudes ahead. Poor liberating lady of the American ideal!" (28). Wells returns to the statue when commenting on what happened to Gorky, the Russian who unlike Svidrigaylov, actually visited

America. Gorky was held by the officials at Ellis Island because he was not married to his traveling companion. He had come to raise funds after the Russian revolution of 1905, and his coming was greeted with enthusiasm, since "that great figure of Liberty with the torch was to make it flare visibly halfway round the world, reproving tyranny" (134), but he was driven out, and Wells had to meet him at Staten Island. Calling Gorky "the Russian peasant in person" brings Wells back to the topic of immigration, his constant fear, and to New York harbor:

> I could imagine how he had felt as he came in the big steamer to her, up that large converging display of space and teeming energy. There she glowed tonight across the water, a queen among cities, as if indeed she was the light of the world. Nothing, I think, can ever rob that splendid harbour approach of its invincible quality of promise. (138)

In the last chapter: "The Envoy," after commenting on the elements of hope that he finds in America, which he lists as "the universities, the turbines of Niagara, the New York architecture," and the quality of Americans, Wells ends on board ship in New York harbor,

> which was my first impression of America, which still, to my imagination, stands so largely for America. The crowded ferry-boats hooted past; athwart the shining water, tugs clamoured to and fro. The skyscrapers raised their slender masses heavenward—America's gay bunting lit the scene. As we dropped down I had a last glimpse of the Brooklyn Bridge. There to the right was Ellis Island, where the immigrants, minute by minute, drip and drip into America; and beyond, that tall, spike-headed Liberty with her reluctant torch, which I have sought to make the centre of all this writing. And suddenly as I looked back at the skyscrapers of New York a queer fancy sprang into my head. They reminded me quite irresistibly of piled-up packing cases outside a warehouse. I was amazed I had not seen the resemblance before. I could have believed for a moment that this was what they were, could have accepted the omen in perfectly good faith, that presently out of these would come the real right thing, palaces and noble places, *free,* high circumstances, and space and leisure, light and fine living for the sons of men. (193, my emphasis)

Kafka's *Der Verschollene* asks, less rhetorically, less sentimentally, about survival in America. For, unlike Dickens or the young immigrant Martin Chuzzlewit, or James, or Wells, Kafka is discussing living in, not just visiting the United States. How does Kafka accentuate what immigration implies and the iconography of the Statue of Liberty? The first chapter, "The Stoker," opens:

As Karl Rossmann, a poor boy of sixteen who had been packed off to America by his parents because a servant girl had seduced him and got herself with child by him, stood on the liner slowly entering the harbour of New York, a sudden burst of sunshine seemed to illumine the Statue of Liberty, so that he saw it in a new light, although he had sighted it long before. The arm with the sword rose up as if newly stretched aloft, and round the figure blew the free winds of heaven. (*America,* 13)[2]

But before discussing this, I would like to give some contexts.

WRITING THE "AMERICAN NOVEL"

The "American novel," as he referred to it in conversation, is unlike other Kafka novels, attached to a specific place, familiar to Germany. Half a million Germans emigrated to the United States in the 1840s, a number increasing until the peak year, 1882, a quarter of a million. In each year of the 1890s, four million letters were mailed back from America to Germany. Between 1870 and 1914, over 90 guidebooks or travel accounts appeared in German.[3] German novelists wrote about America, for example Charles Sealsfield (1793–1864), who romanticized the Indian in *The Indian Chief, Or, Tokeah, and The White Rose* (1828) or Karl May (1842–1912), who though he did not visit America until 1908, popularized the Western in *Winnertou* (1893) with his German narrator as hero, Karl (the same name as Kafka's hero), nicknamed "Old Shatterhand."[4] Kafka's urban America, however, is capitalist and Taylorist, unlike these, as much it is also unlike Whitman.[5] America as technologized defines *Der Verschollene;* Kafka refers to "the iron fist of technology," which means that "we are driven towards truth like criminals to the seat of judgement" (J.71). Kafka's America makes the immigrant subject through Taylorite methods, in which "Time, the noblest and most most essential element in creative work, is conscripted into the net of corrupt business interests. Thereby not only creative work, but man himself, who is its essential part, is polluted and humiliated. A Taylorized life is a terrible curse which will give rise only to hunger and misery instead of the intended wealth and profit" (J.115).

"Kafka" and "America" oppose two contrary principles: Kafka's relationship with language, where he is an exile, and America as the country for exiles. As a Jewish Czech living in Prague where 90 percent of the population spoke Czech and were yet a minority culture within a German-speaking official culture, he experienced alienation. Brought up speaking German, he taught himself Yiddish, Czech, and Hebrew, moving from a "major" toward what Deleuze and Guattari, basing themselves on a diary entry of Kafka for 25 December 1911 (D.148–49) call a "minor literature." Karl Rossmann, in America, must learn English. A "minor literature" designates "the deterritorialization of language, the connection of the individual to political immediacy, and the collective assemblage of enunciation."[6] Language deterritorialized loses its power in relation to place defined nationally and politically; it becomes political because that makes it oppositional to the dominant culture, and it inevitably speaks for a group who have a minority status. Can America be the place for a minor literature?

Kafka and the question of language, and his desire for opposition within language recalls his relationship to literature. He told Felice Bauer in a letter of 14 April 1913, that "I have no literary interests, but am made of literature. I am nothing else and cannot be anything else" (LF.428). Already constructed by textual representations, the subject of writing is lost in writing, as Blanchot brings out, and Kafka knows the impossibility of saying anything within literature. "Hardly a word comes to me from the fundamental source, but is seized upon fortuitously and with great difficulty somewhere along the way . . . how could my writing to you, however firm my hand, achieve everything I want to achieve?" he writes to Felice Bauer.[7] The text can say nothing final, but leads to the loss of the power of interpretation: "the scriptures are unalterable, and the comments often enough merely express the commentator's bewilderment" (The Trial, 240). Walter Benjamin said of Kafka that "he took all conceivable precautions against the interpretation of his writings. One has to find one's way in them circumspectly, cautiously and warily."[8] "Finding a way" through Kafka's ambiguity, where there is no certainty as to what happens to Karl Rossmann is analogous to finding a way in America. To be lost in America is to realize the loss of the autonomous subject who can grasp single meaning; this, Benjamin argued, was something the "big-city dweller" was aware of.[9]

America existed in Kafka's consciousness, as an attraction and a danger. In his first collection of stories Meditation ("Betrachtung" [1913]), came two stories, "Rejection" and "The Wish to Be a Red Indian":

> If one were only an Indian, instantly alert, and on a racing horse, leaning against the wind, kept on quivering jerkily over the quivering ground, until one shed one's spurs, for there needed no spurs, threw away the reins, for there needed no reins, and hardly saw that the land before one was smoothly shorn heath when horse's neck and head would be already gone.[10]

Becoming an Indian permits disappearance of the body. "Rejection" gives a woman's turning away a man:

You are . . . no broad American with a Red Indian figure, level, brooding eyes and a skin tempered by the air of the prairies and the rivers that flow through them . . . (383–84).

Being an Indian implies motion, speed and disappearance, a form of deterritorialization, a line of escape from spaces of power.[11] Such images of Indian liberty, the antithesis of Karl May, match a diary entry (19 January 1911), saying he "once projected a novel in which two brothers fought each other, one of whom went to America while the other remained in a European prison" (D.37). Two destinies and two continents are opposed. Kafka had relatives who emigrated to America: two maternal uncles, Alfred and Joseph Loewy (1852–1923; 1858–1932). Otto Kafka (1879–1939) went to South America and then came to the United States in 1906: In a document about himself in 1918 he said that

> during the twelve years since I landed in this country . . . I relied upon nobody's support or assistance. I did not make a single penny except by hard work and I have tried my best to adapt myself as quickly as possible to American views and ideals. When I arrived I did not know a soul. I had no means and could not speak the language. I started as a porter with a corset concern at $5 a week and worked myself up to become manager of an export department that I created, overcoming considerable opposition on part of the heads of the concern. The former head of the company soon became very interested in the new departure, when results began to show. I stayed there for three years and left because of intrigues of my assistant against me while on a trip abroad.[12]

His destiny was prosperity in New York. Another cousin, Emil Kafka (1881–1963), appears in Kafka's diary when he visited Prague from Chicago. Kafka writes of his "placid life," checking the shipments in the textile department of the mail-order firm Sears and Roebuck, and helping out in the bicycle department. "A wholesale business with ten thousand employees. The Americans like to change their jobs . . . but he doesn't see the point of it, you lose time and money by it. . . . Evenings he generally stays at home, plays cards with friends; sometimes, for diversion, an hour at the cinema, in summer a walk, Sunday a boat-ride on the lake. He is wary of marriage, even though he is already thirty-four years old, since American women often marry only in order to get divorced, a simple matter for them, but very expensive for the man" (D.320). Comparisons can be made with these relatives in America. All three of Kafka's sisters died in Nazi death camps. So it seems did Grete Bloch, whom Kafka had known well, and so did Milena Jesenká. Felice Bauer emigrated to the United States.

Kafka said of some Constructive paintings that they were "merely dreams of a marvellous America, of a wonderland of unlimited possibilities. That is perfectly understandable because Europe is becoming more and more a land of impossible limitations" (J.144). He also wrote about a dream he had of being on a jetty built far out to sea—which implies travel, speed, and deterritorialization:

> on my right, New York could be seen, we were in New York Harbour. The sky was grey, but of a constant brightness. I moved back and forth in my seat . . . in order to be able to see everything. In the direction of New York my glance slanted downwards a little, in the direction of the sea it slanted upwards. I now noticed the water rise up near us in high waves on which was borne a great cosmopolitan traffic. I can remember only that instead of the rafts we have, there were long timbers lashed together into gigantic bundles the cut ends of which kept popping out of the water during the voyage, higher or lower, according to the height of the waves, and at the same time kept turning end over end in the water. I sat down, drew up my feet, quivered with pleasure, virtually dug myself into the ground in delight, and said: Really, this is even more interesting than the traffic on a Paris boulevard" (11 September 1912, D.209–10).

The last sentence opposes two cultures, and since water traffic resembles the traffic of a Paris boulevard, redefines city space, which is New York harbor, the place from which New York can be seen, what Wells evoked: the busiest port in the world.

"THE STOKER"

Kafka's Statue of Liberty in New York harbor Karl Rossmann sees has a different emphasis from Wells's, which guards property. In Wells, the meaning of Liberty has been reduced to "the liberty of property and the subordination of the state to business" (*The Future in America*, 81), and the statue presides over America's "inadequate theory of freedom" (85). Yet that deficiency is in Wells's text too, guarding America against the immigrant. When the Statue of Liberty raises her arm as if newly, and as if in interdiction of Karl Rossmann's approach, the change from torch to sword is not just surreal, but expresses what the torch means; or rather, what the statue means in photographic representation as Kafka has seen it, where a torch might also be mistaken for a sword. The torch/sword change is a reminder that this text is aware that it deals less in nineteenth-century realism than in textual representation, which it cannot get out of—which is the difference from Wells. There are layerings of ambiguities or contradictions here. Whatever Liberty holds can be seen as a beacon of hope or Justice—which demands that the subject should think of itself as under trial, while it also means that Liberty guards the way against both the Promised Land and Eden—including Dickens's Eden, or Cairo—Eden becoming Kafka's city Rameses. Liberty and Justice meet contradictorily in one goddesslike single figure who asserts the impossibility of both or of either. In the "Letter to his Father," Kafka records how the patriarch would say "Not a word of contradiction" (*Dearest Father,* 150). The first sight of America evokes just what the father could not accept—contradiction, the need for a double reading.

On 20 September 1912, Kafka wrote his first letter to Felice Bauer, and two nights later, "The Judgement" ("Das Urteil"), dedicated to her. This leaned on "The Urban World" ("Die Städtische Welt"),[13] left incomplete, but with a significant title, for someone thinking about America. Work on the American novel, started in early 1912 was broken again in November for "The Metamorphosis" ("Die Verwandlung"). In 1913 Kafka published "The Judgement" and, from the American novel, "The Stoker: A Fragment" ("Der Heizer: Ein Fragment"). "The Metamorphosis" followed in October 1915, and Kafka wanted the three texts together in a volume called *Die Söhne* (*The Sons*) since there was "an obvious connection between the three, and even more important, a secret one."[14] "The Stoker" thus read laterally links to other European texts; it also begins a new, American narrative, so it can be accentuated in two different ways.

In *The Future in America,* the sexuality of the Statue of Liberty is unironic; she is the "poor liberating Lady of the American ideal" (28). Kafka, more intent on reading the contradictory implications of the monument, begins with a gender-point. Masculinized with a sword, the statue shows the sexually fissured nature of identity, which emphasizes that liberty and justice must themselves be gender-concepts, and if gendered, they require a contradictory reading. Liberty's sword raises the castration threat for anxious males and makes feminine sexuality commanding; this returns parodically near the end, with the fat and gross prostitute Brunelda, a singer (*America,* 213)—her fatness repeating that of the stoker, Green, and the Head Porter. Brunelda's name makes her a Valkyrie—another goddess with a sword in her hand. Kafka wrote in a letter to Brod (17 July 1912) of the sexuality of singers, which he had heard about at Jungborn, a nature retreat with a feeling of freedom that gave him, as he also wrote to Brod, "an inkling of America."[15] At Jungborn, the doctor had "declared that breathing from the diaphragm contributes to the growth and stimulation of the sexual organs, for which reason female singers, for whom diaphragm breathing is requisite, are so immoral."[16] Karl Rossmann's last acts, before the Oklahoma sequence, are to guard Brunelda, now working in a brothel. The emphasis on the woman's grossness, where she does indescribable things to the porcelain her husband leaves for her, "so that the servant could hardly carry it away for disgust" (214), show that America's interior produces—as symbolized through Brunelda's interior—a profound distaste for the body, and this is warned about by the sexuality and ambiguous gender of the statue at the border, the harbor.

Dickens was challenged by America in relation to sexuality, both through the Mississippi challenging an ability, essential to the bourgeois novelist, to keep the materiality of the body out of his dreams, and through the feminism he encountered, which although he might mock it, also made city space the space of feminine sexuality. James negates the possibility that America posed a sexual question in the way analogous to Europe; yet James's insistence on the maleness of the New York crowd is also an awareness of being pressured by the power of bodies on the move. Karl Rossmann's exile in America has been enforced on him by pruden- tial, antisexual parents, to try to separate him from the body, including the body of Johanna Brummer, who has raped him. He undergoes a history of sexuality, with half-homosexual implications—picking up on hints in *David Copperfield* and on the homoerotic in Horatio Alger—in relation to the stoker; as well as casual gender reversals, as when the sailor loses his dignity on discovering that he has had a girl's apron tied to him (41). Ho- mosexuality reappears with Mr. Pollunder and with the Head Porter at the Hotel Occidental; while the nature of female sexuality is learned through Karl's experiences with Clara, who wrestles him to the ground. All these things feminize Karl Rossmann; all pose threats to identity and alternative forms of identity. There are two Claras in *David Copperfield*, both unlike Kafka's "American girl" (65), though this Clara might be com- pared with Rosa Dartle in *David Copperfield*. Karl Rossmann learns that Mr. Mack, the millionaire's son, is already sleeping with Clara (89). Mr. Mack is Kafka's imitation of Dickens's Steerforth, like Steerforth doing noth- ing; and Steerforth has also, probably, slept with Rosa Dartle. These fig- ures of sexuality have already been evoked in Johanna Brummer's rape of the male, which provides this novel's primal scene, not to be escaped from by the transatlantic crossing since she is in correspondence with the uncle whose existence he discovers in this first chapter. If going to America is attempted evasion of the European body, there can be no escape from it in America. As he goes in the boat with his uncle, "whose knees were al- most touching his own" (43), paranoia and fear of homosexuality (these things were almost the same for Freud, analyzing Shreber) coalesce; he is in near contact with the body of the American uncle, who is also part of his European past, so that the body and the past come together.

Rossmann remembers how Johanna Brummer pressed against him "so disgustingly that his head and neck started up from the pillows, then thrust her body several times against him—it was as if she were part of himself, and for that reason, perhaps, he was seized with a horrible feeling of yearning" (36). There is an upwards displacement here reflecting the boy's fear or hatred of his own body, as that which, "starting up" is the marker of the body's rebellion, its otherness to him. The arm of the not wholly female (in appearance) Statue of Liberty "rose up as if newly stretched aloft," as if the assertion of freedom, and of rebellion against the European order, basic to American ideology, must be codified sexually. So, too, New York's skyscrapers, which can be codified as masculine, also "rose" (21). The boy's attraction and repulsion, hatred and desire, fuse contradictorily in the same moment, and this ambiguity is abjection, deep disgust toward the other, and the other in the self, so that abjection gives the impossibility of founding a single identity. Abject feelings seem to be recalled, and mocked, in a sequence that begins with America's premier architectural symbol, the Statue of Liberty, the image of a single state. America's sexual challenge asks what an establishment of subjectivity would mean.

One metonymic sequence runs through "The Stoker," connecting the sword with Rossmann's companion's walking stick and Rossmann's forgotten umbrella, which makes him dive back again into the inside of the ship, and so disappear as if wanting to be lost, to avoid the familiar (New York harbor, known from photographs), and arriving at the door of the stoker's cabin. It continues with the brooms on the men's shoulders (20), the officer playing with the hilt of his sword and Uncle Jacob carrying a bamboo cane, which is also like a sword (22). The umbrella-less Karl—with no defense against castration (and if we follow Derrida in *Spurs* on Nietzsche's umbrella, no feminine veils which would allow for doubleness and protection) finds himself defending the stoker before seven "men of authority" (30). He is left as a helpless male against superior masculinity.

A second metonymic sequence connects the stoker's paranoia that the chief engineer is not a German but a Rumanian (17) with Rossmann's nervousness about the Irish (14—the point reappears later, 98) and also with his fear that his Slovak companion has tried to get hold of his box on the journey (19). Equally, the Irish and the Frenchman have anti-German sentiments (118). The paranoia continues with Rossmann's glimpse of the harbor and New York, whose "skyscrapers stared at Karl with their hundred thousand eyes" (21), repeating James on the windows of the skyscrapers. Karl Rossmann's temptation, like that of other immigrants—it also confronts James, who feels himself an alien and a nonalien at once—is that which is imposed by a major literature. As Wells's position makes him identify with fear of the Eastern European foreigner, which would, logically, include fear of Kafka's relatives, the danger for Karl Rossmann is to identify with xenophobia, expressed in the fear that "Mr. Schubal gave the preference to foreigners" (25). In the case of Kafka in Prague, this would mean identification with the dominant, anti-Semitic culture. Rossmann is led into advocacy for the stoker, requiring a "guilefulness" on his own part (23), to recognize that he knows that his demand for justice (recalling the Statue of Liberty and her sword) is not quite that, but colludes in the stoker's *ressentiment* and links to his own distaste for the body, as the "other."[17]

AMERICAN ARCHITECTURE

In the cabin, Karl looks out at the harbor through three windows (21) so that the skyscraper windows that look at him can only see him fragmentarily, as he sees things fragmentarily. The paragraph that says Karl looked at New York harbor through the windows ends with, "Yes, in this room one realized where one was" (21)—but that perception is not dependent on the visual, so much as on a sense of the déjà vu—dependent on a sense of New York harbor that has been gathered from photographs—like Kafka's own knowledge. Thus the paranoid sense that Karl Rossmann gets is not quite justified. He is awed by a representation of New York, rather than by New York. This point may be added to the time when, during the stoker's appeal (which is really his trial), Karl Rossmann loses attention, and the text focuses for the third time on the harbor as "restless."

> Meanwhile, outside the windows, the life of the harbour went on; a flat barge laden with a mountain of barrels, which must have been wonderfully well packed, since they did not roll off, went past, almost completely obscuring the daylight; little motor-boats, which Karl would have liked to examine thoroughly if he had time, shot straight past in obedience to the slightest touch of the man standing erect at the wheel. Here and there curious objects bobbed independently out of the restless water, were immediately submerged again and sank before his astonished eyes; boats belonging to the ocean liner were rowed past by sweating sailors; they were filled with passengers sitting silent and expectant as if they had been stowed there, except that some of them could not refrain from turning their heads to gaze at the changing scene. A movement without end, a restlessness transmitted from the restless element to helpless human beings and their works! (26)

The sight becomes an alternative to the stoker's demand for justice and implies the subject's loss of a centered position; Karl has not time to see

what is taking place at speed in front of him, for the scene is "changing."
What is seen appears under the conditions of distraction, which is for
Walter Benjamin the modern and urban mode of seeing (Benjamin associates it specifically with the new media of film and photography).[18]
Nor, because of the windows, can Karl see anything except fragmentarily
(21), which encourages the distracted view. Describing the American city
can only be done by seeing that the urban makes for an incomplete vision; seeing is in time, with no ability to store away momentary and broken impressions and with the simultaneous erasure of memory of what is
seen. The harbor scene begins a response to New York's architecture,
which is continued by the sense that the city cannot be fully visualized. It
cannot be viewed from Uncle Jacob's sixth floor:

> What would have been at home the highest vantage point in the town al-
> lowed him here little more than a view of one street, which ran perfectly
> straight between two rows of squarely chopped buildings and therefore
> seemed to be fleeing into the distance, where the outlines of a cathedral
> loomed enormous in a dense haze. . . . that street was the channel for a
> constant stream of traffic which, seen from above, looked like an inextri-
> cable confusion . . . of foreshortened human figures and the roofs of all
> kinds of vehicles, sending into the upper air another confusion, more ri-
> otous and complicated, of noises . . . all of it enveloped and penetrated by
> a flood of light which the multitudinous objects in the street scattered, car-
> ried off and again busily brought back, with an effect as palpable to the
> dazzled eye as if a glass roof stretched over the street were being violently
> smashed into fragments at every second. (44–45)

Discussing *Martin Chuzzlewit* (p. 61), I referred to *Notre-Dame de Paris* and
the "bird's-eye view of Paris" Hugo gives, imagining how the city could be
mapped in 1482 from the top of the towers of Paris. Hugo thinks of the
"labyrinthine street network" of the city—the city as a labyrinth at
ground level—but then ascends above to the summit to a "dizzy confusion of roofs, chimneys, streets, bridges, squares, spires, steeples." Here,
"everything caught the eye at once, the carved gable, the steep roof, the
turret suspended at the corner of the walls, the stone pyramid of the
eleventh century, the slate obelisk of the fifteenth, the bare, round tower
of the castle keep, the square decorated tower of the church, the big, the
massive, the airy. The eye lingered at every level of this labyrinth, where
there was nothing without its originality. . . ."[19] This prompts the view
from Todgers's, for Hugo's perception of the city, which considers that
the only way to read the city is from above (the point of view of Wells's
aircraft), doubles the space of the labyrinth, particularly as the eye then
moves over the city as a bird flies over. The city is unmappable for the

person in the street, and a vertical labyrinth, which descends to depths that cannot be reached. (Hugo stresses that medieval buildings have as much below them in their foundations as they show above ground.) Yet architecture is a text for Hugo that must be read, unlike Poe's book and man of the crowd, which do not allow themselves to be read, and the labyrinthine must offer itself for analysis.

In Kafka's New York, the labyrinthine is like Caillebotte's Parisian picture, *The Decorators* (1877), where the painter emphasizes Hauss-mann's absolutely straight road going off into the distance to the van-ishing point of the picture, utterly unvaried. It is James's "blank" street, a straight line. The vantage point of Hugo's cathedral is lost in the city as it is replaced by higher buildings, which deny the possibility of vision, and imply a separation between the viewer and the street life below. The gap is imaged in the glass roof continually fragmented and replaced. Just when vision seems possible, that possibility is violently removed in a way that seems to assault other senses (there is the implication of hearing the glass smash). One representation of the city follows upon another, and no one can pass beyond these. The glass implies the glass atrium, which created another city space, neither indoors not outdoors, but it also evokes the cinema screen. The new architecture of New York is in-separable from its evocation in film and in the fragmented space that film offers. The city is as enveloped and penetrated by light. A move has taken place from Dickens's fog, which governs perception of the city, to light where everything is visible; but the visibility is so strong that it is also impossible.

Like Hugo's Paris, Prague, it seems from the quotation, can be read as somewhere that is intelligible. In New York, "the street . . . remained un-changed, only one section of a great wheel which afforded no hand-hold unless one knew all the forces controlling its full orbit" (48). Karl Ross-mann does not know these forces, and the text's modernism, rooted in a perception of America, fuses its emphasis on the fragment with language as estranging, whether it is Rossmann's German, or his English, or the music from home he is trying to play on the piano, which he would like to exert "a direct influence upon his life in America" (48).

The seen has the reality of the photograph. Karl, Robinson, and De-laroche on the road meet "columns of vehicles bringing provisions to New York, which streamed past in five rows taking up the whole breadth of the road and so continuously that no one could have got across to the other side" (102–3). Traffic assumes a militaristic formation, city space can neither be read nor negotiated by the human. The three look back on New York and its harbor, and the description is inverted: Huge buildings squeeze the traffic out of view, and all that remains is the impression of size, as if in another photograph, where everything seen is rendered dead, but, it will be noticed, only in an optical illusion:

> The bridge connecting New York with Brooklyn hung delicately over the East River, and if one half-shut one's eyes, it seemed to tremble. It appeared to be quite bare of traffic, and beneath it stretched a smooth empty tongue of water. Both the huge cities seemed to stand there empty and purposeless. As for the houses, it was scarcely possible to distinguish the large ones from the small. In the invisible depths of the streets life probably went on after its own fashion, but above them nothing was discernible save a light fume . . . (105–6)[20]

The optical illusion makes people disappear, producing the repeated word "empty." The bridge replaces the cities in importance, but joins nothing to nothing. The light fume recalls Dickens's fog, but it also implies that what Karl Rossmann sees is not an unmediated America, but America mediated through photographic illusion.

NARRATIVE AND IDENTITY

Photographs stabilize memory; and memory, following a Nietzschean argument in *The Genealogy of Morals,* is of guilt, as Kafka's unsent letter to his father says: "I had lost my self-confidence where you were concerned, and in its place had developed a boundless sense of guilt" (*Dearest Father,* 170). The text removes the authority of aids to memory and since impressions come so fast, erases memory. Karl Rossmann thinks of Johanna Brummer in terms of a "vanishing past" (35) before his seduction is recalled in the rest of the paragraph. The ambiguity fits with the abject state; he both wishes to erase the memory and to keep it, not to let it vanish, which means the preservation of his guilt.

At the end of "The Stoker," Rossmann has gained an American uncle, which solders him back to his European past and to the body, and he has lost the stoker, as he also feels that he has lost his box and his umbrella. Yet these losses are not the same: Kafka told Janouch that the "only reality is the concrete human being, our neighbour" (a Whitmanesque note) and added that the stoker, "like every concrete human being . . . was a messenger from the outer world" (J.94). Karl's tragedy has been to be reappropriated by patriarchy, and lost to the stoker, who is never heard of again. But, reading beyond "The Stoker," something else emerges. By the end of chapter 3 Karl has finished with his uncle, and with the milieu of Mr. Pollunder and his daughter Clara and Pollunder's future son in law, Mack, where privileged capitalism works by prudent marriage alliances.

Negatively, he learns about Mack through newspapers where "there was excited talk of a strike among the building workers: the name Mack was often mentioned. Karl . . . learned that he was the father of the Mack he knew, and the greatest building contractor in New York. The strike was supposed to be costing him millions and possibly endangering his financial position. Karl did not believe a word of what was said by these badly informed and spiteful people" (107–8). As a comment either on the journalists or the strikers, this means that Karl Rossmann's identifications and interpretations are still on the wrong side (that of paranoia and of order). Yet he has refound his umbrella and box, both through the agency of Schlubal, of all people. The ordinariness of the manner in which these things reappear (91–92) overthrows paranoia, and questions the means by which signs in America are interpreted. It points to another tendency in the text, to see interpretation of signs—which includes interpreting the Statue of Liberty—as European paranoia.

Yet the return of the box is also ambiguous. The box that disappears and threatens a loss of identity imitates Dickens, since it relates to David Copperfield's box stolen in London when he resolves to go to find his aunt at Dover (12.172–73). Copperfield does not get his box back; instead he gets a new identity, leaving his old in the city. Rossmann getting *his* box back is reunited to his European identity; at that point he is unable to effect the break that is implied in Dickens. The one thing subsequently stolen from the box is the photograph of his parents, which in an obsessional way he equates with the value of the rest of the box (121–22).

The photograph has already been described—"his small father stood very erect behind his mother, who sat in an easy-chair slightly sunk into herself. One of his father's hands lay on the back of the chair, the other, which was clenched to a fist, rested on a picture-book lying open on a fragile table beside him." As he considers it, "his father refused to come to life" but "his mother . . . had come out better; her mouth was twisted as if she had been hurt and were forcing herself to smile." That raises questions of interpretation: . . ."how could a photograph convey with such complete certainty the secret feelings of the person shown in it? . . . When he glanced at it again he noticed his mother's hand, which dropped from the arm of the chair in the foreground, near enough to kiss" (99–100). This has Dickens's affectivity, as well as the same gender-distinctions as in *David Copperfield*—the dead father, the mother as if alive, her hand in motion. But the affectivity is in a photograph. It requires a dialectical reading.[21] The mother's mouth and her hand are possible moments of the real, the *punctum* within the photograph, whose ability is to traumatize; but to see the *punctum* here is also dependent upon the subject's reading (on a second view, the *punctum* would not be there); and being held by an image—another element of a "vanishing past"—whose substance is contradictory (one figure seems dead, one seems alive), is also a trap, like the image the Statue of Liberty presents, fixing a memory and a subject position for the viewer.

In Dickens things lost reappear and characters and situations repeat themselves, as if affirming the ability of the text to connect fragmentary experiences. So the narrator in *Bleak House* asks about people and places, "What connexion can there be . . . ? What connexion can there have been between many people in the innumerable histories of this world, who, from opposite sides of great gulfs, have, nevertheless, been very curiously brought together!" (*Bleak House,* 16.235). The narrative tendency appears, to re-unite things that have otherwise lost their identity within city space; the text becomes implicitly a detective novel, a device for mapping the city, before the genre appears unmistakably even if the solution of the detective is also to be seen as part of the problem. Connecting and reconnecting is also played on in *Der Verschollene* with Karl Rossmann's experiences in the last chapter, "The Nature Theatre of Oklahoma" (Brod's title). Fanny, whose name is Dickensian, appears as an angel blowing the trumpets at Clayton (249). Although she has not been seen before in the text, her appearance is treated as a reappearance, through the "delighted surprise" with which Karl greets her and laughs (a Dickensian recognition). Giacomo (264), the Italian lift-boy first met with at the Hotel Occidental (126) reappears, bringing immigrants together into a new community, and another and different space.[22] The companions, Robinson and Delamarche, turn up again after Rossmann thinks that he has shaken them off at the Hotel Occidental. The American uncle is, in essence, "reappearing" in his first appearance, and he means the return of Europe. Yet these reappearances are not like those in Dickens. Their contradictoriness affirms, rather, several possible outcomes to the narrative. Holding onto a photograph is a way of trying to fix one reading, but the text cannot, it seems, be resolved in one way. Brod, in the Postscript to the novel said that the book was destined to end with "reconciliation," that Rossmann would find again "a profession, a stand-by, his freedom, even his old home and his parents, as if by some celestial witchery" (269).[23] This is contradicted by the diary entry, which assumed that Rossmann would be executed (30 September 1915, D.343–44). America is unknown, ambiguous; to go into America is never to be heard of again—but the status of that is also uncertain. The text works in the opposite way from the photograph, where futures are not fixed and connections made and unmade.

EUROPEAN AND AMERICAN FUTURES

America allows people to see that Europe has changed; now, there is no fixed Europe to contrast with America, which is where Kafka goes beyond Wells in his preserving European differences within the new space of America. But that perception is also in James. When the Manageress at the Hotel Occidental meets Karl, she recalls, speaking in English with a German accent, her old European identity as Grete Mitzelbach, working at the Golden Goose in Prague; Karl tells her that it was pulled down two years ago (124). Memory is of what is gone; to be the person never heard of again may be from the standpoint of a Europe that has no longer power to hear. The expatriate has not only no home in the adopted country, but cannot think back to a birthplace, either American—as with James, who has lost not only that, in New York, but also a family house in Boston—or European. James knew it was a "justly rebuked mistake" to return to try and find a home in America; and the reality now is of a place becoming a Deleuzian "any space whatever" (*Cinema* I, 109).

The text embodies more than one narrative, as with the typist, Therese, who works for the Manageress. A virtual orphan, her narrative recalls Dickens; and her relation to her parents recalls Karl's photograph of his parents. She came from Pomerania with her mother, but her father disappeared, leaving them "lost without discovery [playing upon the title] among the tenements in the east end of New York" (140). The text makes the tenements, straight out of *How the Other Half Lives*, impossible to map, labyrinthine, like the ship where Karl got lost, or the view from Uncle Jacob's sixth floor, or like Mr. Pollunder's house where Karl is also lost. As mother and daughter wander round, "Therese could not tell whether between midnight and five o'clock in the morning they had been in twenty buildings, or in two, or only in one. The corridors of these tenements were cunningly contrived to save space, but not to make it easy to find one's way about; likely enough they had trailed again and again through the same corridor" (142). This, with its Poe-like contraction of spaces, is like the space evoked in Dickens's Todgers's; there is no escape from the inside to the outside, and as all the insides may be of one building, perhaps that makes the American city indescribable, like being trapped in and by a body, the body felt as a prison. To be held by the city-as-body, borne down on or suffocated by the weight of buildings,[24] would be another state of urban modernity. To be inside the building or outside it—and the image of the glass roof over the New York streets fractured and replaced suggests that there may be no difference between these things—is equally dangerous. By the end of the narrative the mother has been killed on a building site where she has gone to work, where the "tall scaffolding for the rest of the structure [beyond the first story], still without its connecting boards, rose up into the blue sky" (144). Trying to ascend, as if getting up to where a panoramic view would be possible, she is killed, as if in the vertigo Dickens describes in *Martin Chuzzlewit*. "Rose up" distantly connects with the rising arm of the Statue of Liberty, as the blue sky recalls the "free winds of heaven"; here, however, it is not the male who comes under threat from female power, but the woman who is destroyed. The absent father was a building mason; the mother's death is overdetermined both by the breakdown within America of previously created relationships, and by the buildings without "connecting boards," which, pushing upwards as if in denial of the city, are defining an American future as American architecture. Whatever narrative may be constructed about Karl Rossmann, the novel plots other labyrinths than the one he wanders in, and suggests that nothing in the text can be reduced to a thesis. The intuition is that to be lost without trace is possible anywhere; but that soon, within the normal life-expectation of Kafka (born in 1883), there may be no alternative space in which the European like Kafka or Karl Rossmann can exist in. Unless Europe could be re-created.

Plural narratives and the two possible fates of Karl Rossmann imply several Americas; which one do we take? That which, under the pressure to compete with Europe, has tried to play out a dream of everything being better and nothing impossible, while being at the same time subtly coercive? (As the advertisement says, if you miss your opportunity with the Oklahoma theater you lose it for ever—and the offer closes at midnight, which was significantly also the time when Rossmann was expelled from his Uncle Jacob's protection.) Or the America whose difference from Europe questions it with the possibility of a minor literature? The first America creates a utopia that seems to promise reconciliation, yet always, in its bourgeois construction, it has exclusionary principles behind it, implied in the Statue of Liberty's sword and glanced at in the implications behind Rossmann's irrevocable change of name to "Negro" (257). Both Brod's and Kafka's possible futures for Karl appear likely, reconcilable with each other, though the other America, place of a minor literature, is more fleeting in the possibility that it could lead to another future in America. The text allows for either possibility, that "America" may be different or that it may replicate Europe. No single conclusion could be drawn from looking at Dickens, hostile and yet repeating the experience of going to the United States; or from James, whose *American Scene* has two endings, awed, positive, and hostile, the text's indeterminacy part of its fascination; nor from Kafka, whose hesitations in describing America appear in *Der Verschollene* not being finished. Each has had his memory and unconscious colonized by America, whether he has been there or not, and each responds to the American city as that which threatens to engulf the possibility of representing it. If Kafka does not need to go there to know that he could not represent it, that is because to describe America would be to fit it back into terms that were already known, whereas—as Dickens and James also knew—America had the power to dissolve the preset terms of the subject, producing the man who was never heard of again.

For Dickens, America was utterly different, involving a rite of passage across the Atlantic where the ship nearly went down, and then bringing his own assured subjectivity into question, giving promptings to those elements in his writing which Kafka was not the first to see as sentimentally coercive. James had to learn America's difference afresh, with the sense that America's being eradicated his own past, and *The American Scene* is an autobiographical text attempting to meet and to respond to that difference. Kafka's Karl Rossmann passes into New York harbor via the Statue of Liberty, under the sign of possible castration, the loss of his history, his European past, a loss he partly wills. Can the American city be a place for subjects without power, who have had such a sense of their subjectivity mauled?

Endnotes

1. Theodore Dreiser, *Sister Carrie*, ed. Lee Clark Mitchell (Oxford: Oxford University Press, 1991), pp. 13–14.
2. David Frisby, *Fragments of Modernity: Theories of Modernity in the Work of Simmel, Kracauer and Benjamin* (Oxford: Polity Press, 1985), p. 70. On the planning of nineteenth-century capitals, see Thomas Hall, *Planning Europe's Capital Cities: Aspects of Nineteenth-Century Urban Developments* (London: E. and F. N. Spon, 1997).
3. For Lefebvre, see the translations of his books: *Critique of Everyday Life* (London: Verso, 1991) and *The Production of Space* (Oxford: Blackwell, 1991). See also Rob Shields, *Lefebvre, Love and Struggle: Spatial Dialectics* (London: Routledge, 1999).
4. Landmarks here are Asa Briggs, *Victorian Cities* (1963, 3rd edition Berkeley: University of California Press, 1993); H. J. Dyos and Michael Wolff, eds., *The Victorian City, Images and Realities*, 2 vols. (London: Routledge, 1973); Raymond Williams, *The Country and the City* (London: Chatto and Windus, 1973), pp. 153–63 for Dickens; Sheila Smith, *The Other Nation: The Poor in English Novels of the 1840s and 1850s* (Oxford: Clarendon Press, 1980) for an example of criticism using Williams to read the condition of the urban poor. These are metonymies for a familiar criticism: the city for alienation and social problems, for the creation of the working class, and the question of the knowability of the poor as a community to the middle-class novelist. For a recent reading of Dickens and the city, see Andrew Sanders, *Dickens and the Spirit of the Age* (Oxford: Clarendon Press, 1999), pp. 67–110. Sanders's detailing of Dickens's walks in London gives the sense that Dickens desired more from urban existence than he needed for his novels, and perhaps more than London could give him.
5. For contrasting views of whether the city could be said to be knowable or not, see Christopher Prendergast, *Paris and the Nineteenth Century* (Oxford: Blackwell, 1992), following Raymond Williams on the "unknowable" city; and Priscilla Parkhurst Ferguson, *Paris as Revolution: Writing the Nineteenth-Century City* (Berkeley: University of California Press, 1994). Ferguson's

book details the change in the Parisian *flâneur,* from being the observer within the city to being, in Baudelaire, post 1848, in the increased conditions of commodification, controlled by the city, with a loss of autonomy (pp. 80–114). For the American *flâneur,* see Dana Brand, *The Spectator and the City in Nineteenth-Century American Literature* (Cambridge: Cambridge University Press, 1991).

6. One example of this type of criticism, inflected by the woman's construction as consumer, is Rachel Bowlby, *Just Looking: Consumer Culture in Dreiser, Gissing and Zola* (London: Methuen, 1985); see also Hana Wirth-Nesher, *City Codes: Reading the Modern Urban Novel* (Cambridge: Cambridge University Press, 1996), pp. 65–84 for Dreiser.

7. The topic of Philippe Mathy, *Extrême Occident: French Intellectuals and America* (Chicago: University of Chicago Press, 1993).

8. Repeated in *American Notes* from Dickens's letter to Forster of 3 April 1842, vol. 3, p. 181.

9. For the elements of disgust, see my *Dickens, Violence and the Modern State* (London: Macmillan, 1995), pp. 193–202.

10. Dickens, *American Notes,* ed. John S. Whitley and Arnold Goldman (Harmondsworth: Penguin, 1972), p. 35.

11. Fyodor Dostoyevsky, *Crime and Punishment,* trans. Jessie Coulson (New York: Norton, 1989), 6.6, pp. 427–33.

12. Honoré de Balzac, *Père Goriot,* trans. Burton Raffel (New York: W. W. Norton, 1998), pp. 86, 87.

13. Dostoyevsky, *The Brothers Karamazov,* trans. David Magarshack (Harmondsworth: Penguin, 1958), vol. 2, p. 898–99.

14. Matthew Arnold, "Civilization in the United States" (1888) in *Five Uncollected Essays,* ed. Kenneth Allott (Liverpool: University of Liverpool Press, 1953), p. 46.

15. Anthony Thorlby, *Kafka* (London: Heinemann, 1972), p. 34: the word is "the past participle of the verb *verschallen,* to 'die away' of sound; sounds and silence, noises and listening, had all sorts of symbolic overtones for Kafka's imagination." Roy Pascal, *The German Novel: Studies* (Manchester: Manchester University Press, 1956), p. 220. suggests "Lost Without Trace." Perhaps the idea of not being heard of again is silence, in answer to a call. On the title, see *Diaries,* 324; Kafka used it in an entry for 31 December 1914.

16. *Benjamin Franklin's Autobiography,* ed. J. A. Leo Lemay and P. M. Zall (New York: W. W. Norton, 1986), p. 17. Further references in the text.

17. On Horatio Alger (1832–1899), see John G. Cawelti, *Apostles of the Self-Made Man* (Chicago: University of Chicago Press, 1965), pp. 101–23; Michael Zuckerman, "The Nursery Tales of Horatio Alger," *American Quarterly* 24 (1972): 191–209; Michael Moon, "'The Gentle Boy from the Dangerous Classes': Pederasty, Domesticity and Capitalism in Horatio Alger," *Representations* 19 (1987): 87–110; Glenn Hendler, "Pandering in the Public Sphere: Masculinity and the Market in Horatio Alger," *Ameri-*

can Quarterly 48 (1996): 415–38. Despite the elements of continuity, there are also points of difference with Alger; his heroes are not orphans but have a widowed mother, and they depend less on self-reliance than on finding a nurturing older friend—the homosexual component that is picked up on in *Der Verschollene.*

18. To Janouch's question about what was so attractive in Dickens, Kafka responded: "His mastery of the material world. His balance between the external and the internal. His masterly and yet completely unaffected representation of the interaction between the world and the I. The perfectly natural proportions of his work" (J.185). For Kafka's reading of Dickens, see the diary entries for 20 August 1911, D.51, and 8 October 1917, D.388. See also J.211. It should be added that there has been much discussion about Janouch's reliability, since his book appeared in 1951, and reported conversations held with Kafka when he was just out of his teens some 30 years earlier, supposedly written up as notes. Some reproduce passages in Kafka's journals, which Janouch could not have seen until after he had taken his notes.

19. For the extent to which James's earlier observation of cities had been premised on Dickens's, see John Kimmey, *Henry James and London: The City in his Fiction* (London: Peter Lang, 1991).

20. For Wells and James before and after the journey, and for James's comments on Wells's book, see Leon Edel and Gordon N. Ray, eds., *Henry James and H. G. Wells: A Record of their Friendship, their Debate on the Art of Fiction and their Quarrel* (Urbana: University of Illinois Press, 1958), p. 107–17. For Wells in America, see also his letters, *The Correspondence of H. G. Wells: vol. 2, 1904–1918,* ed. David C. Smith (London: Pickering and Chatto, 1998), pp. 97–101.

21. For Wells on America, see Peter Conrad, *Imagining America* (London: Routledge and Kegan Paul, 1980), pp. 130–58. Wells serialized part of his text on America ("loose large articles") in *Harper's Weekly,* publishing the book, *The Future in America: A Search After Realities* that November, a year before *The American Scene:* both were issued, in similar formats, by Chapman and Hall. Wells had read sections of James's text in magazine form, and he comments on them in *The Future in America.*

22. A difference from James: Wells is fascinated by "muck-rakers" a term given a new currency by Roosevelt in 1906, and investigative writings provide many of the props of the text: Upton Sinclair, *The Jungle* (1906), Ida Tarbell, *Story of Standard Oil* (1902), the journalism of Ray Stannard Baker for *McClure's Magazine,* and T. W. Lawson's novel *Frenzied Finance* (1904)—which tells how he and Standard Oil had joined together to form Amalgamated Copper, a trust that had robbed the American public of millions. He looked at social problems through Robert Hunter and John Spargo and Lincoln Steffens's *Shame of the Cities* (1904) and Henry Demarest Lloyd's *Wealth Against Commonwealth* (1894)—again on Standard Oil.

23. *Diaries* 2:188–89, quoted in Charles Osborne, *Kafka* (Edinburgh: Oliver and Boyd, 1967), p. 56. On *David Copperfield* and *Amerika* see Mark Spilka, *Dickens and Kafka: A Mutual Interpretation* (Gloucester, Mass.: Peter Smith, 1969), pp. 127–98.

24. Maurice Blanchot, *The Space of Literature*, trans. Ann Smock (Lincoln: University of Nebraska Press, 1989), p. 73. Further references in the text.

25. I use the French edition of *Les Fleurs du Mal* with translations by Richard Howard (London: Picador Classics, 1982), pp. 270–72, Translations are mine. T. S. Eliot's "The Love-Song of J. Alfred Prufrock" translates Baudelaire's "brouillard sale et jaune" into "yellow fog" for his American city, while he retranslates it as "brown fog" for London in *The Waste Land*.

26. "Paris change! mais rien dans ma mélancolie / N'a bougé!" (Paris is changing. But nothing in my melancholy has changed), Baudelaire, "Le Cygne." On urban melancholy, which may be linked with indifference (see below, p. 153), see Ross Chambers, *The Writing of Melancholy: Modes of Opposition in early French Modernism*, trans. Mary Seidman Trouille (Chicago: University of Chicago Press, 1993).

27. Andrei Bely, *Petersburg*, trans. Robert A. Maguire and John E. Malmstad (Harmondsworth: Penguin, 1983), p. 26.

28. On nineteenth-century Paris and Petersburg, it is still relevant to consult Marshall Berman, *All that Is Solid Melts into Air: The Experience of Modernity* (London: Verso, 1983).

29. Stephen Crane, *Maggie: A Girl of the Streets*, ed. Thomas A Gullason (New York: W. W. Norton, 1979), pp. 3–4, 17, 53.

30. Emile Zola, *L'Assommoir*, trans. Margaret Mauldon (Oxford: Oxford University Press, 1995), p. 407.

31. Dostoyevsky, *Notes from Underground* (1864) in *Notes from Underground* and *The Double*, trans. Jessie Couslon (Harmondsworth: Penguin, 1972), p. 17.

32. Translation taken from Jacques Catteau, *Dostoyevsky and the Process of Literary Creation*, trans. Audrey Littlewood (Cambridge: Cambridge University Press, 1989), p. 428. The novel has been translated as *An Accidental Family* by Richard Freeborn (Oxford: Oxford University Press, 1994), p. 144 for the passage.

33. Alexander Pushkin, *The Queen of Spades and Other Stories*, trans. Rosemary Edmonds (Harmondsworth: Penguin, 1962), p. 163.

34. Walter Benjamin, *Charles Baudelaire: A Lyric Poet in An Age of High Capitalism*, trans. Harry Zohn (London: New Left Books, 1973), p. 134.

35. The point is taken from Q. D. Leavis, in F. R. and Q. D. Leavis, *Dickens the Novelist* (London: Chatto, 1970), p. 142. For further consideration of yellowness and of fog together, see the discussion of Jean-Louis Forain's picture, "A Study of Fog at a Station" (1884), in Theodore Reff, *Manet and Modern Paris* (Chicago: University of Chicago Press, 1982), p. 66.

36. Friedrich Wilhelm Nietzsche, *Twilight of the Idols*, in *The Portable Nietzsche*, trans. Walter Kaufmann (New York: Viking, 1954), p. 483.

37. See the notes by Susan Shatto, *The Companion to Bleak House* (London: Unwin Hyman, 1988), p. 22, for the fog reaching indoors and for supporting commentary on these paragraphs.
38. Jacques Lacan, *Écrits: A Selection,* trans. Alan Sheridan (London: Tavistock, 1977), p. 264.
39. William Blake, "Poems from the Notebook, 1793" in *Complete Writings,* ed. Geoffrey Keynes (Oxford: Oxford University Press, 1966), p. 166. Keynes shows that Blake deleted the third line in the second verse: "I spurn'd his waters away from me" and changed the fourth from "I was born a slave, but I long to be free."
40. Benjamin, *Charles Baudelaire: A Lyric Poet in the Age of High Capitalism* (London: New Left Books, 1973), p. 176.

CHAPTER 2

1. For Dickens as a Liberal, see his letter to Macready, 22 March 1842, *Letters,* vol. 3, p. 158.
2. Harriet Martineau, *Society in America,* edited, abridged, and with an introduction by Seymour Martin Lipset (1962, New Brunswick, N.J.: Transaction Publishers, 1981), p. 279.
3. Fanny Trollope, *Domestic Manners of the Americans,* ed. Pamela Neville-Sington (Harmondsworth: Penguin, 1997), 3.27. Further references in text.
4. Quoted, *Domestic Manners of the Americans,* p. 361.
5. On American banknotes, see *Letters,* vol. 3, p. 206n.
6. Alexander Welsh, *From Copyright to Copperfield: The Identity of Dickens* (Cambridge, Mass.: Harvard University Press, 1987), pp. 31–38. For Spedding's review, see Welsh, but also Philip Collins, ed., *Dickens: The Critical Heritage* (London: Routledge and Kegan Paul, 1971), pp. 124–29. On the copyright issue, see Gerhard Hoseph, "Charles Dickens, International Copyright and the Discretionary Silence of *Martin Chuzzlewit,*" in Martha Woodmansee and Peter Jaszi, eds., *The Construction of Authorship* (Durham, N.C.: Duke University Press, 1994), pp. 259–70.
7. *Edinburgh Review* 33 (1820): 79.
8. *The Speeches of Charles Dickens,* ed. K. J. Fielding (Oxford: Clarendon Press, 1960), p. 20.
9. Matthew Arnold, *Civilization in the United States: First and Last Impressions of America,* 4th ed. (Boston, 1888), pp. 61–62, quoted in Alex Zwerdling, *Improvised Europeans: American Literary Expatriates and the Siege of London* (New York: Basic Books, 1998), p. 11.
10. "A Word About America" (1882), in *Five Uncollected Essays of Matthew Arnold,* ed. Kenneth Allott (Liverpool: University of Liverpool Press, 1953), p. 2.
11. Martineau, *Society in America,* pp. 164–65.
12. In discussing *American Notes,* the indispensable companion is *The Letters of Charles Dickens,* vol. 3, 1842–43, which gives Dickens's letters to Forster,

many of which became the basis of material in *American Notes,* and comments on Dickens's experiences in America. See also Myon Magnet, *Dickens and the Social Order* (Philadelphia: University of Pennsylvania Press, 1985), pp. 175–202; and Jerome Meckier, *Innocent Abroad: Charles Dickens's American Enlargements* (1990). See the essays by Patrick McCarthy and Nancy Metz in *Dickens, Europe and the New Worlds,* ed. Anny Sadrin (London: Macmillan, 1999), on *American Notes* (pp. 67–76) and *Martin Chuzzlewit* (pp. 77–98). See also Robert Lawson-Peebles, "Dickens Goes West," in Mick Gidley and Robert Lawson-Peebles, *Views of American Landscapes* (Cambridge: Cambridge University Press, 1989), pp. 111–25; and Robert Lougy, "Desire and the Ideology of Violence: America in Charles Dickens's *Martin Chuzzlewit,*" *Criticism* 36 (1994): 569–94.

13. See James Tackach, *Great American Hotels* (New York: Smithmark, 1991), p. 6.

14. See Sander Gilman, *Disease and Representation: Images of Illness from Madness to AIDS* (Ithaca: Cornell University Press, 1988), p. 84.

15. See Michael Holleran, *Boston's 'Changeful Times'* (Baltimore: Johns Hopkins University Press, 1998), p. 17.

16. Benita Eilser, *The Lowell Offering: Writings by New England Mill Women* (New York: W. W. Norton, 1998), p. 22.

17. Quoted, Paul E. Cohen, *Manhattan in Maps 1527–1995* (New York: Rizzoli, 1997), p. 102.

18. On Dickens's account of New York, see Wyn Kelley, *Melville's City: Literary and Urban Form in Nineteenth-Century New York* (Cambridge: Cambridge University Press, 1996), pp. 51–59, 102–7.

19. See Amy Gilman Srebnick, *The Mysterious Death of Mary Rogers: Sex and Culture in Nineteenth-Century New York* (Oxford: Oxford University Press, 1995).

20. Gilles Deleuze, *Cinema I: The Movement Image,* trans. Hugh Tomlinson and Barbara Habberjam (Minneapolis: University of Minnesota Press, 1986), pp. 109–22.

21. *The Encyclopaedia of New York City,* ed. Kenneth T. Jackson (New Haven: Yale University Press, 1995) estimates that after the Napoleonic Wars, there were 12,000 Irish in the city, and in the 1830s, 200,000 Irish arrived. "By 1844, fifteen parishes had been formed on Manhattan Island to serve an estimated eighty to ninety thousand Catholics, most of whom were Irish" (p. 198). The Irish Emigrant Society of New York began existence in 1841; the *Encyclopaedia* (p. 199) notes that Irish dug the channels for the Croton Reservoir. For Dickens's complacency about the Irish laborers, see his comments on them—"jolly and good humoured as ever" in relation to Cincinnati (*American Notes,* II.169).

22. On Melville and Dickens, see Robert Weisbuch, *Atlantic Double-Cross: American Literature and British Influence in the Age of Emerson* (Chicago: University of Chicago Press, 1986), pp. 36–56 especially.

23. Quoted, G. E. Kidder Smith, *A Pictorial History of Architecture in America,* 2 vols. (New York: American Heritage Publishing Co., 1976), p. 195.

24. Compare the English traveler James Silk Buckingham, in *The Eastern and Western States of America* (1842), on "the unavoidable accumulation of soot and dirt upon everything you see or touch. Sheffield, in England, is sometimes called 'The City of Soot,' but its atmosphere is clear and transparent in comparison with that of Pittsburgh, which is certainly the most smoky and sooty town it has ever been my lot to behold. The houses are blackened with it, the streets are made filthy, and the garments and persons of all whom you meet are soiled and made dingy by its influence." Quoted, John W. Reps, *The Making of Urban America: A History of City Planning in the United States* (Princeton, N.J.: Princeton University Press, 1965), p. 206. Reps's work on American cities belongs to a huge bibliography on the subject; for some guidance, see *American Urbanism: A Historiographical Review*, ed. Howard Gillette Jr. and Zane L. Miller (New York: Greenwood Press, 1987).

25. Dickens approves of this Eliot: it is at least interesting to note that he was T. S. Eliot's grandfather. See on him, Eric Sigg, *The American T.S. Eliot: A Study of the Early Writings* (Cambridge: Cambridge University Press, 1989), pp. 3–5.

CHAPTER 3

1. See Mario Gandelsonas, *X-Urbanism: Architecture and the American City* (New York: Princeton Architectural Press, 1999), pp. 59–71.

2. I refer to the full title: *The Life and Adventures of Martin Chuzzlewit, His Relatives, Friends and Enemies. Comprising All his Wills and his Ways: With an Historical Record of What he Did, and What he Didn't: Showing, Moreover, Who Inherited the Family Plate, Who Came in for the Silver Spoons, and Who for the Wooden Ladle. The Whole Forming a Complete Key to the House of Chuzzlewit. Edited By Boz. With Illustrations by Phiz.* For discussion of Dickens against architecture in *Great Expectations* and *Martin Chuzzlewit*, see chapter 1 in my *Dickens, Violence and the Modern State* (London: Macmillan, 1995).

3. The architectural theme in *Martin Chuzzlewit* has been looked at by Alan R. Burke, "The House of Chuzzlewit and the Architectural City," *Dickens Studies Annual* 3 (1974): 14–40; see also Nancy Aycock Metz, "Dickens and the Quack Architectural," *Dickens Quarterly* 11.2 (1994): 59–64; and Steven Connor, "Babel Unbuilding: The Anti-archi-rhetoric of *Martin Chuzzlewit*" in John Schad, ed., *Dickens Refigured* (Manchester: Manchester University Press, 1996), pp. 178–99. On the novel generally, see Dorothy Van Ghent, "The Dickens World: A View from Todgers's," *Sewanee Review* 58 (1950): 419–38; Jonathan Arac, *Commissioned Spirits: The Shaping of Social Motion in Dickens, Carlyle, Melville and Hawthorne* (New Brunswick, N. J.: Rutgers University Press, 1979), pp. 58–93; Alexander Welsh, *From Copyright to Copperfield: The Identity of Dickens* (Cambridge, Mass.: Harvard University Press, 1987), chaps. 4 and 5. The most complete study of the whole text

is by Sylvère Monod, *Martin Chuzzlewit* (London: George Allen and Unwin, 1985).

4. Foucault, *Discipline and Punish*, trans. Alan Sheridan (Harmondsworth: Penguin, 1979) p. 207, quotes Bentham on the Panopticon, "Morals reformed, health preserved, industry invigorated, instruction diffused, public burdens lightened, economy seated, as it were, upon a rock, the Gordian knot of the Poor Laws not cut but untied—all by a simple idea of Architecture!"

5. See Geoffrey Tyack, *Sir James Pennethorne and the Making of Victorian London* (Cambridge: Cambridge University Press, 1992), p. 76. This was not yet modernism: John Summerson, *Victorian Architecture: Four Studies in Evaluation* (New York: Columbia University Press, 1970), p. 8, gives 1860 as the first time when "modernism" was used in relation to architecture. For the history, see Giles Worsley, *Architectural Drawings of the Regency Period* (London: Andre Deutsch, 1991), pp. 1–29.

6. Buildings committees were inadequate to deal with them: see correspondence with Henry Austin, 17 April 1841, *Letters of Charles Dickens*, vol. 2, ed. Madeline House and Graham Storey (Oxford: Clarendon Press, 1969), pp. 262–63 and note. Austin's "Thoughts on the Abuses of the Present System of Competition in Architecture, with an outline of a Plan for the Remedy" (1841) was basically to professionalize the Buildings Committees with members of RIBA. It was written to Earl de Grey (1781–1859), the first president of RIBA. Austin (1812–1861), Dickens's brother-in-law, was an architect and civil engineer.

7. Richard L. Stein, *Victoria's Year: English Literature and Culture 1837–1838* (Oxford: Oxford University Press, 1987), p. 41. "The gaol, it seems to be implied, was not required in the perfect society of the Middle Ages"—Miles Lewis, "Architectural Utopias," in E. Kamenka, ed., *Utopias: Papers from the Annual Symposium of the Australian Academy of the Humanities* (Oxford: Oxford University Press, 1987), pp. 109–32, p. 115. On *Contrasts*, see Margaret Belcher, "Pugin Writing" in Paul Atterbury and Clive Wainwright, eds., *Pugin: A Gothic Passion* (New Haven: Yale University Press in association with the Victoria and Albert Museum, 1994) pp. 104–16.

8. Robin Evans, *The Fabrication of Virtue: English Prison Architecture, 1750–1840* (Cambridge: Cambridge University Press, 1982), p. 409. See also pp. 43–45 for the development of the architectural profession; William Jones is part of the coincidence, since he drew up plans for a new Newgate in 1757. On the prison as a new cultural system in the eighteenth century, see John Bender, *Imagining the Penitentiary: Fiction and the Architecture of Mind in Eighteen-Century England* (Chicago: University of Chicago Press, 1987).

9. Quoted, Kenneth Clark, *The Gothic Revival* (First published 1928; London: Constable, 1950), pp. 201, 202.

10. A. W. Pugin, *The True Principles of Pointed or Christian Architecture* (London: Academy Editions Reprint, 1973), p. 1. On Pugin, see Nikolaus Pevsner,

Some Architectural Writers of the Nineteenth Century (Oxford: Clarendon, 1972), pp. 103–22, and *Pugin: A Gothic Passion,* ed. Paul Atterbury and Clive Wainwright (New Haven: Yale University Press, 1994). On the "principles," see Henry-Russell Hitchcock, *Early Victorian Architecture in Britain,* 2 vols. (New Haven: Yale University Press, 1954), vol. 1, p. 77. Hitchcock aligns Pugin's views with functionalism.

11. Robert Kerr, 1884, quoted Pevsner, *Some Architectural Writers,* p. 302.

12. Quoted, Tyack, *Pennethorne and Victorian London,* p. 33.

13. Donaldson had made this issue the focus of his *Preliminary Discourse Pronounced before the University College of London, upon the Commencement of a Series of Lectures on Architecture,* 17 October 1842. Quoted, Richard Etlin, *Modernism in Italian Architecture, 1890–1940* (Cambridge, Mass.: MIT Press, 1991), pp. xviii, 599. On Donaldson, see Hitchcock, *Early Victorian Architecture,* vol. 1, pp. 544–45.

14. *The Works of John Ruskin,* 30 vols., ed. E. J. Cook and A. Wedderburn (London: George Allen, 1903–12), vol. 8, pp. 251–52. For Ruskin on architecture, see Michael Wheeler and Nigel Whitely, eds., *The Lamp of Memory: Ruskin, Tradition and Architecture* (Manchester: Manchester University Press, 1992).

15. Benjamin Disraeli, chapter 10, *Tancred,* ed. Hughenden, vol. 9, bk. 2 (1882) pp. 112–23.

16. Quoted, Stein (see note 7), p. 191. The series was called "The Poetry of Architecture." See Michael W. Brooks, *John Ruskin and Victorian Architecture* (New Brunswick, N.J.: Rutgers University Press, 1987), pp. 7–13, for Loudon and the *Architectural Review.*

17. *The Works of John Ruskin,* vol. 8, pp. 56, 60, 72, 81.

18. Worsley (see note 5), p. 147.

19. Arthur Schopenhauer, *The World as Will and Representation* trans. E. J. Payne, 2 vols. (New York: Dover, 1957), vol. 2, p. 214. Further references by volume and page are given in the text.

20. James D. Chansley, "Schopenhauer and Platonic ideas: A Groundwork for an Aesthetic Metaphysics," quotes Alexis Philomenko, in *Schopenhauer, Une Philosophie de la Tragedie* (Paris: Verim, 1980), who makes "the tantalising suggestion" that "l'architecture est l'art du ressentiment," p. 150. See Eric von Luft, *Schopenhauer: New Essays in Honor of his 200th Birthday* (Lewiston, N.Y.: Edwin Mellen Press, 1988), p. 77. Nietzsche discusses revenge in *Thus Spake Zarathustra,* Book 2, "On Redemption," and *ressentiment* in *The Genealogy of Morals,* Essay 1, chapter 12.

21. Quoted, J. Mordaunt Crook, *William Burgess and the High Victorian Dream* (London: John Murray, 1981).

22. David J. Rothman, *The Discovery of the Asylum: Social Order and Disorder in the New Republic* (Boston: Little, Brown and Company, 1971), p. 75.

23. Rothman, pp. 83–84.

24. Rothman, p. 90. The Walnut Street jail in 1770 is reproduced in David J. Rothman's chapter, "Perfecting the Prison" in Norval Morris and David

J. Rothman, eds., *The Oxford History of the Prison* (Oxford: Oxford University Press, 1995), p. 113.

25. *Domestic Manners of the Americans,* chap. 2, p. 15; chap. 25, p. 205.

26. Ruskin, quoted Brooks, *Ruskin and Victorian Architecture,* p. 47.

27. "Dickens almost never uses the words 'moral' or 'morality' in any but an ironic sense": Stephen Marcus, *Dickens From Pickwick to Dombey* (London: Chatto and Windus, 1965), p. 236.

28. For Buckingham, see the editor's note for *Letters,* vol. 3, pp. 239–40n.

29. Quoted, Reps, p. 386 (see chap. 2 n. 25): see his discussion of Cairo, pp. 382–89, and his inclusion of Strickland's designs.

30. For a reading of this point, see Victor Brombert, *Victor Hugo and the Visionary Novel* (Cambridge, Mass.: Harvard University Press, 1984), pp. 49–85. Brombert shows that both architecture and print are to be read but that Hugo's figure for both is the Tower of Babel. On the links between Hugo and Dickens's "view from Todgers's" see Richard Maxwell, *The Mysteries of Paris and London* (Charlottesville: University of Virginia Press, 1992), who makes two points relevant for this study: the labyrinth is a figure of return, a line that leads back to the beginning (which gives it the quality of the uncanny), pp. 25–26; and the importance of viewing the city from the air— the panoramic view—which is in Hugo (cf., the chapter title: "Paris à vol d'oiseau" [Paris—a bird's eye view]). Maxwell shows how widespread viewing the city from above was in the nineteenth century: see also his "City Life and the Novel: Hugo, Ainsworth, Dickens," *Comparative Literature* 30 (1978): 164. For a discussion of nineteenth-century photography using aerial views, see Peter B. Hales, *Silver Cities: The Photography of American Urbanization, 1839–1915* (Philadelphia: Temple University Press, 1984), pp. 48, 73–96.

31. John Forster, *Life of Dickens,* IV.2, ed. J. W. T. Ley (London: n.p., 1928), p. 308. My emphasis.

32. Examples of discontinuity: at the beginning of chapter 21 (340–41, the opening to installment 9), and with the end of chapter 30 (485) and the beginning of chapter 31, and with chapter 33 (512).

33. The point is made by J. Hillis Miller, *Charles Dickens: The World of his Novels* (1958; Bloomington: University of Indiana Press, 1969), p. 103.

34. See 40.624; compare 25.403 for Mrs. Gamp's "this Pilgian's Projiss of a mortal wale" and 47.721 for the "shadowy veil" that is drawing round Montague Tigg, near to death.

35. Mark Wigley, *The Architecture of Deconstruction: Derrida's Haunt* (Cambridge, Mass.: MIT Press, 1993), pp. 127–28, quoting from "Cogito and the History of Madness, in *Writing and Difference,* trans. Alan Bass (London: Routledge, 1967), p. 40.

36. For this point about the box, compare D. A. Miller's chapter on *David Copperfield,* "Secret Subjects, Open Secrets," in *The Novel and the Police* (Berkeley: University of California Press, 1988).

37. "The Man of the Crowd," *Edgar Allan Poe: Selected Writings,* ed. David Galloway (Harmondsworth: Penguin, 1967), p. 188.

38. Ned Lukacher, *Primal Scenes: Literature, Philosophy, Psychoanalysis* (Ithaca: Cornell University Press, 1986), p. 306. For "cryptonomy," see Nicolas Abraham and Maria Torok, *The Wolf Man's Magic Word,* trans. Nicholas Rand (Minneapolis: University of Minnesota Press, 1986), p. xxv, my emphasis. For further discussion of Mrs. Gamp, see Pam Morris, *Dickens's Class Consciousness: A Marginal View* (London: Macmillan, 1991), pp. 51–58.

39. Lukacher, *Primal Scenes,* pp. 88–89.

40. Walter Benjamin quotes this from an illustrated Paris guide, in "Fourier or the Arcades," *Charles Baudelaire: A Lyric Poet in the Era of High Capitalism* (London: Verso, 1973), p. 158. For a sustained meditation on Benjamin in relation to architecture and nineteenth-century literature, see Philippe Hamon, *Expositions: Literature and Architecture in Nineteenth-Century France,* trans. Katia Sainson-Frank and Lisa Maguire (Berkeley: University of California Press, 1992).

41. Sigmund Freud, "The Uncanny," *Art and Literature,* Penguin Freud, 14 (Harmondsworth: Penguin, 1985), p. 345.

42. For an attempt to think through this concept, where cinematic architecture has a deconstructive function, see Anthony Vidler, "The Explosion of Space: Architecture and the Filmic Imaginary," in Dietrich Neumann, ed., *Film Architecture: Set Designs from Metropolis to Blade Runner* (New York: Prestel, 1996), pp. 14–25.

43. The Monument was temporarily closed in 1842, after the sixth suicide, that of a servant woman, took place there: the top of it was enclosed with a railing to prevent suicides. See Ben Weinrub and Christopher Hibbert, eds., *The London Encyclopaedia* (London: Macmillan, 1983), p. 942.

44. Quoted, Anthony Vidler, *The Architecture of the Uncanny: Essays in the Modern Unhomely* (Cambridge, Mass.: MIT Press, 1992), p. 224.

45. The word "It" dimly connects to the father, as though the primal violence in this text were father/son related: compare Jonas after the death of his father: "The weight of that which was stretched out stiff and stark, in the awful chamber above stairs, so crushed and bore down Jonas, that he bent beneath the load. . . . he was always oppressed and haunted by a dreadful sense of Its presence in the house. Did the door move, he looked towards it with a livid face . . ." (19.321).

46. "Psychosis" was introduced into medical psychology in 1845. See Victor Burgin, "Paranoiac Space," *New Formations* 12 (Winter, 1990): 61–75, 74.

47. See Brooks (see note 16), p. 22.

48. Freud, "Five Lectures on Psychoanalysis," 1910, Standard Edition (London: Hogarth Press, 1953–74), vol. 11, pp. 16–17.

49. Robert F. Dalzell, *Enterprising Elite: The Boston Associates and the World they Made* (New York: W. W. Norton, 1987), p. 46. I take the point about Lowell from Dalzell.

50. In Norval Morris and David J. Rothman, eds., *The Oxford History of the Prison* (Oxford: Oxford University Press, 1995), p. 118. On the same page,

Rothman quotes Tocqueville saying that reformers had been caught in "the monomania of the penitentiary system."

51. *Society in America*, pp. 315–17. See also *Letters*, vol. 3, pp. 105n and 110n.

52. Lacan, *Ecrits: A Selection*, trans. Alan Sheridan (London: Tavistock, 1977), p. 13.

53. Dario Melossi and Massimo Pavarini, *The Prison and the Factory: Origins of the Penitentiary System*, trans. Glynis Cousin (London: Macmillan, 1981), p. 100. The reference to S. Cooper is to his *A Sermon Preached at Boston: New England, Before the Society for Encouraging Industry and Employing the Poor* (1753).

CHAPTER 4

1. *The Journals and Miscellaneous Notebooks of Ralph Waldo Emerson*, ed. William H. Gilman and J. E. Parsons (Cambridge, Mass.: Harvard University Press, 1970), vol. 8, p. 222.

2. Quoted, Philip Collins, ed., *Dickens: The Critical Heritage* (London: Routledge and Kegan Paul, 1971), pp. 566–67.

3. *Ralph Waldo Emerson*, ed. Richard Poirier (Oxford: Oxford University Press, 1990), pp.101–2 (see the essay, pp. 97–110). See Robert D. Richardson Jr., *Emerson: The Mind on Fire* (Berkeley: University of California Press, 1995), p. 249 (see pp. 245–51 for the Transcendental Club, and pp. 335–36 for *The Dial*).

4. It contained: "History," "Self-Reliance," "Compensation," "Spiritual Laws," "Love," "Friendship," "Prudence," "Heroism," "The Over-Soul," "Circles," "Intellect," and "Art." Emerson brought out *Nature* in 1836. Dickens could have read the essays before coming to America.

5. On this short story, see Robert H. Byer, "Mysteries of the City: A Reading of Poe's 'The Man of the Crowd,'" in Sacvan Bercovitch and Myra Jehlen, eds., *Ideology and Classic American Literature* (Cambridge: Cambridge University Press, 1986), pp. 221–46. Relevantly for the sense of the subject's disappearance in the city, Byer quotes from Emerson's journal for 1842: "In New York City lately, as in cities generally, one seems to lose all substance and become surface in a world of surfaces. Everything is external, and I remember my hat and coat, and all my other surfaces, and nothing else" (pp. 221–22).

6. Poirier, *Emerson*, p. 3.

7. Poirier, *Emerson*, p. 13.

8. Carlyle, *The Complete Works of Thomas Carlyle in Thirty Volumes: Centenary Edition* (London: Chapman and Hall, 1896–99), vol. 1 (11.10), p. 161. *Sartor Resartus* was written in 1830–31. On the subject of the hieroglyph, see John T. Irwin, "The Symbol of the Hieroglyphics in the American Renaissance," *American Quarterly* 26 (1974): 101–26. See also Jonathan Arac, *Commissioned Spirits: The Shaping of Social Motion in Dickens, Carlyle, Melville and Hawthorne* (New Brunswick, N.J.: Rutgers University Press, 1979), pp. 156–63.

9. Kirk Savage, *Standing Soldiers, Kneeling Slaves: Race, War and Monument in Nineteenth-Century America* (Princeton: Princeton University Press, 1997), p. 4. Dickens makes fun of ante-bellum statuary in the fictitious Chiggle's statue to Elijah Pogram, *Martin Chuzzlewit*, 34.531.

10. He borrowed from one of the American Anti-Slavery Society's pamphlets, *American Slavery As It Is: Testimony of a Thousand Witnesses* (1839) written anonymously by Theodore D. Weld, who also advised John Quincy Adams on slavery. The chapter also relied on newspaper reports collected by Edward Chapman. See *Letters* (16 September 1842, to Edward Chapman), vol. 3, p. 342. William Lloyd Garrison in *The Liberator*, 18 November 1842, said that Dickens avoided the abolitionists in Boston (*Letters*, 3:xiv).

11. Dickens is in the shadow of Carlyle's "Occasional Discourse on the Negro Question," *Fraser's Magazine*, December 1849, reissued in 1853 as "The Nigger Question." Carlyle speaks of the "eternal law of Nature for a man . . . that he shall be permitted, encouraged, and if need be compelled to do what work the Maker of him has intended by the making of him for this world," and so identifies "Quashee," virtually, as intended for slavery, while also saying that it is futile to try to abolish slavery—"you cannot abolish slavery by act of Parliament, but can only abolish the *name* of it, which is very little." See "The Nigger Question," in the *Centenary Edition*, 37 vols., ed. H. D. Thraill (London: Chapman and Hall, 1872), vol. 29, pp. 356, 357, 359. On "The Negro Question," see Chris R. Vanden Bossche, *Carlyle and the Search for Authority* (Columbus: Ohio State University Press, 1991), pp. 129–41. On Dickens and Carlyle, see my "Carlyle in Prison: Reading Latter-Day Pamphlets," *Dickens Studies Annual* 26 (1997): 311–33.

12. The women promoting the Stafford House Address to Mrs. Stowe were also compared to Mrs. Jellyby in *The Times*, 13 December 1852, see Deborah A. Thomas, *Thackeray and Slavery* (Athens: Ohio University Press, 1993), p. 127. James's feminist Miss Birdseye in *The Bostonians* is surely in the *Martin Chuzzlewit/Bleak House* tradition; James was accused of having used Elizabeth Peabody, Hawthorne's sister-in-law, as a model for her; see Edel, vol. 3, pp. 79–80.

13. See *Uncollected Writings from Household Words*, ed. Harry Stone (Bloomington: Indiana University Press, 1968), vol. 2, p. 440. The article is anti-slavery, but argues how slavery may be abolished, and shows that return of ex-slaves to Liberia has been only partially successful. Yet it is not difficult to pick up the colonial tone—the new Liberian, ex-American, "may help in spreading the light of civilization among his race." The slave must be allowed to "imbibe in their full freedom the doctrines of Christianity." The conclusion—which Dickens quotes in his letter—is resolutely Utilitarian: "Americans might so abolish slavery as to produce with little or no cost—probably with profit to themselves—results far greater than have been obtained in England with a vast expenditure of money . . ." (442).

14. On the politics of *The Scarlet Letter* see Sacvan Bercovitch, *The Office of The Scarlet Letter* (Baltimore: Johns Hopkins University Press, 1991).

15. Letter of 4 March 1853, to Albany Fonblanque, from Richmond, Virginia; *The Letters and Private Papers of William Makepeace Thackeray,* 4 vols., ed. Gordon N. Ray (Cambridge, Mass.: Harvard University Press, 1945–46), vol. 3, p. 226. Further citations in the text.

16. See Edel, vol. 2, p. 91. See James's account, *A Small Boy and Others,* in *Autobiography* vol. 3, p. 52.

17. The view of Deborah A. Thomas, *Thackeray and Slavery* (Athens: Ohio University Press, 1993), p. 121; see the discussion of Thackeray on American slavery, pp. 115–21. See also Thomas's discussion of Thackeray and Harriet Beecher Stowe (pp. 121–23) and also her reference to Mrs. Stowe in *The Newcomes,* chap. 28 (pp. 125–28). For Thackeray's pro-South views in the war see Thomas, pp. 159–64.

18. Quoted in the essay by Albert Stein, in *Landscape into Cityscape: Frederick Law Olmsted's Plans for a Greater New York City,* ed. Albert Stein (New York: Van Nostrand Reinhold Co., 1967), p. 22, p. 24; and see pp. 15–26.

19. Baudelaire, *Selected Writings on Art and Artists,* trans. P. E. Charvet (Harmondsworth: Penguin, 1972), p. 395.

20. Quoted, Gordon N. Ray, *Thackeray: The Age of Wisdom: 1843–1863* (London: Oxford University Press, 1958), p. 215.

21. Thackeray, *The Virginians* (London: Dent, 1951), vol. 1, p. 22 (chap. 3).

22. Edmund Wilson, *Patriotic Gore: Studies in the Literature of the American Civil War* (1962; London: Hogarth Press, 1987), pp. xxvii–xix, 380–437.

23. Anthony Trollope, *North America,* 2 vols. (London: Dawsons, 1968), vol. 2, p. 197. A cut-down version of *North America* exists in Penguin (1968).

24. See Asa Briggs, "Trollope the Traveller" in John Halperin, ed., *Trollope: Centenary Essays* (London: Macmillan, 1982), pp. 24–52. See also N. John Hall, *Trollope: A Biography* (Oxford: Clarendon Press, 1991), pp. 221–42. See also "Ploughshares into Swords: The Civil Landscape of Trollope's *North America,*" *Nineteenth-Century Literature* (1990): 59–72.

25. Thomas Crawford (1811–1857), sculptor, rather than painter: Trollope may be referring to his *The Indian: Dying Chief Contemplating the Progress of Civilization* (1856). The picture is reproduced as No. 31 in Maurice Rheims, *19th Century Sculpture,* trans. Robert E. Wolf (New York: Harry N. Adams, 1972), p. 198.

26. For Whitman on New York, see M. Wynn Thomas, *The Lunar Light of Whitman's Poetry* (Cambridge, Mass.: Harvard University Press, 1987), pp. 148–77; Alan Trachtenberg, "Whitman's Lesson of the City," in Betsy Erkkila and Jay Grossman, *Breaking Bounds: Whitman and American Cultural Studies* (Oxford: Oxford University Press, 1996), pp. 163–73. Trachtenberg quotes William James's lecture, "On a Certain Blindness in Human Beings," which draws on Whitman to discuss "rapture" in relation to "Whitman's way of being in the city."

27. Quoted, Milton K. Brown, *American Art to 1900: Painting, Sculpture, Architecture* (New York: Harry N. Abrams, 1977), p. 299. This book has useful discussions, as has Dell Upton, *Architecture in the United States* (Oxford: Oxford

University Press, 1998), pp. 71–75, on the Capitol. See also *Worthy of the Nation: The History of Planning for the National Capital* (Washington: Smithsonian Institution, 1977). On the Smithsonian, see Harriet Ritvo, "Gothic Revival Architecture in England and America: A Case Study in Public Symbolism," in *Allegory: Myth and Symbol,* ed. Morton Bloomfield (Cambridge, Mass.: Harvard University Press, 1981), pp. 313–34.

28. See Martin J. Wiener, *English Culture and the Decline of the Industrial Spirit, 1850–1980* (Cambridge: Cambridge University Press, 1981), pp. 88–90.

29. For this tour, see Forster, *Life,* 10:1, 2 (pp. 765–96), which may be supplemented by Kaplan, *Dickens: A Biography* (London: Hodder and Stoughton, 1988) pp. 513–29. See also Michael Slater, *Dickens on America and the Americans* (London: Harvester Press, 1979), pp. 222–45.

30. See the discussion of Simmel's essays "The Metropolis and Mental Life" (1903) and "The Stranger" (1903) in Robert L. Herbert, *Impressionism: Art, Leisure and Parisian Society* (New Haven: Yale University Press, 1988), pp. 50–57. Simmel's essays on the city are collected in Donald Levine, ed., *George Simmel: On Individuality and Social Forms* (Chicago: University of Chicago Press, 1971).

31. Quoted, Philip Collins, *Dickens: Interviews and Recollections* (London: Macmillan, 1981), vol. 2, pp. 318–19.

32. James thought of his meeting with Dickens during his own American tour: see *Notebooks,* p. 238. For the dream of the reversal of the haunting, which leads to James chasing the ghost down a spectral Gallerie d'Apollon, see *A Small Boy and Others* (*Autobiography,* vol. 1), pp. 196–99. I refer to the dream in my book, *Henry James: Critical Issues* (London: Macmillan, 2000) p. 108.

CHAPTER 5

1. A note on chronology. Although James had visited Europe as a child with his family, he first went to Europe independently in 1869–70, and traveled extensively in Europe in 1872–74. In 1875 he decided to settle in Europe, making his home in London in 1876. He revisited America twice between 1881 and 1883, for the death of his parents. His next visit (for *The American Scene*) was 1904–5; he visited again in 1910 for the death of William James.

2. See Hal Foster, *The Return of the Real: The Avant-Garde at the End of the Century* (Cambridge, Mass.: MIT Press, 1996), pp. 132–38 for this. The passage in Lacan is *The Four Fundamental Concepts of Psychoanalysis,* trans. Alan Sheridan (Harmondsworth: Penguin, 1979), p. 53. See Susan Stewart, *Crimes of Writing: Problems in the Containment of Representation* (Durham, N.C.: Duke University Press, 1994), pp. 273–90; "the trauma appears in the break between ego and world, and *is* the break between ego and world" (p. 278).

3. Paul Bourget, *Outre-Mer: Impressions of America* (New York: Charles Scribner's Sons, 1895), p. 19. See James's letter to Edmund Gosse, 22 August

1894, *Letters* vol. 3, p. 486 for James on *Outre-Mer*. See also Edel vol. 3, p. 50, and Kaplan pp. 308–9. For James and Bourget, see Adeline Tintner, *The Cosmopolitan World of Henry James: An Intertextual Study* (Baton Rouge: Louisiana State University Press, 1991), pp. 152–232. See J. C. Fewster, "A Service de l'ordre: Paul Bourget and the Critical Response to Decadence in Austria and Germany," *Comparative Literature Studies* 20 (1992): 259–75. Fewster brings out Nietzsche's appreciation of Bourget, mentioned in *Ecce Homo*, "Why I am so Clever," section 3. See also Walter Kauffmann, *Nietzsche: Philosopher, Psychologist, Antichrist* (Princeton: Princeton University Press, 1968), p. 73n. This contact enables a comparison of James with Nietzsche.

4. James, Letter, 17 August 1902, *Letters*, vol. 4, p. 235–36.
5. James to George du Maurier, 17 April 1883, *Letters*, vol. 2, p. 409.
6. I have discussed this text in my *Henry James: Critical Issues* (London: Macmillan, 2000), pp. 205–20.
7. F. O. Matthiessen, ed., *The American Novels and Stories of Henry James* (New York: Alfred A. Knopf, 1951). The novel not referred to here is *The Sense of the Past*, which opens in New York; however, this section of the novel predated James's visit.
8. I take the quotation from Jean-Philippe Autry, *Extrême Occident: French Intellectuals and America* (Chicago: University of Chicago Press, 1993), p. 24.
9. James to Edward Warren, 19 March 1905, *Letters*, vol. 4, p. 355. James mentions Chicago in discussing Philadelphia, and also in *The American Scene*, chap. 4, sec. 2, p. 129, with regard to the Saint Gaudens "magnificent" statue of Lincoln. On this statue, see Kirk Savage, *Standing Soldiers, Kneeling Slaves* (Chicago: University of Chicago Press, 1997), pp. 122–25; and Barry Schwartz, "Iconography and Collective Memory: Lincoln's Image in the American Mind," *Sociological Quarterly* 32, no. 3 (1991): 301–21.
10. Edel, vol. 5, p. 279. Compare the Dickensian language of Wells on the south side of Chicago in *The Future in America*: "It was like a prolonged, enlarged mingling of the south side of London, with all that is bleak and ugly in the Black Country. It is the most perfect presentation of nineteenth-century individualistic industrialism I have ever seen in its vast, its magnificent squalor. It is pure nineteenth century. It had no past . . . and one wonders for its future. It is indeed a Victorian nightmare that culminates beyond South Chicago in the monstrous fungoid shapes, the endless smoking chimneys, the squat retorts, the black smoke pall of the Standard Oil Company. For a time the sun is veiled altogether by that . . ." (44).
11. James to Edward Warren, 19 March 1905, *Letters*, vol. 4, p. 355.
12. At this point, James made notes for himself of some of the material for *The American Scene: see Complete Notebooks*, pp. 237–42.
13. See Edel, vol. 5, p. 320; Kaplan, pp. 501–2.
14. Attention has been paid frequently to the text in the 1980s and 1990s, an aspect of James being read for his connections with "cultural studies," and

on account of a new attention to James as American: What does this American say about race and gender? A good summary of historical and critical contexts for the text appears in Charles Caramello, "The Duality of *The American Scene*," in Daniel Mark Fogel, ed., *A Companion to Henry James Studies* (Westport, Conn.: Greenwood Press, 1993), pp. 447–73. On *The American Scene*, see Peter Buitenhuis, *The Grasping Imaginations: The American Workings of Henry James* (Toronto: Toronto University Press, 1970), pp. 179–208; William F. Hall, "The Continuing Relevance of Henry James' 'The American Scene'" in *Criticism* 13, no. 2 (1971): 151–65; John Carlos Rowe, *Henry Adams and Henry James: The Emergence of a Modern Consciousness* (Ithaca: Cornell University Press, 1976), pp. 132–65; Rosalie Hewitt, "Henry James, *The Harpers*, and *The American Scene*" in *American Literature* 55, no. 1 (1983): 41–47; Mark Seltzer, *Henry James and the Art of Power* (Ithaca: Cornell University Press, 1984), pp. 96–145, both for the "hotel spirit" and for James on Philadelphia and its prison; Sharon Cameron, *Thinking in Henry James* (Chicago: University of Chicago Press, 1989), pp. 1–31, 169–78; Ross Posnock, *The Trial of Curiosity: Henry James, William James and the Challenge of Modernity* (Oxford: Oxford University Press, 1991), pp. 141–66, 250–84; Stuart Hutchinson, *The American Scene* (London: Macmillan, 1991), pp. 131–44; Donald Wolff, "Jamesian Historiography and *The American Scene*," *Henry James Review* 13 (1992): 153–71; Helen Killoran, "The Swiftian Journey of Henry James: Genre and Epistemology in *The American Scene*," *Henry James Review* 13 (1992): 306–14; Sara Blair, *Henry James and the Writing of Race and Nation* (Cambridge: Cambridge University Press, 1996), pp. 158–210, on Ellis Island, on the "alien," and on the Pullman; Sheila Teahan, "Engendering Culture and The American Scene," *Henry James Review* 17 (1996): 52–57; Beverly Haviland, *Henry James's Last Romance: Making Sense of the Past and "The American Scene"* (Cambridge: Cambridge University Press, 1997), pp. 49–162; and Gert Buelens, ed., *Enacting History in Henry James: Narrative, Power and Ethics* (Cambridge: Cambridge University Press, 1997), pp.166–92.

15. Quoted from Giacosa's "Chicago and Her Italian Colony," in Arnold Lewis, *An Encounter with Tomorrow: Europeans, Chicago's Loop, and the World's Columbian Exposition* (Chicago: University of Illinois Press, 1997), p. 1.

16. Edel, vol. 5, p. 278.

17. See Richard Ellman, *Oscar Wilde* (London: Hamish Hamilton, 1987), p. 171.

18. See in addition to Ellman, Edel, *The Conquest of London*, p. 462.

19. Peter Szondi, *On Textual Understanding and Other Essays*, trans. Harvey Mendelsohn (Minneapolis: University of Minnesota Press, 1986), p. 143.

20. James to George Harvey, 21 October 1904, *Letters*, vol. 4, p. 328.

21. Gertrude Stein, *The Autobiography of Alice B. Toklas* (1933; Harmondsworth: Penguin, 1966), pp. 86–87.

22. Charles Caramello, *Henry James, Gertrude Stein and the Biographical Act* (Chapel Hill: University of North Carolina Press, 1996), p. 129.

23. See Freud's "Wolfman" analysis ("From the History of an Infantile Neurosis,") *The Penguin Freud 9* (Harmondsworth: Penguin, 1979), p. 317, "A repression is something very different from a rejection" (*Verferfung*) and p. 323, where Freud speaks of the child having not repressed but simply repudiated the idea of castration. In contrast, elements of James's hysteria, and his awareness of the past as castrating appear not only in the suggestions of having his past amputated (*The American Scene*, 2.2.71) but in the account of his visit to the Cambridge cemetery in 1905 (*Notebooks*, p. 240); also see my *Henry James* pp. 109–10.

24. The thesis of Richard Poirier in *A World Elsewhere: The Place of Style in American Literature* (Oxford: Oxford University Press, 1966).

25. For James and architecture, see Ellen Eve Frank, *Literary Architecture: Essays towards a Tradition* (Berkeley: University of California Press, 1979).

1. Ross Posnock reads this as a pun, "Affirming the Alien: The Pragmatist Pluralism of *The American Scene*," in Jonathan Freedman, ed., *The Cambridge Companion to Henry James* (Cambridge: Cambridge University Press, 1998), p. 230.

2. James to Howard Sturgis, 17 October 1904, *Letters*, vol. 4, p. 325.

3. Edith Wharton and Ogden Codman Jr., *The Decoration of Houses* (New York: W. W. Norton, 1997). On Codman, see Dianne H. Pilgrim in *The American Renaissance, 1876–1917* (The Brooklyn Museum; New York: Pantheon Books, 1979), p. 149. This discussion places him in the context of Newport houses; see below. See also Judith Fryer, *Felicitous Space: The Imaginative Structures of Edith Wharton and Willa Cather* (Chapel Hill: University of North Carolina Press, 1986).

4. Quoted, Cynthia Griffin Wolff, *A Feast of Words: The Triumph of Edith Wharton* (Oxford: Oxford University Press, 1977), pp. 64–65. On the use of interiors, see Fryer, *Felicitous Space*, and Annette Larson Benert, "The Geography of Gender in *The House of Mirth*," *Studies in the Novel* 22 (1990): 26–42; Claire Preston, *Edith Wharton's Social Register* (London: Macmillan, 2000), pp. 52–73. See also, in relation to this chapter's reference to art nouveau, Reginald Abbott, "A Moment's Ornament": Wharton's Lily Bart and Art Nouveau," *Mosaic* 24 (1990): 73–91.

5. In New York, James speaks of his "artful evasion of the actual" (*The American Scene*, 2.2.68) through memory, since past buildings have gone.

6. For James on California, see the letter to Mrs. William James, 5 April 1905, *Letters*, vol. 4, pp. 356–57.

7. See Charles E. Beveridge and Paul Rocheleau, *Frederick Law Olmsted: Designing the American Landscape*, ed. David Larkin (New York: Rizzoli, 1995), pp. 96–108.

8. James, *Collected Travel Writings: Great Britain and America* (New York: Library of America, 1993), p. 761. Further references in the text as *Travel Writings*.

9. The term "the City Beautiful" seems to have been first used in 1900 in relation to the improvement of Harrisburg. See William H. Wilson, *The City Beautiful Movement* (Baltimore: Johns Hopkins University Press, 1989), p. 128.

10. On the Casino built for James Gordon Bennett Jr., son of a New York newspaper owner, see Jane Mulvagh and Mark A. Weber, *Newport Houses* (New York: Rizzoli, 1989), pp. 92–101.

11. See Paul R. Baker, *Richard Morris Hunt* (Cambridge, Mass.: MIT Press, 1980), p. 366.

12. See James's letters on Biltmore, 4 February 1905 and 8 February 1905, *Letters,* vol. 4, pp. 344–48.

13. See John Bryan, *Biltmore Estate: The Most Distinguished Private Place* (New York: Rizzoli, 1994), p. 111.

14. See Baker, *Richard Morris Hunt,* p. 424. See also Bryan, *Biltmore Estate,* p. 133, for references to tapestries and evocations, in Vanderbilt's and Bitter's mind, of *Tannhäuser.*

15. I refer here to my discussion of *The Golden Bowl* in *Henry James: Critical Issues,* pp. 185–91.

16. Flaubert, *Selected Letters,* trans. Geoffrey Wall (Harmondsworth: Penguin, 1997), pp. 213–14.

17. Saint-Gaudens, the sculptor, said of his meetings with these architects, "This is the greatest meeting of artists since the fifteenth century"—an indication of the awareness of power in the "American Renaissance"— quoted, Richard Guy Wilson, in *The American Renaissance* (see note 3), p. 12.

18. On the Louisiana Purchase Exposition, see Robert W. Rydell, *All the World's a Fair: Visions of Empire at American International Expositions, 1876–1916* (Chicago: University of Chicago Press, 1984); Eric Breitbart, *A World on Display: Photographs from the St. Louis World's Fair* (Albuquerque: University of New Mexico Press, 1997).

19. The point (not with reference to James) is made by Wilson (see note 9), pp. 57–59.

20. Henry Adams, *The Autobiography of Henry Adams,* ed. Ernest Samuels (Boston: Houghton Mifflin, 1973), p. 343.

21. Rudolph Arnheim, *The Dynamics of Architectural Form* (Berkeley: University of California Press, 1977), p. 227, quoted in Philip Fisher, *Hard Facts: Setting and Form in the American Novel* (Oxford: Oxford University Press, 1987), p. 137. Frank Lloyd Wright's work, beginning in 1889 with his house designed for himself in Oak Park, Chicago, contrasts with the description of American houses in James, in that Wright designs for families as a unit; but Wright's work, in suburban rather than urban contexts and his utopist sense of creating the family rather than the individual through architectural structures, cast him very differently from James. Wright and Sullivan, along with Richardson and Root are examples of architects James does not speak of; it will be recalled how Lewis Mumford in 1931, puts them, along with La Farge, whom James does discuss, against the

Chicago Exhibition, which Mumford reads negatively as "the easy mechanical duplication of other modes of architecture," *The Brown Decades,
1865–1895: A Study of the Arts in America* (New York: Dover Publications,
1955), p. 141.

22. Walter Benjamin, *Charles Baudelaire: A Lyric Poet in the Age of High Capitalism*
(London: Verso, 1973), p. 168. For this reference, and the subsequent one
from Nietzsche, see Irving Wohlfarth, "'Construction has the role of the
Subconscious': Phantasmagorias of *The Master Builder* (with Constant Reference to Giedion, Weber, Nietzsche, Ibsen and Benjamin)," in Alexandre Kostka and Irving Wohlfarth, eds., *Nietzsche: 'An Architecture of our Minds'*
(Los Angeles: Getty Research Institute for the Study of Art and the Humanities, 1999), pp. 141–98.

23. See Michael Egan, *Henry James: The Ibsen Years* (London: Vision, 1972), pp.
66–69.

24. Nietzsche, *Twilight of the Idols and The Antichrist*, trans. R. J. Hollingdale
(Harmondsworth: Penguin, 1968), p. 74.

25. James makes reference to its unveiling in a letter of 7 June 1897 to
Frances Rollins Morse (*Letters*, vol. 4, p. 46) and to the point that his
brother, Garth Wilkinson, was wounded in the charge. James saw a photograph of the image in *Harper's Weekly*—a reminder of how much the
America he saw in 1904 was already available to him in images.

26. For Roland Barthes on the punctum, see *Camera Lucida*, trans. Richard
Howard (New York: Hill and Wang, 1981), p. 41.

27. For a comparison between Boston and New York, in their post–Civil
War developments, see Mona Domosh, *Invented Cities: The Creation of Landscape in Nineteenth-Century New York and Boston* (New Haven: Yale University
Press, 1996). She sees Boston as controlled by far fewer figures and
therefore more homogeneous than New York, which had many capitalists working upon it in competition in order to change it; she sees, however, in both, the creation of the city as spectacle (p. 156).

CHAPTER 7

1. James signed a contract with Macmillan in 1903 for a book on London,
to be called "London Town," but it was never written: see *Notebooks*, pp.
273–80.

2. The phrase recurs: see also *The American Scene*, 2.2.76, 2.3.83, 3.3.102.

3. Another word to link James on New York and Ballard on Shanghai is
"gaudy"—James refers to the hotel where Montieth stays at in *A Round of
Visits* as "gaudy" (vol. 1, p. 896): the word is also used to describe Shanghai.
See J. G. Ballard, *The Empire of the Sun* (London: Granada, 1985), pp. 351, 11.

4. LCI, p. 893. The essay (pp. 871–99) appeared first in 1903. For James on
Zola, see Vivien Jones, *James the Critic* (London: Macmillan, 1985), pp.
92–100.

5. Amy Kaplan, *The Social Construction of American Realism* (Chicago: University of Chicago Press, 1988), p. 44. With her view of *A Hazard of New Fortunes,* compare Emily Fourmy Cutrer, "A Pragmatic Mode of Seeing: James, Howells and the Politics of Vision," in David Miller, ed., *American Iconology* (New Haven: Yale University Press, 1993), pp. 259–75. See also, on the subject of getting to know the city by walking, Timothy L. Parrish, "Howells Untethered: The Dean and 'Diversity,'" *Studies in American Fiction* 23 (1995): 101–17.

6. On Hassam, see Warren Adelson, Jay Cantor, and William H. Grelts, *Childe Hassam: Impressionist* (New York: Abbeville Press, 1999).

7. See Lisa N. Peters, *American Impressionist Masterpieces* (New York: Hugh Lauter Levin Associates, 1991), p. 58. In this volume, compare William Merritt Chase, *Prospect Park, Brooklyn* (1886) (p. 48) and compare James's description below of the obviously comparable Central Park: Chase keeps out from his painting any heterogeneity. On Chase (1849–1916) see Barbara Dayer Gallati, *William Merritt Chase* (New York: Harry N. Abrams, 1995), pp. 71–76. She points out that when Chase paints Central Park, he looks for architectural features in it, rather than showing it as a place for everyday use; in that sense his vision of New York is the tourist's.

8. Quoted, Dorothy Norman, *Alfred Stieglitz: An American Seer* (New York: Aperture, 1990) pp. 35, 38. A selection of Stieglitz's photographs of New York appears in Dorothy Norman, *Alfred Stieglitz* (New York: Aperture, 1976), pp. 23–33.

9. See *America and Lewis Hines: Photographs 1904–1940* (New York: Aperture, 1977). Sara Blair discusses Hines in her *Henry James: The Writing of Race and Nation,* pp. 165–73. For the comparison between Stieglitz and Hines, see Alan Trachtenberg, *Reading American Photographs: Images as History, Mathew Brady to Walker Evans* (New York: Hill and Wang, 1989), pp. 164–230.

10. For James on photography, see Ira B. Nabel, "Visual Culture: The Photo-Frontispieces to the New York Edition," in David McWhirter, ed., *Henry James's New York Edition: The Construction of Authorship* (Stanford: Stanford University Press, 1995), pp. 90–108.

11. Emile Zola, *L'Assommoir,* trans. Margaret Mauldon (Oxford: Oxford University Press, 1995), p. 73.

12. Zola may be reworking Caillebotte's painting *Le Pont de l'Europe* (1876), his impression of the bridge overlooking the Gare Saint-Lazare; here it is impossible to see either the bridge whole, or the railway line; for Zola and Impressionism see William J. Berg, *The Visual Novel: Emile Zola and the Art of his Times* (Pennsylvania: Pennsylvania University Press, 1992). For Caillebotte, see Robert L. Herbert, *Impressionism: Art, Leisure and Parisian Society* (New Haven: Yale University Press, 1988), pp. 22–23. James's positive sense of Impressionism seems to relate to his question of how to represent America (see *The American Scene,* 1.5.37).

13. I have discussed this aspect of *The Portrait of a Lady* (13.105) in my *Henry James: Critical Issues,* pp. 55–56. The New York edition appeared in 1908; the original novel in 1880–81.

14. On the setting and context of this novella, see Curtis Dahl, "Lord Lambeth's America: Architecture in James's 'An International Episode,'" *Henry James Review* 5 (1985): 80–95.

15. "Between its opening on 1 January 1892 and 1924 [it] was the point of entry for sixteen million immigrants, or 71 per cent of all immigrants to the United States." In *Encyclopaedia of New York City,* ed. Kenneth T. Jackson (New Haven: Yale University Press, 1995), p. 372.

16. Compare W. D. Howells, describing his Bostonians, Basil and Isabel March, walking through Washington Square, less prestigious than at the period of which James wrote his novel: "they met Italian faces, French faces, Spanish faces, as they strolled over the asphalt walks under the thinning shadows of the autumn-stricken sycamores. They met the familiar picturesque raggedness of southern Europe with the old kindly illusion that somehow it existed for their appreciation and that it found adequate compensation in this. March thought that he sufficiently expressed his tacit sympathy in sitting down on one of the iron benches with his wife and letting a little Neapolitan put a superflous shine on his boots, while their desultory comment wandered with equal esteem to the old-fashioned American respectability which keeps the north side of the square in vast mansions of red brick, and the international shabbiness which has invaded the southern border, and broken it up into lodging houses, shops, beer gardens and studios." W. D. Howells, *A Hazard of New Fortunes* (1890; New York: New American Library, 1965), p. 48. Note Howells's punctuality with each adjective; his balance is the attempt to describe the city by noting every detail. He does not mention the Washington Arch, which James comments on, and which Childe Hassam painted in 1895, since this, the design of Stanford White, was begun in 1889. See H. Barbara Weinberg, Doreen Bolger, and David Park Curry, *American Impressionism and Realism: The Painting of Modern Life, 1885–1915* (New York: Metropolitan Museum of Art, 1994), pp. 181–83.

17. Quoted, Alan Trachtenberg (see note 9), p. 212.

18. Amory Mayho, *Symbols of the Capital; or, Civilization in New York* (New York, 1859), pp. 40–43, quoted in James L. Machor, *Pastoral Cities: Urban Ideals and the Symbolic Landscape of America* (Madison: University of Wisconsin Press, 1987), p. 124. See also Machor's discussions of nineteenth-century American urbanization.

19. Rem Koolhaas discusses the Waldorf-Astoria, pulled down in 1929, and replaced by another, in *Delirious New York: A Retroactive Manifesto for Manhattan* (Rotterdam: OIO Publishers, 1994), pp. 132–51, and he sees the hotel as Hollywood's favorite subject in the 1930s. "A Hotel *is* a plot—a cybernetic universe with its own laws generating random but fortuitous collisions between human beings who never would have met elsewhere. . . .

With the Waldorf, the Hotel itself becomes such a movie, featuring the guests as stars and the personnel as a discreet coat-tailed chorus of extras. . . . The movie begins at the revolving door—symbol of the unlimited surprises of coincidence; then plots are instigated in the darker recesses of the lower floors, to be consummated—via an elevator episode—in the upper regions of the building" (pp. 148–50).

20. "Provisional" wraps the chapter round: *The American Scene,* 2.1.61, 2.3.84; 2.3.85 for "stop-gap."

21. James's "cauldron" may be compared with the title of Israel Zangwill's play *The Melting-Pot* (1908): on James seeing ethnicity as a relation, rather than as a thing in itself, see William Boelhower, *Through a Glass Darkly: Ethnic Semiosis in American Literature* (Oxford: Oxford University Press, 1987), pp. 11–40.

22. It is worth comparing James here with Rem Koolhaas, who uses "bigness" in *S.M.L.XL,* taken over from *Delirious New York,* for the scale of buildings then beginning to be realized in New York that "can no longer be controlled by a single architectural gesture, or even by any combination." Bigness means the impossibility of interpretation. "Where architecture reveals, bigness perplexes; bigness transforms the city from a summation of certainties into an accumulation of mysteries. What you see is no longer what you get." Bigness is defined by Koolhaas as "urbanism vs. architecture." Rem Koolhaas, *S.M.L.XL* (New York: Monacelli Press, 1995), pp. 499, 501, 515.

23. Jacob A. Riis, *How the Other Half Lives,* ed. Luc Sante (Harmondsworth: Penguin, 1997), pp. 47, 73. On the dual aspects of this text, as both surveillance and serving a consumer culture, see Keith Gandal, *The Virtues of the Vicious: Jacob Riis, Stephen Crane and the Spectacle of the Slum* (Oxford: Oxford University Press, 1997). The book brings out also the topicality of work on New York slums: Riis being hardly a pioneer.

24. This visit was not his only one: he returned for two months in 1921 as a journalist covering a conference in Washington on disarmament; and again in 1934, again to Washington, pursuing an interest in the New Deal; and in 1936, going to Hollywood to publicize his film *Things to Come;* and in 1940, giving a lecture, "Two Hemispheres or One World." He continued to write about America, in *The Shape of Things to Come* (1933) and in his polemical writings, *Outline of History* (1920), *The Short History of the World* (1922), *The Work, Wealth and Happiness of Mankind* (1932), and *The New America: The New World* (1935).

25. On Jacob Gordin, see the work of urban sociology by Hutchins Hapgood, *The Spirit of the Ghetto* (1902), ed. Moses Rischin (Cambridge, Mass.: Harvard University Press, 1967) pp. 113–76. Hapgood's account of the ghetto is illustrated by charcoal sketches by Jacob Epstein. For further details on Yiddish theater—the first company in New York began in 1884— see Moses Rischin, *The Promised City: New York's Jews 1870–1940* (Cambridge, Mass.: Harvard University Press, 1962) and Irving Howe, with Kenneth

Libo, *World of our Fathers* (New York: Harcourt Brace Jovanovich, 1976), pp. 460–96.

26. "Between 1880 and 1910 about 1.4 million Jews fleeing pogroms and economic discrimination in eastern Europe moved to the city. About 1.1 million stayed, and by 1910 Jews accounted for almost a quarter of the city's population. Between 1880 and 1890 three of four Jewish immigrants, or about sixty thousand altogether, settled on the Lower East Side" (*Encyclopaedia of New York History*, pp. 620–21).

27. I take it that the sense of this last sentence requires an "it" or an "and" before "suggests."

28. Beverly Haviland, *Henry James's Last Romance: Making Sense of the Past and The American Scene* (Cambridge: Cambridge University Press, 1997), p. 149.

29. Compare with James, George Bellows's *Rain on the River* (1908) and *A Morning Snow: Hudson River* (1910)—two attempts to capture the doubleness of Riverside Park, including the park as wholly constructed. See H. Barbara Weinberg, (note 16) pp. 170, 172. See discussion, pp. 168–72.

30. Richard N. Murray, in *The American Renaissance* (note 3, chapter 6), pp. 175–76, compares the Shaw memorial in Boston by Saint-Gaudens with the Sherman statue, seeing both as presentations of the heroic. He says of the "Victory" figure that it suggests "Sherman is riding into an exalted realm. . . . [The monuments] propose that the men portrayed were destined for historical greatness even before they performed their celebrated deeds." They express, in other words, the values of the American Renaissance—inherently opposed to those of James, and with a capacity for creating trauma through the implied comparison with the viewer's passivity.

31. It should be noted that in all this discussion of the European "alien," he never registers the black, though the reference to the "blackamoors" in the Veronese painting (*The American Scene*, 4.4.138) suggests a blindness of attention.

32. The cage image has appeared twice before, in relation to Trinity Church (*The American Scene*, 2.1.61) and the fire escapes on the Lower East Side.

33. In *The Bostonians* (1886), Olive in New York (on Tenth Street) with Verena and Mr. Burrage envisages a drive in the park (Central Park) and a visit to the Museum of Art in the morning, and in the evening, dining at Delmonico's and going on to the German opera (*The Bostonians*, p. 256). James describes now a different city.

34. Walter Benjamin, *Charles Baudelaire: A Lyric Poet in the Age of High Capitalism* (London: Verso, 1973), p. 37–38, on interpersonal relationships marked by the eye's activity over the ear's (because in the new conditions of transportation, people have to look at each other for long periods without speaking to each other). The point is repeated on p. 151. All else proceeds from this particular type of detachment Simmel registers.

35. T. J. Clark, *The Painting of Modern Life: Paris in the Art of Manet and His Followers* (London: Thames and Hudson, 1985), pp. 238–39, 310. See my *Henry James: Critical Issues* p. 162.

1. Compare Manhattan as "the vast bristling promontory" (*The American Scene*, 2.1.58). Another sense of "bristles" is implied in the account of Washington: see 12.13.280. See also 3.3.100, for "bristles" in relation to the population of Jewish people in New York.

2. See Freud, "The Uncanny," *The Penguin Freud Library*, 14: *"Art and Literature"* (Harmondsworth: Penguin, 1985), p. 364.

3. Jacques Lacan, *Ecrits: A Selection*, trans. Alan Sheridan (London: Tavistock, 1977), p. 4.

4. 29 January 1884, *Notebooks*, p. 24. On James and Adams, see George Monteiro, ed., *The Correspondence of Henry James and Henry Adams, 1877–1914* (Baton Rouge: Louisiana State University Press, 1992).

5. See Charles E. Brownell, Calder Loth, William M. S. Rasmussen, and Richard Guy Wilson, *The Making of Virginia Architecture* (Charlottesville: University of Virginia Press, 1992), p. 204.

6. See Edel vol. 2, p. 459; see also Ellman, *Oscar Wilde*, p. 171.

7. For Henry James on Marion Clover Hooper, see his letter to William James, 8 March 1870, *Letters*, vol. 1, p. 208. But it may be that James associated her with Minny Temple, and with the sense of her nonsurvivability, a point implicit in the letter to Grace Norton, 1 April 1870, *Letters*, vol. 1, pp. 231–32. Marion Clover Hooper took her life in December 1885. James visited the Saint-Gaudens statue put up in Rock Creek Cemetery (Edel, vol. 5, pp. 264–65); the statue is reproduced in Ernest Samuels, *Henry Adams* (Cambridge, Mass.: Harvard University Press, 1989), following p. 272.

8. Richard N. Murray, in *The American Renaissance* (see note 3, chap. 6), pp. 181–86. Murray discusses the library at Boston and the Congressional Library (designed by Thomas L. Casey, Edward P. Casey, and Bernard Green) in relation to their murals—a new, post–Columbian Exhibition art form, and celebratory of American history.

9. For this picture, see Robert L. Herbert, *Impressionism: Art, Leisure and Parisian Society* (New Haven: Yale University Press, 1988), p. 53.

10. On this passage, see Lewis P. Simpson, *The Brazen Face of History* (Athens: University of Georgia Press, 1997), pp. 270–71 (and see also pp. 72–74).

11. On the mythologizing of Lee, see Thomas L. Connelly, *The Marble Man: Robert E. Lee and his Image in American Society* (Baton Rouge: University of Louisiana Press, 1977). On the iconography of "the Lost Cause," see Mark E. Neely Jr., Harold Holzer, and Gabor S. Boritt, *The Confederate Image: Prints of the Lost Cause* (Chapel Hill: University of North Carolina Press, 1987). See also Edmund Wilson, *Patriotic Gore: Studies in the Literature of the American Civil War* (1962; London: Hogarth Press, 1987), pp. 442–49.

12. See Robert A. Colby, *Thackeray's Canvas of Humanity: An Author and His Public* (Columbus: Ohio State University Press, 1979), pp. 394–95.

13. Other Virginian creators of the legend included George Cary Eggleston (*A Rebel's Recollections,* 1874—an account of life in Robert Lee's army) and Thomas Nelson Page (*In Ole Virginia,* 1887, six stories giving local color, one, "Marse Chan," told by an obedient slave). These nostalgic accounts meshed with the changes taking place with the Southern Historical Society, which began in 1869 in New Orleans, but was reshaped after 1873 to become Virginia-dominated.

14. The hotel was Beaux-Arts style, built with tobacco-money and completed in 1895, the work of John Mervin Carrère and Thomas Hastings, architects who had begun with McKim, Mead, and White. See Charles E. Brownell and others, *The Making of Virginia Architecture,* p. 320.

15. Richmond was burned during the Civil War. See Dennis Malone Carter's picture, *Lincoln's Drive Through Richmond,* discussed by Barry Schwartz in William Ayres, ed., *Picturing History: American Painting 1770–1930* (New York: Rizzoli, 1993), pp. 144–46.

16. Quoted, Brownell and others, *The Making of Virginian Architecture,* p. 48; the discussion of Jefferson (pp. 47–53) brings out reactionary elements in his Palladianism and his setting of architecture against the city in his view of Paris: "the style of architecture in this city is far from chaste" (quoted, p. 50).

17. Brownell and others, *The Making of Virginia Architecture,* p. 70; see also p. 63.

18. James's comments on the monumentalism of the Capitol, "the unassorted marble mannikins" that decorate it, each from different states, and reflecting the absence of artistic "discretion" in the mid-Victorian period (11.5.266) may be compared with this passage.

James on the statue may be compared with Hawthorne's comment on the model he saw in Crawford's studio: Again this reflects on the work's provincialism.

> It is certainly in one sense a very foolish and illogical piece of work—Washington, mounted on a very uneasy steed, on a very narrow space, aloft in the air, when a single step of the horse backward, forward or on either side, must precipitate him; and several of his contemporaries standing beneath him, not looking up to wonder at his predicament, but each intent on manifesting his own personality to the world around. They have nothing to do with one another, nor with Washington, nor with any great purpose which all are to work out together. (quoted, Wayne Craven, *Sculpture in America* [New York: Thomas Y. Crowell, 1968], p. 131)

19. The Church was St. Paul's Episcopal, Greek Revival style, designed by Thomas S. Stewart in 1845. Lee surrendered to Grant on 9 April 1865.

20. Threatened with demolition in 1889, the White House of the Confederacy became a museum in 1896. Today, it is on display as the home of Jefferson Davis and has memorabilia associated with him; there is a sep-

arate Museum of the Confederacy adjacent. The number of museums has doubled since James's time.

21. On the history of the statue, see Kirk Savage, *Standing Soldiers, Kneeling Slaves* (Princeton: Princeton University Press, 1997), pp. 128–55: the discussion of James here seems inadequate in its placing of James.

22. Compare V. S. Naipaul on the house in Charleston: "The staircase was in the center of the narrow house, separating the front room from the back room. The entrance to the house was on the side. That central side entrance and staircase was fundamental to the idea of a 'single' Charleston house, a single house being . . . [one] in which, for the sake of privacy, the entrance was not at the front but at the side, and in which there was a single room on either side of the entrance and staircase" (*A Turn in the South* [New York: Alfred A. Knopf, 1989], p. 88).

23. This aspect of *The American Scene* is the focus of Mark Seltzer, *Henry James and the Art of Power* (Ithaca: Cornell University Press, 1984), p. 109.

24. James's use of this technical architectural term will be noted: the OED cites *Roderick Hudson* for another reference.

25. See James's letter to Wister on *The Virginian*, 7 August 1902, *Letters*, vol. 4, pp. 232–34; and see Lee Clark Mitchell, "'When You Call Me That . . . ': Tall Talk and Male Hegemony in *The Virginian*," PMLA 102 (1988): 66–77. See also Sanford E. Marovitz, "Unseemly Realities in Owen Wister's Western/American Myth," *American Literary Realism, 1870–1910* 17 (1984): 209–15; and on *Lady Baltimore* see Julian Mason, "Owen Wister, Champion of Old Charleston," *The Quarterly Journal of the Library of Congress* 29 (1972): 162–85. See Owen Wister, *The Virginian* ed. Robert Shulman (Oxford: Oxford University Press, 1998).

26. Wells, in *The Future in America* also refers to W. E. B. Du Bois's *The Souls of Black Folk,* but he met Booker T. Washington in Boston and distinguishes between Washington's belief in separate rights and Du Bois's stress on "equal citizenship and equal respect," finding Du Bois "more of the artist, less of the statesman; he conceals his passionate resentment all too thinly." Wells's preference for Washington's "statescraft" over Du Bois accords with his fear of immigration; racial attitudes revealed in chapter 8 dictate a position that implicitly sidelines Du Bois. Wells identifies the black as the figure of infinite submission.

27. For an informative (though uncritical) look at Florida architecture and Flagler, see Hap Hutton, *Tropical Splendor: An Architectural History of Florida* (New York: Alfred A. Knopf, 1987), pp. 20–33.

28. William Blake, *Complete Writings,* ed. Geoffrey Keynes (Oxford: Oxford University Press, 1966), p. 585.

29. Quoted, Jon Morton Blum, *The Republican Roosevelt* (Cambridge, Mass.: Harvard University Press, 1977), p. 32. James reviewed Roosevelt's *American Ideals and Other Essays Social and Political* (1898) critically for its "making free with the 'American' name" and for "the puerility of his simplifications" (LCII, p. 65).

30. Edward Bellamy, *Looking Backward, 2000–1887* (Harmondsworth: Penguin, 1982), p. 55.
31. H. G. Wells, *The Time Machine* (London: Dent, 1995), p. 18.
32. H. G. Wells, *The History of Mr Polly and The War in the Air* (London: Odhams, 1930). Wells dates the events as "191-" (p. 216).
33. German; directed by Fritz Lang; designed by Erich Kettelhut, Otto Hunte, and Karl Vollbrecht.
34. For Taylorism, see Martha Banta, in *Taylored Lives: Narrative Productions in the Age of Taylor, Veblen and Ford* (Chicago: University of Chicago Press, 1993). Banta also shows in readings of *The Wings of the Dove* and *The Golden Bowl* how much Taylorism subtends James's writing.
35. Wells reviewed the film in the *New York Times Magazine,* disliking it for its belief in spontaneous enlightenment and social rapprochement between workers and bosses. See Frank McConnell, "Realist of the Fantastic: H. G. Wells About/In/On the Movies," in Michael Mullin, ed., *H.G. Wells: Reality and Beyond* (Champaign, Ill.: Champaign Public Library, 1986), p. 29.

CHAPTER 9

1. On the Statue of Liberty, see Albert Boime, *The Unveiling of the National Icons: A Plea for Patriotic Iconoclasm in a Nationalist Era* (Cambridge: Cambridge University Press, 1998), pp. 82–133.
2. A newer translation of the text has appeared: *The Man Who Disappeared (Amerika),* trans. Michael Hofmann (Harmondsworth: Penguin, 1996). I have worked from the older translation as it is more familiar and cite it throughout, but I also refer to Hofmann's version as Hofmann plus page number. The most detailed account of the novel appears in Jack Murray, *The Landscapes of Alienation: Ideological Subversion in Kafka, Céline and Onetti* (Stanford: Stanford University Press, 1991). For the stress on photography, see Franca Schettino, "Photography in Kafka's *Amerika,*" in Moshe Lazar and Ronald Gottesman, *The Dove and the Mole: Kafka's Journey into Darkness and Creativity* (Malibu: Undena Publications, 1987), pp. 109–33. See also Stanley Corngold, *Complex Pleasure: Forms of Feeling in German Literature* (Stanford: Stanford University Press, 1998), chap. 6, pp. 121–38.
3. For these details, see David E. Barclay and Elisabeth Glaser-Schmidt, *Transatlantic Images and Perceptions: Germany and America Since 1776* (Cambridge: Cambridge University Press, 1997), pp. 82–83, 116, 126—and see the essays by Hans-Jürgen Grabbe (65–86), by Wolfgang Helbich (109–29), and by James T. Kloppenberg (155–70) and generally; see also Jeffrey L. Sammons, *Imagination and History: Selected Papers on Nineteenth-Century German Literature* (New York: Peter Lang, 1988), p. 218, and generally. On German-Jewish immigration, see Avraham Barkal, *Branching Out: Jewish Immigration to the United States, 1820–1914* (New York: Holmes and Meier, 1994).

4. For Sealsfield, see Sammons, pp. 219–24 (note 3 above), who suggests the importance of other German writers. The Viennese Ferdinand Kürnburger wrote *Der Amerika-Müde* (1855). The novel's hero, Moorfield, is "the America weary" of the title, revolting against American coarseness and capitalism, and derives from the poet Nikolaus Lenau, who farmed in western Pennsylvania in 1832. Sammons speculates that *Martin Chuzzlewit*, translated into German immediately after its publication, might have influenced Kürnberger. (For Dickens in nineteenth-century Germany, see H. R. Kleineberger, "Charles Dickens and Wilhelm Raabe," *Oxford German Studies* 4 [1969]: 90–117). Kürnburger reacted to Ernst Wilkomm, *Die Europamüden* (1838), where Sigismund is the "Europe-weary," who would set up a more pure Germanness in America. Friedrich Gerstäcker (1816–1872) spent two periods of time in America, and *Nach Amerika* (1855) is positive about the situation of Germans in America, of American agriculture and the frontier, and Indians (some of the knowledge derived from Cooper). Berthold Auerbach (1812–1882) in *Das Landhaus am Rhein* (1869), used Benjamin Franklin (whose biography he published in 1876) and self-help ideas: see Sammons, 177–91. On Karl May, see for instance Richard H. Cracroft, "The American West of Karl May," *American Quarterly* 19 (1967): 249–58 and Carolle Herselle Krinsky, "Karl May's Novels and Aspects of Their Continuing Influence," *American Indian Culture and Research Journal* 23 (1999): 53–72.

5. Kafka gave *Leaves of Grass*, in Czech translation, to Janouch, saying Whitman "combined the contemplation of nature and of civilization, which are apparently entirely contradictory, into a single intoxicating vision of life, because he always had sight of the transitoriness of all phenomena. . . . I admire in him the reconciliation of art and nature. When the war between the Northern and Southern States in America, which first really set in motion the power of our present machine world, first broke out, Walt Whitman became a medical orderly. He did then what all of us ought to do, particularly today. He helped the weak, the sickly and the defeated. He was really a Christian and—with a close affinity especially to us Jews—he was therefore an important measure of the status and worth of humanity" (*J.*167).

6. Gilles Deleuze and Felix Guattari, *Kafka: Towards a Minor Literature*, trans. Dana Polan (Minneapolis: University of Minnesota Press, 1986), p. 18. In late 1911, Kafka had made contact with a Yiddish theater troupe performing in Prague (D.64) and had become aware of a Judaism whose spontaneity was outside a relationship both to Christianity and to the assimilationist tendencies of Western European Judaism: This was the moment of thinking about a "minor literature."

7. Kafka to Felice Bauer, 17–18 March 1913, in Franz Kafka, *Letters to Felice*, ed. Erich Heller and Jurgen Born, trans. James Stern and Elizabeth Duckworth, including Elias Canetti, *Kafka's Other Trial*, trans. Christopher Middleton (Harmondsworth: Penguin Books, 1978), pp. 340–41.

8. Walter Benjamin, "Franz Kafka," *Illuminations,* trans. Harry Zohn (London: Jonathan Cape, 1970), p. 143.

9. Benjamin, "Max Brod's Book on Kafka," *Illuminations,* p. 145.

10. *Kafka: The Complete Short Stories,* p. 390. The text was written some time after 1905. See on this story Benjamin, "Franz Kafka," *Illuminations,* pp. 119–20.

11. See Syed Manzural Islam, *The Ethics of Travel: From Marco Polo to Kafka* (Manchester: Manchester University Press, 1996), pp. 39–42. Islam compares the two Kafka short stories, "The Bridge" and "The Departure."

12. Quoted, Anthony Northey, *Kafka's Relatives: Their Lives and His Writing* (New Haven: Yale University Press, 1991), p. 54. See the chapter, "Kafka's American Cousins," pp. 51–67. For Kafka's knowledge of America, there was also Arthur Holitscher's *Amerika: Heute und morgen,* which had already appeared between 1911 and 1912 in *Die Neue Rundschau,* and gave a positive sense of America, especially Canada, which he referred to as Canaan; Kafka bought the book in 1913.

13. The text appeared in the diary after the entry for 21 February 1911. See D.40, 213.

14. Quoted, Gerhard Kurz, "Nietzsche, Freud and Kafka," in *Reading Kafka: Prague, Politics and the Fin de Siècle,* ed. Mark Anderson (New York: Schocken Books, 1989), pp. 142–43.

15. Letter of 9 July, quoted, Mark. M. Anderson, *Kafka's Clothes: Ornament and Aestheticism in the Habsburg Fin de Siècle* (Oxford: Oxford University Press, 1992), p. 86: see Anderson's discussion of Jungborn's Christian revivalism and naturism. See also Anderson's essay on *Der Verschollene,* pp. 98–122.

16. Quoted, Anderson, p. 110.

17. On Jewish hatred for the body, see Sander L. Gilman, *Franz Kafka: The Jewish Patient* (London: Routledge, 1995).

18. Benjamin, "The Work of Art in the Age of Mechanical Reproduction," *Illuminations,* p. 240.

19. Victor Hugo, *Notre-Dame de Paris,* trans. Alban Krailsheimer (Oxford: Oxford University Press, 1993), pp. 133–34.

20. Hofmann, p. 74, reads Boston for Brooklyn and the Hudson for the East River. The geography is essential, not specific, and may fit the sense of the impossibility of mapping America.

21. This recalls Benjamin, "Franz Kafka," in *Illuminations:* Kafka writes "fairy tales for dialecticians" (p. 117).

22. Karl Rossmann's age is relevant, for Kafka told Gustav Janouch that the subject of the story was "youth . . . Youth is full of sunshine and love. Youth is happy because it has the ability to see beauty. When this possibility is lost, wretched old age begins . . . happiness excludes age." He added that "*The Stoker* is the remembrance of a dream, of something that perhaps never really existed. Karl Rossmann is not a Jew. But we Jews are born old" (J.30). Karl Rossmann, like America, embodies another possibility of life.

23. Compare Max Brod, *The Biography of Franz Kafka,* trans. G. Humphreys Roberts (London: Secker and Warburg, 1947), p. 108: "it was to be the sole work of Kafka's that was to end on an optimistic note, with wide-ranging prospects of life."

24. Compare Alice James feeling in her hysteria that the sea's "dark waters closed over me" (quoted, my *Henry James,* p. 110). It cannot be a coincidence that parks are referred to so often as the "lungs" of a city. The notion of being trapped in a body—which is akin to what mother and daughter suffer from when they cannot get out of the tenement—is like the nineteenth-century homosexual's perception of being one sex trapped inside the body of another. See D. A. Miller, *The Novel and the Police* (Berkeley: University of California Press, 1988), pp. 154–56. This would return to the single sexual subjectivity that the Statue of Liberty evokes as an impossibility.

Index